D0398095

THE POWERS

Sayers, Valerie.
The powers : a novel /

c2013.
33305227967886
gi   07/08/13

THE POWERS

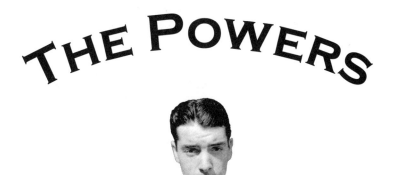

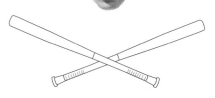

a novel

VALERIE SAYERS

Northwestern University Press
Evanston, Illinois

Northwestern University Press
www.nupress.northwestern.edu

Copyright © 2013 by Valerie Sayers. Published 2013 by Northwestern University Press.
All rights reserved.

Photography design by Christian Jara, Center for Creative Computing, University of
Notre Dame.

Printed in the United States of America

10 9 8 7 6 5 4 3 2 1

Library of Congress Cataloging-in-Publication Data

Sayers, Valerie.
    The powers: a novel / Valerie Sayers.
        p. cm.
    ISBN 978-0-8101-5229-8 (pbk. : alk. paper)
    1. DiMaggio, Joe, 1914–1999—Fiction. 2. Baseball players—United States—Fiction.
    3. Baseball stories—United States. 4. World War, 1939–1945—United States—
    Fiction. I. Title.
    PS3569.A94P69 2013
    813.54—dc23

                                                                    2012036262

This is a work of fiction. Characters, places, and events are the product of the author's
imagination or are used fictitiously and do not represent actual people, places, or events.

⊗ The paper used in this publication meets the minimum requirements of the American
National Standard for Information Sciences—Permanence of Paper for Printed Library
Materials, ANSI Z39.48-1992.

For my magnificent sons
Christian and Raúl

In memory of Phil Rizzuto and Helen Levitt

CONTENTS

Acknowledgments

Warm thanks to Henry L. Carrigan Jr. and Peter Raccuglia at Northwestern University Press and to the following:

The publications where portions of this novel have previously appeared in different form and the editors who shepherded them: *Zoetrope: All-Story* (Tamara Strauss and Michael Ray), *The Pushcart Prize XXX* (Bill Henderson), *Commonweal* (Mollie Wilson O'Reilly and Paul Baumann), *Carolina Quarterly* (Lindsay Starck), and *Image* (Mary Kenagy Mitchell and Gregory Wolfe). Thanks, too, to Tim Morris, who runs the estimable online site "Guide to Baseball Fiction."

All who have written about Joe DiMaggio, especially Maury Allen, Richard Ben Cramer, Joe Durso, Herb Goren, Jack Moore, Michael Seidel, and Glenn Stout. Though this portrait of Joe DiMaggio is entirely my own, I am especially grateful for their versions. Actual events depicted here are reported in multiple sources. Accounts of the games are based on box scores and descriptions in the *New York Times* and the *Sporting News*. Any baseball errors are doubtless my own.

Recorders of the Holocaust and pacifist movements, especially Robert Abzug, Scott Bennett, Robert Coles, Gregory Conti, Dorothy Day, David Dellinger, Paul Elie, James Forest, Ruth Kluger, Rosetta Loy, William Miller, A. J. Muste, Mel Piehl, J. F. Powers, and Susan Zuccotti. Special thanks for the gracious assistance of the United States Holocaust Memorial Museum.

Janet Sayers for memories; Casey Fuetsch and Sealy Gilles for the generous offers of family pictures; Esther Newberg, Kari Stuart, and my colleagues and students at the University of Notre Dame for support. Christian Jara, without whom this book could not have been conceived or completed, and the Center for Creative Computing, University of Notre Dame.

THE POWERS

RIP

JOSEPH PAUL DIMAGGIO

"He must have been dying inside."
—Lefty Gomez

His whole life, everybody thought they knew who Joe DiMaggio was: DiMaggio the Hero, walloping the ball to left and saving the season; DiMaggio the Saint, bone spurs digging in like Christ's crown of thorns; DiMaggio the Noble Faithful Lover, bowing his head in unspeakable dignity at Marilyn's funeral.

But we're not that innocent, not anymore. We can't pretend we knew him, and it's way too late to go all exposé. By now everybody's heard the dredged-up stories about the babes and the mobsters and the brittle coldness, the charges that he made himself a human profit center (Mr. Coffee! Bowery Savings Bank! Old Timers Day!), that he cut his friends cold and wouldn't even say what they did wrong.

Maybe we could just give the guy a break. The man sprang Monroe from a mental ward long after she'd divorced him, was kind to a few people who needed kindness, grieved and held a grudge and struggled to be a human being same as the rest of us. Rest in peace, DiMaggio.

Let's face it, now you're more idea than man, and that idea says more about our own need for a saint and a hero and a noble faithful lover than it says about you. Maybe you were just an idea back then too, back when a whole country followed your impossible hitting streak and believed in it as some crazy ideal of goodness and order and beauty, back when we believed in you as if you were some movie star, some Greek god, some Superman come to rescue a brutish murderous world from our own icy hearts.

PART I

BASEBALL SEASON, 1941

HOCUS

POCUS

DiMaggio's been drifting in and out of a wretched queasy sleep for an hour at least, since Dottie woke up weeping and fled their bed. What did he do? Something he said last night, drunk? Some way he touched her? He can't even remember the cab ride much less a tussle.

Now he has to plot his own escape: has to get himself shaved, dressed, and out the door before she starts in again. He stretches to reach under the mattress before he remembers that the *Supermans* aren't there, that he hasn't kept comic books under his bed since he's been old enough to keep women between the sheets. Dottie hasn't said a word about the comics—a couple of times he's left the new one out before he stashes it—but she's sure as hell raised an eyebrow, and you wouldn't call it her *aren't-big-ballplayers-who-act-like-little-boys-adorable* eyebrow. Cut a fellow some slack. Superman takes his mind off all his mind's been on this year, with a kid on the way (that he still can't believe) and the radio bleating *DRAFT* night and day.

"Joe. Joseph. Did you hear that about Greenberg? Did you hear?"

She's been calling like that every few minutes from their vast new living room, where she perches on the new velvet loveseat and listens to the radio the way other women listen to their fortune-tellers. *Pazza*, his mother would say: nuts. God knows he's a slave to her perfect white leggy curvaceous showgirl body—well, her perfect body till recently—but he has no idea what to do when she goes on a tear like this. When the women in his family get pregnant, they get happy, they get crabby, whichever, they get on with it. Jesus God, it's life. But Dot carries on like she's the first girl in history to ever get herself in the family way.

His right temple's throbbing, but it's not his right temple he's worried about, it's the shoulders, the neck, the way a hangover can work its way from the front of the head to the back and then down and before you know it: nothing for him to do but take a deep slow breath, hold his temper, hold off the pain. Deny it. Pad to the john, pick up the razor. She knows it's a game day. She knows he's got to lay off the boozing with the season started but last night they had to go to just this one opening night party, just this one time. And her belly already pushing out the satin, her boobs spilling. Breasts. Her breasts, she's his wife, not some gold digger, not some cheap slut with boobs, and he's not a monster either, not the cold punishing monster she's lately accused him of being.

"Joe!"

He runs the water loud enough to block her out, to block the radio and its news about the draft, shakes out three aspirins, forces them down without water, looks himself in the other eye. One foot after the other. Do your job and forget your troubles. Straighten up and fly right. He parts his hair three times before he's got it the way he wants it, a fraction to the right of his widow's peak. He's always been a meticulous sort of fellow, and at a time like this, the hangover pushing in like a wolf at the door, it's the little precautions at the bathroom mirror that will save you. His pop, tying the ropes. His mother, kneading the dough.

The hair's good. He's ready now, ready to stick his damp head out into the day. When he heaves the window up, the air comes at him fresh and clean: recrimination, almost, for his carousing last night. He peers up West End Avenue, where Lefty's already hung out their signal, the big white towel flapping from his own bathroom window.

"Joey, they're drafting Hank Greenberg! Can you hear me?"

God knows he can hear her. But he can't have a conversation about Greenberg now, not before a game, not about Greenberg of all people,

and Dottie should damn well know that by now. He retucks his shirt, swings his jacket one-fingered over his shoulder, steps into the long hallway silent as a spy in his own apartment. Sometimes he feels that strange in the new place, all the furniture stiff and grand, the walls still bare. She has some decorator coming, some decorator who'll put up something else to make him feel like an intruder in the apartment he pays for.

The acid smell of the coffee she's brewed him just about makes him gag, but he appreciates the gesture, terrible as Dottie's coffee is. He doesn't have the heart to tell her he'll get his coffee in the clubhouse, so he keeps it simple: calls out a good-bye (OK, maybe it's more of a mumble), then scoots to the front door before she can catch him and make it more complicated than it needs to be. The only thing they have to remember, either of them, is the game. The game, the game, the ever-loving game: their meal ticket, this baby's future. All on his shoulders, the very shoulders that rise now, tightening, against his will.

The getaway elevator awaits and he darts inside, the Negro attendant impassive and unblinking, a big man who's never once given a sign that he recognizes Joe DiMaggio. What a relief, that somebody in the world, somebody who goes to work every day for a living, doesn't really give a shit who rides in his lift. He returns the fellow's nod, trying and failing to match his self-possession. The great Joe DiMaggio is nothing but a guilty little kid.

It just slays him—an elevator waiting to whisk him away, silk roses in the private foyer fresher than real flowers—but it makes him wonder too what his pop, who still can't believe that his sons make a living playing a child's game, will think when he finally sees the new penthouse digs. Somebody's made him feel guilty since the first day he ever picked up the stick to hit the ball. If not his pop, his teachers. If not his teachers, his wife. He hears Dottie rattle the apartment door above, but she's too late. The elevator man has long since latched the gate and cranked the lever. The car has long since begun its descent. His gut lurches, his temple throbs.

He has the strangest premonition: that Dottie's going to make him pay for running out on her—not just tonight but on and on and on. And with the premonition a judgment: maybe he deserves it.

Downstairs the doorman peers out to make sure no fans are lurking, then gives him the all clear. The doorman's name is Sal, or else Sol: he never can remember which. "You're gonna make mincemeat of those Athletics, Mr. DiMaggio."

"Sure we are. Thanks, uh. Thanks." Mr. DiMaggio blushes like a girl to the roots of his perfectly parted hair. He hates that he doesn't know the doorman's name and even more that he won't just ask him to repeat it. What's the matter with him?

He winces, stepping off the curb. The air's spun from gold, perfect day for a ball game, and all he can think about is the needle digging into his right eye. Gomez's big Caddy waits as usual to whisk him away, but the ride's going to be torture with his back twisted so tight. He's too young to hurt this much.

Gomez leans his head out of the driver's side window and clucks his tongue like an old man. "Sheesh, Dago. You look like a bowl of cold turkey soup."

DiMaggio grunts out his misery. Yeah, so he was drinking last night. Yeah, so Gomez was pitching today and knew enough to stay home and hit the hay. So what else is new? He climbs aboard, slams the door shut, tucks his head so some passing fan won't recognize him, so Lefty won't razz him any more than he already has.

Not that Lefty would. No, Gomez has more ingenious ways to punish him: he jerks away from the curb and lurches all the way to the West Side Highway. DiMaggio doesn't know if he can make it to the Stadium without puking. The right eye must be twice its size, and the back of his neck's a steel rod. He's dying. It's another premonition, and not the first time he's had it: the neck and the shoulders and the feet are too far gone for a man in his twenties, this must be cancer rotting out his spine or else one of those mystery diseases like the one that snuck up on Gehrig. Either he's dying like Lou or he's making himself crazy again: what he can't help doing before a game, especially at the start of the season before he's got the rhythms down, before he's remembered how to drink without having to sleep it off.

Gomez picks up speed on the Henry Hudson, and DiMaggio lifts his head infinitesimally. The green-gold light pours down on him, the Hudson River slapping behind Lefty's shoulder. The balmy day, the haze burning its last off the river: reminds him of home. Gomez is a San Francisco boy too. They never talk about it, because if they did, they'd both be back on the first train heading west. More than anything, he misses the smell, which is funny when you think about it. He told his pop he couldn't, wouldn't, work with him on the *Rosalie* because of the stink of diesel and fish, because of his queasy stomach. And his pop gave him a look of disgust such as Dottie herself couldn't screw on her face, not if she practiced for a hundred years.

Lefty's having a fine old time to spite him, weaving in and out of traffic, chortling to himself, waiting for DiMaggio to say: *What are you snorting about, Gomez?*

"What are you snorting about, Gomez?"

Lefty giggles like a girl. "The kid."

They've been talking about *the kid* since the first week of spring training. Rizzuto. Little squirt, the only one of the new bunch worth noticing. Ballplayers are funny that way—they can take a rookie or leave him, and most of the time they'd rather leave him. You can't waste energy on a kid who might get busted back down in two months' time. His own rookie season, when he drove all the way cross-country to spring training with Crosetti and Lazzeri, the other two dagos didn't have two words for him the whole trip and he didn't expect to be spoken to, either. Not even if he was the shits that year, his name plastered over every paper in the country. When they got to Florida they acted like they never saw him before in their lives.

The only two vets who even bothered to say hello were Lou Gehrig, who made a point of shaking his hand and would have done the same for any nameless rookie, and Lefty Gomez, who flat-out claimed him. Lefty could see he was scared nutless, walked up to his locker, gave him the ritual punch in the arm with his pitching fist. *So this is the boy wonder, huh? You look like an ordinary mortal to me.* DiMaggio could have grinned from there to October.

He owes Lefty big time. All this time Gomez has kept him steady, kept his mind off the pressure, roomed with him on the road, chauffeured him up to the Stadium, shown him the show, the town, the clubs. How to answer the big-mouth reporters, where to rent a room, how to pick up a showgirl and get himself laid by same. It was Gomez who found him the penthouse apartment on West End Avenue so they could be neighbors and double-date with June and Dot.

Which is why Gomez might drive like a maniac, but DiMaggio, dying or not, losing his mind or not, will never tell him to take his foot off the gas. Lefty looks out for him the way his brothers have looked out for him his whole life, though face it, no DiMaggio was ever as big a nut as Gomez. Gomez, at the moment, is still giggling like a dame.

"The look on Rizzuto's face when he's trying to get Pop to let him in. *But I'm on the team,* he says." Lefty runs his mouth the days he's pitching, can't shut up, but it doesn't bother DiMaggio the way Dorothy's yakking can. Gomez doesn't want an answer from him, doesn't even care if he laughs at the punch line. He's been telling this same story about Rizzuto getting locked out of his first day of spring training for six weeks now, and he'll tell it for the next six years. All Lefty wants at the moment is to keep his mind off the game, to proclaim that maybe his passenger's seasick but their rookie pal is really green, that he's looking out for Rizzuto the way that he once looked out for DiMaggio. It occurs to DiMaggio that maybe Lefty's even asking him in his goofy way to join the welcoming committee. Which is A-OK by him—he likes Rizzuto, who's playing his heart out at the top of the season, playing like it's October—and the truth is he wouldn't mind being the older brother for a change. But he knows what's coming, and he's pretty sure that Lefty can't see it:

"McCarthy's gonna yank him soon."

Gomez shoots him a look, a sarcastic, *oh-no-not-that-again* look. It's true, he knows he's always doing this: predicting who's about to get benched, who's about to take off, but he knows that's not what really gets to Lefty. What really gets to Gomez is that DiMaggio's always on target, that he bats 1.000 with his predictions, that it's creepy, how right he always is about the future.

"What, you been consulting psychics again? The kid's on fire." Gomez passes a cop car stylishly, with a breezy wave, and DiMaggio stiffens. They recognized him. Every now and again a squad car will pull him over just for the signature, the autograph that's worth more than a year of double time. But today there's no siren, no hot pursuit, and DiMaggio resumes breathing. The neck's loosening up. The aspirin must be kicking in.

"McCarthy's not going to pull the kid now," he says, slow and almost patient. "Soon, though. When he slumps."

"*When he slumps?* He goes into a slump, he'll climb his way out, Signor DiMaggio. Skip's been sailing this boat long enough to give the kid some time."

DiMaggio holds his own counsel, presses the heel of his left hand to his right eyelid. He doesn't know the how or the why of it, but already he's got the feel of the kid and he knows that Rizzuto's going to shut down sure as he knows his own batting average. He practically knows the timing: a month or two, give or take. The Scooter will burn brighter and brighter these next few weeks, riding the team train, getting the come-hither look in hotel bars, seeing the insides of ballparks he's been hearing about since he was ten years old. Then one day, probably in one of those strange new cities, maybe after a rough night, the kid'll flash so hot he'll scare himself silly. Won't remember how he holds his own bat much less how he ever hit a fastball off that looming goon on the pitcher's mound.

DiMaggio should know. He knows that Rizzuto's gonna go deaf, dumb, and blind with panic, that McCarthy won't have any choice but to take him out of the lineup, cool him off. He knows what's going to happen to Rizzuto the same way he knows when he himself will hit the inside curve. It's part of this special power he's always had. He doesn't sit around analyzing shit the way the other ballplayers do, doesn't run the numbers. Breaking it down would be kryptonite against what he knows. He knows it whole—the man, the body, the attitude—and he knows that a guy who gets this hot this fast gets the heebie-jeebies pretty quick too. You'd think a pitcher would see it for himself: for crying out loud, Gomez knows the first thing a ballplayer has to do to stay alive is to size the other fellow up. You'd think he'd know it's not just Phil Rizzuto who's going to slump soon.

They're crossing 155th already and Macombs Dam, that moat separating the Stadium from Manhattan, looms up ahead. The first day he drove up to the Stadium in a Checker cab they came this route, and when he crossed the dam he just about pissed his pants. That day the Stadium looked like the castle on the hill, looming over the Polo Grounds across the river. Today it looks like it's looming over the whole shining city, over the Empire State, over the U.S. of A. All the writers call them knights and heroes and they are, pretty much. Look at Gomez, watching out for the kid, refusing to believe he's gonna slump. That's why people resent them, because they're powerful and loyal and they won't hear crap about one of their own. The Yankees shut their ears to bad news: they just go out and get the job done.

Lefty swings into the players' lot as stylishly as he waved at those cops and hops out of the car, as if to prove DiMaggio's point. DiMaggio waves him on and watches him trot toward the clubhouse, boinging up and down like he's on a pogo stick, like he's a kid again. He wouldn't be a bit surprised to see Lefty kick up his heels. They've lost the first two games of this home stand, but this is the day that Gomez—who's getting old for a pitcher, who's looking at retirement whether he wants to retire or not, who hasn't finished a game in two years—will go the distance. He knows it whole again. This is the day the Yankees get the win and settle into the season.

How many predictions does that make for the morning?

Well, any fool can take what information he's given and make a reasonable prediction. That's a ballplayer's job and that's why he's a good ballplayer. He's been reading too much *Superman*. He sends Lefty out to buy the new one every Wednesday, cause he doesn't want some newsstand bozo telling the world that Joe DiMaggio, Yankee hitting sensation, reads a kid's comic that makes his wife raise one eyebrow. But he's no Superman and he's no psychic, as Gomez is the first to remind him. Sometimes he goes a little pazzu and thinks he has some kind of magic powers, some kind of hocus-pocus, but he's just very good at what he does—the best, he would venture, only you don't want to come off conceited.

Inside the locker room, Lefty's already disappeared. They're early and the place is deserted: he likes to get there first and leave last, and Gomez is happy to oblige, happy to hold court, to hold their teammates at bay while DiMaggio goes into his pregame trance. The clubby, Pete Sheehy, plays guard dog too. Not that anybody even tries to strike up small talk with him anymore.

Everybody including the rookies—especially the rookies—knows DiMaggio's routine. By the time he gets his second leg through his uniform pants, Pete shows up with a half cup of coffee. The smell makes him gag the same way Dottie's did but this time he sips it anyway. He still has to go out and play this game.

"Hear about Greenberg?"

God knows he heard about Greenberg. He gives Sheehy a wary nod.

"Good thing you got a kid on the way or they woulda drafted you too." Pete's the only one besides Gomez who even considers joking around with him, or lighting his Camel as he does now. "They're making an *example* of you fellas."

"Think I'm OK, though?"

"Course you're OK, and not just on account of the kid. They're not about to send guineas to fight Mussolini."

"Hunh." Maybe Pete's joking, but he's not that far off the mark. It's going to be a complicated war with Italy on the other side. His pop's all churned up about a draft too, but it's not Roosevelt's draft that has him hot and bothered, not when he's got nephews and cousins all over Palermo eligible to play for the other team.

"I wouldn't wanna be in a tank with Greenberg, the big galoot." Sheehy, a little wraith of a man himself, drifts away.

And DiMaggio, belt still unbuckled, finally sits to finish the half cup of coffee. He's not letting on to anybody, not even Sheehy, how much this Greenberg news rattles him. Last month the reporters said Greenberg would get an exemption on account of flat feet, which is funny in the first place but funnier still when you picture how the big lug runs the bases.

Today, that radio Dottie was blaring says Greenberg's gotta go. Flat feet or no, baseball season just getting underway or not, Greenberg's in the Army now. And Greenberg, the radio told him, says OK. That part just slays him. Greenberg says he's not going to appeal it. You've gotta hand it to the guy, class act all the way—not that DiMaggio himself has any interest in being a class act. War will always be with us, and he'd rather not be the one getting shot at, not in a season when the shot he has in mind is the Triple Crown. They all think he's looking over his shoulder at Ted Williams, but they're all wrong. It's Greenberg he's seen breathing down his neck. Greenberg, the big sunnuvabitch in all the ways you could possibly be big and just coincidentally the only guy in either league who slams the ball as far to left as he does. He'll have a better shot with Greenberg out of the way, and Dottie knows that, and that's why she was screeching down the hallway when she knew better. What she doesn't know is how complicated it is, what he feels for the man. He held his breath when Greenberg got close to breaking the Babe's record, mumbled more than one Hail Mary: maybe not the first time somebody asked her to make the other guy strike out, but probably a sin to use a Hail Mary that way. He never had much feel for the religion business. It's a woman's game. Probably he should have asked his mother to do the praying, to stop the home runs from accumulating—but the Virgin, let's say she followed baseball, was Jewish herself, wasn't she? She'd be on Greenberg's side if she was inclined to get into the game.

He's just insecure, Dottie would say (*has* said), cause Greenberg knows how to work the fans and how to work the press. Because Greenberg—like Gomez, like Sheehy—is good with the gab, whereas DiMaggio's good with the silence, with sitting and brooding while the locker room fills up with big men with big jaws out-loudmouthing each other. Look at Gomez right this minute, holding Bill Dickey captive with the Phil Rizzuto story. Look at Dickey, yucking it up like it's the first time he ever heard the tale. And here sits DiMaggio in the darkest, farthest reaches of the room, keeping his clam shut. The fans hate it, the other players hate it, but there's nothing he can do about that. It's what he's known since the third grade, that people—broads especially—will turn your words against you, will mock them, will mock you. But if you don't say it, they can't misquote you and they can't see that when you're rattled you don't know how to say it in the first place. *DiMaggio unn parra. Don't say nothing.* The reporters call Greenberg "Hankus Pankus," but what do they call DiMaggio? "Deadpan." *The Sourpuss,* they might as well say.

Well, he's not afraid of them and neither is Greenberg, and between them is that bond, and that's what makes it complicated. You can't play the Tigers without hearing some rube in the bleachers yell *The Hebe can't hit* or *Throw the Sheenie a pork chop.* He's heard them yell it in the Bronx—in New York, fer Christ's sake—and in Detroit, in the man's own backyard. The louder the catcalls, the looser Hank gets. Hankus Pankus, hocus-pocus. Talk about magic. Greenberg shakes them off the same way he himself had to shake them off over the contract business, when they booed him in the Stadium and then out on the street, the real kick in the teeth. One thing watching Greenberg has taught him: he'll never say *kike* again.

Sheehy returns and holds out a hand for the empty cup, to half-refill it. Before DiMaggio walks down the ramp into the dugout, before he takes that field in the dazzling April light, he'll have a dozen half cups.

"Gonna burn your fingers there, Joe, you smoke that butt down any further. Gonna be like the diathermy."

He grins but he cringes too, in case somebody heard. The other men are showing up like pimples, one at a time and then in clusters. Tommy Henrich, who kidded him plenty when his foot got sizzled in the diathermy, has stripped to his skivvies not fifteen feet away. Henrich insinuated he was too shy to tell anybody he was burning up. *Shy's* an inappropriate word to use about a ballplayer and anyway he's not shy, he's reserved. *Reserved* was Dottie's favorite word when they were engaged, but now that she's pregnant she resorts to *cold*, to *mean*. But the point isn't that he's reserved or shy or cold or mean, the point is that he keeps pain to himself, and he can take a lot of it.

God knows. It's his back and shoulders he feels the most now, but another day it will be his old man's feet, shards of broken glass jabbing at his heels when he picks up speed to round first. And his gut—sweet suffering Mother of Jesus, his gut started rotting away when he was just a kid, younger than Rizzuto. That first year playing pro ball, he was in a terrible slump, worried the Seals would cut him, and the only way he knew to climb out was by hitting in sixty-one games in a row. Sixty-one. Unheard of. The photographers used to crowd him at the plate. To this

day he can taste the flash powder they blew in his face. That was the year the acid started dripping on raw sores, the year he didn't sleep for six weeks. And they wonder why he doesn't want to talk to reporters.

Sometimes he feels the same pressure—don't kid yourself, DiMaggio—sometimes he feels more pressure, playing for the Yanks. Everybody in New York thinks Joe DiMaggio can part the Red Sea. Doesn't matter whether he reads the comic or not: they all think he's Superman anyway.

They don't have a clue what it means to feel your body, your paycheck, give on you, to know what you're going to have to do if you want to keep in the game. Sure as his ma believes what the fortune-tellers tell her, he believes what his body's telling him, and his body's been on high alert since the season started. He has a feeling—no, stronger: he has another one of those premonitions. This is the year he'll bring his minor league act to the majors, this is the year he has to make his move if he wants to stay on top. He knows it the same way he knows about Rizzuto, the way he believes somewhere down in that rusty gut that he and Dorothy maybe won't make it after all, the way he smells something putrid, some smell of diesel and rotten fish, in this war news. The acid's already dripping and the steam's already building and the season is barely underway. He hasn't even gone through the slump yet, and he always has to fall down low before he can claw back up, before he can do what he hasn't done since he was a kid like Rizzuto: this is the year he's going to take off on a hitting streak the likes of which this town has never seen. Pete's already back with his second half cup.

"Gonna be some year, Sheehy."

"You're gregarious today. And here I been keeping my distance."

DiMaggio lights another cigarette to steady his hand and bends his neck gingerly. All around him lockers click open and shut, the reassuring mechanical sound that means it's getting closer to game time. He can almost see Lou standing there, stripping his broad back bare, but Gehrig hasn't been near the locker room all season. Lou can't walk anymore. He's dying: everybody knows it.

He's got to stop with the weird stuff, the seeing things, the fortune-telling. He bends to tie his laces. He's OK once he's down the ramp, once the ball's in motion. He sees that Rizzuto's all suited up, standing back till the vets make room for him, and he feels a clutch of affection for the kid, the way he sometimes feels about Gomez or McCarthy or, face it, Dottie when she's not on a rampage. He gives the Scooter a nod, acknowledged likewise. Good kid. Good instincts. Keeps his distance, respects a man's privacy.

Halfway across the locker room, Lefty's playing court jester as usual. He's high as a blimp, which he has to be, to go out there and hurl balls at ninety miles an hour. Gomez has to start clowning in the clubhouse, the way DiMaggio has to go as deep down into himself as his self will let him go. Lefty spots the Scooter—maybe spots DiMaggio watching the Scooter—and calls out, "Uh-oh, Rizzuto. You better watch out, young man. You better get yourself a wife and kids quick as you know how."

Rizzuto answers Gomez with a wary *what-are-you-talking-about* grin.

"Army's drafting anybody in pants, my friend," Lefty intones. "Ballplayers even. Hank Greenberg even. The draft board cometh."

The draft board cometh and Hank Greenberg goeth and Joe DiMaggio stayeth, hammering the ball into left field, where Hank always hits it. Nobody ever said there was any justice in baseball. And nobody ever said Superman played for the Yankees either, but everybody's looking for a hero. DiMaggio feels the top of his head lift off.

"Rizzuto." The Scooter stands there on his toes, ready to come tie DiMaggio's cleats if he so much as lifts a finger. DiMaggio says what he never says, what it's bad luck to say: "We're gonna win this one today."

"Yes sir." He watches Rizzuto catch himself and grin. "Holy moley. You bet."

DiMaggio rises from his bench to go play ball. In five minutes, he'll forget he ever had a hangover. Too bad Dottie's not going to be out there today in her usual spot, wearing one of her big classy hats and her tomato-red lipstick, surrounded by the crush of photographers who think she's so swell. Underneath the hat her blond hair would shine like Christmas tinsel, and when he planted his feet wide, when he let loose his fierce last-minute swing, she'd see again that he's not the puny mortal she believes him to be.

A SPY

ON THE LEXINGTON AVENUE LOCAL

"I like the looks of this rookie Rizzuto," Joe D'Ambrosio says, and Agnes O'Leary swallows back a sigh. It's not enough that her grandmother pines for Joe DiMaggio night and day. Now Joe-and-Bernie, a pair of boys she's so crazy in love with she thinks of them as one, are filling her Saturday night with baseball talk. She sits mute while they lean over her to make themselves heard, two male thighs pressed against her own. So maybe it's not the worst thing in the world to be squeezed between two boys on the subway, even if they are talking baseball.

The train clacks along and they slide against each other, Bernie's shoulder sinking into hers. He grins at her, but he's talking to Joe: "I thought you liked the looks of Peewee Reese. You can't go touting a Yank and a Dodger at the same time."

"Sure I can. I can admire any shortstop I choose."

Agnes doesn't need to know baseball to know what points Joe thinks he's scoring there: he was a shortstop himself, before he gave up baseball to become a track star. And he thinks that she must be a Dodger fan because she comes from Brooklyn, when the truth of the matter is that baseball bores her to tears and she couldn't find her way to Ebbets Field if she had a police escort.

Funny she's thinking police escorts. Even before the three of them began making this pilgrimage on Saturday nights, she felt the thrill of danger every time she rode the train. Everyone feels it these days. Everyone knows the world is about to crack open. The question now is not if the Germans will bomb New York, but when. *Those Huns know no bounds,* her father says. This month it's Greece and Yugoslavia, and if the Nazis can send panzers across the breadth of Europe, why not fighter planes across the Atlantic? Lately she spends her time underground imagining what it will be like when that happens. She pictures the dim cave blackening: she fumbles for her glasses, stumbles through the smoky tunnel, calls out for Bernie, calls out for Joe. She knows it's wrong, deeply selfishly wrong, to be excited by this fantasy, but the truth is, she's excited. They've been waiting—for the Nazis, for the war—forever.

And that man across the aisle, halfway down the car, has been staring at her forever. Or so she thinks. She can't say for sure because, actually, she's not wearing the glasses she would have to fumble for in the event of an air strike. Glasses are unthinkable under a new hat or a new hairdo, and Agnes has both tonight: pin curls courtesy of her little sister Loretta, and a green tam meant to bring out the blue in eyes boys sometimes mistake for gray. She senses the stranger sneering at her vanity.

"I've seen that fellow before," she says. Joe-and-Bernie press themselves harder against her. The man's middle-aged, pale and rumpled, but he's jumpy as a schoolboy, and every few seconds he registers a slight satisfied smile. As they all three stare, he fiddles in the pocket of his spring coat. Agnes says: "I think he's taking pictures."

"What's he got up his sleeve, a line to the shutter? By jove, that chap's spying on us." Bernie just slays her. He's always putting on an accent, playing the fool. In the contest over Agnes (she doesn't mean to be vain about it, but it's true, Joe and Bernie *are* fighting for her), Bernie believes he's already lost. Because unlike Joe, he's short and slight; because unlike Agnes, he wears his glasses instead of slipping them into his pocket. Doesn't Bernie know he's brilliant, for God's sake? He speaks German and Latin and French and this spring he's been admitted to Columbia, but he says he'll go to City College if the war hasn't started by September. His widowed ma cannot possibly afford to clothe him for the Ivy League, much less cough up the tuition—as if any of their families could cough up the tuition. No wonder Joe-and-Bernie spotted her at the Dominican-Xavier dance. No wonder the three of them can travel the city without explaining to each other the weight of every dime in their pockets.

Tonight, as they do every week, Joe-and-Bernie waited for her on the sidewalk outside B. Altman, where she sells stockings afternoons and Saturdays. Every Saturday, she slips her hands into their crooked arms, one on either side, and allows them to escort her downtown. Every Saturday the three of them pretend, without a word, that they're the kind of swells who might actually enroll at Princeton, who might actually wear the shoes they wear at Sarah Lawrence. (And what kind of shoes might those be? Crocodile pumps with toe cleavage?)

Every Saturday, Joe-and-Bernie talk baseball, which makes them forget her till she brushes up against one or the other. The three of them bound out of the train at Bleecker Street and march off to one ornate coffee house or another, where they sit at little marble tabletops to ogle dark paintings, to suck soup, to suck coffee, to suck talk, talk, talk for their Saturday night supper—and then at last she can lay down the law. No baseball talk in a coffee house. Sometimes when they've finished their soup Joe orders a monte bianco. She never tasted chestnuts before she met him, and when she licks the cream off his spoon she thinks indecent thoughts involving nipples. Agnes's three sisters, who never leave Brooklyn, do not imagine that such a world exists.

Joe-and-Bernie go into a reverent trance, watching her eat her dessert,

and then they're running late. They must trot to deliver her on time to her Saturday night job at DeRobertis, where she boxes cannolis for the hoi polloi of First Avenue. Agnes O'Leary is the only O'Anything who's ever worked the counter: Joe, who lives around the corner, knows the family and got her the job, only sometimes she wishes he hadn't. By nine o'clock her feet are so swollen that she slips out of her pumps (which certainly aren't made of crocodile) and, leaning on the glass counter she has just polished, strokes one stockinged ankle with the other. Joe and Bernie come in at ten P.M. acting like customers—sometimes they even order a cannoli—and at eleven they walk her out to the Packard waiting at the opposite curb: her father's friend, Matt McClary, who miraculously and coincidentally gets off his Consolidated Edison shift at ten forty-five and who can deliver her straight to her door in Brooklyn. Agnes suspects that Mr. McClary gets off at nine P.M., or eight P.M., or doesn't even work a Saturday shift but roams the streets of Manhattan until it's time for her to go home just so that he can say, as they pull away from the curb:

"The Italian one—what name did you say? Damn Romeo?"

Agnes will giggle as she is expected to. "D'Ambrosio. Joe D'Ambrosio."

"What's this, DiMaggio fever?"

She has recently noticed how attentively Mr. McClary watches her when he tells a joke, how suddenly the whole world wants to tell her the punchline. She is one of the world's designated listeners—and a good thing, too. Her lack of glasses, her view of the world as pleasantly out-of-focus, has led to some merry money mistakes behind her sales counters. But meanwhile she's been listening so closely, smiling so appreciatively, giggling so *blithely*, as Bernie says in his British accent, that she's never once been called on the carpet for her blind change counting. It's a strange power to hold over people.

Joe D'Ambrosio inclines his head toward their mystery man, trying to be suave. "Look at the fedora on that fellow. Who does he think he is, a private eye?"

"Stop staring," Bernie mutters. "He's got his private eye on us."

"Are you saying he really is a spy?" Now that Joe's spoken the word it's too delicious. A Nazi spi. "Who would he be spying on, on the Lex?"

"Jews." Bernie says it sharply, without a funny accent, and Joe leans over Agnes this time not to hear him but to study the look on his face. They do this all the time, too—stare at each other's face to read the intention there—and Agnes is sharp enough to know that, much as she's in love with the pair of them, they're in love with each other too. Oh, not that way. Not like the skinny mustachioed fellows you see prancing with each other on Waverly Place. But in love nonetheless. This entire year they have been carrying on a debate (sometimes heated, sometimes so cool it's wordless) about the war. Bernie—Bernhard—has a German mother who says she'd assassinate Hitler herself, if she could get close enough, and Bernie's willing to do the deed on her behalf. He'll be first in the enlistment line.

But Joe's becomes a pacifist over the last year (only the Jesuits could turn him into a pacifist in a military school). He says he won't go to war even if he's drafted. He'll find a way over to Europe, to fight the fascists by smuggling people out, and if it's too late to do that—which it is, of course, by years—why then after graduation he'll go down on the bus to the Mexican border and he'll escort refugees (the lucky few who have bribed their way in) back to New York. Bernie rolls his eyes at this foolishness. *Look. If you're too pure to fight you're not going anywhere but a jail cell, once this starts.*

Joe sneaks another look. "Aryan perfection. Of course he's a kraut."

"Really, Joe. What do you think he's doing, sending snapshots back to Germany?"

"Did you know in Berlin women in *evening* gowns stood around on the sidewalk, pointing out men for the brownshirts to pummel?"

No of course she didn't know and neither do any of the other girls at the Dominican Academy or anybody else who pays a nickel for the subway. Everything she knows about Germany, about Austria, about Poland or France or the Sudetenland, she knows from Bernie-and-Joe, who apparently read seventeen newspapers a day. When they have a second to spare on their Saturday night jaunts, Bernie even dashes over to Christopher Street to pick up a *PM* and a couple of foreign newspapers for good measure. He's showing off, but she's impressed just the same. The nuns do not discuss international politics—though they can't stop moaning about the priestly blood that ran so recently in the streets of Barcelona.

Bernie gives the man another once-over. "Maybe he works for America First. Maybe he's taking pictures of people *suspected* of being Jewish."

"Bernie, Joe, Joe, Bernie—" Agnes is in the habit of mixing up the order, so they won't guess which one she's soft on—"he's not a spy. He thinks he's another Weegee." She's pleased to move the conversation from politics to pictures, though Weegee is the only photographer she's ever heard of. She won't be able to keep this up for long.

"Couple of months ago they rounded up . . ."

"You told me."

"Ten thousand in Vienna. *Times* didn't even put it on the front page—why do you think they buried it?"

"I don't know. Too much war news?"

"Took all their jewelry and shipped them east. Why, do you suppose?"

She hates these quizzes, which she never answers correctly. "I know it's terrible, but Bernie, I don't know what we can do about it this minute."

"Don't be naive, Agnes." Lately, this is why she's leaning toward Bernie, because he's so firm with her. He has a dark beard that begins to emerge, bristle by black bristle, late on a Saturday afternoon, emphasizing his authority.

"Let's none of us be naive, shall we?" Joe understands that Bernie's won a momentary advantage and retaliates in his best imitation-of-a-Jesuit. "If he's just some innocent photographer, he'll say so."

"You're not going to ask him."

"Agnes. You'd let him get away because you're *embarrassed*?"

She's a little tired of all the sanctimony. They're eighteen years old, for heaven's sake. She's seventeen. Can't they ever just have a laugh? There's nothing they can do about the poor Jews in Vienna, not a thing in the world, and before every boy she knows gets drafted they might as well . . . She hears her father's sweet tenor voice gathering in her own throat—*break your heart, poor bastards*—and remembers why she lets these two toy soldiers trail her around. At least they don't lie flat in the steamroller's path, the way her father does.

She giggles and then, confused by the false sound of her own laughter, gazes past Joe to study the out-of-focus photographer. He's finally settled down, engrossed in the women opposite him. She knows, more or less, how he works: he hides the camera in his coat, the lens between two buttons. Sometimes he stands and pretends he's studying the map or ogling the lush girl in the Chesterfield ad, which means he's about to shoot the length of the car; but mostly he sits and fools with his pocket. It just kills her how many women stare right back at him. Well, he is attractive in a skittish, nightclubby sort of way, a rich layabout amusing himself by spying on the subway class. His clothes are expensive but wrinkled. She imagines him throwing them on a chair at night, a woman in a negligee watching him from beneath silk sheets. She can't say for sure, but from here his profile suggests a ski-slope nose. She herself has a Roman nose—large, maybe not Roman exactly—and with her dark hair maybe she too could be taken for Jewish by a spy snapping pictures.

Their spy grins, as if he knows he just got himself a good mug shot. How can they move ten thousand people overnight? She calculates how many people could squeeze onto this subway car at rush hour: a hundred and fifty? How could you feed thousands of people, along the way?

"Joe," she says, "when you go down to Mexico, what will you eat?"

"What?"

"When you go down to Mexico on the bus, to escort those refugees. Have you figured out how many meals that will be?"

"Agnes, don't. Just when he's given up on it."

"I haven't given up on it." It's hard to know anymore if Joe is just being stubborn in the face of Bernie's disdain. "You'll send me off to Mexico with a box of cannolis." Joe laughs that manly low-register laugh he and Bernie have been trying out: Bernie's is a little bitter (Gary Cooper) but Joe's is delighted with itself (Clark Gable). She lets his knee dig into hers. Other lovers whisper sweet nothings, but this pair of Romeos is trying to drag her to the altar by her conscience.

Their spy leans back, looking for new prey. Photographers are always spying, even when you know they're taking the picture: a photographer's always trying to steal something you want to hide. That's why she's never been able to recognize herself in a picture. She's the happiest of the four O'Leary sisters, merry and blithe, and yet the line of family portraits in their dim entryway shows a very unmerry Agnes, a grim, lips-set, murderous Agnes, an Agnes who threw a tantrum every year when it was time for the O'Leary girls to queue for a new photo down at the parish hall. How she resisted: her uniform blouse tugged on over her arched back, her lank hair brushed and watered and brushed some more (Loretta hadn't perfected pin curls yet), the long walk from the South Slope to SFX to stand in line with other families who all knew perfectly well that her grandmother didn't go to confession and said rude things about the Dodgers. Out loud. In Brooklyn. Agnes hissed at Loretta not to smile for the camera. She was beside herself with dark fury, and there is the evidence on the grimy apartment wall: year after year, the merry child revealed! She was really a miserable child after all, her jaw set so tight that her face looked plain as a turnip, her nose looming and bulbous, her far-set eyes watery and . . . gray. Well, who wouldn't be a little gloomy, without a mother?

Their spy turns, suddenly, and she's pretty sure that he's staring directly at her. Or no, that he's reaching in his pocket and pressing the line to the shutter. Criminy, she hasn't even told Bernie and Joe that her mother was a suicide. The first one she tells will be the one she marries.

Beside her, Joe draws in his breath. "C'mon, he knows we're onto him."

"I don't know . . . I'm a little scared of him." She raises a gloved hand to Joe's sleeve to restrain him, or maybe just to touch him. The photographer's already turned away, toward a pair of squirming little girls, and she sees a picture her father showed her once: two little girls leaning on their elbows at an open porthole, two little girls dressed in raincoats, trapped on an ocean liner. Refugees on the SS *St. Louis*. Her father said FDR wouldn't let them in, and after they left the port of New York, Havana and Buenos Aires wouldn't let them in either. One of them—the blond child, a prisoner on a big boat—looked like Loretta, and Agnes imagined a kinship. Her father called them *poor bastards,* the same way he calls his daughters *poor motherless girls.*

"Whatever happened to those refugees from the *St. Louis?*" Though she knows exactly what happened. The boat sailed back to Germany.

"Some of them got to France." Bernie doesn't hide his frustration with her. "But if they're rounding them up in Vienna . . ."

The train pulls into Astor Place. The photographer rises languorously and dances with the pole on his way out the doors. Joe's on his feet, and now so is Bernie, and Agnes has no choice but to follow them, though this is a stop too early.

The spy pauses on the platform, as if to let them catch up. He pats his pockets, but what he retrieves is not his secret shutter-closing device but a box of cigarettes (Chesterfields?). He lights one with a wry Fred Astaire face, amused at himself. The three of them tumble toward him.

"Look here," Joe says, and the spy nods as if he's been expecting this.

"You blew my cover." How easily he laughs at them. She was right. The man's coat is crumpled and expensive, his hat pushed back at the angle men adopt when they've had a martini or two, the fringe of hair that shows strangely tousled, boyish. He takes a drag and tilts his head slightly to blow the smoke out of their range. He must be the same age as her father and she sees now—finally—that he wears rimless glasses: that's why she couldn't make them out from half a car-length away. She takes his glasses as permission to remove her own from her pocket, but her ears burn scarlet as she hooks on the humiliating horn rims.

"We just need to know," Joe begins anew, smooth as a radio announcer, "whether you were taking pictures of Jewish passengers."

The spy jerks his head with a sense of wonder that strikes Agnes as fake and real all at once, as if the only way he knows how to register shock is to repeat a gesture he's rehearsed a thousand times before. "Jewish passengers."

Now Joe's confused. "Because at a time like this—"

"That's what you thought I was doing?" The spy takes his time unbuttoning his coat, motions them in, co-conspirators, and reveals a dull black camera: "My Contax," he says. With her glasses in place Agnes can see that the shiny parts have been painted dull for camouflage. He pulls from his pocket a slender cord to which is attached . . .

" . . . a shutter release," Bernie says.

"Precisely."

"We thought you were spying," Joe says, not embarrassed in the least though he's the one who's really garbled things.

"Well I suppose I *am,* but good grief, not on Jews."

"That's a relief," Joe says. "We were just checking."

The spy shakes his head in wonder—Agnes decides this time that the gesture's completely authentic—and considers his words. "Look, let me send you a copy of my new book. So you'll know I'm legit." He pats his pocket, this time for a pen, and withdraws a scrap of paper so that they can write an address.

Bernie shakes his head and retreats a step. "No need."

"No need," Joe repeats. "Sorry to trouble you. Can't be too careful."

" . . . In this day and age?" The spy looks directly at Agnes for the first time. He's as old as her father, and she falls in love with him too while she's at it, with the glint off his glasses and the way he smiles without his teeth. "It was you, wasn't it? *You* were onto me."

She thinks to say: "I'd like a copy of the book. If it's not too much trouble."

She's never done such a thing and knows that Bernie-and-Joe are shocked by her forwardness. Probably they're shocked at her glasses too: and underneath a *tam*, of all the comical hats. It's hard to get her address down—the pen keeps slipping between her gloved fingers, especially when she gets to *Brooklyn*, and naturally it's a good pen, sleek and silver. When she hands the slip back she meets the photographer's eye through two layers of glasses and sees that his are as smudged as her own. And as she moves down the platform after Bernie she hears, from a distance: "Good *somebody's* paying attention." She turns to acknowledge him, but he's disappeared, vaporized.

"He's never going to mail you a book," Bernie says. But Agnes, in love with three men now, knows that Bernie's just jealous and that the photographer will keep his word.

And she looks for the package, for a week or two, when she comes home at night, shaky with hunger after the school day and the stocking counter and the long train ride home. After a while she begins to forget about the book, the way worldly men forget schoolgirls in glasses. She's been distracted, anyway. She splurges on the *Times* almost every day now, so she can keep up with Joe-and-Bernie on Saturday nights. She pretends that the paper's a gift for her grandmother Babe, who's started a photo collection of Joe DiMaggio twisting his long body into one graceful audacious swing. Babe doesn't think much of the so-called sports reporting in the *Times*, but a picture's a picture.

And Babe's never read so much as the front page of the *Times,* but she seems to pick up world news by osmosis, just walking the neighborhood. She appears, for instance, to know as much about Hitler sympathizers as Joe-and-Bernie do. Sometimes Agnes thinks she knows more. Last year her grandmother ran into a pair of Christian Fronters hawking the *Christian Index,* wearing the swastika in broad daylight. As Babe told the story, she jabbed one of the boys, then the other, in their skinny cowardly chests, till they turned tail.

Agnes wasn't there, but it's the most important memory she has of her grandmother, the one she holds to the light, the one she pores over for clues. It's taken her years—and Joe-and-Bernie—to sort out her grandmother's contradictions. Father Coughlin, according to Babe, is a cretin, but his followers need something to hang onto. Jews are tight; Italians are—*God knows after what what your mother did*—hysterical; but teenage boys hawking the *Christian Index* have to be stopped.

Babe does not herself attend Mass but the girls must, under pain of the back of her spoon. And speaking of silver spoons: FDR is an arrogant bastard leading us into war so his pals can get richer than they already are; but anybody who votes Republican is a traitor to working people. Those other Republicans, the Spanish ones, were fools and Communists and priest-killers, not that there aren't a few priests she'd like to murder herself. Babe has raised her four granddaughters, even as they're kneeling at the altar rail and thrusting out their plump pink tongues for communion, to mistrust priests, to mistrust all men while they're at it. *Men are weak:* they die too soon, the way Babe's husband did, or turn to mush on a barstool the way Agnes's father did. You're going to have to marry one, and the sooner the better, but that doesn't mean you have to respect them. The only men worthy of respect are ballplayers. Agnes's grandmother follows DiMaggio's numbers the way brokers used to follow the market—adoringly—but she complains too that Joe's a big Italian goofball, *with those teeth.*

Dinner's on when Agnes walks in the door: the sweet smell of carrots and turnips night after night, Babe's fidelity to root vegetables meant to balance her father's infidelity to his jobs. At least he's working at the moment, as an insurance investigator (Babe found him the job, the way she finds the girls scholarships and hand-me-downs). Just now he sits at the kitchen table stunned by the effort of his day. They all look a little stunned, the six of them squeezed around a wobbly card table. In the corner Loretta wears a face suggesting, as it often does, that she might burst into tears any minute.

"So, Aggie, let's have the news," Babe says. Mame and RoseMarie promptly examine their fingernails for chips. They are file clerks downtown and they are not interested in Agnes's news, a recent feature of the

dinner hour, one she suspects is designed to keep providing Babe with newspaper photos.

"I thought you were going up to the Stadium today," her father says.

"Ladies Day." They all know what Babe thinks of Ladies who need a Day to lure them to the ballpark. "I thought better of it."

Agnes says: "They rounded up five thousand Jews in Paris, and it wasn't even on the front page. I didn't notice till tonight."

"Can't you get in free on Ladies Day?"

"I could get all the way up there and McCarthy pulls Rizzuto? I like the little fella. Give him time."

"Five thousand," her father says, and shakes his head. "Poor bastards. That man knows no bounds."

"Agnes! I forgot. Package for you today. Something from the college, I suppose."

"May I be excused?"

"Leave it for later," Babe says, and Agnes knows it's because her hoity-toity Manhattan academy has already caused enough bitterness.

Agnes rises. "No, for the bathroom." She'll grab the package from the hallway and take it with her to the bathroom, the only room in the apartment where the door fits properly into its frame, the only room where four sisters who live in one jail cell can retreat when they want to hoard a secret.

She sits precariously on the curved side of the clawfoot tub and unwraps the brown paper as quietly as she can. It's the book, finally. Looking for a note, an inscription, she shakes out the packaging, but there's only the book itself, a little portfolio of pictures at the beginning.

He's famous. She knew it. She's shaking with anticipation but already feels cheated. If he went to all the trouble of having the book sent, he could have signed it for her. *To the charming blue-eyed girl who spied me first. Your accomplice in crime, Walker Evans.* Men like that always have last names for first.

She flips through the picture pages in front and sees that the spy Walker Evans has sent her pictures of poor country people. She feels again the weight that Joe-and-Bernie have been suggesting she should carry. Is she supposed to do something about these people too? Her family's broke but she can't imagine this kind of poverty, posing for a rich man with your own face grubby and your clothes streaked and torn. The Depression is over but this Mr. Walker Evans is still groveling in it the way the wealthy sometimes do. Only the rich don't stay awake at night: she's the one who'll lie sleepless in bed with Loretta, who twitches with all her sorrows.

The apartment's quiet, as if they're waiting in the kitchen for her to betray herself by turning the pages of her book. This bathroom, she feels certain, is very like the one they fled when her mother killed herself. That was a mansion practically and this is a tenement but the shape of the room is surely the same as the one where her mother hanged herself from a sturdy steam pipe. And isn't she her mother's daughter? Probably she'll always have a long narrow bathroom in her life: a coffin. At her scholarship interview, she said she might study psychology and was surprised to hear the word come out of her own mouth. The committee thought that was grand—women have a gift for counseling and there'd be plenty of need during wartime. Or was she perhaps interested in the moral development of children?

In the silence she sees Joe D'Ambrosio enter a jail cell, Bernie Keller ship out. In the paper tomorrow (but not on the front page) she'll read how they arranged the food when they rounded up the Jewish families: they sent the women home for provisions, as if they were being sent to pack for a picnic.

She flips the front of the book again, but now a dark fury rises. It's not just that the photographer wants her to imagine what he's witnessed—he wants her to imagine what it's like to live that life, when she can't even imagine what it was like to be her own childhood self.

She shifts and the brown paper makes a racket, only now she doesn't hear it. Now she's riding a train in the dead of night. She sits in the terrible silence as if she might imagine moving past this helplessness, as if one day she'll decide the way Bernie and Joe have decided what it is she's supposed to do. She's riding a train. When Bernie comes home from the

war beyond the reach of language, she'll sit with him in a silence darker and deeper than this one, a silence suffused with shame. When Joe goes to federal prison, she won't have a single word of consolation for him.

She's riding a train in the dead of night but she doesn't know what she can do about it. *Poor bastards.* She slaps the book shut—she's not ready for any of this—and the doorknob rattles. Mame's fuming: "Aggie, it's your night for the dishes and you know it."

In a few minutes, Babe will commandeer the radio again, and then Marty Glickman's voice will rumble through the apartment with the replays of Ladies Day on "Today in Baseball." Maybe DiMaggio has roused himself from his slump, and then the mood in the O'Learys' will lift.

In the hallway, she stops in front of the portraits of the poor motherless O'Leary girls, row after row in the dim bare-bulb light. She looks her eight-year-old self in the eye, her glasses in her pocket even then: a mysterious scowling girl who wants to raise holy hell but grows up giggling instead.

"Da," she hears herself bellow, though no one but Babe is allowed to bellow in this household. "Dad," and even before she hears the scrape of his chair the sentence has formed: *I'm going to lose my mind if you say* poor bastards *one more time.* Even before she sees his confused face appear in the hallway she understands that it isn't just her father she's admonishing, that it isn't just Joe-and-Bernie she's choosing between.

THE

BABE-LOVER

Babe O'Leary is going up to the ballpark and it's probably going to kill her. Well, there are worse ways to die.

Getting downstairs is slow torment, one step at a time so the kneecaps won't scream. She shifts her weight as if it's a sack of laundry. Before she deals with the subway steps and the climb up the bleachers, she'll have to deal with the mile-long walk up to the Grand Army Plaza to catch the IRT, a walk she'll break into five-block segments, with two rest stops on stoops and a second breakfast at the Purity to sustain her.

"Mrs. O'Leary, you must be going to that American Day. If I was feeling stronger I'd go myself."

That's Nosey Bruscelli, a shameless spy on the first floor. She's been standing in her doorway, her wrapper gaping, since Babe ventured onto the third-floor landing.

Babe intones the same crisp line she speaks every time Bruscelli interrogates her: "I make it a practice to keep my plans flexible and private."

For some reason Bruscelli always thinks this is a joke. "You're a card."

Babe drags her foot for effect. "Jesus, Mary, and Joseph. *I Am an American* Day? My people have been in this country a hundred years and more." This is gross exaggeration—her mother was pregnant on the journey over—but called for under the circumstances.

"Well, we're all Americans, just like La Guardia says, and we'll beat the crap out of anybody says different." Bruscelli beams a pleasant confused smile and, with a little wave, pulls her wrapper tight before she disappears.

Beat the crap. It is humiliating to live among such coarse people, but Babe has no one but herself to blame for the apartment. She was a younger woman with better knees when she rented it, and Bruscelli was not then in residence. The deal she made with her only son after his wife killed herself was this:

First, she would not live above the Calabrese funeral parlor. She would not under any circumstances allow the girls to stay in the apartment where Gloria killed herself, and she would not, furthermore, have anything to do with the Calabreses, who were all out of their heads.

Second, she would only stay till the girls were grown and not a minute longer. She already despised Brooklyn in general and Park Slope in particular: the hordes of adorable Dodger fans, the prim houses of the Gold Coast, the lace-curtain Wall Street Irish at the top of the Slope looking

down their pert noses at the O'Learys, O'Schmearys, O'Dearys at the bottom. Not to mention the likes of the Bruscellis. Or the Newfie fishing families down on Third Avenue.

Speaking of Third: (she knew this would not come to pass but felt she must include it for her son's dignity) if he found a new wife she would move out immediately.

Fourth, once a week during baseball season she would require a trip to the Bronx. She was willing to sit in the bleachers, as always, but Mickey had to know that the money would come out of the household budget and that it was not an indulgence. It was a necessity.

Mickey—poor dear mush-face Mickey—agreed to all the terms as pleasantly as Bruscelli might have. As if pleasantness were appropriate when his histrionic wife had just hanged herself in front of the girls.

No wonder he was so pleasant. It worked out just fine for Mickey: it was only a bad bargain for her. Back then she didn't have a clue what the journey to the Stadium would cost her. The subway's still a nickel, but the stairs are worth a decade of her life, so once a week has become once a month.

She picks her games carefully. Ordinarily she wouldn't consider a crowded Sunday, but on "I Am an American" Day she calculates that the fair-weather fans will be going to Central Park to see Eddie Cantor and Bill Robinson for free. Let them. DiMag needs her more in Yankee Stadium than La Guardia needs her in Central Park. Joe's just starting to hit again and even though today they're playing the lowly Browns he could get rattled.

DiMag needs her because she has a special gift that soothes a ball-player and allows him to go about his business. It's not as if the boys see her out there in the bleachers, or exchange a word with her. She's never been a clinging, autograph-hounding kind of fan. She'd die before she'd wave a lace hankie at them the way other women do. No, she makes a brain-wave connection. She shows up at the Stadium, and the Yankees win. Over the past ten years, which is as long as she's been keeping statistics on this phenomenon, the Yankees have won fifty-one of the sixty-one games Babe O'Leary has graced with her presence, which makes her winning percentage .836. Even if you take into account how carefully she picks the games, even if you take into account the Yanks' winning records, even if you take into account the home-park advantage, it's a record that points to, if she does say so herself, unusual powers.

"Mrs. O'Leary." She returns Raymond Connelly's nod and hello. He's a handsome young fellow, super of a big building up on the park, and he's handsomer still in his slate-gray suit, his shoulders wide as a door-frame. His girls played with Mickey's girls when they were all younger: there they are with their mother, trailing their father half a block, wobbling home from Mass on their high heels. "How's that neighbor of yours holding up? Mrs. Bruscelli?"

"She's the very same busybody she was yesterday, Ray."

"You didn't hear, then. Her nephew was picked up last night at El Morocco. All anybody talked about at St. Saviour's this morning."

"Who'd he murder? Whom, I should say."

"They rounded up all the busboys who didn't have papers, which was pretty much all the busboys. Three from the parish. Stupid wops."

Babe draws herself up. She doesn't like Italians better than anyone else in the neighborhood, especially the ones who don't trouble to learn the language, but she doesn't like the debasement of English, either. It's hard to say whether she objects to *stupid* or *wops* more. The two words are forbidden at her table, but only Agnes remembers, which is why Agnes is going to college and her sisters are going to be file clerks all their lives. First she gives Ray a hard stare, and then she gives him a little squeeze to the forearm, so he knows she forgives him his manner of speaking. She moves along with a (God help her) pleasant smile for Mrs. Connelly and the girls, who are catching up.

So that's why Bruscelli went on about being an American. Does the woman even have papers herself? Who knows what Italian spies Bruscelli could be hiding in her dim little hovel. Ironic that Babe is on her way to see the Dago. She was not inclined to like DiMaggio in the beginning—not because of his nationality, she's bigger than that—but because he was so sullen and full of himself. Or so she thought. Now she understands that he is just sufficiently full of himself to ask for more money, God bless him. And he's not as cold as people say. He's shy, because he grew up speaking two languages—who wouldn't be confused?—and because every time he opens his mouth those teeth loom. (She's a sucker for homely fellows. Dorothy Kilgallen can say till the cows come home that DiMag is handsome, but she, Babe, knows a looker and Joe DiMaggio is no looker.) He's the proud quiet type, which is what Albert was and what Mickey is, the type who requires a forceful woman. She's seen Mrs. DiMaggio at the ballpark: a cheap blond siren, a showgirl. A Midwesterner they say. There's something about the cruel set of her scarlet lips that makes it clear poor Joe has fallen under a spell. The marriage won't last—she'd stake her powers of prediction on that. Mickey fell for the same *opposites attract* with Gloria, when what he needed was a good Irish

girl with a sense of humor, a firm grasp of grammar, and a head for bookkeeping, someone who—as her husband lost job after job—would take a firm stand and send him back out the door to find another. Instead Mickey picked himself a tragic, keening Italian who shouldn't have borne one child much less five. Mickey's never admitted it, but Babe is absolutely certain that Gloria was pregnant when she died. That was when her daughter-in-law carried on the most, in pregnancy and then after the deliveries. She stayed in her nightgown all day, had her mother deliver meals from

downstairs, sent her babies out to the greengrocer's. She wanted Mickey to go into the undertaking business with her father—as if that was a calling you could just fall into—and when he wouldn't she hanged herself. The bitch. Babe retracts the word, even though she has not actually spoken it. It's a coarse word that doesn't pass her lips. Or rarely, in any case.

Five blocks. Here's the first resting place, a good broad stoop on which a large woman in her sixties can sit for a moment without looking common. It's never crossed her mind before, but her journey to Yankee Stadium is something like the Stations of the Cross, a ritual she has always considered another opportunity for the pious to weep and moan and congratulate themselves.

She arrives at the Stadium forty-five minutes before game time, according to plan. It's taken her three hours to traverse Brooklyn, Manhattan—where she changes trains—and the Bronx. If she were perfectly honest about it, she'd admit that second breakfast takes up a good chunk of time. The descent from the El is the hardest part of her journey, but the smell of sauerkraut is in the air and the hawkers below on 161st distract her hip, her knee, her shoulder. This is a glorious Sunday. This is her morning Mass, her Broadway musical, her "I Am an American" Day. She makes steady time along River Avenue, where they are selling flags-on-sticks by the fistful. The I AM AN AMERICAN banners are everywhere. In the bars across the street men are pouring back patriotic pints. They'll be weepy in time for the national anthem.

She stands in line for a seat. It's nothing like the old days, when the wooden bleachers stretched across the outfield, but she'll still be perched in center left, where she has a good view of DiMag's profile when he's in the outfield and a chance of seeing a homer whiz by when he's at bat.

"Hello, Babe."

"Tom." She has been going to the same box-office window for eighteen years: since the week the Stadium opened. "Who's scoring today?"

"My sources tell me it's Daniel's turn." Tom winks, and she winks back. "Beautiful day for a ball game." The beauty of their exchange is its economy. Her gestures, too, are economical as she backtracks round the ballpark toward the bleacher entrance: she crooks an elbow, ready to push past out-of-towners. Her shoes linger on the concrete, sticky with spilled ginger ale, and burp as she releases them. She's tempted by a bag of peanuts but indulges, as always, in a program instead.

They're already admitting the bleacher bums. She bypasses the line, ready to invoke the privilege of age if anybody so much as looks at her funny. She knows every usher in this end of the park. Nick, a hairy gnome who guards the portal, tips his cap to her, and she tips her own black boater in turn.

She must descend another short flight of steps. *Offer it up,* the nuns would say, offer it up for the poor suffering souls in purgatory. She'd like to offer the Sisters of St. Joseph up. She proceeds around the field and then up to her seat with her shoulders throbbing. As she hauls herself up, row by row, lopsided and limping, middle-aged men slide across to give her a hand, but she wields her pocketbook as weapon and waves them off with a scowl. The pocketbook is nearly empty: it contains one ruby lipstick, one subway token, one smuggled box of Cracker Jacks that must last her nine innings, one pencil to score the game. One foot up the steps, then the other. Breathe. It's a glorious May day, fair and cool, and she draws her spring coat around her as she makes her slow ascent.

She always sits low enough that she won't collapse en route, high enough to ensure that no one with a small child will try to keep her company. She can bear any insult but a toddler. Even Mickey at two or three—face it, children are not attractive at that age, with their incessant questioning and their streaming snot. Mickey was five and a perfect gentleman when she took him to his first game in Hilltop Park, back when the Yankees were the Highlanders.

Two more rows to go. She takes a deep dignified breath. The trick up here will be to avoid thinking of the toilet or her rumbling stomach: no turning back, once she's settled. Next to her spot a tall lanky teenager is just claiming his place. She heaves herself down with a great thud of displeasure, but the boy's oblivious. He scans the field, his cap pushed back over a high forehead, a lick of sandy-colored hair escaping. The angles

of his nose and chin are sharp enough to give him a movie-star look. Ballplayer himself, she'd wager.

She sees with alarm that they are setting up a pregame "I Am an American" ceremony. La Guardia and FDR, the warmongers, are whipping people up—though of course there's nothing else America can do now but go to battle Hitler. That ridiculous mustachioed man. She has a sudden vision of his little shriveled penis. Sometimes she has visions of the Yankees as naked men, too, though of course they are not shriveled—just the opposite, they are alarmingly . . . robust. Would Albert be horrified? She thinks not. He was a playful man in bed and he liked to prance in the nude himself.

She sighs, loudly, and in response some knucklehead comes to the microphone to remind the fans how blessed they are to be Americans. To break the monotony of his speech, she pictures him without his pants, too. She feels her young neighbor's eye on her and senses that he would like to strike up a conversation. Just let him try.

"I don't think DiMag's heart is in it," the young man says, and she makes a point of not answering. He's right, though. The rest of the Yanks, in martial lineup, at least make a show of patriotic sentiment, but DiMaggio stares at the ground, wincing, as a soprano breaks into "I Am an American."

Finally, the Yankees are allowed to take the field. Gomez is pitching, which is a big reason she has deigned to come to a Sunday game. Lefty's days are numbered, and his last few outings have been disasters, but he always puts on a show, win or lose. And she's figured out another thing: when Gomez pitches, DiMaggio hits.

Gomez is aging well—Irish and Spanish, an excellent if explosive combination of genes—and he's hurling them hard today. She feels the boy lean forward: "Put it in there, Lefty." Lefty puts it in there and gives up a double. She consults her program: the runner is Lucadello, the new batter Estalella. Have these mellifluous names been arranged especially for "I Am an American" Day? As if to answer her, Estalella promptly scores Lucadello. A poor start, but Lefty settles down, and the Browns are kept to the one run.

The boy turns to her as the Yanks head for the dugout. Without the least encouragement he says: "I wish McCarthy wouldn't bench Rizzuto. That's who I came to see."

Babe cannot resist: "Whom."

"Actually—if I'm not mistaken—it's *who*. Predicate nominative."

Babe gives him a withering stare. She cannot for the life of her remember what a predicate nominative is, though surely the nuns beat it into her.

"*That is who*," he adds helpfully. "The way you might say *This is he*."

Her cheeks flare. Can he possibly be right? It wouldn't be the first time her grammar school education let her grammar down.

"I see you're getting a good education," she sniffs. "Christian Brothers?"

"Jesuits."

"Regis?"

"Xavier."

She feels some measure of superiority again. Mickey was a member of the first graduating class at Regis, which even then was establishing itself as the best high school in the city. Xavier was a poor pretender, for those who had to have the Jesuits but couldn't get past the Regis gatekeepers. A terrible, terrible worry, getting Mickey an education. Someone told her the Jesuits were starting a new scholarship school for the children of immigrants, and she didn't sleep till she'd wangled his way in there. Mickey was not, strictly speaking, the child of immigrants—she and Albert were both born on these shores—but he was one smart whip of a lad.

And nothing, nothing she wouldn't do for him. After Albert died, she found a salesclerk's job at a tiny hosiery store on Broadway. Then, when B. Altman opened its grand new doors, she talked her way into the stocking counter there. Her paycheck might have been puny, but Mickey would get an education and she would be the best-dressed woman in Spuyten Duyvil, even when she became portly. From the matrons of Park Avenue she learned which hat draws the eye up. If a woman is going to get fat, she might as well do it in style.

And Mickey was proud of her, even when she was scrubbing the priests' toilets, her Mondays off, to pay his tuition. The Jesuits saw that he went on to Manhattan College, where they were able to coax a baseball scholarship for their star pitcher. But he played, she sensed even then, only to affirm all those mother-son outings to Hilltop Park and the Polo Grounds. He might have been fatherless, but she gave him baseball. Who could have predicted that it was she, not he, who would fall in love with the game? He was nineteen years old when he choked. Nineteen when he gave up on baseball and college and married Gloria Calabrese, who only encouraged the self-pity. A year later, he baptized his first baby, and at the christening he gave his mother a new name too, in honor of the new love of her life. Babe Ruth put on Yankee pinstripes that very year, and Mickey introduced her as *my ma, who loves Babe Ruth. My ma, the Babe-lover.* Before the afternoon was out, he shortened it to *Babe.* Her grandchildren would never know her by any other name.

She feels herself drifting away from the game, but the boy who sits beside her buzzes in his seat like radio static and brings her back. Tommy

Henrich, Old Reliable, has doubled, and here's Joe up to bat. She groans as his grounder beelines for third base, but the ball bounces off Harland Clift's glove.

"Error!"

"We'll see about that." Babe is more secure about the capricious rules of scoring than she is about the rules of grammar.

"Sure looked like an error to me."

"Dan Daniel's scoring today, and that's a whole lot of latitude. Not to mention attitude."

"Dan Daniel."

"*World Telegram,* big DiMaggio booster."

"You mean he just gave Joe the hit."

"That would be a fair call," she says, firm as a Josephite. "Joe walloped the ball, and that's why Clift couldn't scoop it up."

The boy says nothing but looks at her sidewise with a kind of wonder. The Yanks have pulled ahead, but in the top of the second Clift makes up for his bumbling with a homer that sails by them into the left field stands. They both shake their heads: now it's two–two, which means she must really focus. If the Yanks lose to the Browns, they'll be seriously shaken up, and Joe's dubious hit will only drive him, doubting, back to his slump. She lowers her head, as if in prayer, and wills the Yankees to pull themselves together. She wills DiMag to hear her, and Lefty, and even Rizzuto, riding the bench.

Lefty Gomez hears her. Leading off the bottom of the second, he actually gets a hit. The boy says: "I don't believe it. Usually Lefty can't even *bunt.*"

If only the boy knew what she was up to when she bowed her head and summoned her forces. The Yankees turn fierce before their very eyes. You can see them all crouching at the plate like bobcats: Sturm walks, Rolfe doubles. And already DiMag is up again. Babe goes into a near trance when Joe is at the plate.

"Home run, Joe," the boy hollers. The crowd goes silent. Babe watches what she cannot see from this distance but imagines is DiMag's steady effortless breathing, knows he will crack the ball long and hard, toward right—no, center. No, center-right. Impossible to follow it from their angle, but they can make out the right-fielder tearing toward it and, you have to give the guy credit (who's that, Laabs?), that is one swell catch he stretches his glove to make.

Only then Laabs drops the ball. The bleachers let out hoots and bleats: derision, contempt, awe. "Well, *that* was an error," the boy says.

Babe smiles the slightest of smiles. "We'll see."

"Don't tell me. Joe hit it so hard Laabs shouldn't have caught it in the first place."

The Yankees are ahead now, four–two, and Babe knows the danger has passed. You can see the Browns shriveling in the outfield, diminished already, as the mighty Yankees do what the mighty Yankees are supposed to do. The Browns thought they had a shot today, on account of the Yanks being so spooked lately. They didn't know Babe O'Leary would be sitting in the bleachers watching over her fellas. Maybe she should have sent them a telegram.

The boy reads her mind: "Looks like Joe's got somebody watching out for him today."

If he only knew who—whom?—Joe had looking out for him today. She feels the affection she used to feel explaining the infield-fly rule to Mickey, who as a child was, like this young man, completely trusting of her authority. She had to be the final word for her son, the Supreme Court, the president, the pope. She leans a little closer to her neighbor. "You know what?" He turns toward her with the lopsided grin of a charmer and she says, "DiMaggio's going to walk out of this game ready to break some records."

"I hope you're right," the boy says, but then, seeing her glare: "I *know* you're right."

"What are the odds?" She's starving, walking through the apartment door, through the living-room arch. The Cracker Jacks ran out before the seventh-inning stretch, and even though she allowed herself a push-cart hot dog on her way to the subway, by the time she was standing in the crush at Grand Central, waiting to change trains, she thought she might keel over. Now, at last, after the final climb up the final mountain to the third floor, the smell of Sunday pot roast soothes and agitates her at the same time. It's a cheap cut she haggled cheaper from the butcher, but thank God she managed a sizable hunk for their Sunday dinner. Thank God it was Agnes's turn to take her grandmother's place in the kitchen, which means that dinner is ready on time. She could collapse into the armchair, always left vacant for her, but she might never rise again.

The family's gathered in the living room, waiting. Mame and Rose-Marie, resentful, hunch over the nail polish they apply to each other on Sunday nights.

"Odds of what?" Mickey, at least, listens to her.

"The odds that I'd spend the afternoon with Agnes's sweetheart."

Loretta lets loose a rare smile, Mame and RoseMarie raise their heads in unison, and Agnes tears out of the kitchen, her spoon a weapon as surely as Babe's pocketbook is one. "I heard that! But I don't have a sweetheart, so how could you spend the afternoon with him?"

Babe advances on her slowly, for effect. "Joe? D'AmBROsio?" The syllables rise and fall like a wave.

Agnes is ashen, and then flaming: she's always registered her embarrassment in reverse order. She used to be the sunniest of the girls, but in the last year she's become positively . . . emotional. "What makes you think he's my sweetheart?"

Babe's already in love with him herself, so how could her granddaughter not be? She's already planning the meal she will make for him when he treks out to Brooklyn: a fat roast chicken, surrounded by rutabagas. Maybe Agnes has been keeping it secret because she thinks Babe won't tolerate another Italian in the family. But Babe wants these girls married off, and Joe D'Ambrosio's a fine catch, Italian or not. He loves Agnes, too, Babe's sure of it. What else causes a young man to turn scarlet?

She feels a little more pressure than she might, ordinarily. The country's on the brink of war. Joe D'Ambrosio will be drafted, and Agnes might never see him again if she doesn't move in quickly, if her family doesn't make a fuss. The very worst that could come of such a marriage is that Agnes will have widow's benefits for the rest of her life—of course Babe doesn't like to imagine such a charming boy lying dead in a trench, but you might as well be practical. How many times, facing the light bill, has she wished she had the sense to marry a civil servant? Agnes's college plan looked sensible twenty-four hours ago, but now this plan looks more sensible still: a handsome smart young man who respects Babe's baseball knowledge. Agnes should snag him while she can.

"I know he's your sweetheart because of the way he blushed all over when we got to chatting and he figured out that I was connected to you. The way you're blushing now."

Agnes flounces off. "You'd be red-faced too, if you spent the afternoon over the stove."

"They'll be calling him for military duty, so if I were you I wouldn't act so above-it-all. Boys need to know where they stand before they ship out."

"You've got it all wrong," Agnes hollers back from the kitchen. "Joe D'Ambrosio's a pacifist. He won't be going to any war, ever."

Babe feels the breath sucked out of her. Could that possibly be? The boy with the grammatical rules tripping off his tongue? Agnes might as well have said he's a Red. In fact, if he's a pacifist, he probably is a Red. Unless he's a Mussolini fan as so many Italians must be, in private.

She feels more light-headed still. Everything's all wrong. Agnes has been cavorting with Reds, or possibly fascists, after school every day. Agnes reads her mind, thrusts her belligerent head through the opening between kitchen and living room. "And he's not a communist either. He's getting all this from the Catholic Workers."

Babe does not ask what a Catholic Worker is, because if she finds out the answer she might faint dead away. That's all the family needs, another religious nut like Gloria, who plastered the walls with Sacred Hearts and covered every light switch with a gilded guardian angel. Her heart races at the thought of Agnes under the influence of religious mania. So she doesn't have to marry the boy. So she can go ahead and take the scholarship. But she feels betrayed by Agnes's hot fury, when she's always been

on Agnes's side. She feels betrayed by Joe D'Ambrosio's passing himself off as someone he's not.

"What was the score?" Mickey says.

"Twelve–two. A romp. DiMag went three-for-three."

"DiMaggio's dreamy," Mame says, currying favor.

RoseMarie purses her lips like an old nun. "He's a married man with a baby on the way."

"I wasn't going to *marry* him."

"No, you're not going to marry anyone."

Babe watches Mame consider stabbing her sister with the nail polish brush. Those two are unspeakably tiresome. "We had to endure 'I Am an American' Day."

"We heard a little of that, on CBS. La Guardia sounded grand."

"A lot of claptrap. A ridiculous young woman sang at the Stadium." Babe hears herself and reconsiders. She doesn't want Mame and RoseMarie and Loretta to get the impression that she's some kind of pacifist too. "Not that we don't have to get behind the president, however conniving he is. We're going to have to go to war, but I won't tolerate putting ribbons and bows on it. It was an ugly war last time, and it's going to be an ugly war this time, too."

The three girls in the living room tilt, in unison, and look up at their grandmother. It's the first time in a long time that she's seen fear on their faces: not the childish panic that used to appear, after Gloria, but a subdued fear, a long-term fear, the same kind of fear they've probably seen on her own face when Mickey's between jobs and the gas has been shut off. It occurs to her that maybe the girls have sweethearts too, fellows they won't bring home because they think she won't approve. She wants to tell her granddaughters they should grab the first man who asks them: Italians, Romanians, Armenians for God's sake. Who would quibble, at a time like this? She only had a year with Albert, before they hauled him off to Hart's Island, and wasn't it the best year of her life? Pacifists. What kind of nonsense is that?

She hears Agnes clattering the dishes down from the cupboard, and she pushes herself toward the kitchen. The hip is worse, after her outing. Both hips are worse, and the knees crack like snapped wishbones with every step. She doesn't know if she'll be able to sit more than two minutes at the cramped kitchen table. She doesn't know if Agnes is telling fibs about Joe D'Ambrosio to throw her off the trail. She doesn't know how she'll get herself up to the ballpark next time, if it takes it out of her this way.

Mame wails: "Agnes, isn't the food ready yet? I can't stand to wait another second."

"Then sit for it, you ninny," Babe snaps, and has to suppress the urge to smack Mame while she's at it. She hasn't even revealed to Mickey how Joe DiMaggio was handed his third hit of the day: how, in the fourth, Joe slammed the ball at Harland Clift, how Clift—ready this time—pocketed it neat as you please. But the catcher's mitt had grazed Joe's bat, and the plate umpire called interference, an automatic single. Agnes's sweetheart was dumbfounded—Babe could see he thought it was an injustice, even if it was DiMag, and she herself was taken aback, though she knew the rule well enough. For the first time she felt the weight of her powers, of tipping the world her way.

Babe O'Leary doesn't often feel guilt, but she felt a little guilty in the bottom of the fourth, and she feels a little guilty now. Three at bats, three hits: undeserved, manipulated, summoned. Gold spun from straw. She is the wicked witch, the fairy godmother, the cruel stepmother. She has committed the worst kind of interference you can commit in baseball, and the best kind: psychic interference. Most likely the pot roast will take the edge off that. And most likely, after all those questionable calls, Joe DiMaggio left the ballgame, on "I Am an American" Day, determined to hit the ball fair and square from here on in.

BLOOD

Manhattan is crawling with policemen. Joe D'Ambrosio's never seen so many cops, and he's seen a few—he's felt the sting of their nightsticks too, in Union Square, but he doesn't hold it against them. His cousin Vince, who failed the exam twice, is finally a rookie.

At the corner of Fifty-Fourth and Eighth, he stops to see what the cops will do with the Socialist Democratic Youth of America, Columbia students mostly, marching from uptown toward Madison Square Garden. They look like young lawyers in their jackets and ties. The careful schoolboy print on their signs reads: GIVE CHURCHILL A HAND and STOP HITLER'S HENCHMEN.

The cops (no sign of Vince among them) stretch across the sidewalk in a line as straight as the Rockettes', and the marchers hit the brakes. From across the street, he can't hear their conversation—but eventually the picketers yield to authority. One of the Socialist Youth steps off the curb to hail a cab.

Joe turns the corner, heading south. He himself has never been in a cab in his life. They must be loaded with dough.

From the looks of Forty-Ninth Street, it's a good thing he has a ticket. They've set up loudspeakers for the overflow, and already the streets are mobbed. It takes him awhile to push through to the entrance, but he's always pushed through city crowds alone, often walking solo—as he did tonight—from his folks' place on Twelfth Street to midtown or farther. An unwritten rule controls space in the four railroad rooms of the D'Ambrosio household: if you miss the evening meal, that's more room at the table for everybody else. Uncle Fran saves a plate for him, *in the cupboard, Joey, where I hid it from the vultures. Lemme warm it up for you.*

Lately, in his wandering, he's come to see himself as a solitary soul. He takes in baseball games and movies alone, and last week stood by himself for the first time at the back of the City Opera for *The Barber of Seville.* If he were perfectly honest, he'd admit that he strikes up a conversation wherever he goes, that he's a talk-magnet for middle-aged businessmen and foreign tourists and colored shoeshine men. But lately, every time he has a jolly encounter with a stranger, he imagines himself standing outside the picture frame. Even with Bernie and Agnes—especially with Bernie and Agnes—he's not all there.

If he could just get his hands on her he could win her back, he knows he could, but when does he ever have a chance? If he could trace the curve of her breasts under the white Dominican blouse, if he could squeeze them—he stops right there. He shouldn't be going beyond a chaste kiss, which would be a victory in itself, but instead he lies in bed night after night picturing himself raising her plaid skirt, running his hand up the length of her white thigh till he touches the nub of her garter. His hand proceeds—she's not wearing any drawers (some nights she's not wearing anything) and he's doing more solitary sinning than he's ever done in his life. Does Agnes know somehow how far he went with other girls, back before Xavier? Girls from the building, nasty girls from the street, when he wasn't much older than his little brother Petey. The things he did with those girls. The nipples he squeezed.

Now he shares the bed with Pete and Pauly—he's got the wall—and he suspects that they both feign sleep when the mattress quivers. In the dark you can see the crucifix over the doorframe, Jesus's white body a beacon shining down on him. He could use confession every day of the week. At Xavier the other guineas swagger, mouthing off about their latest visit to Eileen's on Forty-Fifth Street, where the whores take off their silk stockings twenty times a night. He never knows whether to believe them, or whether they've conjured those whores doing the same thing he's doing, under the same shining crucifix.

Inside the Garden, he scans the crowd for girls. The truth is, he's attracted to all females under the age of forty, unless they're fat or have a mustache (Agnes's grandmother was pretty scary in both regards). They're attracted to him too. The last few years they've been making eyes at him in the Gotham Book Mart, in Washington Square, in Caffè Reggio. Older women, usually, secretaries and clerks, the seams of their stockings as straight as their souls. Prettier women, sometimes, than Agnes, who is not beautiful but who just . . . *shines.*

No one in this mob could touch her, and anyway, there are no girls for him here, only married couples or men coming from work. He's never seen the Garden so crowded or so imposing: huge flags hover high above, bunting swoops from the balconies. His seat's in the second section, far back from the bandstand, but he'll have a fine view of Norman Thomas at the podium. He's come to see why a socialist would agree to share the platform with Charles Lindbergh. He squirms, a spy in the house of isolationism.

And he fingers the little notebook he's carrying in his pocket. Tonight he's an observer, a reporter. At the very least he'll have an essay for philosophy class, but if it turns out well maybe he'll even submit it to the *Catholic Worker.* Meanwhile, he'll strike up a conversation, as usual, with one of his neighbors.

This time it's a stocky middle-aged fellow in a black suit and a black hat: an insurance adjuster or an accountant who looks more like an undertaker. They pop up together, straining to see a commotion down front. Joe can make out cries of: "Throw him out!" and even "Throw the bastard out!"

"What's going on?"

For answer, Joe leans forward till he hears a name rustle through the crowd, a name that's in the tabloids often enough. "McWilliams," he answers the fellow. "They're trying to throw him out."

"And who's this McWilliams when he's at home?" The man has a bald spot like a tonsure.

"Head of the Christian Mobilizers. Calls himself the führer. You might've seen his picture in the *Post*."

"I don't read that rag. And I don't like the sound of *führer*."

"That's what the ruckus is all about."

"You seem to know a lot about it."

"We have to read the papers for school." That, he thinks, will account for his notebook and his scribbling.

"Much obliged." The man leans back. His shoes could use a shine, and they're cordovan which, as Joe's father would be quick to point out, is all wrong with a black suit. Not that Joe's father is ever in a suit himself, except for funerals, but he cares desperately how other men carry themselves. "Haven't followed the war too closely, this time around. I was in the big one."

Joe regards him, as he does all strangers he meets, face-on, which requires twisting in his seat. "I bet you've got some stories."

"I wouldn't repeat what I saw," the man shoots back. "Certainly not to a lad like yourself."

Meaning a lad who might ship out to the next war soon. He knows he won't tell the man that he plans to resist, to go to jail if he has to. It gets too complicated, distinguishing himself from the isolationists. "Look at all the cops," he says instead.

They're lined up everywhere, two deep by the podium, scattered along the walls like human pillars holding up civil order. No sign of Vince. "Alien squad," the man says, but this crowd does not look alien. This crowd looks like it trooped over from Wall Street. "The wife wouldn't come near the Garden tonight. *You'll get thrown in jail with all the reds*, she says. But I want to hear what Lindy has to say. And I'll tell you something else." Here he leans in close. "I'm not inclined to help the English, not after what they've done to my kind."

Joe D'Ambrosio counts tawny heads: Irish, like this man? German? It's not just a matter of helping the British, he wants to say. What about the Poles? What about the Jews in Paris? Do you let them fend for themselves? Am I my brother's keeper? He hears himself making the case for war and almost laughs. Pacifism might be too complicated for a conversation with a stranger, but it's the only conversation he has with himself anymore.

The band moans, tuning up, and the crowd sits straighter. Someone comes along to pass out miniature flags. Joe and his neighbor practice-wave and then grin stupidly at one another. When the bandleader in his white suit is satisfied, he turns to face the audience. The balconies fall silent, then the floor. The bandleader clears his throat. "Shall we open with 'God Bless America'?"

The crowd bellows back a resounding *No!* Interventionists sing "God Bless America," but America Firsters stand and belt out "America the Beautiful." Joe belts it out right along with them. He loves to sing. He has inherited from his father a clear unpretentious tenor, but he hardly ever gets the chance to let it loose this way. When he finishes the tune, he's light-headed.

He has the strangest fleeting sensation, that they're all prisoners in an enormous courtroom, waiting for the judges. When the platform party enters from stage left, the crowd's murmur becomes a low ecstatic cry. Lindbergh's high forehead appears. And that has to be Norman Thomas with the glasses, settling into his seat next to Lindy. In the front row a cardinal perches, red beanie bobbing. Joe nudges his neighbor. "Alice Roosevelt Longworth. Crossing the stage."

His friend's mouth pops open and stays open. The crowd's delirious, straining to see who's who. The roaring and the foot-stomping go on and on, two minutes and then three and then five. The balconies chant: "We want Lindbergh, we want Lindbergh," till the Golden Boy finally rises grinning from his seat center stage and waves, all his gleaming teeth on display. Joe catches a glimpse of the wife in the row behind. Poor grieving Mrs. Lindbergh. The fans at the Stadium last week didn't make half this much noise. You'd think Lindy was Joe DiMaggio, Jimmy Stewart, and Glenn Miller rolled into one.

Lindbergh's speech is just what the crowd wants. It makes Joe's jaw go rigid, the way it does when he's anchoring the relay and they've fallen so far behind he can't possibly save them. Something so *golly gee* about the man—couldn't he even come up with a new line? *America first, America first.* He tunes out till he hears Lindbergh take a deep breath.

"We deplore the fact that the German people cannot vote on the policies of their government." The crowd pants its approval. "But have we been given the opportunity to vote on the policy our government has followed?"

The crowd roars its answer and Lindbergh echoes: "No!" The audience pops to its feet again, chins and fists raised, but Joe only half-rises from his chair. He wants to propel himself right through this crowd, right down to the stage to grab the mike. *We haven't said one word about the refugees.* He writes *Nothing about the refugees* and sees that his handwriting, with its looping letters, is a child's. He's as golly gee as Lindbergh, with his fantasies. What did he expect, coming tonight? He knows who these people are. Agnes keeps a tally of the Jewish refugees who've been rounded up and shipped out and fenced off, in Vienna and Paris and Warsaw, and Bernie asks how you could save them with your bare hands. From this side of the ocean. He doesn't have an answer. This week the Germans barred Jewish emigration from all the occupied territories. He keeps a smeared, rained-on copy of last year's *Catholic Worker* statement in his back pocket. He has the lines memorized—*We are opposed to all but the use of nonviolent means*—but he has Bernie's taunt memorized too: *Don't be a fool, D'Ambrosio. What nonviolent means?* Even his Uncle Fran, the old fussbudget: *What if somebody threatened your wife and kids, Joey? I'll tell you what. You'd pull out their eyeballs from their sockets, that's what, and then you'd squeeze them till eyeball juice ran down your fingers. And you know what? You'd feel good about it. You'd feel good about it, because that would be justice.*

He's squeezing Agnes's breasts, hard this time. Norman Thomas, in bow tie, approaches the microphone at last, and the audience turns the same adoring gaze on him. They don't have a clue he's a socialist.

When Thomas begins with a ringing cry—"Peace now!"—Joe springs up with everyone else. This is where Thomas should come in with the refugees. There must be twenty thousand bodies in the Garden tonight. If every one of them stood arm in arm, they could stop Hitler's tanks. Or maybe not his tanks—he's getting carried away. He has a hard time picturing where in Europe twenty thousand people could go to stand arm in arm. Norman Thomas leads the crowd in a recitation, a repeat-after-me chant of FDR's pledge not to send our American boys into any foreign war. The speech is over before it began. Thomas finishes by being *sarcastic*.

Some lady novelist rises from the bank of speakers, and he feels himself float away from the Garden, from his own body. "Never again!" the audience chants, but Joe D'Ambrosio's not listening anymore. He's retreated to his own solitude, doodling in the margins of his notebook, a wiser man than he was when he entered the hall. He sketches Agnes in her ridiculous tam, then stabs her pompom with his pencil point. Surprised by the depth of his rage, he abandons her to draw Superman. Superman? It's a word that's floated through Xavier all year, ever since they read Nietzsche. Father Phelan, who thinks he's droll, said *Adolf Hitler has himself confused with Superman,* but if he read the comic he'd know that Superman's *against* the Nazis and fighting for world peace.

Onstage, one of the roman collars stands. Joe can't bear to look at the priest. He can't bear to hear a prayer at this unholy gathering. His eye falls on his sketch of DiMaggio at home plate, bat extended so far he looks as if he might spin around in a full circle. After all those weeks of watching his batting average plummet, DiMag has begun to wield his bat like a weapon again. There's a superman.

It comes to him easily then, and all in a rush. What he has to do is write to Joe DiMaggio, make him see that war's not the way to go, not the way to stop Hitler. Surely a man who plays with that measure of grace is already leaning in the direction of peace. Surely a man whose family saved years for the passage will want to save refugees. If it's hard to get through by mail—DiMaggio must get letters by the sackful—he'll find a way to talk to him in person. DiMag lives up Bernie's way, on West End Avenue. He pictures himself haunting the West Side till Joe and Mrs. D drive up in a cab. No, a limo. They'll issue a joint statement: *Schoolboy*

and Slugger Team Up for Peace. Or better, they'll have a rally to top this one. *Resist Hitler, Resist War.* Not bad. He'll ask Agnes to try it out on her grandmother for a typical fan's reaction (as if Agnes's grandmother is a typical anything). And he can screw up his courage to ask Dorothy Day herself for her blessing. She looks so humorless, but you never know. She might go for baseball and she might go for DiMaggio. One thing you hear a lot of gossip about, around the Catholic Worker House, is how many lovers Dorothy Day collected, back before she decided to become some kind of a saint.

On Saturday he shows up at the Worker House early, with his article about the Lindbergh rally in his pocket. He's down at Mott Street every weekend, spooning out soup, but he's never approached the great Dorothy Day about writing for her paper. He can talk to anybody about anything, can charm the pants off any fierce Xavier priest including the Prefect of Discipline, but he has never made Miss Day, with her dark unrevealing eyes, so much as crack a smile. She's given him permission to move in, come graduation, but she's never looked kindly on him. Maybe if he can thrust the finished article into her hands, she'll warm up.

His pop is ready to come down to Mott Street and throttle Dorothy Day with his bare hands. The way his father had it worked out, after graduation Joe would keep working at the vegetable stall, only full-time, and when he had enough money for four years' tuition, plus lost wages, then he could start college: the pay-as-you-go plan that has transformed the D'Ambrosios, as he never tires of reminding them, from wage earners to vegetable-stall-proprietors. It's precarious proprietorship, his father struggling to pay the rent on the hole-in-the-wall behind his sidewalk display, unloading crates with a sore neck and once, even, a three-week stretch of pleurisy. But it's proprietorship nonetheless. His pop regards the piddling scholarship offer from Fordham as an insult. After the Jesuits lured him to their military high school, after they collected their track medals, now when the D'Ambrosios need them they can't come through. They've thrown his son out with the garbage, and now the boy wants to live in a flophouse with a bunch of crackpots. Pious Uncle Fran has no patience either: *Joey, take a look at them Jesuit priests you don't know what I'm talking about. Sure, they take their vow of poverty. But, excuse me, the finest wines and silk sheets on the bed? They'd let you live in poverty, all right, and they'd think you was a sucker.* He only has to walk Mott and Mulberry to see what makes his pop quiver with rage. Down here they still sell the vegetables from carts.

Today he's parked himself in the kitchen. The House is actually two houses squeezed on the one lot: one with a storefront that used to sell dry goods when it wasn't a speakeasy, one in back with twenty rooms where whole families crammed not so long ago. Now the back house is the men's residence, and the fellas who live there are not what you'd call swells. He'll room back there in the smell of piss that's missed its mark and aftershave that's swallowed, not applied. It's a dark, dank building with long, narrow halls, and he can't wait to claim his space.

This time of the morning the men are still holed up (sleeping it off?), but a few drift through. The girls from Cathedral High scrape carrots and celery, flicking the dirty skins onto newspapers, and the women who live in the front house poke their noses in to criticize the cooking. He used to show up with a bag of onions and turnips his father let him take—just starting to soften, perfectly fine for soup—and if his pop was in a good mood he'd throw in a handful of kale or escarole, barely yellow. But no more. Not a parsnip, his pop says, not a sprig of parsley for these misguided holy moleys.

So now Joe shows up empty-handed, but the Saturday girls don't hold it against him. Only two are in the kitchen at this hour. His job is to amuse them while they cook, and if amusing them amounts to flirting, God knows they could all use the attention. The girls are there every Saturday, radiating efficiency and energy. From their capable bustling he infers strict orderly home lives from which they, too, long to escape. Sometimes he imagines that one or the other of them will come live in the front house, that late at night they'll rendezvous. One's pretty—Julie, with blond curls, a high forehead, Rita Hayworth lips—and the other, Jean, has darting green eyes.

"Yesterday in Boston," he tells them, leaning against the icebox, "they called DiMaggio *meatball*."

"I'll tell you who the meatballs are." Jean eyes him sharply.

"Exactly. Can't they see his neck is killing him? He's only out on the field cause he doesn't want to let McCarthy down."

"Who's McCarthy?" Julie asks.

He'd be glad to review baseball's cast of characters for the lovely Julie, but Jean jumps in first. "The Yanks' *man*ager." She pours enough vinegar on the words to indicate that Julie must have been living in a cave the last few years. "Say," she goes on, knife stopped midscrape. "How about that streak of Joe's?"

He's taken aback. He knew Ted Williams was on a hitting streak, but there was nothing about a DiMaggio streak in the *meatball* article, only Joe's four sensational errors in yesterday's doubleheader.

"He's been hitting up a storm." He strikes a neutral tone, in case he's missed something.

"Fourteen straight going into yesterday's doubleheader. Which means that Boston made it—"

"Fifteen and sixteen." As if he's known about the streak all along. He's fired off three letters to Joe since that night in the Garden, and even though it's too soon for DiMag to have even opened them all, much less replied, he can't stand the wait.

They hear a flutter of voices in the front room and Julie says: "Guess who's back from Mass." The girls scrape faster, and Joe straightens himself against the icebox. Voices approach and there she is, Dorothy Day herself, swinging into the kitchen with her dreary scarf still tied under her chin and another schoolgirl in tow.

The girl is Agnes. Joe can't stop a ludicrous grin from stretching. "What are you doing here?" It's Saturday: she's supposed to be working. And she's in her work clothes, the gray spring Altman's suit and—here he could weep with gratitude—a new beret that matches her buttons and trim, a smart beret the color of raspberries. Her hats are either adorable or so silly that it slays him, how she can't see which is which.

Before Agnes has a chance to say what she's doing there, Miss Day thumps the kitchen table and lets out a low gurgle of laughter. Dorothy Day, who's forever scowling at him, has the *giggles*.

Miss Day unknots her scarf. "I found your friend taking pictures of the soup line." When she looks at Joe her sternness reasserts itself, as if he were the one taking illicit pictures with the Brownie he now sees

clutched in Agnes's fist. "One fellow says, *Soup ready, miss? I can't stand to wait much longer* and she says, *Then sit for it, you ninny.*" This fractures Dorothy Day all over again. Her laughter tapers off the same way Agnes's does. Great Day's wearing a suit, too, only hers is the color of rust. She makes wearing it look like a challenge: go ahead, ask me which dumpster I raided for these rags. She removes the hideous flowered scarf, snapping it like a whip, and gazes at Joe with a look he interprets as disgust. "So. Off with you. I told your friend we could spare you this one Saturday." Her tone suggests they could spare him every Saturday.

"No, no—"

"Oh, for goodness' sake, take the day off. Then persuade her to come back with you the next time. Only no romancing in the kitchen."

"Gracious, no." Agnes's eyes are merry—and wonder of wonders, Miss Day's eyes are merry too under that stern part in her graying hair. But what are she and Agnes saying to each other? That Joe's her sweetheart? That he isn't?

He takes Agnes's elbow and steers her through the kitchen door and out of the house. She doesn't look back at him once. On the narrow Mott Street sidewalk he waves to the waiting men but angles her away from the soup line. They travel a block in silence, Agnes matching his long strides. He notices what he never notices, the air so pungent you're breathing smells instead of oxygen. His hand still guides her elbow, till it's safe to say, "What are you doing here?"

She pulls her elbow out of his clutch. "I don't know, exactly." She stops dead on the sidewalk, one step away from a wooden cellar door that picks this moment to rise into the air like a drawbridge. A butcher's boy emerges from the depths, hauling up a side of beef. Joe takes in the Saturday crowds around him, the pushcarts, the bouquets of Italian ices. He smells syrup, fish, cheese, bread, blood. Mott Street is the most beautiful street in New York. He nods at the grannies rocking baby carriages from their stoops, woolen shawls around their shoulders though summer's almost upon them. A grubby brown boy in shorts and filthy saddle shoes rushes along, a tall girl chasing after. Their jostling pushes him into Agnes. He stretches one hand to her shoulder, balancing, and she finds her voice at last. "I told her I…had to *talk* to you."

"What's the matter with that?"

Agnes's cheeks flush the color of her beret. "She gave me a *look,* and I knew just what that look meant. She thinks I'm pregnant."

His heart stops. He still feels the soft light wool of Agnes's suit, though he has withdrawn his hand. He can't think what she means. "Are you?"

"Joe!" She laughs his name in a way that starts his heart again. No, she's not pregnant, she's a virgin, of course she is, how could Bernie have possibly found a place and a time. "How could you *think* such a thing?"

"I didn't mean you'd… I mean if you did, do you think I'd. . .?" Of course he can't say *love you any less,* but she hears it anyway, hears the unspoken words and lowers her eyes, ashamed. Ashamed because she doesn't love him back? Ashamed because she knows he's just a lousy hypocrite?

"Oh, Joe." She sounds as if she's going to collapse into a pool of despair on this sticky sidewalk, as if she knows how, sometimes, he dreams of holding her so tight, digging into her skin, that he draws blood.

"What's wrong?" He sounds like his old man, helpless.

"I don't know. I don't know why I came down here. This old lady threw up at the counter, and when I rushed around to help her I slid on the. . .mess. And I cracked my arm hard, going down, everybody heard it, and they all said I must go get an X-ray."

He waits.

"So I told my manager all right, knowing perfectly well I can't get an X-ray. Who would pay for that?"

"But Agnes, if you've broken your arm . . ."

She thrusts her arms out from her sleeves, the white skin startling, a violet bruise spilling along her left forearm down to her wrist. "Oh for goodness' sake, I'm perfectly fine."

"But why'd you come down here then?"

She bites her lower lip.

He finds himself walking again, walking in the direction of the old Cathedral with its catacombs. It looks like Agnes is walking beside him. He takes her hand before he knows he's done it, and she doesn't pull back. He's elated—they've never held hands, not once—and here come the little boy in the dirty shoes and the tall girl on their return journey, still in hot pursuit. The sidewalks are so narrow that even the pushcarts totter, struggling to decide whether it's safer to roll among hooligan children on the sidewalk or monstrous sedans honking like rowdy geese in the street.

"I never saw you with a camera before."

In answer she pulls her hand back and whips the black box around. She aims up and shoots before he knows it. "I've been looking at that book."

"What book?"

"*You* know." He does know. The photographer they met on the subway.

"I've been shooting the salesladies—they take *forever* to rouge up—and then I thought, why not go see that Catholic Worker House you're always talking about. Then when I was coming up to it I kept thinking *What the heck is that mob of people? Isn't the Depression long gone?* And then I just started taking pictures. I'm as bad as him, I guess."

"The photographer?"

"Bad as he," she corrects herself, and it just slays him. They're walking very fast, as fast as he travels from the lockers to the starting blocks. What race does Agnes think she's heading to?

"Boy, she's tough, isn't she? Miss Day. She was all over me. *What are you doing, this isn't some tourist attraction.* I had to work hard to soften her up."

"She's tough all right."

"It's so expensive, bringing the film in. Mr. McClary said he'd show me how to develop in his basement, he was a photographer in the Army—"

"I don't want you in the basement with Mr. McClary."

"I don't think I want to be in the basement with Mr. McClary either." She's giggling, laughing at him.

"I didn't mean—"

She casts him a reckless sideways glance. "My mother...."

Somehow they're up to Kenmare already and they turn west together, as if they both know where they're going. He wants to reclaim her hand, but she's clutching the camera. He waits for more about her mother but there isn't any more. And he knows enough not to push it, knows that she was just a little kid when her mother died, that she and Bernie shut down fast before they'll talk about their dead parents, as if it's shameful to be the child of someone who passed away too soon. He stumbles. Agnes and Bernie, the dead parents. He flails about for a dead relative of his own.

"I found a picture of my mother."

A long pause, and he tries gallantry to cover it: "I bet she was beautiful."

"A lot more beautiful than me. Than I."

"You're—"

"No, Joe, you're sweet, but you don't have to say those things. I don't know, I guess other girls want to hear them but..." She's still giggling. "*My mistress' eyes are nothing like the sun.*"

She has about a thousand sonnets memorized, and finally, this is one he's studied. *If snow be white, why then her breasts are dun.* He too would take dun breasts, oh wouldn't he just. *Mistress.* He reaches for her hand again, but it's floundering along this time, too hard to catch, so without knowing he's going to do it, he swings her round by the shoulders and kisses her, hard, right in the middle of the sidewalk on Kenmare Street, out in the open in the bright day. He's never kissed Agnes before, and he's out of practice, surprised all over again by the soft flesh, by the way her lips simultaneously yield and push back.

"Hey! Ya mind?"

A passing workman regards them over his shoulder, teasing, enjoying their kiss, and it's then that he realizes Agnes has curled her hand up around his neck. A movie pose. She's learned how to kiss from the movies. She pulls away, embarrassed, and skips along as if she's still on

the screen, darting ahead, flirting. It's just as well—he's moving along the sidewalk with a hard-on, trying to subdue it, but how can he when he realizes that if *he had just grabbed her before* he could have won her back months ago. He can speak with his hands, he knew he could. She glides through the Saturday shoppers and he sees a small spot on the back of her skirt. The old lady's vomit. Even that doesn't deflate him.

Finally he's up to her and slings an arm around her shoulder, but she slithers out. Won't be pinned so easily. "Good thing I didn't have my glasses on for *that*," she says.

For that. He's won her back, he knows he has, he's won.

"But you should see my pictures! They're all out of focus. I say I don't need your sweet-talk but then I won't even put my glasses on to take a picture."

He has to get her into a coffee shop, someplace where he can slow her down and coax her into connecting these spilling thoughts. She turns away from him, and this time he sees that the spot on the back of her skirt is not sickness, it's blood. She's *on the rag*. That's it for the stiffie. But knowing this about her has made them close as an old married couple, and he wants to spread a great flowing cape over Agnes's back so she won't be embarrassed walking through the streets. When she gets home and finds the stain, she'll know he saw it. That too will bind them.

"Agnes." Suddenly he's ravenous, as hungry as the men on the soup line. "Let's sit down someplace. Let's get something to eat."

"I want to tell you something, something about my mother." She's gazing up at him now, every muscle on her face straining into what she needs to say. He imagines wrapping her in his arms again, but he hesitates, and in his pause her face resettles itself, comes to some resolution.

"What about your mother?"

She smiles a little too brightly and slips her arm through his the way she does on Saturday nights, when she divides her touch like half-a-loaf for Bernie and him. He understands that his victory was momentary. She doesn't answer him, just clams up. He waits and waits and . . . nothing. They walk along, and she looks here and there, like some tourist slumming. It's as if she's completely forgotten him, completely forgotten she was going to tell him something big.

"Oh, never mind," she says, finally. "It was nothing."

He steams a little, under his collar. Nothing. She has nothing to say to him.

They trudge along the sidewalk in silence, like drunks sobering up. All the dashing children have disappeared, and so have the old ladies. So has the crowd. Even the horns have stopped their honking. His sense of smell shuts down. He walks across Kenmare Street with a stranger, a girl who showed up on his doorstep to tell him something and then changed her mind, a girl in a bloodstained skirt.

PART II

IRON  MAN

Saturday they're rained out in Cleveland. It's always raining in Cleveland. DiMaggio slumps on his hotel bed, watching dirty water streak down the window, watching Gomez rummage through his duffle for another deck of cards.

Lefty says, "Sure you don't wanna go snooker those suckers?"

DiMaggio grunts out a *Nah*. He droops his eyelids and tries to loosen the hardball knots in his neck. The door slams behind Lefty, whistling down the corridor. DiMaggio pretends he's going to take a nap, but if he can't sleep at night, he sure as hell can't sleep in the middle of the day.

Last month, when he was slumping, he never missed a card game. This month, right on schedule, he's got the start of the streak going, and the word is that Lou Gehrig's dying, really dying this time, dying fast. Every time he gets the hit now, he has the ungodly sensation that it's Lou waiting for him on the bag: a ghost, a *spiritu* at first base, playing for the other team. He can still feel the press of Lou's handshake, that rookie season: "Glad to have you, Joe." That was it. Say what you have to say and then stop. The man has class.

The rain sliding down the window stands still, and he tries to picture Lou's funeral in the Bronx, as if he's inoculating himself for when the time comes. He has no idea what picture to summon for the church: Lou's people are German, so he makes it Protestant, not Catholic. Talk about the other team. Maybe not so much blood and gore on the walls? An empty cross? If he's on the road—and odds are he will be—Dottie will have to represent the DiMaggios.

So Dottie, sashaying up a church's center aisle like it's their wedding day, only she'll be wearing some black maternity dress. She'll really be showing by then. She'll go with June Gomez, but June will still look like a showgirl: he can't take his eyes off June lately, feathers swooping out of her broad-brimmed hats, her little tummy nice and tight. That's OK. Dorothy, in her pregnant-lady suit, will look like Mrs. DiMaggio for Lou Gehrig's funeral. Dottie's always liked Lou best of the Yanks: because he's never run his mouth. Dottie, evidently, likes the quiet ones.

She'll wear a black veil, probably. He makes it small and tasteful, but when he pictures her face beneath he puts too much rouge on her, the way she's been doing herself lately, big round circles to compensate for the big round belly. If he knows Dot, even in her condition she'll be eyeballing every last reporter in the pews. Maybe he doesn't have a way with the press, but his wife thinks they're swell.

The rain in Cleveland makes him decide that it will rain for Lou Gehrig's funeral in New York, that the air will smell like pennies. The fans will gather on the sidewalk in their raincoats and boots and slickers: no shelter, no comfort, on the day they bury Gehrig. Cops will bar the door, the way they do whenever the Yankee brass show up. Christ's sake, Ellie should hold Lou's funeral in St. Patrick's Cathedral. Who cares whether he was Catholic or not? They should bury him from Fifth Avenue, where the city could say a proper good-bye.

Well, you can't suggest funeral arrangements before the man's dead. DiMaggio hasn't been up to see Lou and Ellie lately. Gehrig's been decent to him, God knows, but he just can't bring himself to sit by the bedside anymore. Can't take looking down on Lou, can't take the way Ellie smiles when she hands the big ballplayers the little china cups. They all pretend Lou's gonna beat it when he can't even lift his head and shoulders anymore. Jesus Christ, how do you stay sane with your body going dead on you like that? His own head weighs a thousand pounds lately, just trying to imagine it.

Why'd he ever think he could be the same kind of guy just by keeping his own mouth shut? He sees the difference between them now clear as he sees the funeral: when Lou opens his mouth, he never talks about himself. He's *sweet,* that word you could never imagine using about a little guy like Rizzuto—who is, to tell the truth, pretty sweet himself. But you'd never in a million years call Rizzuto *sweet:* you wouldn't want to make a pansy of him. A big guy like Lou can hold the word, can wear it on his back like his number, can hold that word *decent,* that word *good.*

It was all over the papers a couple of months ago when Lou said Joe DiMaggio was the best outfielder playing the game. Inside a week, DiMaggio's neck and shoulders cramped, began to weigh him down, as if a dying man's praise was too much to bear. That was when he started making errors like nobody's business. Against his own pop's resistance to baseball, he's played like a demon, like a man possessed, a man who has to prove himself. But Lou Gehrig says he's the best and what happens? He shuts down in center field.

He should say a prayer for Lou, lying paralyzed across the country: it's all he can think to do. He starts an *Our Father,* the only prayer he can remember all the way through anymore, but it feels fake. *Thy kingdom come?* This is the kingdom, this life in locker rooms, this life on the road. This is the kingdom, where Lou wakes up one morning and can't lift the bat. This is the kingdom, Lou's broad back withering. In the Bronx, Lou Gehrig struggles for every breath, and in Cleveland his teammates play rummy. Lou loved bridge, so they've been playing rummy, canasta, pinochle, poker, euchre: anything but bridge.

His teammates play cards and lie on their hotel beds imagining his funeral. A laugh pushes up from deep in DiMaggio's spine. Maybe when his own body's too broken for baseball he can go into the fortune-telling business. Put out a sign: Signuri DiMaggio Knows Your Future. The laugh goes south on him. Sometimes since this streak started he feels like he's losing his mind. Did that happen the first time? When he was small and trying to get out of going to school, his mother used to ask if he was *malatu* or *malu: sick* or *bad.* What's Gehrig done to deserve this?

Lou, Lou, Lou. Next thing he knows he's like a newborn babe rolled up in a clammy ball, fist in his mouth and the taste of bloody knuckles like copper on his tongue.

He's lucky if he gets four, five hours of sleep, and this is only the start of a frigging streak. Sometimes it's Lou in his nightmares, sometimes he wakes up paralyzed himself. Sometimes it's those refugees: before he left San Francisco for spring training this year, he sat with his father at the kitchen table, translating the war news for pop. They were shipping Jews out of Vienna, ten thousand Jews, and his pop couldn't believe it, couldn't believe he was reading the words right. "*Comu? Perchi?*" How could you even feed them all? How could you send ten thousand people out of a city overnight? And why? That's Krauts for you, his pop said. A Sicilianu would never do such a thing.

DiMaggio tipped his chair back into the icebox door like he was still a little kid, the little kid who kept quiet while his pop ranted on. He pictured the crowds in the train, in a Europe he's never seen, tried to imagine what it would be like to be moved overnight, what it would be like to pack your own food for the journey. He saw the refugees carrying paper sacks full of peaches that smashed when they crowded up against each other. The smell of crushed fruit came right off the newsprint—but that was only because his mother had put out canned peaches in red wine for her boys, for her Joe.

Now that he's started this streak, now that Lou Gehrig's dying, they come to him at night, those refugees the Germans rounded up, bewildered travelers who crowd their way into his dreams and swarm there. Lou would know what to say to them. Sometimes when he's sitting in the dugout or loosening up in the batter's box, he pictures them out of nowhere, the way he pictures Gehrig. They're in their best clothes, lugging suitcases tied with string, paper bags leaking peach juice. Sometimes *they* are paralyzed.

The look on his pop's face that gray spring day: not possible, inconceivable, that you would round up human beings and ship them off. Ship them where? The same look of stubborn refusal that used to come over his dark fisherman's face at the pazzu idea that his sons might not join him to earn their livings on the *Rosalie,* that they might shun his little boat and spend their time instead in dusty ballparks, that they might someday lie around hotel rooms dreaming of women and corpses.

Sunday the sun comes out, sort of. Must be fifty thousand fans at Municipal Stadium for the doubleheader. He smokes half a pack of Camels in the locker room and swivels his head from side to side. He's been up since four thirty. Neck feels like it might lock up on him again, the way it did in Boston. Right now he should be lying flat on his belly while Doc Painter works out the kinks, but he can't bear the thought of another man's touch. Cleveland fans maybe aren't as loud as New York fans, but they're more obnoxious, smug and fat and self-satisfied. He pictures them counting their dough. They call down to him on the field like they own his contract. *Hey Joe, bring your butterfingers?* It's all he can do to keep from leaping into the stands and pummeling that asshole. Only one way to shut the punk up: he'll have to make his move early in the game.

In the third inning, with two out, he whacks a swifty to left. He feels it leave his bat nice and clean, and knows he's got the single. The streak's alive. Like anybody in Municipal Stadium gives a shit. Like he gives a shit. If he could just get one night's sleep. Taking his lead off first, he can hardly hold his head up.

Back on the bench in the fourth, he lowers the neck, jiggles his shoulders. Clods of dirt descend on Lou Gehrig's coffin and then Lou stirs in that coffin, alive, alive and breathing, his big shoulders struggling to raise up the coffin lid. They're going to bury Lou alive because he's paralyzed and he can't tell them to stop.

Joe DiMaggio makes himself raise his head. It's just that he didn't sleep last night. Snap out of it. Grow up. We're all gonna die. The dirt's coming down on all of us, one day.

They shut out Cleveland two–zip.

He smokes another half-dozen Camels between games, drinks four half cups of coffee, moves the grit around his throat. Rizzuto smiles at him vaguely, closest acknowledgment anybody's going to make that the streak's still on.

On the train to Cleveland the rookie Priddy walked the aisle on his way to DiMaggio's seat with the *World Telegram* in his hand, but other hands reached out to stop him. You don't say something about a streak. You certainly don't say something about a streak to Joe DiMaggio. Anyway it's so early—seventeen hits—it doesn't even count. It's not a streak till you're up to twenty, and Dickey had twenty on "I Am an American" Day. That went nowhere. He doesn't even know why the papers are talking about it, and he's sure as hell not going to keep it up with his neck jamming, not if he keeps waking up in the dead of night. Ted Williams has eighteen, wouldn't you know, so the reporters are setting up a battle royal. Williams is batting .430 besides. Bastard can't shut up about it. Maybe at least he can keep his own streak going long enough to deny Williams the satisfaction.

In the second game, the weight shifts some, from his neck to his shoulders. Mel Harder's pitching—always gives him a hard time—and the bat's uncentered in his hands. DiMaggio can make other pitchers disappear, but over and over Harder somehow catches his eye at the last second, all but winks. Well, let him wink. If Harder stops the streak, at least he'll get some sleep.

Top of the eighth, out of nowhere, he starts reading Harder instead of the other way around. The man's back leg isn't rising high enough: he's winded. Before he takes the batting box DiMaggio knows he's about to slam one of Harder's sluggish fastballs past Ken Keltner at third. One-two count. There it goes. He hears the stadium shake its collective head.

They lose five–three, but now DiMaggio's hit in eighteen consecutive games. He knows before Gomez checks the paper the next day that Williams has nineteen. What he doesn't know is that tonight, in the deepest middle of the night, he'll sit bolt upright on his bed in a trance. Doesn't know that Lefty will stand over him, snapping his fingers: "It's OK, Dago. Wake up. It's all jake."

Doesn't know that after Gomez plays nursemaid he'll spend hours breathing in rhythm with Gehrig's breathing, his windpipe rigid as metal. He'll drift in and out of sleep for the rest of the night, but it won't be Lou he'll see in his dreams. He's on his father's boat, but it's his mother at the tiller: Rosalie on the *Rosalie*. She gives him a net full of empty paper bags for the refugees. They crowd the hull and hold their hands out,

looking up at him the same way the fans look at him, wanting something from him, wanting everything, wanting him to part the waters.

By Monday he's lost so much sleep he keeps seeing things out of the corner of his eye. Get a grip. Don't let on. He waits till Lefty goes down for breakfast and has the operator put him through to New York.

Dottie must be standing over the phone: she grabs it up on the first ring and he can see her, in her white negligee, her big new pregnancy breasts powdered and spilling. "Oh, Baby," he says.

She starts to cry. "Joe. I've been waiting for you to call all week. I've been going out of my mind with worry. What if they draft you, honey? What if they want you to go fight this terrible war?"

He could laugh with gratitude: Dottie, who follows his batting average almost as closely as he does, doesn't know about the streak. "Don't you worry, sweetheart. We've got a baby on the way. They're not going to touch me."

"Are you *sure?*"

Well, that's the deal, isn't it: he's expected to read Uncle Sam's mind the same way he reads the pitcher's. "I'm sure, Dorothy. They're not taking this baseball man for the Army."

"Baseball man," she breathes as if she's auditioning for one of her shows. "I like the sound of that."

And when they finally hang up, he chuckles—that's the only word for it—chuckles at the idea that he's Baseball Man out here in Cleveland, Ohio, twenty-six years old and so famous already the fans think they can call down to him on the field. But he didn't ask Dottie how Lou was faring. So much for the chuckles.

All right. Be Baseball Man. Move that body around like a mechanical toy. He doesn't even feel stiff anymore, just directs the welded joints where he wants them to go, and where he wants to go is downstairs to get his breakfast before it's time leave for the park.

At the stadium, he looks up at the brown Ohio sky and out at the well-upholstered Ohio fans and feels like shouting, "Here I am, suckers. Baseball Man." He fell off an assembly line and he can hit it anywhere he pleases.

Top of the second, he singles, just to toy with them. That makes it nineteen games in a row. That makes it almost a streak. Child's play.

In the fourth, he slams the ball into the left bleacher seats, a sweet long wallop that travels over four hundred feet, deep into Greenberg territory. He rounds first in a cold clicking heat. They think he's arrogant? They think he's standoffish? He's a boy's best friend, he's Sluggin' Joe DiMaggio. Two hits, two runs. Nothing to it.

But back in the clubhouse, he hears the rattle in Lou's throat. What kind of friend, that he hasn't been to see him? That he doesn't ask his wife how Gehrig's doing? He stares into his locker till he hears the others watching him, unbuttons his uniform with what used to be his fingers. Now they're struts, more nimble than the real thing.

The rattle in Lou Gehrig's throat recedes.

It's late, time they hit the lobby in Detroit. An undulating mass of Yankees gathers on the sidewalk, lined up to move through the revolving doors. When DiMaggio swings through and sees that time has stopped in the lobby, he knows.

Nobody says a word. Not a syllable. They all stand there, scattered among the poofy chairs and the dainty sofas, under the twinkling chandeliers. They line up like chess pieces, taking in Lou Gehrig's death. Somebody at the desk must have told McCarthy—he's always first through the door—but he stands like any of them, short and stout and tired, looking out just beyond any man in his line of sight. They don't lower their heads or remove their hats. They stand there.

Until DiMaggio feels the flesh soften over his tender joints, and glides over to his manager. Gomez follows. Dickey, Henrich, Rolfe, Crosetti. They stand by their manager, watching the rest of the team clunk their armor through the revolving door. Any other lobby, they'd be mobbed, but here the guests hurry past, mute, understanding there's been a terrible tragedy—a fire? a war?—understanding that the Yankees mustn't be interrupted while they contemplate their battle plan.

It's DiMaggio, of all the guys, who speaks first. "You got to be there for Eleanor," he tells McCarthy. Not for the team, not for Lou, for Ellie. He's astounded by his own wisdom and by the fact that he's spoken it. He looks at Dickey: Lou's roomie, his best friend. Everybody knows it.

"Bill," he says. "You have to be there too." He watches Dickey swallow.

It's settled, then, a done deal. McCarthy and Dickey heading off to the funeral, Art Fletcher managing, Joe DiMaggio leading the team against the Detroit Tigers. Unreal, that they'll actually play a game at Briggs Stadium, but somehow right. Briggs is where Hank Greenberg plays, when he's not off getting ready to fight a war. Briggs is where Gehrig took himself out of the lineup for good, two years ago May.

They're all metal now, all iron men.

"'Member dropping those paper bags full of water out the window in Cleveland? What floor were we on? Eighth?"

"Jeez, Lefty, how old are you?"

"I'm an old, old man," Gomez says. He's standing by the window, looking down, calculating a bag-full-of-water's trajectory. It's raining again, rain in Detroit, rain in New York, rain for Lou Gehrig's funeral. Merciful rain: means they won't have to play the Tigers while the Yankee brass are singing hymns for Lou Gehrig in Christ Church, Riverdale, the Bronx. Joe DiMaggio and Lefty Gomez and the boys can stay here in the hotel, refraining from rummy and euchre, refraining most of all from bridge.

They're going to cremate Lou, Dottie says. It gives him the willies—Catholics aren't allowed—but at least he can't be suffocated in a coffin. He'll be ashes. Maybe he is ashes by now. Like a hallucination, Lou stands naked in front of his locker at Yankee Stadium, his broad back laced with fierce muscles.

Yesterday at Briggs DiMaggio led off the fourth and, without blinking, slammed a home run off Dizzy Trout. So now he's hit the ball twenty games in a row. It's official, it's a streak, and it's all over every paper in the country, twinned with Gehrig's death. This morning the funeral and the streak were on the front page and the war news was inside somewhere, buried. So to speak.

STIFFS

Agnes O'Leary marches down the hill from Seventh Avenue to Fifth, from the Irish blocks to the Italian, past the stoops where the middle-aged mamas drag their chairs to sit, past the swarming dark-haired boys flinging their Spaldeens. Along Fifth Avenue the vegetables spill out lush in front of the greengrocer's. *Italians.* Babe still pronounces the word the way she says *Protestants,* as if such people have a nerve claiming space on the sidewalks of Park Slope.

Agnes is on her way to Calabrese Funeral Services, where Babe's always forbidden the O'Leary girls to go. The last two Wednesdays, her afternoon off, she sneaked down to Fifth Avenue to get a good look at her grandfather's business. It's a big corner building, a handsome wood-trimmed brick rising four stories above the sidewalk and stretching back deep. She can't imagine she's related to someone who owns this kind of property, even if it is in the Italian part of the Slope.

This Wednesday, she's made up her mind, she's going to stop and go in. Her grandfather couldn't be worse in the flesh than he is in Babe's stories: *He tried to kill your father! As if one dead body weren't enough.* The only problem is, the closer she comes—the corner looms, the full building comes into view—the more foreign she feels. Irish girls have always been forbidden to walk this far end of the neighborhood. *You've seen the way those men stare. Why, even the ten-year-old boys ogle you, and that's not all they want to do.*

But the only man out on the avenue today is an old barber holding up his pole across the street, and he doesn't so much as glance her way. Calabrese's front door opens to the funeral parlor. Close to the back, there's a side door that must lead up to the apartment where she lived as a little girl. Babe says her mother used to tie the girls' wrists together with a length of clothesline and send them out to the butcher's or the baker's.

She considers putting this visit off till next Wednesday, or the week after, when she'll be out of school and will have all the time in the world. She considers putting it off forever, but the next thing she knows she's pushing open the front door, gilt letters on glass spelling out *Calabrese.* She walks into a room that's mostly parlor, plump armchairs and sofas upholstered in dark velvets underneath a swell chandelier. At one end is a mahogany counter, grand as the front desk in the Waldorf, flanked by a door on one side and, on the other, a long hallway with a small sign above: CHAPELS.

She strains to see without her glasses. Is she supposed to sit down? Does someone come out? She clutches her camera and then sees the bell on the countertop. Two choices: ring the bell or flee.

She rings the bell and presently the door creaks open. She knows him right away. *Has* to be her grandfather, with the puffy mouth and the big eyes. He even has her mother's arched eyebrows, and above them a full head of black hair. Babe's always called him *the old man,* and instead he's in his prime, a robust worldly man in a well-cut suit.

He's her height exactly, and from behind the counter he stares straight into her eyes. She watches his puzzlement grow. Why doesn't she say something? Out loud? Why doesn't he? A slight smile—merry?—plays at his mouth. She must be smiling too, because a funeral director doesn't beam unless someone beams first. Then her grandfather begins to weep, tears flowing profusely though the smile never wavers.

"Oh my God, I prayed for this day. I hoped and I prayed." He has a deep scratchy Brooklyn voice, a shock. She imagined an Italian accent. "Mame," he says.

It's not till she shakes her head no that she knows she's close to crying too and doesn't trust her own voice.

"RoseMarie?"

Another shake, and then they're *laughing* together. He chokes out: "Agnes? Agnes, Little Miss Independence, Little Miss I-Can-Do-It-My-self?"

She hears herself gasp, and on her exhale he comes out from behind the counter, opens his arms wide, then squeezes her tighter than she's ever been squeezed, even by Joe D'Ambrosio on Kenmare Street. She feels the press of Joe's shoulders, sees her father's undershorts, breathes in her grandfather's smell. He wears *perfume*. She might pass out.

"Just look at this little girl. Just look at you." How can he see her—she's squeezed flat against his chest, under the wing of his dark suit jacket. Finally he releases her and takes her by the hand to the clumps of high-backed couches and wing chairs. It's very bright for the first floor. Light bounces off the largest mirror she's ever seen, sitting atop a fireplace tiled in robin's-egg blue. The chandelier beams more light. The late afternoon sun streams through the long front windows: Calabrese Funeral Services faces west. The Dominican Academy is in an old mansion too, but the Sisters would never paper the walls in ivory and gold, or upholster a couch in velvet. Her grandfather certainly came through the Depression all right: there's always a market for funerals.

Though they're the only two here, her grandfather puts a finger to his lips and whispers, "Right back. Stay here." They grin like fools at each other. He pops back behind the counter, through the door into the room beyond. She catches a glimpse of office.

He's gone forever. Surely she's been in this room before, in another life, but she can't summon a vision. She counts backward. Her mother killed herself in '28, a year before the Crash, Babe reminds them, as if one catastrophe brought on the other. She tries to call back the shape of the O'Leary rooms on the top floor, but no shapes appear. She was four years old. How can she remember?

She hears a crowd passing through the hallway. Here they come, a jolly boisterous gang of middle-aged men and women who sure don't sound like they're mourning. They merge into the big front room and look her up and down frankly, as if they're trying to recall whether she belongs to them. Her grandfather brings up the rear, and sees them out the front door as if he's saying good-bye to party guests.

When they're gone, he comes over and sits in a wing chair facing her. "Agnes. Sweetheart." He leans forward, as if he can't tolerate space between them. "I don't know what to say, sweetie. The sight of you!"

"I'm sorry I didn't come before."

He waves her off. "You! A child! You musta been wondering why your old grandpa didn't put up more of a fight to see you."

"No, no . . ." Yes, yes.

"Agnes, she said such terrible things. About your mother. You wouldn't believe the things your grandmother said."

"She's very—."

"She barred the door, sweetheart. And your father—." Her grandfather shakes his head in sorrow and Agnes finishes the sentence for him. *Your father never fought for anything.*

"Your other grandmother's funeral? We held it up, fifteen, twenty minutes. I was sure the four of you would walk in with your father. What was I, crazy? She wouldn't even let Fulvia say good-bye to the four most precious . . ."

"She didn't tell us till a long time after."

This time he shakes his head in anger. "Who does she think she is?"

"I'm sorry. I'm sorry I didn't think to just come before."

"She told you not to, didn't she?" Her grandfather's still working himself up, neck reddening under his stiff white collar. "I prayed maybe one of you would write, that's the most I ever hoped for. And here you are! It's Saint Joseph, I'm telling you." Agnes smiles politely, clutching her camera, pretty sure that's not how it works in the prayer department.

"You brought a camera?"

"I thought I could show a picture of you to my sisters," she says, though she doesn't have any intention of showing them a picture, not till she knows everything she needs to know.

"They might come too, you think so? You take a whole roll of pictures, that's what you want. A whole roll of the old undertaker. Where you want me?"

This grandfather Babe's painted as a monster is mushy and merry and not at all who she came looking for. He doesn't begin to answer why her mother killed herself—but maybe she'll see, in a photograph, what she can't see with the man himself in front of her. Ever since that photographer sent her the book, she's been staring at faces, staring at portraits of strangers till they've become familiar as family. Now she'll be able to stare at the stranger in the family till he becomes familiar too. "If you could just stand there, by the window."

"You got enough light? Wanna go outside maybe?"

"I think I'll be fine." In the library, she's been studying how photographers use sidelight, and this late afternoon sun's just what she needs to wash out one side of her grandfather's face and reveal the other. "I'll have to wear my glasses," she apologizes, digging in her pocketbook.

Her grandfather leans against the glass to strike a pose. "Nearsighted? Your mother sometimes couldn't tell her own children apart, unless you got up close."

Agnes bends one knee, fixes this stranger through the little Brownie lens. His skin's as smooth as his crisp pinstriped suit. A little sag pulls at his throat, but it's no more extra chin than her father has, and there must be twenty years between them. The shadow of his beard and his eyelids are charcoal smudges. No wonder Babe despises him, a swarthy Mediterranean man, sure of himself. His hands, she sees for the first time, are weighted down with rings. My God, six rings, and she's always thought the only men with manicures like that live on Park Avenue. He leans forward again, as if he's about to speak, as if he's a kind wise judge about to render a difficult decision.

———

It's torment to sit next to Babe at dinner and not tell her what she's done, who—whom—she's seen, but Agnes doesn't want a showdown, not yet. Babe says: "Gehrig tribute tonight. They're sure to mention Joe's streak."

Agnes sees her father stiffen. "I'm sorry, Ma. Willkie's Chicago speech is on CBS the same time."

Babe lays down her fork, RoseMarie and Mame roll their eyes in each other's direction, and Agnes watches her father and grandmother unsheathe weapons for a battle they're always threatening but never actually fighting. Looks like tonight's the night.

"You want to listen to *Willkie?*"

"Ma, we're on the brink of war. I'd like to hear what he says."

"We've been on the brink of war for five years. What could he possibly say?"

Usually Mickey bows out right about now, but this time he meets Babe's eye. "He could say he supports the president."

He's so flippant that Agnes is dumbfounded. Babe's dumbfounded too. She rises slowly and makes an even bigger show than usual of limping over to the coffee pot. But as soon as she raises it, she lowers it again. "I suppose I'll have to go down to Margie Shaughnessy's to see if they've tuned in. I suppose I'll have to grovel." They all know what this means—Tim Shaughnessy downstairs is a Dodgers fanatic who would sooner drink sewer water than listen to a Yankees tribute, and when Babe shows up at his door he'll grab his hat and leave the radio to her.

"That's a good idea," Mickey says, and Mame actually smirks. Even Loretta tugs back a smile, which gives their father the idea of pulling a dollar from his wallet and handing it over, grandly, to his youngest. "Run down the corner and get your grandmother a coffee cake she can bring Mrs. Shaughnessy."

Babe's face pulses with color, a neon sign flashing agitation as she snatches the dollar from Loretta. "I'll pick it out myself."

"I'll walk you to the avenue, Babe," Loretta offers, but Babe glowers.

"I'll walk along just fine. Me, myself, and I," she says. "And maybe I'll keep walking. Maybe I'll walk all the way back to Spuyten Duyvil."

Mickey lets her have the last word after all. He stares down at his plate, feigning sorrow, but Agnes sees that he's hiding a look of smug self-satisfaction. It's a look that oddly mirrors Babe's grim pleasure at her parting shot. Agnes is transfixed by this turn of events, and so are her sisters, but at the sound of Babe's clunking down the steps their father breaks the spell.

"Twenty-one games," he says, turning toward Loretta with a crooked smile, "is only the start of a streak. We'll hear plenty of Yankees games the next few weeks."

For the first time in forever, Agnes sits in the living room and listens to the radio with her father. It's her night off kitchen duty, and maybe it's the night she'll tell him that she's betrayed the O'Learys, that she's visited the Calabrese camp, like the enemy camps in *Henry V* and *Julius Caesar*. She had to read them on her own, because the Sisters don't like to wallow in gore.

The Sisters prefer Shakespeare's poetry to his drama: next week her final examination will require her to identify a dozen sonnets. A snap— she's long since memorized them all and devised elaborate theories about the numbers. "When in disgrace with Fortune and men's eyes," for instance, is Number 29 because '29 was the last year her father cursed his fate. *I all alone beweep my outcast state.*

In his grief, Babe says, her father raised hell for an entire year, carousing and palling around with the likes of Matt McClary. Then one morning just after the Crash he staggered in, hung over. Babe said *Look at you!*

A disgrace to your own children. She made him stand over the breakfast table to behold his little girls, ashamed to look him in his bloodshot eyes. As Babe tells the story, he never took another drink.

Sometimes Agnes thinks maybe he should. The way he sits tonight— so still, so vacant in the airless little room—is enough to make her believe the poor man could do with any comfort he could find. She's been trying hard to practice the virtue of patience with her father, biting her tongue when he makes one of his bland pointless remarks, but ever since the night she hollered at him that he mustn't say *poor bastards* one more time, she's sensed him backing away farther still than he's already backed away from her. When she was little she knocked herself out—made a clown of herself, belted out "It's a Long Way to Tipperary"—and all because she sensed he had a special feeling for her, of all the girls. If she tells him she's been to see Vito Calabrese, what kind of feeling will he have for her then?

The program's long and she listens only intermittently, but she perks up when the announcer introduces Carl Sandburg, *the renowned poet.*

"Who's that?" her father says.

"The renowned poet," she repeats, giggling.

"Weisenheimer." Her father makes a face: pleased? They haven't bantered in a long, long time.

Willkie gives an odd, tight-lipped speech attacking anyone who attacks the president. He means Lindbergh, doesn't he, and he probably means Joe D'Ambrosio too, and Dorothy Day, and all those pacifists at the Catholic Worker. Her father listens, rapt, and when the speech is finished, he stands—*stands*—in front of his straight-back chair, and applauds as if he's in the Chicago arena where Willkie can hear him. Then he lectures her in a rush of fervor: "He's a mean little Republican, attacking labor that way, but by God, he's getting behind the president and so should we all. So should we all."

She nods, confused—alarmed—by this new authority. How suddenly her father's come to life. She's pretty sure she agrees with him, but she hears Joe D'Ambrosio's objections, Joe calmly countering that slaughtering millions is no way to save anyone, least of all the refugees. Handsome charming Joe is kissing her on Kenmare Street and she's yielding, she's feeling the alarming thrust of his hard body right there on the sidewalk. Bernie's voice snaps in: *That's why we should have taken him out in '38, when he bit off Austria. Should have taken out Franco and Mussolini while we were at it.* She hates wavering, can't abide it in her sisters or her father, and here she is wavering. The press of Joe's mouth, his thighs. The way that flap of hair falls over. She came so close to telling him that her mother was a suicide.

Her dad leans over to turn the dial off. "Some speeches, huh, kid?" It must be about a million years since he called her *kid*. How can she possibly bring up Calabrese Funeral Services now?

Her grandfather proposes that she come back on Sunday morning— *Visiting starts at two*—so she lies to Babe that she must go to Manhattan, to a special Mass for the graduating seniors. She walks all the way to the train station, in case Babe's sent one of her sisters to trail her, and looks over her shoulder as she heads downhill. It's the first time, not counting bedridden feverish mornings, that she's missed Mass since she turned seven, the age of reason. She used to love Mass—the rolling Latin, the rustling vestments—but lately she's so irritated by the priests, by how they turn their backs to the world's woes, that all her thoughts are positively unchristian. She's supposed to be consumed by guilt over the enormity of her lie—missing Mass is a MORTAL SIN—but she is after all Babe's granddaughter. If Joe or Bernie were to know she's thinking such thoughts . . . They're so devout, or anyway Joe certainly is, with his novenas and retreats. Look at her, skulking through the neighborhood. Babe has informers everywhere, and eyes in the back of her head.

She's still looking behind her when she rings her grandfather's bell. This time he doesn't even pause at the counter.

"There she is. Look at you. An asparagus, skinny as your mother."

She's not skinny. She leans into his hug the way she's never leaned into a stiff O'Leary embrace. He kisses one cheek and then the other, steps back to look at her, repeats the entire process.

"Come in, come in, dollface." He sounds like James Cagney. This is harder than she thought, the second time around.

"Nobody's giving us a break *this* Sunday. We got one already in the back chapel—and Tom's downstairs working on a delivery got here the crack of dawn."

"Should I come back . . ."

"No, no, sweetie. Tom's dying to meet you—listen to me, I catch myself all the time."

She doesn't know who Tom is or why he wants to meet her. Her grandfather leads her into the front parlor. Should she make small talk before she asks about her mother? Her grandfather gives her another one of those goofy grins and then she's all right. "What does he have to do to the body?"

He laughs. "With this one, what *don't* he have to do is more like it."

"And you talk to the families?"

"That's it. I used to do all the body work myself, back when we made house calls, but now I keep my hands clean. You remember this place, Agnes?"

She evades the memory question. "It's gorgeous," she says. She isn't one to gush, but she means it. A little flashy, after all, she allows herself to think on this second look, but why not, to mourn the dead?

"I couldna designed the house better myself."

"I was hoping I could—see more?"

He beams. "Come, come on, you want to take a look? You're not scared of stiffs?"

She shakes her head though she's never considered the question before, much less the word. Already her grandfather's popped up to lead her past the counter. The rooms open up into each other, the next one his office, with a green banker's lamp on his desk. "I bring the relatives in here to talk turkey. Listen to me. *Talk turkey.* That don't sound right."

Then they pass through to the first chapel—"Don't worry, this front one, the body's not in there yet. Give you a chance to get used to the . . . atmosphere."

She draws in a big swallow of undertaking air. The chapel's nearly as dark as the hallway, papered in a purple so deep she thinks of bruises. Crosses everywhere. She walks around from holy picture to holy picture. Her grandfather favors madonnas and pietàs: Mary's broad lap, holding the dying Jesus, reminds her of Babe when she used to hold two or three O'Leary girls at once. She *is* a Judas. She should be kneeling at the communion rail right now.

Her grandfather stands back, watching her circle the room. "The other one, we got a customer in there—wanna see?"

The second chapel's like the first, only papered a dark forest green, and since it's at the back of the building it gets the morning light. As they enter her nose swells and her eyes stream, assaulted by the thick sweet smell of lilies. Her grandfather throws a switch that sends a spotlight down, a circle of yellow like a body halo. When she approaches she sees an old man laid out, grotesque and unreal, a big wax doll. She bends for the kneeler, but her grandfather says: "Don't worry, nobody's looking. Stand up. Stand right on the kneeler! You'll get a better view."

She pulls her glasses from her pocket. Against the white satin the corpse's skin is the color of rust. He's fat, with pleated chins and a belly that rises up like a cushion for his hands, clasping a crucifix: on top of all that corpulence, Jesus on his cross looks even more emaciated. Along the dead man's forehead she thinks she sees a narrow line of black hair dye. It's occurred to her that she might someday like to take pictures of the bodies in Calabrese's, but a picture of this fellow would just be . . . lifeless. The mysterious Tom, down in the basement mortuary, has painted the stiff's cheeks with circles of rouge as bright as the Altman's salesladies use. Poor fellow looks ready to appear onstage.

"Did you know, Agnes, they displayed Caruso for six years after he croaked? Six years! Every year they gave him a new suit of clothes."

"No," she giggles. "I didn't know." And then adds, "What do you have to do to them?"

"You really want to know?" Her grandfather bends to wipe the kneeler with his handkerchief, then takes her elbow. They move through the rooms in reverse order. "First off, Tom disinfects the whole body. Then he shaves the men—the women too, you might as well know. They wouldn't want nobody to see those mustaches. Let's see. Mop up the fluids. Stuff the throat, pad the mouth, sew the lips. You all right there? This is maybe more than you want to know?"

She smiles. She's all right. This is the way death should be, out in the open. Her mother, dead, would have been treated like any other body—though surely her grandfather didn't do the job himself?

"Plugging the orifices was not my favorite, believe me. Did I say cement the eyes? Let's see. Drain the blood! How could I forget drain the blood. The last thing you do, outside of the paint, you pump it up full of preservative—first we do the arteries, then the guts. I tell you, we get through with you, you don't got to worry about waking up in your grave. This one today, Tom's gonna have to bleach the bruises. I don't wanna tell you how she died."

They're back in the front parlor and her grandfather's ruddy with pleasure. "How'd you get in the business, Grandpa—is that all right, to call you Grandpa?"

"Listen to her. Is that all right?" He swipes dramatically at his eyes, and the gesture reminds her of someone. "I been waiting fifteen years."

Thirteen years. It's thirteen years since her mother died.

"Babe too ashamed to tell you I came over when I was a kid? The dago side of the family. Bet she don't like to talk about that."

"She doesn't allow us to say that word." Does she sound too prim? "Unless it's DiMaggio, cause he doesn't mind . . ." She's making a mess of this and he'll think she's a Yankee fan besides. "I thought you'd have an Italian accent."

"Aw, I was young enough to lose it. Misplaced the language too, I'm ashamed to say. My uncle and me, we had the name of a carpenter, supposed to give us jobs making wooden boxes, crates. Turns out he makes *coffins.* Oh my God, Agnes, if I'd hadda dime in my pocket I woulda run back to mama." Again the eyes glisten, but now she knows why his outsize gestures look so familiar. No wonder he and Babe couldn't get on.

"Listen," her grandfather says, and reaches over to squeeze her hand. "I hear Tom coming up the stairs."

She can't take it all in—or maybe she just can't make it fit. *She sent you out for a loaf of semolina,* Babe's always sneered, and Agnes pictures the four of them, tied together at the wrist, trudging up that back staircase. She drags Loretta along behind her. They were two-four-six-eight, she and her sisters, two years apart from one another. It was only last year that it came to her whole: if Loretta was two, her mother must have been pregnant. There must have been another baby on the way.

She sits on a park bench in Washington Square with Bernie, waiting for Joe to get back from the Yankee game, and for once she's glad he's running late. If the two fellows were here together she'd never get a word in edgewise, but alone, Bernie's perfectly willing to listen. He lost his own father when he was seven. They've always had that between them.

"It's not just a grandfather she kept from us," she tells him. "The mortician turns out to be my Uncle Tom. My mother's little brother. And two more brothers besides—one's a marine. I don't know, Bernie. She robbed me of a whole family."

Bernie shakes his head. For once, he seems to know a funny accent won't console her. Anyway, she's not Agnes the Listener today. All her powers of empathy have deserted her, and now she only wants somebody else to listen for a change. "The strangest thing is how I'm walking around feeling Italian." She could almost rise and prance along the walkway—*sashay,* the way the Italian girls do, getting on the train in the morning. Hasn't she worn her most uncomfortable high heels tonight? Isn't this her tightest summer jacket? All year at DeRobertis, she's been the outsider. Now she's one of them. "Only, what a time to feel Italian. As long as I don't start feeling fascist."

Bernie laughs at her. "How you think *I* feel?"

She puts a hand to her mouth, demure and Irish. "You're right—German's worse. They're not giving you grief, are they, in the building?"

"Just funny looks. I don't think they'll run us out." Agnes has never been sure whether Bernie's proud or ashamed of living where he does, a swell building on West End Avenue filled with lawyers and doctors. All she knows is, his father was the porter. After he died, the owners decided they didn't need another porter but, having realized that economy, let his mother stay on in the little apartment on the ground floor. She doesn't know a lot: he doesn't chatter on the way she's doing. "Bernie," she asks, not knowing she's about to, "how'd your father die?"

He laughs one of his Gary Cooper laughs. "My mother told everybody he fell on the tracks because he had a heart attack."

Fell on the tracks. Her own heart stops. Does he mean—jumped? "Did people believe it?"

Bernie shrugs. "They sure felt sorry."

"Oh, Bernie, I never knew." Imagine, that she and Bernie should both have parents who killed themselves and that she would never know until this moment. The way he throws it off so easily, the story of his father's death, when all these years Babe's made her feel she'd turn to stone if she told anyone. She's so sick of keeping it secret, of her mother's very face hidden away all these years, under her dad's shorts.

She can't stop seeing the picture. She found it a few weeks back—well, all right, she *hunted* for it, because she knew her father couldn't possibly live without some reminder. And there it was, in one of the two drawers he's allocated in Babe's back-room dresser: a gilt-framed photo, facedown, that showed her mother as a girl of, maybe, seventeen: Agnes's age. She wasn't surprised to see that her mother was beautiful—Loretta, after all, is beautiful, and even Mame and RoseMarie are pretty in a thoughtless, standard kind of way. No, she was surprised by how un-threatening her mother's beauty was: even features in an oval face, dark hair curled off high temples. Huge eyes, big as a baby's, light enough that Agnes imagines they must have been green or maybe even blue, like her own. Her mother's brows arched perfectly, but they weren't plucked so sparse you'd think she was vain. The part that just kills Agnes, the part that just slays her, is how a smile played at her mother's full lips, how the smile held, after all these years, the terrible power to make a daughter think for one fleeting second that she knew who her mother was. It was a *merry* smile, the very word Babe's always used to describe Agnes. But a merry mother wouldn't have done it. A merry mother wouldn't haunt her this way.

"Agnes? You OK?"

No, she's not OK, she's back at Calabrese's, trudging up the stairway. Mame and RoseMarie trudge ahead of her, Loretta behind, the clothes-line cutting into her wrist. Mame stops dead at the top of the stairs. Their mother has tacked up another note and Mame reads it aloud: *Don't come in. Get your father. I love you always.* The little girls wring their bound hands. It's the fourth time their mother's left a note and always before Mame has dutifully dragged them around to the speakeasies to find their father. Why don't they just fetch their grandfather? Are they so scared of the stiffs? Babe says their mother tried three times before—twice the oven and once phenobarbital—but Mame mustn't understand this, be-cause this time she decides that they'll rescue their mother themselves.

This time she pushes the door open and skips down the hall that runs the length of the apartment, the other three girls bound to follow her all the way to the end. They run their grimy fingers along the wallpa-per till they reach a high square of light skittering from the bathroom window. Mame enters first, and stops: the other girls pile up, derailed like train cars. Their mother's found a good sturdy steam pipe this time.

She's used the rest of the clothes-line. Is she dangling above them, tongue bulging out the way you see in pictures? Are there pictures of such things? Don't people . . . soil themselves? Does Agnes hide her eyes? Is it so horrific that she screams or sings or giggles? To this day she can't be trusted in the movies, where her sisters cast her the evil eye when she bursts out laughing at the tragic mushy bits in *Rebecca* or *Wuthering Heights*.

"My mother hanged herself," she hears someone say, in a fluty voice. "Aw no. Aw Agnes."

Wasn't it Joe she meant to tell first, Joe who would have known she didn't need him to answer, she didn't need him to *say* something, she only needed arms wrapped around her, the smell of boy, a broad chest?

Bernie doesn't offer his chest. He removes his glasses, then promptly returns them to his nose. "Agnes, jeez. Awww, that's terrible. Oh I'm sorry, really I am." No funny voices today from Bernhard Keller. She's turned him inside out.

"I've never told anyone, I wasn't allowed. But if your father . . ."

"Oh, but Agnes he didn't—aw. My mother says he was drinking, he'd been drinking all day, he was . . . a drunk, is what my father was. But—" there, he's finding his old sure voice, the Bernie she's never seen so flustered is finding his way out—"but in a way he did kill himself. Sure. I mean, abusing himself like that."

Agnes gives him a weak smile, and knows she won't say another word all night. Maybe she won't say another word for the rest of her life.

But Bernie takes her by surprise when he grabs up both her hands: "Agnes, I love you for telling me that." He swallows hard, presses ahead: "I love you." He looks at her desperately, as if to say *Would I be an oaf if I kissed you now, after that?* She's turned to stone just as Babe has always said she would. But they're both saved from the oafish kiss, because here comes Joe D'Ambrosio, entering the park at the arch. He spots them right away—Joe *would*—and waves a piece of paper as he advances. He's calling out a number: "Twenty-seven! Twenty-seven!"

In her stupor Agnes thinks he means Sonnet 27: *Looking on darkness, which the blind do see.* She casts her eyes to the ground, and her field of vision narrows, she and Bernie caught red-handed at this love-and-death business. But Joe keeps coming, oblivious, and when he reaches them he throws his arms around them both.

"Friends, comrades, countrymen. DiMaggio's streak is up to twenty-seven games. We're witnesses to history!" He waves the paper, which must be his scorecard.

She exhales, and for all she's sick of Joe DiMaggio, wishes she had the slightest interest in whatever it is he's supposed to be doing, wishes that she could feel the press of Joe D'Ambrosio's arm on her shoulder forever, wishes she'd told Joe first about her mother. He stands there radiating such an uncomplicated joy.

Hasn't she always known that the first one she told would be the one she married?

BEANED

Always before, it's been Mame and RoseMarie Babe would like to throttle. Lately, it's Agnes. Does Aggie think her own grandmother doesn't suspect who's been rummaging through Mickey's drawer looking for that picture of Gloria? About the trips down to Calabrese's? Could Aggie possibly believe Babe doesn't see the furtive way she holds the Brownie (which, it's worth mentioning, Babe took off a neighbor's hands when her Brownie-wielding husband died)? Could Aggie possibly imagine that her grandmother didn't notice the defiant tilt to her chin when she announced she had to go to Manhattan for the "graduation Mass"?

Graduation Mass, my ass, Babe wanted to say, but of course she resisted. Resists still, because she and Agnes are well matched in this battle they're fighting, and *discretion is the better part of valor.* Who said that? Doesn't matter, what matters is that she can wait out Agnes's trips to Vito and emerge the victor. The old man will show his temper soon enough and then Agnes won't be so inclined to sneak off and visit him. If she gets a few dollars for college out of him in the meantime, so much the better. It's always been Babe's only regret, that she didn't negotiate a better deal for the O'Learys on the way out of that funereal hellhole.

Agnes is so complicated lately, so childish. Tonight, she's practically having a temper tantrum.

"Look at this!" Aggie says, stabbing the classifieds. "Look."

"I'd be happy to look if I weren't at the sink scrubbing." She doesn't lower the acid content in her voice on Agnes's account. Agnes thrives on acid. It's after dinner and after cleanup: Loretta's night at the sink, which means nothing has been done properly and they will none of them, not even Babe, mention her slovenly ways. Better simply to do it all over for her. Any criticism sends the youngest O'Leary deeper into the grip of Demon Melancholy, and they all know that if anybody's going to repeat what Gloria did, it's Loretta. "Read it out to me, for goodness' sake."

"Situation wanted," Agnes reads, begrudgingly. "Chambermaid. Jewess. Refugee."

Babe waits.

"Jewess?" Agnes hints. "Refugee?"

"Read down the column. Tell me don't some of them say Christian. Don't some say Protestant?" She doesn't turn away from the sink but she can hear Agnes spluttering and knows she's seen the words rise up from the newsprint.

"That's not the point!"

"You'll have to tell me what the point *is* or we'll be standing here when the sun comes up tomorrow morning."

"Oh Babe, you know exactly what I'm talking about. All these refugees reduced to applying for *chambermaid* jobs. Doesn't it sound like the last century? Can't we do something for them?"

"What do you suggest?" She knows she's sneering. "Hire a chambermaid for the O'Leary apartment?"

"I can't stand it when you joke about it."

"Then sit for it, you ninny."

Agnes stamps her foot. *Stamps her foot.* She really has decided to become that impossible motherless child again.

"Don't you get fresh with me, Miss. I'll have you know—as a matter of fact you already do know—I scrubbed the priests' toilets so your father could be educated. And what *situation* do you suppose my own mother took when she came to America? She'd have been thrilled to bits if someone dignified her job with the title *chambermaid*."

"All right, I forgot."

"Forgot!" She's only winding up. "You're turning your back on this family and where you came from, Agnes O'Leary. All you talk about lately is the Jews this and the Jews that. O the poor Jews. Excuse me, the poor *Jewesses*. We can't all come to this country bankers and money-lenders."

Aggie gapes but answers in a voice that's eerily calm. "You could at least come up with an original insult. They come here stripped of everything."

"Most of us who came to America didn't have anything to be stripped of in the first place. I've had quite enough of your carrying on about the Jews. I'll have no more mention of them in this household."

A strange deathly silence seeps through the kitchen. Babe tightens every muscle, standing at the kitchen sink, and behind her she can feel Agnes doing the same. She knows exactly what reply she's handed her granddaughter, and here it comes:

"Then I won't be part of . . ." Aggie doesn't even trouble to finish.

Babe holds her rag paralyzed above the scouring powder. If Agnes leaves, they'll lose the two paychecks she hands over to Babe. If she leaves, Mickey will despair and they'll let him go from the agency. If she leaves, no one will be able to rouse Loretta from her weeping. But it's none of those realities that finally chokes off what's in Babe's throat—*Exactly where do you think you could go, on an afternoon salesgirl's salary*—because she knows exactly where Agnes will go and precisely how she'll pay for her education. She'll run to Vito, and he'll buy her velvet frocks from Best & Company the way he did when she was a toddler. A spasm in her left hip, a terrible clenching of muscle and bone. Maybe he's already given her money. Maybe he's already bought her a dress that she hangs in another closet.

Slowly she lowers the rag. Slowly she gets it out: "You know I didn't mean that. You know it was only my temper talking."

Because you have to be patient and you have to be canny. She forces herself to turn around—in her hip, the torments of the damned—and sees that tears threaten to stream down Miss Independence's cheeks. But this can't be: Agnes never cries. If Agnes falls apart, all will be lost.

"Agnes," she says crisply. "Don't carry on like this, over one harsh word."

When Agnes finally answers, her own voice is crisp, too, and she looks her grandmother in the eye. Good girl. "Didn't you chase the Christian Front boys, Babe?"

Babe nods and feels her dignity returning.

"Who else did I learn it from?"

From whom did I learn. This time Babe doesn't trouble herself with the correction. Who else indeed? Hasn't she been the moral beacon for these girls? Hasn't she taught them whom to mistrust?

"You know I don't begrudge the Jews," she says. "Aren't I putting together a pile of Loretta's outgrown clothes for the refugee drive?" It's a lie—the shabby pile was, until this very moment, destined for the rag bag—but having said it she comes to believe it. The warm glow of virtue makes her expansive. "It's only the talk-talk-talking I can't abide, the talking instead of the doing."

Agnes looks startled but holds her tongue. Babe waits. Silence. The silence builds, like moisture in the air, and Babe waits for the thunderclap, but finally Aggie drifts away to the back of the apartment.

The silence grows, the truce holds, the porcelain gleams. If Babe's not mistaken she's scored several points in this round.

In the bleachers, in Babe's usual spot, the sun streams down on her game and the seventh-inning stretch. She daren't rise, because if she does she'll never sit again. It's a decent crowd for a weekday, but the place should be standing room only. No matter it's Wednesday—the whole town should take the afternoon off to come see DiMag go for the Yankee streak record. Today will make thirty games in a row, and even though Joe's hitless heading into the seventh, she has every confidence he'll come through in his next at bat. After today, he'll go on for the major league record. Last week Ted Williams folded his own streak away at twenty-three games. Ha. Ted can keep his gargantuan batting average, his testament to consistency. What Joe's doing is inspired.

The game's not going her way—Chicago's leading seven–two—but she counts her blessings. Rizzuto's back in the lineup after all these weeks on the bench. He's bungled a few, but he'll find his rhythm. Whenever she beams him grace, he looks sharper straightaway.

She's taking a chance, going up to the Bronx on a Wednesday—one of these days Agnes is going to visit Calabrese Funeral Services and not come back—but she's decided to give Aggie a very long length of rope with which to hang herself. So to speak. Terrible turn of phrase, considering Gloria. And Babe's been thinking of Gloria—she doesn't want to think of Gloria, she just can't seem to stop herself—since she found the picture disturbed in Mickey's drawer. Those baby-face eyes, those puffball lips.

For weeks now she's found herself pondering Gloria's two mystery pregnancies: that first baby she claimed to lose—only to get herself pregnant again as soon as the ring was on her finger—and the one she was most certainly carrying when she hanged herself. She's always suspected Gloria had some neighborhood crone take care of the first one. Now she sees that must be what happened the second time around too. Gloria must have been so terrified by the thought of another pregnancy—and well she should have been, the way she fell apart—that she went to one of those peasant women who scrape it out. The way she has it calculated, Gloria was so overcome with guilt for killing the baby that afterward only hanging would do. It all fits together so neatly that Babe's almost forgotten it's a theory she's spun out of air. She believes it now as established fact.

The way she believes that she chased those Christian Front Nazis when she only thought to herself that someone should chase them, the way she believes she was saving the clothes all along for Jewish refugees.

She has, at Agnes's request, begun to refer to them as *Jewish refugees,* not *those Jews,* a fine distinction which strikes her as akin to the rules of grammar, hence another piece of evidence that Agnes takes after her. As a nod to Agnes, she's even approached some of the better neighbors about adding to her pile of old clothes, a pile that grows daily in the corner of the kitchen. Babe herself doesn't refer to its presence. She doesn't need to, since it is visible to all, and at the dinner table Mickey praises her nightly for her community spirit, her generosity, her patriotism. Agnes, of course, is silent on the matter—but Aggie's off balance, which is all Babe needs her to be to keep her in the household.

When DiMaggio finally takes the plate in the bottom of the seventh, Babe beams him the hit, but instead he grounds the ball to short. She's stunned—she was sure this was the one—but then the ball bounces hard off the ground and she's hopeful all over again. It beans Luke Appling, who clutches his shoulder at short. Joe tears off to first like the fire department. It's over so fast she can't quite believe it.

The crowd goes wild over the safe hit, the safe streak, the team record. Joe makes some aborted movement that might or might not be a tip of the hat, and the fans reluctantly sit again. The game of baseball must go on, Yankee hitting streak notwithstanding.

King Kong—Charlie Keller—follows DiMag to the plate and, inspired, gets a good chunk of the ball. Then Joe Gordon draws the walk. Her boys are back in the game and so is she—or maybe it would be more accurate to say *because* she's back in the game they're back. Here's Rizzuto. She wills him to keep the rally going and he obliges.

But as Rizzuto hightails it for first, Babe O'Leary lets out a cry of pain and surprise. Her own shoulder's been hit, from above. Her shoulder, the last (barely) functioning joint in her body, and it's been pulverized by (oh, the irony) a baseball. Not Rizzuto's—she can't even claim a sacrifice for the team. She wails full force. She has too much class to let the appropriate words out, so instead she cries, "Damn! Damn! Damn!" The ball's landed in the broad glove of her lap and she picks it up to hurl it back from whence it came. If it breaks some punk's nose, some punk deserves that and more.

All around her middle-aged men, bleacher bums, unemployed lay-abouts, cheapskates in cheap suits, come to her aid. She beats them off with her flailing pocketbook and her ball-holding arm. "Don't touch me. Jesus, Mary, and Joseph. O the pain." The men who think they're lending a hand are torn: the Yankees are closing the gap and this could be the turnaround inning. She wails again to keep their attention. From above, a decent-looking if shabby man in a fedora climbs down two rows and approaches her tentatively.

"Lady!" he calls. "Lady I'm terribly sorry." Behind him is the culprit—a ten-year-old with freckles peeking around from his father's jacket. Really, a cute kid is too much to bear. "Are you all right there?"

"I'll live," she says. "In pain, for the rest of my life."

The man blanches, the child disappears behind him.

"It just slipped!" she hears from behind the man. So a smart-alecky kid let his ball drop onto her shoulder. Already the pain has eased—in truth, the ball only dribbled down a few rows—but she gives a good grimace.

"We'll see what the police have to say to that." She would never be a stooge, but it can't hurt to invoke the police where small boys are involved.

"Lady, he's sorry. If there's anything we can do."

"You can stay out of my sight." What she would really like to do is watch the game. She's completely missed Sturm's at bat, and Rizzuto's already advanced to third. The score is now seven–five.

"Lady, if he could just have his ball back."

The other fans are leaning around their conversation to follow the game. "You've got a nerve," she huffs, without looking at him.

"Lady, *DiMaggio* hit that ball foul last time we were here."

She feels the weight of it in her palm. Joe's

bat has connected with this piece of leather and she cannot stop herself from stroking it with her fingertips, a direct line to DiMaggio. The ball has a spiritual weight, a power of its own. She cups her hand tighter and feels the power increase. "What in heaven's name are you doing carting it around to the ballpark?"

"Would you shuddup already!" some jackass yells at them. She's heard worse in the bleachers. Down in the infield—good heavens—Sturm's caught in a throw out on his way from first to second. When did that happen? And Rizzuto's trying to sneak home. Shite. They nail Phil at home plate, though it's a beautiful feet-high slide. A silly courageous thing to do, demonstrating precisely the spirit she knew he had. The boy's ball, the ball emanating Joe DiMaggio's power, is now pressed against her chest. In her excitement she must have raised it there. Her heart beats against it.

"We were going to get Joe to sign it," the man begs. He sounds very close to tears.

She turns to the man as the Yanks take the field, gives him a withering pitying look. "Joe DiMaggio hides out in the clubhouse till everyone's gone home. He hates autographs."

The man grovels. "Can we have the ball back please?"

"Yes, I suppose you are able to receive the ball, if I choose to give it to you. The real question is *may* you have the ball back."

"May we have the ball back?"

What sort of manhood is this fellow demonstrating to his son? She considers. The ball is magical, but it's ill gotten and it would be bad luck to keep it from a child on the day that Joe broke the team record. She stares at the boy's adorable wavy hair. "Sit back down," she says, "and if you're perfectly behaved for the rest of the game and *if* you promise you won't torment Joe DiMaggio with a pathetic autograph request, I will seriously consider returning your ball."

The father slumps, raises a hand as if to protest, sees that it's useless. Reminds her of Mickey when he turns around and leads the child back to their own seats. She has half a mind to put the ball in the depths of her pocketbook and keep it for herself.

She doesn't, of course. DiMag wouldn't approve. In the eighth, the Yanks pull even, but the Sox put another run on the board, and when her Yankees come up for their last chance, they strand two. Final score: eight–seven, a travesty the fans stick around to boo, but one to which she has already resigned herself. All that counts today is Joe's streak. She sits absolutely still, looking neither to the left nor the right, as the bleachers empty. The boy and his father wait in her row and then, in frustration, move down to the row below her so they can confront her.

"I suppose you're going to keep it," the father says bitterly. "He was perfectly behaved. I should call an usher."

"Well, I should call an attorney and ask him what a lawsuit for my maimed shoulder would yield." She's only toying with them. She pounces on the boy. "Are you going to bother Joe DiMaggio?"

He denies it with a vigorous shake of the head.

"How many stitches in a baseball?"

She's sorry to see a panicked look in his eye. "One hundred and eight!" she barks. "Repeat it."

"Hundred and eight," he says, and now there's resentment in his voice, a surly bad attitude that convinces her he's already growing the spine his father lacks. She underhands it to him—thank God he doesn't fumble—and says to the father: "See that you sit lower in the bleachers next time you come."

The two of them get going while the going's good, and Babe heaves herself down, row by row, behind them. Nick the hairy usher waits discreetly for her as she plunks herself down the last two rows. She must be the last soul to depart this ballpark, and he grins up at her with his wizened face, then extends his elbow for her to grab.

"Thank you, Nick, but you know I don't take a man's arm."

"You'll take this one," he says, his usual reply.

The utter self-confidence that makes her rejoice in the male sex. Why is this simple lesson so hard for some men? She takes Nick's arm and knows that, leaning on him, she's making her limp more pronounced.

"I got beaned today, Nick."

"No kidding. Where?"

"Shoulder."

"Why'n't you holler bloody murder?"

"I did holler bloody murder."

"We'd a gotcha the ball or another one, and maybe an autograph besides. You OK now, Babe?"

"Throbs a little."

"Jeez. Well, who hit the ball? Maybe I can still get you the goods, I ask extra nice."

"It wasn't like that. A kid dropped it on me." It occurs to her that she could say *It was a ball Joe DiMaggio hit foul,* but if Nick had any self-respect—and clearly he does, walking along so jauntily, a head shorter than she—he'd point out that Joe didn't hit any into her section today. Wheedling an autograph would be cheating and anyway she's never had any interest in the paraphernalia of the game, the sad dependence on stuff, on the man's mark. She's already in brain-wave communication with Joe DiMaggio and how could she possibly acquire more than that?

"Well, it's funny you getting hit in the shoulder," Pete says. "On the day DiMag bounces one off Appling's shoulder. Funny coincidence. You and Appling, you're connected."

For heaven's sake, Babe wants to say, Appling's not the connection, but Nick's never personally witnessed her powers, so she lets it slide. Still, it's almost as if she's been cheated twice today: once of the ball, and once of the recognition that's due her.

Out on River Avenue, she sees how much time has elapsed while she was chitchatting. The hordes of autograph-seekers have thinned out and the ballplayers themselves are probably halfway home by now. She considers crossing the street for a glass of beer. Mickey put an extra dollar in her hand this morning. As a younger woman she never would have entered one of these dark bars unescorted, but she's finally achieved an age that allows her to walk into that all-male domain and find an amusing conversation.

It's getting late, though. She stands there weighing it, dipping her toe into the traffic, when a big sedan rolls by and brushes her. Would have run her down, if she'd been standing one inch off the curb. The peculiar thing is *that could have been Joe DiMaggio sitting in the passenger seat.*

The car came so close that all she could really make out was a young man's pale face, staring hard from the passenger seat to make sure they *did* miss her. But the more she thinks about it, the more she's sure it was Joe. She tarried so long, DiMag would have had time to dress and to hide out from the fans. And Lefty would have been driving him, of course—he's always Joe's chauffeur. What a driver he is. Didn't even slow down to see if he'd committed vehicular homicide.

She could sit on the sidewalk, she's that taken aback. The man who sped by in a blur was definitely Joe DiMaggio. What clearer sign could she possibly have that DiMag knows about her? The way he stared. That was a cold frank stare between equals, a stare that said *I know who you are and you know who I am but it will be better for both of us if we don't acknowledge that fact.*

And, she reflects, she stared back pretty blankly herself. Possibly she looked a little put out. Lefty did come close to running her down.

She laughs out loud and turns for the subway instead of a saloon. Run down by Lefty Gomez and stared at, with respect, *with a message,* by Joe DiMaggio. The family needs to hear about this as soon as possible.

But when she arrives in Brooklyn, RoseMarie has barely started supper and Mickey isn't even home yet. Her shoulder throbs and she pops four aspirins—when in doubt, double the dose. "I ask for very little," she says to RoseMarie, and goes to lie down till dinner in the tiny back room.

Outside the evening is still bright but in here, facing the courtyard, she languishes in twilight. She knows full well that Agnes is tormenting her by staying late at Vito's. The only smell in the apartment, aside from the ever-present mothballs, is the insipid white rice RoseMarie's cooking. Babe despises rice. An unbidden memory of Gloria, showing her how she makes rice the Italian way, with oil. O the airs. Gloria was so eager in the beginning: shy but craving Babe's approval. Like Loretta that way, always wanting to brush up against you or touch your hair. Babe can't tolerate an uninvited touch.

She slips into an anxious sleep and dreams that Joe DiMaggio has climbed onto her shoulders. He jumps up and down for Lefty Gomez's amusement, and her bones crunch beneath his heels. She cries out, but doesn't wake, and when her eyes finally open, the little bedside clock says 9:41 AM. She's confused. Through her window, a clear day presents itself.

She springs from the bed and travels the hallway with a spryer step than she's had in years. But she's panicked, too. She's slept fifteen hours and more. She's forgotten her shoulder, and even the bad hip acts as if it's had a vacation.

It's not only morning, it's late morning. They've all cleared out for the day without so much as waking her for a good-bye. She's like the princess who falls asleep for days, months, years. She should be starving, but she's strangely uninterested in food. She walks the apartment in a trance. All she wants to do is see how the papers cover Joe's record, but Agnes has only left her yesterday's *Times*. She's almost afraid to check the date, but she forces herself to look. Thank God, she hasn't missed more than the one dinner.

And now she knows what to do. She'll walk over to Seventh Avenue and nurse a cup of coffee—by this hour, two or three morning editions will be left behind on the counter. She can read competing descriptions of the game, and find out besides if the country's gone to war while she was sleeping.

All day she practices the story she'll tell at dinner: Joe's safe hit, the crowd's ecstasy, the two injured shoulders, the sign from DiMaggio. She'll have to change his stare to a raised finger—come to think of it, she's quite sure Joe did raise his hand as he passed by. Mickey and Loretta will love every minute of the telling. Even Agnes will have to offer her some begrudging respect. How has it come to this, that she's in such a bitter battle with her favorite?

She doesn't know how bitter till that night, when they all wait for Agnes to return from Altman's. Aggie's not there at six thirty, when she usually walks through the door, and she's not there at six forty-five. At seven, the meatloaf is a dried rock, the cornflakes Babe uses to stretch the ground meat protruding like the scales on an armadillo's back. She paces back and forth from the kitchen to the living room, where Mickey sits listening to the radio and Mame and RoseMarie regard her with resentment. They know better than to suggest eating without Agnes.

"Don't worry, Ma. Train's probably delayed."

"I'm not worried," she snaps, but even Loretta can see through that. At seven fifteen, she serves them the cold meat and potatoes, but she doesn't have the heart to start her story without Agnes there. They eat in silence, and by seven thirty the table's cleared.

"Subways get stalled an hour or two all the time. Every day of the week," Mickey offers. But at eight thirty she still hasn't shown up. Aggie's graduating from high school this weekend, a ritual Babe herself has never experienced (by the end of grammar school she could not tolerate one more minute of the nuns' despotic rule). Is this what young women do when they graduate from high school? Pull stunts to torment their grandmothers?

"Should we tell the police?" Loretta whispers.

Mickey says, "She's only two hours late. Tell you what, Loretta. Let's you and I walk down to the station. Aggie'll want the company, in the dark."

Babe wonders if Agnes has stopped by Calabrese's on her way home. She wonders if Agnes has left home for good after all, but she resists the urge to say anything. After Mickey and Loretta leave her shoulder throbs again. She works on another theory, some snippet she heard on the radio earlier today, some headline her eye caught on the way to the sports page this morning. She can't remember for the life of her—were they worried about attacks on the subway?

Something about Roosevelt and the refugees.

"Mame! RoseMarie!" she cries out, though they sit in front of her nose. "Run knock on the neighbors' doors and see does anyone have today's *Times*."

Mame gives her that infuriating passive look she's perfected, her *don't-blame-me-for-the-bad-news-I'm-about-to-tell-you* look. "Nobody in the building buys the *Times*."

Nobody buys the *Times* but Agnes, they're all thinking. And Aggie will be home any minute, surely she will, and then they'll have two copies of one paper, a ridiculous waste and indulgence. Why does she want a newspaper at a time like this, Mame's raised eyebrow asks. Babe says, "Run, you two. Find an open newsstand. Today's paper, not tomorrow's. And don't come back with a *News* or a *Telegram*."

Even the Dour Sisters must be worried, because they go out the door without further complaint. When they return there's still no sign of Agnes.

Mame hands over the paper and there's the front page:

U.S. Bars Refugees with Kin in Reich.

Babe sits, heavily, and Mame puts a hand to the hurt shoulder, one of those uninvited touches she'd ordinarily shake off, even if the shoulder weren't sore. But this night she decides to offer it up, an act she hasn't seriously considered performing in thirty years.

"Your sister's gone a little crazy over these refugees," she says. "That's all this is. It's not—"

"Not what?" they ask in unison.

It's not that she's at Calabrese Funeral Services, Babe doesn't say. *It's not that she's gone and hanged herself,* which, she realizes for the first time, is what she's really been dreading. Maybe it's what they've all been dreading. But it's Loretta who gets the blues, not Agnes! Babe laughs a little recklessly and Mame and RoseMarie regard her with their usual suspicion.

RoseMarie says, "I wish she'd stop trying to make us all feel so guilty."

Mame dismisses it all with a wave of her hand. "Oh, she's probably just sitting with a boy somewhere."

Agnes is at a meeting of those Reds, is what Babe's thinking. She's been brainwashed by that Joe D'Ambromeo. But she doesn't say that either. Sometimes you just have to have faith. She allows herself to believe that Agnes is safe, and hasn't gone over to the other side, and then for good measure she allows herself to know that DiMaggio's streak will hold. But even as she's believing, she knows that she has more control over Joe DiMaggio than she has over her own granddaughter.

Aggie's becoming a stranger, slipping away from her, and there's nothing she can do to grab her back.

WHAT

GOOD DOES IT DO?

Joe D'Ambrosio's packing for the rest of his life when he hears his little brothers screaming bloody murder from the front of the apartment. He hotfoots it out there and finds them all gaping down through the window: Pete and Pauley, his mother, Uncle Fran.

"He's coming, he's coming," Petey calls.

"For the love of Christ get down there already," Uncle Fran says. "What kinda girl stands there calling up?"

His mother turns: "She's pretty, Joey." Joe suspects his mother would find any girl calling up for him pretty. Between his birth and Pete's, she delivered two baby girls too premature to survive in this world and ever since she's been dying for female company.

Did he give Julie from the Catholic Worker House his address? He squeezes his ma, but he's down the stairs fast, once he gets going. And when he bursts out the front door, wouldn't you know it's Agnes he sees standing there in the middle of East Twelfth Street. If she doesn't want him, why does she torment him this way? He stifles a fury he recognizes as a direct genetic link to his old man.

"I'm sorry Joe, I couldn't find the bell." She's acting all this out for the benefit of his mother who, he sees when he glances up over his shoulder, is still framed by the window above, hair pulled back tight from her strong jawline. His mother's the one who gave him the golden hair and the high forehead, and when he turns to wave his family off (you'd think they were in a movie balcony, the way they gawk), she's the one with the sense to back them all away. It stokes his fury to know that his mother looked down from five flights and called Agnes *pretty*, that she'd approve of what's not going to happen.

Agnes holds out a folded newspaper. He takes the paper but doesn't even glance at it, walks back to the sidewalk and out of window view just in case Uncle Fran decides to take another peek. "Let's get out of here."

Agnes can see how furious he is. "Joe, I'm sorry, I shouldn't have."

"Yell up for me? That's not the problem."

She casts her eyes down. She knows exactly what the problem is, and in the knowing holds her tongue. They're walking already, most natural thing in the world for a pair-of-lovers-who-won't-ever-be-lovers. He knows they'll drift toward Washington Square, *their* park, and he sees again the way Bernie was all over her on that bench. Maybe he's so mad he'll keep going, up to Union Square. Maybe he's so mad he'll walk to the top of the Empire State Building and dump a pot of Catholic Worker soup down on Manhattan.

"I was heading home but I had to get off the train and come talk to you."

"About what."

"About the news."

"I don't know what the news is." He sounds *exactly* like his father.

She has to practically run to keep up with his long lope. Good. Let her run, hand to her hat. Good she came today. Good he can tell her about Julie, and they can finally for once and forever say these good-byes he keeps threatening. He'll never have to babysit the pair of them again.

"The refugees." She pants it out, skipping along. "Roosevelt."

"What."

"Turning back. Anybody. With relatives." Maybe he's been running too. He feels sweat slide down his forehead. Must have hit ninety today. Already the city stinks, of dog shit on the sidewalks, of rotting meat the restaurants have tossed into barrels, of human sweat. His sweat. And it's only June. The air presses down, a smothering damp wave of it. When did he become his old man? When did everything start enraging him this way?

He stops on the sidewalk. If he's going to become his pop, he might as well sing the whole song: "Slow down Agnes. Take a deep breath. What are you saying?"

"I'm saying. FDR won't take any refugee with. People over there."

He understands the disaster immediately. "Sheesh." And in understanding doesn't even realize that he's turned back into himself, that he's gone instantaneously from fury—all he feels now whenever Agnes is in the picture—to calm. Well, why not? He's been otherwise calm for a whole year, watching his best friend steal his girl, watching the world at war. He'll have to be plenty calm to go to prison, but he doesn't even understand himself how it descends on him now so completely, so unbidden. "Let me get this straight."

They walk west, toward the setting sun, New York ablaze in flashes. They walk from the tenement blocks to the brownstone blocks, a slide

so smooth he doesn't even register the brightening anymore. The changing facades, the tidy shutters don't matter. Today they walk toward the bright, clean streets. Tomorrow he'll walk toward Mott Street, toward the crowds and the filth. He won't be living at the Catholic Worker House long either. After a few months he'll be on a bus, bound for Mexico. A fool's errand. By then a war will rage all around him, maybe even in Manhattan.

"I'm so ashamed," she says.

They stop again. He puts two hands to her shoulders, pressing her down onto a high step on the nearest stoop. They're almost up to Fifth Avenue: the moneyed blocks, the moneyed houses, the flower boxes above swollen with yellows and purples, jolly and oblivious. He sits her down where nobody ever sits—these are not the stoop-sitting blocks. He feels like Uncle Fran fussing. He's found the only girl in New York City who understands what's going on in the world and to her he's just some kindly old relative.

Only he felt her yield to his touch that day, he did. He felt her kissing back, not just following his lead but pushing herself forward too. What made her pull back? Is she picking Bernie because he's the safe one? Does she know somehow that he and Julie smooched for an hour last week?

"It's not just Germany," she says. "They can't come if they still have family in Norway or Holland or Belgium. Or France. Or Czechoslovakia." She's memorized the list the way she memorizes those sonnets. "The State Department says the Nazis threatened to torture any relatives left behind."

"So the refugees would spy on us? To keep their relatives from being tortured?" He snorts. "That's cockamamie. We have to write letters. Tonight."

"Write to who . . . m?"

"Cordell Hull. And who's your congressman?"

"Joe. Don't those Catholic Workers of yours write letters all the time?" He doesn't like where this is going. "Didn't you tell me fifty thousand people demonstrated in Union Square when Hitler came to power? And didn't the Catholic Workers go down to the docks to picket when the German ocean liners came in?"

"Are you saying they shouldn't have bothered?"

"I'm saying, what good did it do?"

"Well, what do you suggest, Agnes?" He can't stand her darting evasive eyes any more than she can stand his. He turns his face to the street. This side of the Village, people don't trudge home, they step lively, lawyers and bankers and, he fancies, songwriters and poets and jazz clarinetists.

Agnes says, "They're in Lisbon, the refugees. They're in Lisbon and Casablanca—I don't even know where that is. They had to buy tickets a year ago, and wait for visas, and now they'll never get out."

A fat old man in a linen suit veers off the sidewalk—Joe's afraid they're sitting on his stoop—but the man turns in one house before he reaches them.

"It's in Africa," he says.

"Joe."

"What."

"If you'd been in the Blitz—or let's say they started bombing us here—what would you do?"

"I guess I'd get myself to a bomb shelter. Hide under the bed."

"No, seriously. What's a pacifist supposed to do when somebody's dropping bombs on them?"

"Do what everybody else does. Take cover."

"But after. When you come out from under the bed."

"When everybody else says, now we'll bomb them back to smithereens? What's the point of that? Twice as many people dead?"

"The point," she says drily, "is to make them stop."

"But does it? Aren't there only more dead bodies when you answer bombs with bombs? You see what's happening."

The only problem is, he sees what she wants him to see too: the dank crowded hotel room in Lisbon, the father snapping at the children, the money running out. Her knee swings back and forth, pressing his in a steady rhythm, her signals as garbled as the way he feels about this war.

"It's the priests who made you believe this pacifist stuff."

"Jeez, it's a *military* school. This is a *just* war. This is a *good* war. As if every miserable war that's ever been fought hasn't been a good cause."

"But Joe—*Hitler.*"

"As if we didn't wink when he passed laws against the Jews. When he marched into Czechoslovakia. As if Wall Street didn't pay us to wink."

"You're so cynical."

"You might think about the refugees, but nobody else does, not even FDR. Especially not FDR. We're not going to war to save any refugees. We go to war, they'll all get slaughtered."

He's scared her into silence. He's scared himself, a little. And of course she's seen through him, of course there's a priest who got him thinking this way—there's always a priest. He won't talk religion with her, makes him sound like a sap. So naturally the most sanctimonious thing he could possibly say pops out: "I don't know how you could read the Gospels, be a Christian, and think that we should go to war."

Her knee, he realizes, isn't swinging against his anymore. "I'm not so sure I am a Christian. I'm not really sure I believe in God anymore."

The sidewalk in front of him turns into a movie set, celluloid, framed, real-but-unreal. All these well-heeled householders of Greenwich Village: movie extras. He and Agnes, sitting on a stoop, having their—what? Lovers' quarrel? Political discussion? Actors too. They're only reading lines. She can't mean that. It's not that he doesn't know any atheists—though come to think of it, he doesn't know any atheists. They're crawling all over the Village, but he's never had a conversation with one, not in the cafés, not even at the War Resisters League, which is as a matter of fact crawling with believers so fierce they're willing to defy their own country. Even Uncle Fran, the fairy, Christ! The most pious member of the family. Daily Mass, when he's feeling guilty about his prowling. His mother, his father, his brothers: it's the air they breathe, from the morning bells to the nighttime prayers, his mother invoking her dead little angels. Maybe they're atheists on this side of the Village, but there's not a soul on his end of East Twelfth Street who doesn't believe. In every sip of coffee, every crust of bread.

"I've tried to see it your way, I have. But how can you ask the refugees to turn their children's other cheek?" Her voice reverberates the way the radio does sometimes. "Sometimes I think you're, I don't know, crazy."

They both go quiet. And then she finishes in a rush:

"But mostly I think you're too good, and I'm not good at all."

Through a megaphone, from a distance. Like an old-timey bandleader. Nonviolent resistance means resist, not roll over. He should fight for her. Dimly he hears *You're too good*. She doesn't mean that. She means what Bernie means, that he's too naive. He's about to move in with winos, and she's about to go to college. She'll never be without money in her pocket and an extra job and a plan for the rest of her life.

"I'm going to write to my draft board."

This time she's the one who takes his hand, and he almost jumps off the stoop. She strokes one finger at a time, nice and slow. Where'd she learn to do that? The spring light dims, just for them. If only there were somewhere they could go, some hotel. If only he could persuade her the way he did that last time, with a squeeze and a kiss, only this time in the dark . . . He doesn't have a dime for a hotel (as if she'd agree to *that*). He doesn't have a dime for a café even, since his father banished him from the vegetable stall.

"You're going to tell them you're a conscientious objector?"

"I'm going to tell them I refuse to register."

They'll be lowering the age to eighteen any day, everybody says so. Sure he's a c.o., but that's not the route he's going to take. Everybody at the House expects he'll go to a c.o. camp. What could be cozier than that? Doing useful work and being with like-minded souls and not doing a damn thing to help the refugees. Well, he's not going to one of their safe camps. The doors begin to shut behind him. And if she keeps doing what she's doing with her hand . . .

"You're going to jail," she whispers. "You really are."

"First I'm gonna run like hell. To Mexico."

The light falls faster now. Even a dark alley would do (as if Agnes is the sort of girl who follows you into a dark alley). He saw Bernie all over her, saw them with his own eyes. Do they think he's blind? She leans down against him, presses her cheek into his knee, mute again. Don't do that, put your head on me. Don't do that, then lean your cheek against Bernie's.

"Getting dark," he says, his old man again. "They'll be worried about you in Brooklyn."

"Can't go home," she whispers, and she's worn him down. He can't even summon his fury against her. She's brought him a challenge—do something—and then given him a list of all the somethings she holds in contempt. He'll do something all right. *Facta non verba.*

"Come on," he says, back to being her kindly older relative. "Take a walk with me." He coaxes her up till they're descending the stairs, till they're headed west again into the dying flashes of light. He puts his arm around her shoulder, and she slides his arm around her waist, as if that's the way they always walk. If she'd done that a week ago, he'd have been out of his head with joy and lust. He tries to picture Julie, but Agnes is the one whose shoulder is warm beneath his hand. With a single squeeze, he could bruise her slender arm. With a single squeeze, he could win her back.

Of course they end up in Washington Square. On the same bench, for all he knows, where he smooched with Julie a few nights ago. Or maybe it's the same bench where Bernie had his mitts all over Agnes.

Hip to Agnes's hip, he forgets Julie and after a while he even forgets Bernie. When he draws his arm around her, she all but flings herself at him and through her light summer blouse he feels her breasts flatten into his chest. When he leans down to kiss her, she presses harder still and feathers her hand along the back of his neck. That movie pose.

They kiss for hours, days, weeks, months. They kiss as twilight turns to dark night. They kiss for kissing's sake and they kiss so they won't talk about war and Bernie and the rest of their lives. She's forgotten how it's supposed to look on camera and instead she's just feeling him, every inch of his skin through his shirt, as if the shirt doesn't exist. She reaches his waist and tucks four fingers in just below his belt. Her soft damp flesh is crazy about him.

He's bursting. Bursting. Burst.

Not much for him to pack after all. At the bottom of the brown paper sack, three books given him by three different priests: *The Imitation of Christ, Mahatma Gandhi His Own Story, The Spiritual Exercises of Ignatius Loyola*. Resting atop the books, three shirts, undershorts and socks, Sunday Mass pants. He folds his gray gabardine uniforms for his little brothers, but when it comes time, he'll tell them to go to any school but a military school, no matter how big the scholarship.

―――

When he moves into St. Joseph's House, he becomes a monk. Isn't that what he wanted? He doesn't sleep all night with the bedbugs gnawing. Then the bites torment him all through morning Mass, and once he's back in the kitchen Dorothy Day has a long list of errands for him to run. First she sends him off to Tony at the corner grocery, where the food has to be put on their tab. He finds this humiliating, but the grocer doesn't blink an eye.

"What am I gonna do, Joe?" Tony says. "Is it Joe? You're all Joe down there. I'm gonna turn down a saint when she asks me for a crust of bread?"

Miss Day with a halo: he can't picture it. Now that he's moved in she's invited him, finally, to call her *Dorothy*, but he chokes on the three dry syllables.

"Where you go to school, Joe?"

"Just graduated Xavier."

"Hey, good for you. Where you going to college?"

Joe grimaces. "Not sure I will."

"Best thing I ever did, philosophy at Fordham." He must see Joe's surprise. "I know what you're thinking. Four years slaving over the books, I come back here and run the family grocery?"

It's exactly what he's thinking. "I thought they'd give me a good scholarship, but no dice."

"They like you to work for it."

As if he hasn't *worked* for it. As if he hasn't worked every spare minute for his pop and now for Dorothy Day. "Yeah well. I'll save up."

"Keep up your Latin while you're saving, that's my advice." Crazy. The corner grocer, giving away a box of food like that—his pop would be appalled, milk on the house—is telling him to keep up his Latin.

"Got any Greek?"

"Greek what?"

"The Greek language, you goofball. Learn yourself a little Greek. You're gonna need it."

Mott Street: one long surprise. Miss Day runs him ragged delivering papers, scheduling baptisms, peeling potatoes. He might as well be in the

Army. At night he hears rats running through the cellar and thinks of his mother, who begged him to come visit the first weekend, and his father, who told him not to show his face till he could admit his folly. Uncle Fran took him aside the morning he left: *Your papa was gonna expand, and how's he supposed to do that without your help?*

Now that he finally lives in the House, he sees what he never saw when he was volunteering: six, seven times a day he has to break up fights between the men. He thought he'd spend most of his free time jawing with the other pacifists, but everybody's off in two thousand different directions. Sunday he oversleeps by fifteen minutes and by the time he comes downstairs everybody else has taken off for Mass and Sunday visiting, the visit his pop nixed.

At nine A.M. Crazy Louie, a guy of indeterminate middle age who rooms two doors down, comes into the kitchen with blood dripping down his wrists. Joe doesn't have a clue what to do but grabs a couple of dishtowels and ties them up as neatly as he can over the man's trembling forearms before he realizes the rags aren't what you'd call clean. Never mind. He heads off, walking Louie to Bellevue, then trips to a halt on the sidewalk when he imagines Miss Day finding out he didn't take him to a Catholic hospital. The two of them turn west—if Louie starts to pass out, he'll just have to holler till someone calls the cops to take them to St. Vincent's. Louie's exhilarated by the walk, by the slashing. His bleeding stops, but he can't shut up about how he saw worms crawling along his white flesh, *death worms, they was oozing green filth.*

Joe paces the emergency room for twelve hours while the doctor contemplates committing an indigent. Finally, at ten o'clock, they release Louie to his care. Swell. Eighteen years old, on his own for the first time in his life, guarding the drunken loony would-be suicides of the world.

Wednesday he's been there a week. Dorothy Day takes one look at him after lunch, hauling in a box of winter clothes in the steaming New York summer, and says, "You'd better take the afternoon off."

"I'm fine."

"Didn't you ever hear of resting on the seventh day? Out. Out you go."

For the first time in his life he thinks of retreating to bed in the middle of the afternoon but knows it's as unthinkable here as it would have been at home. He's flat out broke, and what a day to be broke. If only he'd known she was going to give him the afternoon he could have begged some pocket change off the other Workers. The Yanks are in town, last game of a home stand, and DiMaggio's closing in. Today will make thirty-seven games. Four more after that and he'll have Sisler's record. The city's going nuts over the streak. He pictures Agnes's grandmother, Her Cranky Royal Majesty, in the bleachers. What he would give to be sitting next to her.

But nobody's around to bum three bits off of, and he's sure as shooting not going to bum them off Miss Day. Nothing to do but submit, go out, out. Walk himself silly. Maybe at least he'll sleep tonight.

Mott to Kenmare, Kenmare to Sixth, up through the Village, replaying Agnes's kisses. He's up to West Twelfth Street already when it hits him anew, that without their Saturday night routine he might not ever see her again. Her family's had no phone since her father's last run of bad luck, so she has no way to reach him now, not unless she writes or shows up and risks the wrath of Dorothy Day. He despairs, picks up the pace, despairs all over again. He can feel her nipples against his, pictures figs, doesn't know whether to laugh or cry. For the rest of his life, he'll see fruits and vegetables on a woman's naked body. All that wasted time and now, when he finally gets his hands on her . . .

He heads toward Times Square, where at least (if DiMag hits safely, which he will, he *will*) he'll see the news flash above him. He hasn't thought about news in a week, hasn't stopped once to wonder if America's gone to war. Hasn't, he realizes with a pang, thought about the refugees or his unanswered letters to DiMaggio.

He crosses Fortieth Street and the headlines flash:

       ... Roosevelt to Aid Russia ...

       ... Hitler at Soviet Front ...

He feels worms crawl over his own wrists. Agnes would say *We have to stop him,* but Agnes won't be the one riding a tank. He pictures her in his narrow little cell in St. Joseph's House, on his bedbuggy mended sheets, naked, pink. Her figgy breasts. She can't mean that about not believing in God anymore. Maybe he should get on the subway and go find her in Brooklyn. Surely he could beg a nickel—but he doesn't even know her address, only the funny coincidence they both live on a Twelfth Street, in two different boroughs.

He's not the only one standing on the sidewalk, neck craned, waiting for the news of the world. Colored fellow next to him says, "Bet you waiting to see does DiMaggio hit the ball."

He shakes the man's hand. "That's exactly what I'm waiting for."

"Me, I'm waiting for them to flash Satchel Paige's name up there."

"You might be waiting a while."

"You even know who he is?"

"He's having a helluva year."

"You must be a serious student of the game."

Joe beams and in that flash of his pride the news appears:

... DiMaggio Homers in Fourth ...

A cheer goes up from the street. "He's gonna catch that record," the colored fellow says sadly. "And you gonna have to tell your friends about Satch cause *his* name is not gonna be in the headlines in Times Square."

"Will do," Joe says, trying to match the fellow's sadness. But he can't squash his own exuberance, and the man trudges off alone. A cloud of shame descends on him: he wouldn't have ever known about the Black Yankees if Bernie hadn't told him. It was Bernie who first spoke Satchel Paige's name. Hasn't seen Bernie since graduation, when he stood on the sidewalk next to his mother, looking miserable. They did not exchange good-byes.

He doesn't stop to think, he just takes off. Has to be the most crowded sidewalk in New York, but he pushes his way through, running the way he hasn't run since track practice, running to go see his old friend and stop this foolishness once and for all. He pounds the pavement in his button-down shirt, struggles to find his rhythm in his stiff street shoes. Every few feet a tourist gawks at him. He runs up Broadway round the park side of Columbus Circle, runs—for old times' sake—along Central Park past the Mayflower Hotel, where DiMaggio lived when he was a bachelor. Now his breathing's steady and even, though that might be a blister starting up against his right instep.

He heads back across Sixty-Sixth Street to reclaim Broadway. Definitely a blister, and the possibility of another on his left heel. He runs west at Seventy-Second Street, takes the broad deserted sidewalks of West End Avenue north to Bernie's building.

A block short, he slows to consider the extent of his sweat and stink, decides to ignore them both, lets his blisters settle. He shouldn't be this out of breath. One week off his routine, and he's an old man at eighteen. The doorman knows him, salutes, throws his arms out to say *Go right ahead.* He heads past the mailboxes, down the long, dark corridor behind the elevator where the porter's apartment sits, rings Bernie's bell. He doesn't smell that bad. He's not breathing that hard.

Bernie's mother answers the door. She starts a little, peering into the dark ground-floor hallway, then smiles wide. "Joe." Funny how you can hear the German in a single syllable.

"Mrs. Keller."

"Come in, come in."

She skips over the usual stiff interrogation in the dark entryway, proceeds to the dark living room. Mrs. Keller, the Flaming Red, is actually a pale brunette. She's a formal person—Joe's always imagined she's a stern taskmaster in her Lower East Side classroom. Her local's been kicked out of the union, supposedly because they're all flaming Reds. Bernie swears she's just an ordinary socialist and anyway, Catholics *can't* be communist. Whatever she is, she's always been sweet on him.

"We missed you around here, Joe." She knows. How long can Bernie stay on here, telling his mother every little detail of his life? He pictures the long-dead Mr. Keller fleeing this mole hole. Agnes says Keller was a drunk. Impossible to imagine Bernie's mother, with her severe, round glasses and her tight curls, her bust cantilevered and protruding at such a precise angle through her white summer blouse, with a drunk.

"I've missed seeing you as well." He hears himself reaching for a William Powell pitch to his voice, and sees this middle-aged woman he's known since he was fourteen buckle a little. He should knock it off, this strange power he has over women. Over any woman whose name isn't Agnes O'Leary.

"I will go find Bernhard."

Funny expression—find Bernie, in an apartment this size—but unnecessary anyway. Bernie stands under the lintel in his gym shorts for some reason, a goofy expression on his face.

"Hear about DiMag? Homer in the fourth."

"Saw it in Times Square. That's what I came to tell you." And that's it: rift mended in a pair of manly laughs. Next thing he knows they're back in Bernie's room, Bernie tugging on long pants to walk outside.

Mrs. Keller has faded away in most uncharacteristic fashion and remains faded while they drift onto the avenue, heading uptown.

"Where we going?"

Bernie says, "DiMaggio's."

"What are you talking about?"

"I thought we'd walk up to his building. Maybe you can catch him getting out of his car. How many times have you said you want to talk to him about the refugees?"

"About as many times as you poured cold water on me. What gives?"

"He'll be in a good mood today."

"Seems like you're the one in a good mood." He looks down on the top of Bernie's head. Mutt and Jeff, Father Phelan calls them.

Bernie doesn't stop walking, but he slows. "Got something to tell you."

"Shoot."

"I asked Agnes for a date finally."

"A *date?*" Maybe it's the shock, but it strikes him as hysterically funny: the word, the concept, the bashful look on Bernie's face. He whoops and hollers. "Bernie's got a date with Agnes," he sings up West End Avenue. "Bernie and Agnes up in a tree."

"Knock it off, D'Ambrosio."

"Jeez, Bernie, is this your first *date?* High school graduate like yourself?"

"Shut up, D'Ambrosio. Who are you seeing?"

"Agnes, as a matter of fact."

Bernie stops dead on the sidewalk, pounds one fist, like a gavel, through the air.

"Not *formally.* She showed up at my folks' last week. We spent the night together." He hears himself draw out the word *night,* caressing it, which might account for why he doesn't see it coming: a sucker punch right to the gut. The next thing he knows Bernie's all over him, pummeling.

He slams the back of his hand against Bernie's right cheek—it's the way you'd hit a woman—and Keller's glasses go flying. Without them

Bernie looks older, his boyishness vanished with the flying specs, and he lowers his serious blank face and comes at Joe with a head butt. Knocks him right off his feet and then they're going at it on the sidewalk, bodies entwined like lovers, one head and then the other clunking down hard on concrete. He's caught off guard by Bernie's fury: he feels a jagged fist crack into his cheekbone and hears, dimly, the protests of middle-aged ladies who stand back and cluck their tongues. If Bernie would let up for a second with the windmilling fists, he could hop to and reclaim some dignity. But now he's on top: he feels his own hand pressed against his best friend's windpipe and hears a barking sound below.

A screech of brakes. Approaching footsteps. The female bystanders point and shriek and moan. A big middle-aged fellow in a sports coat pulls Joe off Bernie by the scruff of his neck. He stands at last, stiff as an old man.

"You don't go creaming a little guy like that," the big man says, disgusted. Joe turns away, his cheek rebelling against the rest of his face. He's disgusted himself. Some pacifist. He doesn't have a breath left in his body but he's still awake, by God, still conscious that the man who stopped the fight, the man with the slicked-back black hair, retreating to his big sedan at the curb, bears a distinct resemblance to Lefty Gomez.

He must be dizzy from the crack on the noggin. If that was Lefty, then the leg protruding from the passenger seat, that foot perched on the sidewalk, waiting for Lefty to do the dirty work, would belong to . . . Cannot be. That would be a crazy coincidence, the stuff of screwball comedies. He's just got DiMaggio on the brain.

He stands exiled at the curb, watches Bernie wiggle himself into standing. The ladies of West End Avenue remove hankies from their pocketbooks, dab at Bernie's face, minister to him, the little guy, the poor dear fellow. They're only a couple of blocks from DiMag's building. Maybe he should just proceed as if nothing happened. The hell with Bernie.

His face is starting to crack apart. Maybe this is a sign from God. Maybe this is St. Paul knocked off his horse. He should march up to 400 West End Avenue and ask Joe DiMaggio to help the refugees right here and now.

"Lousy stinking crumb bum," Bernie spits at him.

Joe D'Ambrosio lets out a yowl that's half-laugh, half-you-know-what. Then he doubles and throws up every last ounce of Catholic Worker soup all over the sidewalk. It goes on and on: he's made himself sick down to his soul. His gut clenches so desperately he's briefly sure he's dying. But when it's over he pulls himself erect, cleared out. Cleansed. He'd wave good-bye to Bernie if Bernie were still there, but he's already run home to mama.

D'Ambrosio wipes his mouth with his sleeve and on he trudges. He's pretty sure Joe DiMaggio is waiting for him.

PART III

HEAT

June 29. On the way to Griffith Stadium, the red-faced cabbie tells them that the Nazis are pushing hard into Ukraine and White Russia, and Gomez gives him a conspiratorial look. What the hell's a "White Russia"? Anyway, DiMaggio can't think about Russia today, can't think about Latvia or Estonia (cities? states? countries?). The cabbie drones on, but Joe DiMaggio's two games away from breaking the major league streak record, two games away from hitting safely in forty-two consecutive games. Today the Yanks and the Senators play a doubleheader in D.C. Today's the day.

In the locker room, Henrich says it might get up to a hundred degrees. The other Yankees groan, but DiMaggio grins into his coffee. Name him an Italian who doesn't heat up with the thermometer. Sweat beads behind his knees and pours out from deep in his groin. This heat wave just won't let up and he doesn't want it to. The hotter it gets, the hotter his bat.

McCarthy barrels through, looking a little drunk in the steamy locker room, and announces: "Thirty thousand paying customers waiting for you, boys." He directs a sarcastic waggle of his finger at the entire team and not, of course, at Joe DiMaggio. Not a syllable about the streak, but if the manager wants to mention the ticket sales . . .

McCarthy rallies his troops, DiMaggio lights another Camel. Today he needs to double his luck for the doubleheader, even if now the papers are saying it's only the *modern-day* record. In the last few days somebody's dug up the niggling bit of news that Wee Willie Keeler had a forty-four game streak all the way back in eighteen-ninety-something, when they didn't even count fouls as strikes. What the hell. Sisler's record—forty-one—is the one everybody's been waiting for all season long. He'll deal with that one, and then he'll deal with Wee Willie Keeler.

He woke up every half hour last night, the sweat pooling on him, and when he rose from his bed this morning he was sure he was living on a different planet. His gut's a rusty bucket shot through with holes and Gomez had to call the front desk for more toilet paper before he could leave the bathroom this morning. But when he got to the ballpark the heat just shimmered and a crazy kind of peace shimmered with it. He's still clenched—every muscle in his body including his culu and if he lets go of that it's all over—but now he thinks that he might actually break Sisler's record.

Usually Lefty's the one who stops the others from blathering on around DiMaggio, but today he waves a *Washington Post* he's picked up somewhere: "Jeez louise, they're gonna draft a million men. FDR's gonna come after you the way he went after Dom." DiMaggio gazes up at Gomez but drifts away. His brother just ducked the draft on account of bad eyesight, which slays him and all the sportswriters too: Dominic DiMaggio can see enough to play major league baseball, but not enough for the U.S. Army.

DiMaggio waits for Lefty's hot air to cool off, and soon it enough it does, and then he's left alone the way he always is before a game, the way he wants to be. Joe DiMaggio doesn't have time to waste on chitchat, not even talk of wars and drafts. DiMaggio's got a major league record to break. Forty-five games in a row is a nice round number, but it's not enough. Isn't he the same Joe D who hit in sixty-one games straight in the Pacific Coast League when he was a kid? That's the number he'd really like to crack open, his own minor league record: he'd like to go for sixty-five at least. And lately he sees a rounder number still, a number farther along the page of numbers facing him. Seventy-five. He'd like to hit in seventy-five games in a row and he'd like to lay down the seventy-five hits in front of the Yankee brass, in front of the fans, in front of Dottie, the way a cat lays down a mouse.

There you go. Maybe this'll satisfy you.

When he heads out to take batting practice the damp glare of Washington's heat wave dazzles him and he fears, briefly, that he might have to dash back to the crapper. The liquid in his gut hardens. (Somewhere in White Russia bayonets must be glistening.) The ballpark's gone nuts: fans  crawl everywhere, lean over the box seats, jump down onto the field, prowl past the batting cage. Crazy! Anarchy in our nation's capital.

Joe, Joe! For my kid.

I got money riding on you, Dago. Don't let me down.

You can do it, DiMaggio!

The streak has turned him into a patient man, and when the fans manage to get up close, when they stick out balls and programs and bats and dirty envelopes they find in their pockets, he signs away. Why not? He doesn't need batting practice today. He doesn't need loosening up anymore. He even grins at them the way he grinned at his coffee. The cameras click and flash and he sees the pictures in tomorrow's papers: he's a charmer for a change. The Roamin' Roman. Joltin' Joe DiMaggio. Cops and security guards march across the field. (The Panzers advance on Latvia.) The look on his pop's face that spring day he had him translate the war news: not possible that this will happen, that this *is* happening.

Sign here, Joe.

Sign mine.

A little smile plays on his lips when the teams line up for the National Anthem, only now the ground beneath his feet slopes toward oblivion, and he makes the mistake of looking down. (The trains head east: from Paris, from Vienna. Why does he keep seeing the frigging trains?) How much is one man supposed to carry, anyway? It's been more like dying, living through this streak, every day another little piece of him hacked away and served up raw.

Hey Joe DiMaggio.

You can do it, Dago. Do it for the fans.

Dutch Leonard's pitching for the Senators. Any other day he'd have already clobbered a fastball off Leonard, but suddenly he can't remember why he thought he had it in the bag, can't remember, now that he's one long cramped muscle, how he's ever managed to loosen his twisted neck or shoulders. It's already the top of the sixth, and the whole crowd's lost faith: if you wanted, you could reach out and touch the stickiness of defeat in the air. DiMaggio usually takes care of business in the early innings. Now the fans think they're gonna walk out of here without getting what they came for. *So close,* they'll say. *So close but no cigar. What a heartache. Poor Dago.*

He swings hard at the first pitch, misses. (His pop shakes his head in disbelief.) What a fucking heartbreak. Deep breath, but not so deep anybody can see. He slides his feet wider, pumps the bat once. Takes the ball. One–one. Leonard winds up again. DiMag focuses on the low fastball whizzing toward him till it's ten feet away, leaves his body, snaps his wrists without actually being *attached* to them. He hears the crunk of bat against ball but he's already taken off as fast as his legs—no longer anywhere in the vicinity of his torso—can move and makes it safe to second. The double ties Sisler's record.

The crowd, as they say, goes wild.

And Joe DiMaggio allows himself one last brief grin from his safe base and knows that he's back inside his own skin. Why does he have to put himself through that? Why's he have to do it this way? He pictures his disappointed pop boarding a crowded train, ducks his head, feels the ground shift again beneath his feet.

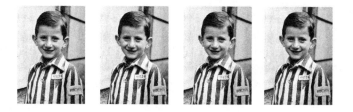

Between games, he showers in another trance, doesn't remember turning the water off. Towel draped, he holds the fresh uniform shirt in his fingers and breathes in the faint smell of bleach, which calms him the way the smell of fresh bread or wine calms him.

He takes his time, buttoning up, before he faces the reporters. When he turns finally they all beam at one another like little kids.

"Say, how'd that feel?"

"You had us sweating there, Joe. Think you'd have to wait till the sixth?"

"Now that you've tied it, how far can you go? What's the limit?"

"Think I better break the record before I make any predictions." They

all chuckle, men of the world. He hears himself tell them he's been nervous the last couple of games. He hears himself say the word *tense*, and he catches a glimpse of Gomez yucking it up. Yeah, yeah, so maybe he's been nervous a little longer than the last couple of days. The scribblers don't have to know everything about him. They don't have to know that since the streak started flashing in headlines all over the country, women show up at the front desk of every hotel they stop in. If he tells the desk to send them on up, the dames are already ripping off their blouses by the time he opens the door, cradling their own luscious tits. His teammates all put out the same story, even Gomez: *That Joe, you wouldn't know there was any pressure on him. He comes to the clubhouse, he drinks his coffee, he reads the paper. You'd never know he was feeling any heat at all.* They don't have to know, the reporters, that his guts are rotting away, that his wife hounds him, that he smells crushed peaches, that he dreams of crowded trains and his father's bewilderment, that he thinks he's losing his mind.

They don't have to know that yesterday in Philly, he and Gomez went to the hospital to see a kid who probably wasn't going to make it—but they do know. Somebody in the front office must have tipped them off, the way they tipped him off that a kid named Tony, who wasn't having a lot of good days lately, wanted to meet his hero. His dying wish: something out of a movie, a three-hankie sob story at the Astor.

"How 'bout that little Italian kid, Dago? Think he's gonna pull through, now that you tied the record for him?"

He'd never seen a dying kid before, pictured the tyke lying in an oxygen tent or hooked up to a bottle of blood or something. He didn't want to go, but you hear the word *dying,* you hear the kid's named *Tony:* what can you say? And it wasn't like he imagined at all. Tony managed to sit up, wearing pressed pajamas for the occasion, his eyes sunk in blue hollows but a big, goofy smile on his face. Nine or ten, maybe. A little tongue-tied, like Joe himself, and resigned to his fate. Knew he was on the way out—you could tell. What do you say to a dying kid? Not much. Lefty did most of the talking as usual, but on the way out the door DiMag told the boy that when he listened to the game tomorrow he'd hear a record smashed. And when he heard that magic crack of bat against ball, he should know that DiMag-gio in D.C. was sending Tony in Philly his regards.

"Listen fellas." He hears something he's never heard before in his talking-to-reporters voice. "Don't write about that. Don't play that up. The kid's . . ." He doesn't need to finish. The men with the fedoras pushed to the backs of their foreheads all look up at him, nodding solemnly, the way they'd nod to the boss, pretending they'll honor Joe DiMaggio's one heartfelt request on the day he's trying to break the streak record. And he knows they'll write it up anyway. Won't be able to help themselves, anymore than he can help himself hitting the ball.

When they file back into the dugout for the second game, his bat's gone, vamoosed, the fourth slot in the rack empty. His eye falls on the absence just as the bat boy trots over in a panic, his freckles like ashes scattered on his pale sweating face. The bat rack's right below the box seat railings: all some bastard had to do was lean over, maybe have a buddy hold his ankles so he could stretch far enough to grab Joe DiMaggio's bat.

McCarthy bellows about security in this two-bit town, but after he's done screaming the bench starts to look like wake night at the funeral parlor. Nobody wants to meet DiMag's eye. This is it, then. Some punk's reached into the visitors' dugout and stolen his chance to break the record. Everybody knows he's got to have a top-heavy bat, custom sanded. Everybody knows DiMaggio's bat is one of a kind.

"We'll fix you up," McCarthy blusters, but how's he gonna fix it? DiMag charges after Tommy Henrich, already on his way to the batting box, and asks to see his bat: Tom borrowed a couple of Joe's new bats when his swing was off, and now DiMaggio prays that he grabbed the wrong one. But the one in Henrich's hand isn't the magic bat DiMag has been hitting with. Baby Face asks him why doesn't the Dago take one of the borrowed bats back now?

Why doesn't the Dago go ripping through the stadium till he finds the son of a bitch and then really show him what he can do with a bat? What, he thinks it's funny? Thinks it's cute? Some joke, mister. Some funny joke, a guy sweats blood for forty-one games and then you lean down over the rails and pull his bat out of the rack. The biggest hole in his rusty gut rips open and for a second he thinks he's actually shitting his pants.

Tony with the blue hollows around his eyes had a big, goofy grin on his face when Joe DiMaggio walked in the room. And what do you know, Henrich's bat doesn't feel half-bad. It's not worn in, the handle's a shade thicker than he likes, but it's not half-bad. It is what it is.

This time Anderson comes in to relieve for the Senators, one of those wise guys who likes to throw at his head. Anderson knows how many pitches DiMaggio's had steam by his earlobes, knows how the Dago stands there and takes it and never flinches, but still he keeps them coming high and tight. DiMag respects the man for throwing tough but, staring him down, he sees the punk who stole his bat.

It's already the seventh inning, already his fourth at bat. The seventh inning is what you'd call late in the game. The seventh inning is when fans start leaving in disgust. Not that anybody's leaving the ballpark today, not even with the thermometer stuck at ninety-six, the humidity at a zillion. They'll stick around, all right. They'll stick around to see if he can do it, and part of them will want him to break the record and part of them will hope he doesn't quite make it. Maybe they'll hope for a high fly that looks as if it might go the distance but gets snatched at the last split second. Maybe they want to see him go down swinging. It's good to see a man break the record, but it's satisfying, too, to see him fail. If he can't pass Sisler, he's a real mediocrity. Oh sure, fine hitter, but not quite the hero everybody thought he had the potential to be. Couldn't even do it for a dying kid.

Anderson and the punk and the rest of the fans merge into one moving target. (The tanks rumble, the bayonets shimmer. Cities, states, nations tremble.) Big deal, the *modern-day* record. Couldn't even take on Wee Willie Keeler. Wee Willie. How's a man go through life with a name like that?

What he wants is for this to be over. What he wants is for Dorothy and the photographers and Gomez to stop looking at him with that pitying smile that says *What a shame that would be, if you came this close and didn't make it. What a lot of stress you've been under.* What he wants is for bloodied kids to stop accosting him on the sidewalk yelling *You can do it, DiMaggio! You can save the refugees!* As if they're mind readers. Everybody and his brother thinks he can read Joe DiMaggio's mind.

Anderson sure thinks so. He makes like a flamethrower, gets one in so close even Joe DiMaggio has to duck—but he doesn't flinch. The crowd boos Anderson, their own pitcher, and then they tense up again. But up at the dish Joe DiMaggio isn't tense anymore. DiMaggio isn't even there. DiMaggio resides in another zone of the universe. Rivers flow through his body. Birds perch on his head. The stadium is silent and the heat is balm for his soul. He rips open on the second pitch for a hot, sure single. And stands on first base not entirely sure how he got there.

There you go, Dottie. There you go, FDR. There you go, Mr. and Mrs. America. There are your forty-two games in a row and now will you please get out of my way so I can take on Wee Willie Keeler for you.

He hears the crowd's roar as golden as Caruso's high notes. And when Keller behind him whams Anderson for a triple, and DiMaggio crosses home plate, the other Yanks jump up and down like ten-year-old boys, like that kid Tony in his hospital bed. They're jumping for him—for Deadpan DiMaggio, for Mr. Lost in His Own Universe, Mr. Standoff-ish, for Oh That's Joe He's Just Shy—tooting and yippeeing and clapping their hands together like girls.

He feels he could grow wings. He feels he could hold his arms out like Superman and take off into the stratosphere: scoop up refugees, stop trains in their tracks, shield his brothers from the draft, win the war before America even joins the fight.

Lying next to Dottie who loves him again, now that he's broken a major league record, now that he's the toast of Manhattan, he tries again to loosen his stiff shoulders. It is what it is, this streak of his.

His wife gurgles love sighs in her sleep, her big pregnant belly pushed up against his broad back. His son—he's as sure this is a boy as he's sure he'll hit the ball in game fifty-five—gives him a good kick in the kidneys. Will this boy sit with him one day at the kitchen table and see bewilderment on his face? His father sailed oceans, left his home behind, only wanted one of his sons to fish with him on the *Rosalie*. Instead they picked up bat and ball. A boy's game, which Joe DiMaggio will teach his son—and his son will recoil from it the way he himself, the great man, recoiled from the smell of fish in the San Francisco Bay. He has disappointed someone as long as he can remember.

It still bugs him, the way that kid came at him downstairs. *You can do it, Joe DiMaggio. You can save the refugees.* What's he supposed to do? Use the superpowers everybody seems to think he has? Pick up the phone, call the Pope? March in the street and be arrested for a Red?

Joltin' Joe DiMaggio lies as still as he can in his penthouse on West End Avenue and hears, somewhere down on Broadway, the rumble of convoys in White Russia, wherever that is. Whatever that is. He stares out his window at what must be, under all that thick night, a tranquil summer sky.

He doesn't hear for almost a week that the kid was dead in Philly before that first game in D.C. even started. So much for hocus-pocus and superpowers. So much for saving anybody.

PERVERSE

It's Agnes's first official boy-coming-to-the-front-door date, and she spends half an hour debating whether to wear the dark green linen dress with a broad black belt to cinch her waist. Does it make her look too ordinary? She knows exactly what she wants to look like, but B. Altman does not carry the clothes that gypsies and jazz singers might wear. She snaps her stocking top into her garter. She's dreamed of marrying Bernie since the first night she met him, but when she thought of *flesh,* of caresses in the dark, it was Joe she pictured. Now she wobbles into the sexy high heels she treated herself to for graduation and decides that they redeem the dress. They'd better: she hasn't anything else.

She's still nowhere near ready when the buzzer rings ten minutes early. The vision of Babe and Bernie in the same small room, her father hovering silent in the background, makes her drop an earring. When Babe comes to the doorway of the girls' room, she and Loretta are still on their hands and knees, searching for the fake pearl. Babe grabs both sides of the door frame and looms.

"Is that boy Jewish?" she hisses.

Agnes looks up from the floor and stares, dumbfounded. "He goes to *Xavier.*" She watches Babe hide a smug smile of triumph: once again she's tricked Agnes, who should have said *So what if he is?*

"He seems perfectly nice," Babe says, in a voice intended to carry to the living room and, if need be, the hallway beyond.

And that is how Agnes comes to be without her earrings and without her dignity when she finally leaves the apartment with Bernie. She doesn't know till they're on the subway that she's left without her glasses, too. She was sure the case was inside her pocketbook.

Never mind. The trip to Forty-Second Street is a happy blur, Bernie's leg pressed tight against her own just the way it would be on one of their Saturday night jaunts: familiar but different, too, without Joe's pressed on the other side. She's dying to ask Bernie what news he's had, but she can't exactly bring that up on their first just-the-two-of-them date. She can't tell Bernie that when it's slow at the stocking counter she imagines that every man or boy entering the doors of B. Altman is Joe D'Ambrosio, come to whisk her away to another park bench for another smooch.

Anyway, she's crazy about Bernie—wasn't she leaning toward Bernie in the first place?—and it slays her to see him in a suit, looking like a thirty-five-year-old lawyer for the Justice Department. He takes her elbow, getting off the train, and by the time they're out on the street he's grabbed her hand. They walk stiffly toward the heart of Times Square, her hips forced to sway by the hand-holding and maybe by her new

shoes. She'll just have to let them. Bernie points out the billboard for *Sergeant York:* the biggest billboard she's ever seen, Gary Cooper looming so large that standing down below they can't even make out what he looks like.

No wonder the Astor's jammed, with that sign. They queue up, speechless. They're both shy now that they're out on a date, and Bernie's decided to forego all accents, so he doesn't even seem like himself. When they finally take safe possession of the tickets, he wanders off, stiff and formal, to buy a popcorn to share. She could eat two bags all by herself. Bernie said, *Sergeant York, and maybe we could get some ice cream after.* He didn't say anything about dinner, and she wouldn't expect him to either. Who could afford that kind of date? She has to remind herself not to grab the bag from Bernie's hand when he reappears.

"He was here last night," she whispers.

"Coop?" He does a big exaggerated Cooper double take, a good impression. Maybe they'll both loosen up before the night is over. She'll have to squint without her specs, but the Astor's the Astor, grand and carefree. The ushers twirl smartly and they claim their seats. It's July third, the crowd already on holiday, the women as glittery as sparklers. She's glad she left her glasses at home. She'd rather not see the newsreels too closely, anyway: it's Russia, Russia, Russia (and White Russia and Latvia and Estonia) and though the narrator tries to pretend the Soviets are all brave and noble fighters, it sounds like Germany's winning. How else could the Nazis have gone that far into Russian territory? Bernie leans forward and pounds a fist on his knee without, she suspects, even knowing he's doing it.

Finally, the feature starts to roll and she leans back. It's hard to relax with her whole body braced for a first date and a war movie in the bargain. Bernie's been talking about *Sergeant York* for weeks, but she didn't know it was going to be about a pacifist. He might have warned her. When Gary Cooper says he won't go to war, *can't* go to war, her heart races. Then in the second half, when he sees that sometimes you have to fight for your country, she feels her cheeks flame. Bernie's brought her to this movie to score another point against Joe, maybe the last point he thinks he'll ever need to score. By the time the battle scene looms over them, she could weep. It's all forced and pretty and fake, Cooper killing all those men single-handed. She doesn't believe it happened that way for one minute.

In the dark, she squirms in her seat, not sure if she's mad at Bernie, or mad at Joe, or so caught up in Gary Cooper's new folksy charm that she doesn't know who she is much less who she's mad at. Bernie responds to the squirming by resting his elbow next to hers on the armrest, but he doesn't reach for her hand the way he did in the street. Thank God.

They're both silent as the credits roll and the applause rings out. A sailor rises and sings "Anchors Aweigh" to the biggest audience he'll ever capture. All around her, she hears the vast departing crowd murmuring to each other, murmuring that they've never seen Gary Cooper play somebody so *simple,* so *sincere,* that they didn't think he had it in him, that it really makes you stop and think, *Maybe we better just go ahead and fight this war already.*

On the sidewalk Bernie says, "Did you read Bosley Crowther?"

Agnes doesn't trouble with the movie reviews—it's hard enough to keep up with the war news—but Bernie wasn't really looking for an answer anyway. "Crowther said it was *dignified.* What did you think?"

Agnes thinks she'll pass out from hunger if they don't get something to eat soon, and if she doesn't watch it, she'll bite Bernie's head off too. "I don't know what to think," she says. She's turning into Babe.

"How about we head to Schrafft's then?"

"Tell you what, let's go down to DeRobertis. They'll give us two for one on the cannoli and I bet they'll throw in a cup of coffee too."

A funny look crosses Bernie's face, and she sees her gaffe. *Let's go to DeRobertis, where you and Joe used to come call for me.* Bernie hasn't said a word about Joe all night, after four years of finishing his sentences. Something bad's happened between them. It was building at the end, before they all went off to the rest of their lives, and now it's come to pass. She can read the word *trouble* on Bernie's face.

"Sure," he says. "Let's go down to DeRobertis."

She hasn't worked at DeRobertis since Altman's put her on full-time, and, much as they treat her as the prodigal daughter, hugging and kissing the way her grandfather does, just being in Joe's neighborhood makes her tremble. She and Bernie sit, finally, in the back corner, close enough at the little table for their knees to bump, a big plate of on-the-house pastries between them. She wants to run up past the counter and gaze out the front window every two seconds, to see if Joe's strolling past, to see if he's just dropped by Twelfth Street to say hello to his ma.

They chomp away on wedding cookies to avoid looking each other in the eye, and soon enough their lips and fingers are dusted with sugar. Bernie must be reading her mind, because finally he says, very softly, in a Cockney accent: "We had it out, me old pal Joe and me. Din't we just?"

She raises her eyes. Bernie wavers before her, dear, corny Bernie, his wire rims reflecting the overhead lights. She can't make out much of his face, can't even tell whether he's shaved for their date or has let his beard go bristly the way she likes.

"Over the war?"

He shakes his head: she can see that much. "Over you."

A large chunk of cookie lodges in her throat. She sputters and grabs for coffee. "Oh Bernie . . ."

"He told me you spent the night together."

She can just hear Joe saying something like that. "We didn't spend the night together! We spent a couple of hours walking around the Village."

Bernie lets out a huge old-man sigh. "But it was a date, wasn't it? I didn't know you were dating him. I wouldn't have . . ."

It just kills her, the weight he gives the word. He's worried about whether they had a date and doesn't have a clue what he should really be asking: *Did he tell you he's going to jail? Did he swoop to kiss you the very moment you were hoping he would? Would you have run away with him that night, if he hadn't walked you to the subway?*

"It wasn't a date, Bernie." She says it as gently as she can, and knows in the saying that she can't keep on doing this to herself, much less to the pair of them. She chose between them that night, when she descended the subway stairs at West Fourth Street without saying what she wanted to say: *I've just cashed my check, I have twenty dollars in my pocket, I know there are fleabag hotels down here where you can rent a room . . .*

What she couldn't say because Joe, for all the body heat he generated, is a good Catholic boy who belongs to the sodality and says the rosary and adores the priests. Because he'd run from her as fast as he possibly could if she suggested such a thing. If he even knew she was thinking such a thing. And he'd be right. There's something wrong with her, the way she thinks about lovemaking every minute of the day. She could have gotten pregnant that night and she didn't even care—no, worse. She would have been ecstatic if Joe had made her pregnant. Then she'd have to go live with him among the bums and stop worrying about every dime. Then she could forget about college and stocking counters and handing over the money to Babe. There is definitely something wrong with her. She *needs* to study psychology.

"I haven't seen him since that night."

"I haven't seen him since we had a fistfight on West End Avenue."

Somehow she's not surprised. Only she won't ask who won: Joe towers over Bernie. She's feeling a little ill from all the popcorn and sugar. Bernie's got a white streak in his left eyebrow.

"Lefty Gomez broke it up. Can you believe it?"

"I think I can. But who's Lefty Gomez?"

"Agnes. Big pitcher for the Yanks. He rooms with Joe DiMaggio. Haven't you heard? DiMag broke the last record yesterday."

"The record, the record. All I've been hearing all summer. You know what? I don't even know what the record's *for*."

"Agnes, you're the limit."

Maybe it was the way he said she was *the limit.* Maybe it was going to DeRobertis. She finds herself snuggling into Bernie on the train going home as if they've been snuggling for years. He cuddles his arm around her shoulder and for one horrifying second she even pictures her wedding dress, an ivory dropped-waist in Young Sophisticates she's been coveting for weeks. Babe is truly insidious, the way she's managed to interject her grandmotherly marriage plans into this first date.

Bernie picks Babe up on his radar. "I heard your grandmother ask you if I was Jewish."

"I'm surprised she didn't ask you for a blood sample. She thinks she's descended from the kings of Ireland."

"What if I were Jewish?"

"What if you were?"

"I think about it all the time, what if I were Jewish."

It's a curious thing to say, but it rolls out for Agnes as stark if it's one of the newsreels they've watched tonight, what Bernie's imagining: what it would be like to be pointed out on the street, corralled into a train station. "I love you for that. I wish FDR could imagine *he* was Jewish."

Now she's gone and said the same thing he said, in Washington Square: *I love you for that.* Bernie lifts his chin and leans down to kiss her—on a *subway* car. Their teeth clink, their kiss an awkward aborted meeting.

It's Joe whose mouth is still pressed against her own. Bernie's sweet and decent and good and for some reason she doesn't seem to want sweet and decent and good. She has to stop dreaming about wedding dresses and leading Bernie on. It's just a date they're having. It's *just a date.*

They're just doing the things that other people do, she's just being normal for a change. It's Saturday night, and she's one of 2.5 million New Yorkers stepping out for a squeeze. She grabs Bernie's hand, but sees with a panic how gratefully he squeezes back.

What she feels for Bernie is a mystery, endlessly complicated. It's love all right, some kind of love, but which kind? She's the one who reached for him but she'd pay him, this minute, to give her another lecture rather than hold her hand.

And she'd pay her grandfather to let her photograph a corpse but for some reason she doesn't need to: he likes the idea. He's all for it, as long as she promises she won't sell the pictures or show them to anybody outside the family. Certainly not the stiff's family.

"Sure, I see it," he said, when she first proposed the idea. "Part of your training. Believe me, I had my training too."

"I know. Plugging the orifices."

"Hey, that wasn't my favorite part."

"So you said." What a relief, this kidding around, after the O'Learys: the muffled sobs, the resentful sidelong glances. Her grandfather's willing to get a good laugh out of an orifice and out of his customers too, the living and the dead.

Even better, he liked her idea so much he promised he'd find her a good face for the camera. Every morning this week she's phoned from the corner call box to check in, and today, when he says she ought to come and get a load of this one—*You don't mind an old lady, do you?*— she doesn't even need to dial Altman's and make her excuses. It's the Fourth of July and she has the holiday. She's the only O'Leary up this early: the whole world is sleeping in. Twelfth Street is deserted.

She skips up Fifth Avenue in the halfhearted rain. Another relief, after all the heat they've had. By the time she lets herself into Calabrese's it's coming down in earnest. She shakes herself off and makes her damp way back to the second chapel, where they're still fussing with the final presentation, her Uncle Tom retucking the burial dress into the side of the casket, the old lady it holds so tiny Agnes thinks briefly that her uncle's embalmed a child.

"Agnes, honey! You're all wet." Tom's like her grandfather, only more so. When he puts his arm around her shoulder, he hangs on, squeezing. "Happy Independence Day, Miss Independence. You're soaking wet, little girl. Getta load of who we got for you."

"She's perfect."

"You woulda loved the hairs growing on her chin. I measured one ten inches long."

"Uncle Tom, I don't believe you."

"You're right. I guess it was twelve inches. Now *that* would make a picture."

"So next time maybe you'll let me come downstairs? Grab a shot before you fix up the body?"

He removes his hand, finally, from her shoulder, and presents the corpse with a deep bow, but he's only trying to distract her.

"Do you think, Uncle Tom?"

"Awwww, honey. We been through that. First see how you do taking your snapshots up here."

They're not snapshots—they're portraits, Portraits of the Unliving. She plans a whole series of them and sometimes when she's falling asleep at night she even imagines a gallery showing like the ones she's been working up her courage to attend. Maybe she'll ask Bernie to go with her. She's starting to recognize the names of photographers and to roll them round her tongue: Berenice Abbott, Helen Levitt, Margaret Bourke-White. *Life* magazine uses someone named Lotte Jacobi. Has to be a German refugee. Wouldn't she love to meet Lotte Jacobi in the subway, the way she met Walker Evans? She can't believe she's so dumb, but it never occurred to her before that women could be photographers, not photographers for *Life,* not big-time photographers with shows on Madison Avenue, anyway.

When she has her own show, she'll invite Walker Evans, and when he sees her he'll remember: the blue-eyed girl who was onto him. He has a corpse in his book, doesn't he? The first prints in her show will all be corpses, too, prim and properly embalmed. Dressed for their own funerals, you might say. See, Mr. Evans? Homage. Or maybe she'll pronounce it in French: *hommage.*

And then: if you're walking through this show, if you're looking at Agnes O'Leary's corpses, Mr. Walker Evans, you'll turn the corner and you'll see that this show is more than an homage to the first photographer she ever met. You'll see something startling: naked corpses *before* the mortician gets to them. You'll suck your breath in, you'll be so surprised, and maybe you'll even be shaken. Because not only will the bodies be naked, they might even be bruised or battered, gaunt from sickness or poverty, twisted with fury or sadness. Who knows how you might find a corpse, before its face has been pumped full of chemicals, pickled and settled into its false good-bye?

It's only a fantasy. She has a pretty good idea what's ahead of her, once she has a real camera and not a toy. She'll practice at her grandfather's, maybe for years, and eventually she'll work her way up to knocking on a strange funeral director's door. She'll introduce herself: "Perhaps you've seen my pictures in *Life,* in *PM.*" She'll charm her way in and she'll get her shots of the unsuspecting dead, sure as Weegee gets his fully clothed murder victims lying in their pools of blood.

But she'd certainly like to practice on some of the bruised corpses that arrive at Calabrese's back door before she goes knocking on a stranger's door. Lately, she's come to the conclusion that Tom will never let her into the mortuary, not so long as he's guarding the premises. He's already brought up the Health Department, but that's not the real reason. It's the nakedness they don't want her to see, the groins and the genitals, the ideas she'll get. These Calabreses know her somehow, know her better than she knows herself. She's never seen a naked man in her life. Maybe they're right. Maybe a real man won't measure up to the statues in the Met. Maybe she'll faint dead away when she finally sees that dangling organ.

She almost fainted dead away at the sight of her mother's face, didn't she? But once she'd seen it, once she had the breath knocked out of her, she picked herself up and stared some more.

Now she allows herself a good, long look at the little old lady, who can't be more than four feet tall. Her people have provided her a stiff gray silk to be buried in, and against her neck rests a cameo pin: a delicate young woman's profile to decorate a tough old bird. The neck itself is an accordion, layer upon layer of skin folded down into itself.

Tom, as usual, has painted her exactly the wrong color for this wallpaper. All the corpses in the green room look green. Still she'll make a fine portrait, her white hair coiled and coiled some more atop her green beaked face. She's a mynah bird, the tip of her nose hanging over her upper lip with utter contempt for anyone who would cross her. Agnes hears her cackling, mimicking her husband, her children, her grandchildren. Even the layers of hanging flesh can't disguise her ferocity. She sighs, happy.

"What do you think?" Tom says.

"Bee-yoo-ti-ful." The old dame's lips are set so tight they're practically white. As usual, Tom's daubed on the rouge in perfect circles. And isn't it ironic? Her uncle works from a photograph—he always asks the family to bring one—so Agnes's portrait will be an homage to an unseen picture, a picture doubling back on itself. A good picture of the dead triggers something, something deep and unspeakable, something even Dr. Sex-on-his-Brain Freud couldn't call forth with language. And the photographer's job, her job, is to step outside her own sensible self and connect with that dead body, to receive the mysterious message that body wants her to deliver, a message that isn't written in words. No book in the Brooklyn Public Library can tell her how to do it: she's in the dark, feeling her way.

"Lucy Carelli, meet Agnes O'Leary."

Her grandfather has a sudden attack of business sense: "The Carellis aren't showing up early?"

"Relax, relax. She's got all morning. But say Agnes—where you get them developed? Hey pop, we never thought of that. What if somebody in the drugstore—"

"Not to worry. I'm developing everything myself. And I'm getting better with the prints."

"So when are we gonna see some."

"When they're perfect. Like your stiffs." She's made Uncle Tom smile.

But her grandfather's not smiling, not even close. "Uh-oh. Still with that friend of your father's?" When her grandfather's not joking, he's all business, and he's all business right now. Agnes hears in his question the clean and simple mistrust of one worldly man for another. Funny. Her grandfather's the one who encouraged the photography—if she gets good with the Brownie, he says, he'll buy her any camera she wants. Maybe she can take up photography in college. Maybe she can combine photography and psychology! Why not? Little did he know that his enthusiasm would send her to Matt McClary for darkroom instruction, would make her dream about galleries and frames and the way she'll sign her name in pencil on the mat, the way she'll autograph her first book the way Mr. Walker Evans forgot to do.

She aims for offhand. "He lets me use it on Saturdays. After work."

"Agnes, I told you before. I don't like it. Who else is down in that basement, Saturday nights?" The funny thing is, he has his finger on something, but how'd he know? How'd he know, without ever laying eyes on Matt McClary, that she too has been uneasy about the way he hovers outside the little closet he's rigged up? How'd he know that Mr. McClary likes to brush up against her as she lines up the negatives, that he still wants to check her focus even though she always wears her glasses in the darkroom—always—and doesn't even need the contact sheets to know which shots, and where she'll crop them. It's not that she thinks he'll try something. These old bachelors her father befriends aren't scary because they're going to make a pass. They're scary because they think they should, and they have to worry it, and worry you in the bargain. They have to make her feel guilty with all their naked longing, with all their corny jokes: and when she feels guilty about them she feels guilty about Bernie all over again.

"It's just the two of us," she admits.

"Nah, that's no good." She knows what he's biting his tongue not to say: *Your father should know better. Your father should take care of you.* "We'll get you your own darkroom, right here. Sure, why not?"

"You don't need to do that."

"I don't need to do nothing, sweetheart. Don't you know it would give me more pleasure than just about anything?"

Agnes could swoon. She's never had anyone buy her the secret things she covets, the things she's never been able before to name out loud, for fear of the pain her wanting would cause her father. She must stop her grandfather, pretend she doesn't even care about printing pictures, that she isn't already some kind of drug addict addicted to the smell of fixer . . . only she's already figured out where the darkroom would go, in Calabrese's, and what that would mean. Darkrooms go in basements, in the dark. They'll have to set it up in some corner carved out of the mortuary, or down below in the cellar, and either way she'll pass by dead bodies every time she comes with a roll of film. She'll be able to do what she's wanted to do since the first time she set foot in here, which is to get a good look at a *real* stiff, at an unadulterated dead body. A nice naked corpse. If she'd seen a naked man maybe she wouldn't have held back with Joe. Maybe she would have told him about the twenty dollars, proposed that fleabag hotel, stripped off all her own clothes for him.

And if she had the chance to see another naked woman—even in her household of women, all the dressing's done behind doors or sheets or towels or hands spread wide—she'd be able to imagine what her mother was able to imagine: how a body's just a body, once you squeeze the life out of it, how if you can't bear living in your body anymore you can just step out of your suffering flesh. You can just abandon the prison your body's become. Why not, her grandpa would say. Leave it. Leave it for Tom to paint, to falsify. Leave it for Agnes to photograph. The way they left her mother alone and let her fall into her darkness. The way they've all left the refugees alone to fend for themselves. That's why they hover over her now—they're guilty about Gloria—and that's why one day the whole world will be guilty for what they haven't done.

"Mr. McClary wouldn't dare lay a finger on me," she hears herself say, and sees by her grandfather's face that she's just confirmed his worst fears.

"It's already decided."

So she'll have to acquiesce, won't she? She'll have to assuage her grandfather's guilt, be gracious, take his gifts. She'll have to have what other people have for a change. She raises her camera to cover her confusion, her finger still moist on the metal. She gazes down on Lucy Carelli in her silk, but through the lens she sees her mother, that girl in the picture hidden away in her father's bureau drawer. The girl who teases the photographer that any minute she will let loose a merry smile. She sees her mother naked, slender as Loretta, big breasted, sees her walk right into the arms of the white, naked body of her young father. Oh what is the matter with her, she is truly perverse.

> *Thou art thy mother's glass, and she in thee*
> *Calls back the lovely April of her prime.*

She steadies the camera, and now it's Lucy Carelli who's naked. Now the old lady rips her gray silk asunder to reveal her shrunken breasts and hairless mound, the corpse a child once more.

Agnes can't stop herself from shuddering, and in the flash of time her damp body trembles, she sees beyond the stiff, beyond her mother and father, beyond the vision of herself and Joe on dingy sheets. She sees what she's spent her whole life trying not to see: another body, fully clothed, rope burns festering on her long bruised neck.

THE

FIRST SHOTS

Now it's really war. This morning—a holiday, when they should all be sleeping in—Aggie's up at the crack of dawn, and after her late night too. It's not difficult to guess what she's up to. Babe bides her time in bed, listening to the light summer rain as Aggie flushes the toilet, runs the water. Water, water everywhere. Aggie's very efficient in her movements. Babe hears her creep down the hall and out the front door.

Babe's already rising herself. She limps to the bathroom before anyone else can claim it. Efficient in her own movements, she tugs her dress on and tiptoes past Mickey sleeping on the living room couch. In the hallway the one functioning umbrella in the O'Leary household is waiting where she left it, thank God. At least Agnes has not had the effrontery to steal that away from her.

No sight of Aggie by the time she makes her slow way downstairs, but Babe trails her nonetheless. She knows exactly where Aggie's going. She's followed her granddaughter three times in the last three weeks, three times as the balmy spring has turned to hellish summer, and this morning makes four. This morning the rain lets up as she walks along Twelfth Street, but as soon as she turns the corner the lightning crackles and the skies open.

Up ahead, Agnes is no doubt drenched, but behind her Babe hobbles along under the big black umbrella. By the time she struggles all the way up Fifth Avenue, Agnes has disappeared into Calabrese's with her grandfather and the corpses. Maybe she's hiding behind one of Vito's fancy schmanzy funeral drapes, peering out at her grandmother on the sidewalk across the street. Babe lingers there even as the rain pummels her.

Aggie's still bringing a paycheck home, but how long will that last if she keeps this up? If Vito keeps this up? Babe pictures him setting out little cups of thick, bitter coffee, untying a box of sticky pastries—but no, that's all backward. That was Fulvia who saw to it that the guests had their mouths full. Vito's wife was a timid, skinny, pretty woman like Gloria, always tittering. Not a thing in the world to say for herself, and not that much English to say it with, either.

Vito, on the other hand, knew what was what. He always attracted her—physically, not romantically. A man like that's impossible: imposing his will on a wife and daughter with no wills of their own. But let him try to tell Babe what to think. She'd have none of it, and he liked it when she defied him, liked it so much that he flirted with her shamelessly, right up to the moment when they fought so bitterly over Mickey, his intrusion into her son's life the end of any attraction whatsoever. Vito wanted Mickey to sign up for the funeral business, which would have meant *embalming,* for starters. Her son would have done it, too, if she hadn't stopped him. Embalming. She's not at all sure it's a sound practice in the first place, and remembers with fondness her own mother's body on ice, when they lived (and, in her mother's case, died) in a Bronx boardinghouse. The landlady was kind enough to keep her mother in the parlor, a tin liner round the coffin. Terrible mess, draining out the melted ice and all those pools of water she mopped, but worth every puddle to have her mother's body with her a few more days. She was barely eighteen and about to face the world alone. Nowadays the Vitos of the world steal the body away, just when you most need its comfort and its advice, and then they pump it full of lies. It's not right. She remembers rising in the middle of the night to go stroke her mother's cold cheek. That's how we should take our leave, not in some gaudy funeral parlor stinking of lilies.

It would have been one thing if Vito suggested Mickey greet the customers, or send the bills out, but no: he wanted her son to stick his hands deep into dead bodies so his own fingernails could stay clean. She didn't give her son a Jesuit education so that he could handle corpses but Vito—it still steams her to remember—Vito asked if the Jesuits couldn't at the very least have trained him to bring home a paycheck, then. He said—she can remember it word for word, as if he's still blowing hot air over her at the Calabrese kitchen table—he said,

Let your son live his own life, Babe. Get out of the way.

He might as well have slapped her. She rose from his kitchen table, gave Fulvia a curt nod, took her silent leave of Mickey in the hallway, both their heads shaking their mutual regret. Planned never to darken the Calabreses' door again, never to haul herself down from the heights of Spuyten Duyvil to the lower depths of Brooklyn—but within the month Gloria hanged herself and Vito blamed it all on the O'Learys.

Thank goodness she arranged to stay with the girls during those first dark days, or who knows what Vito might have done to Mickey. He came clattering up the stairs after the funeral, didn't so much as knock on the door. Stood by Mickey's window sobbing the way only a barrel-chested man can.

I might as well jump out the fucking window myself. That such a word should be spoken around those little girls!

She was calm the way you have to be around that kind of hysteria: *Wouldn't be very effective from the fourth floor, would it now? Then Fulvia would have a cripple on her hands.*

He lunged at her—lunged—and as she sidestepped him she wished she'd said what was really on her mind: *At least Gloria finally got* something *right.*

"Ha!" She surprises herself, blurting out a silly cartoon word when anyone on Fifth Avenue might hear her. Not that anyone *is* out on Fifth Avenue in this onslaught. It's the sight of Vito's flag, hanging ostentatiously over the avenue, that has her exclaiming. He's not even a citizen. How dare he fly Old Glory, and in the rain? *His* country's on the brink of war with hers and he has no idea how to show respect.

It seems to her that the rain is letting up, if only ever so slightly. She crosses over to his side of the street, so that she'll be harder to spot if they peer out. She briefly contemplates sitting across from Joe DiMaggio at a kitchen table, seeking his calm advice about her errant granddaughter. Her picture of Joe is surprisingly like the picture she remembers of Vito Calabrese, thirteen years ago. They're both sharp dressers, both men of the world in their broad-shouldered pinstripes. They shave with Mollé shave cream and don't mind smelling sweet, either. Maybe Joe even gets a manicure the way Vito always did. Every time Vito leaned over her, she wondered if he wasn't going to lean a little further.

Well, he never did. He only tormented that dimwit Fulvia with his oozing charm. She wonders what he'd say to Agnes if he knew she'd just had a date with a dark-bearded bespectacled boy, a boy named *Bernie* no less. In these times! And Agnes pretending that it's never crossed her mind he might be Jewish. Everybody knows about the false converts. You can't blame them—they did what they had to do—but that doesn't mean her granddaughter should be traipsing around town with one of them. He goes to Xavier, indeed. Keller, indeed. That boy might be German, but she knows exactly what *kind* of German.

She begins to doubt that the rain has let up at all. It will be a long walk home, the better part of a mile, and if she's going to survive the weather she'd better get started. Other women her age take the streetcar, but Babe saves her nickels for the subway, for the Stadium. She wouldn't have the patience to wait for a streetcar to show up anyway.

No game today: it's hard to say whether she's disappointed or relieved. She wasn't with Joe for the final glory—the second of July was blistering, and DiMaggio wouldn't have expected a crippled lady to brave the ovens that the trains become. She wasn't the only one to stay home, either: it was a sparse crowd to see Joe bust Wee Willie's record. But that's because New Yorkers know what's what. That old record didn't count—they didn't even charge fouls as strikes in Willie's day—and she has nothing to feel guilty about.

She planned to pay her respects to Joe today, on the Fourth of July, to mingle with the crowds she normally shuns. They were supposed to unveil Gehrig's statue. Every seat in the Stadium would have been gone, and if that doesn't prove her loyalty . . . But there'll be no doubleheader in these torrents.

Mickey, brewing his coffee, is the only one up when she returns, and in the kitchen she watches him try to hide his disappointment that his solitude's been broken. Well, isn't life a trial, and hasn't she felt the same discouragement herself whenever one of the girls barges in? They'll all learn patience before they die. A good thing she's caught him before the other girls are up, because Agnes has really passed the limit now.

She peels off her sopping raincoat, the damp hat. "How'd you sleep, Mickey?"

"Fine, ma. Pretty good. Course Aggie woke me up, going out. And then you—why so early with you gals? On a holiday."

"I thought I'd breathe the air." She finds herself taking an exaggerated swallow. "What do you suppose Aggie's up to?"

"Maybe she's breathing the air too. Only it's pouring rain outside."

"Ha, ha. Hilarious."

Mickey takes a bow and she makes her move. "What about that boy last night?"

"Aw, I couldn't get an impression. Should be all right—Xavier."

"If he's not another pacifist, like the first specimen."

"Well, I never met the first specimen. But I doubt they could field a team of pacifists at Xavier."

"Didn't you think he was a little . . . odd?"

"Quiet, you mean?"

"No, not exactly."

Mickey waits. Maddening the way he waits, padding around, spooning out his sugar so cautiously, so precisely. Mickey waits and waits and waits.

"Didn't he look a little Jewish to you?"

Mickey stares at her with an expression that's even more maddening than his movements, a slack-jawed disbelieving blank-eyed disrespectful look no man should ever give his mother. And then he turns his back.

"I have no idea what you're talking about, ma."

Maybe she'll learn patience before she dies, but she's not going to learn it this morning. The rage builds so quickly that she doesn't feel her rising temperature, only the sweat pouring off her. How dare he.

"Mickey, maybe you can turn a blind eye but I will not. I. Will. Not. And let me be the first to inform you that Aggie's made contact with Vito. Where do you think she sneaked out this morning?"

Now Mickey turns to face her. Now he leans against the icebox in that mild-mannered pleasant way he has, more maddening than any small defiance he might occasionally muster. And says the most astounding thing he could possibly say:

"Good for her."

"Mickey, that gorilla took his hand to you."

"He *raised* his hand to me. And I raised mine back."

"He tried to throttle you."

"Well, he didn't succeed. He was out of his mind with grief."

"He said you—"

"I know what he said. You don't need to."

"Oh no? That man accuses you of driving your wife to suicide and we don't need to *remember?*"

"Maybe he was onto something. We all turned our backs, even Vito. Pretended it wasn't happening. All of us."

"You, maybe."

"For Christ's sake, ma. You wanted me to *institutionalize* her."

"Maybe you should have taken my advice, instead of drinking yourself silly."

He glares, a child's stubborn, resentful rebellion screwing his usually placid features into distortion. His words sound distorted too, scratched out: "I didn't know what to do. She was on another planet."

"Who was on another planet?"

Loretta's somehow appeared, out of thin and quiet air, wavering between them in the tiny kitchen without Babe's so much as registering her arrival.

"And good morning to you, Loretta."

"Sorry. I . . ."

"Yes. Well. Your father and I are having a painful and I might add *private* conversation, so if you would be good enough."

Too late. Mickey, hearing the word *private,* has drawn his youngest to him and there they pose, against the icebox, in hateful and silent solidarity, Mickey behind, leaning his head on his daughter's head, his thick arms resting on her slender ones. Loretta knows better than to appear in the kitchen in her nightgown, but there she stands in filmy white. She's sixteen years old with substantial breasts. Entirely inappropriate.

Loretta gazes at the floor (at the shabby wooden kitchen floor, with knotholes big enough for the passage of rats) rather than meet her grandmother's eyes while wearing her nightie. Babe's rage has nowhere to go now except out through her ears, and they fill with a surge. She shakes her head, feels liquid slide, hears the inevitable ringing, a peculiar mysterious din that sends her fleeing to the living room.

Where she plops herself in the so-called easy chair and contemplates the Victrola—Gloria's Victrola, wouldn't you know, a special present from Vito—so long unplayed that they've all forgotten it sits there. The horn mocks her, mocks her ringing ears and her family's base disrespect. After all these years she's given them. In *Brooklyn,* refuge to Italians and Jews and coloreds. Home of the *Dodgers.* She's faint with her rage, until she remembers that she's tramped through this infamous borough without her breakfast.

The pressure in her ear ceases. Hunger. That explains the momentary loss of control. She rises with more speed than she thought possible, her dignity restored with the diagnosis, and returns to the kitchen.

"I'll thank you both to give me a moment's peace," she says. "I'd like to fix myself a bite to eat."

All day, neither Mickey nor Loretta acts as if any harsh words have been spoken—worse, the pair of them are elaborately and falsely polite. When Agnes returns at six o'clock, she is more polite still.

"Where have you been?" Babe demands.

Do Mickey and Loretta signal to her behind Babe's back? How else does Aggie know to answer as she does? "I've been visiting on Fifth Avenue."

"Fifth Avenue? Where I've asked you all these years not to venture?"

"Oh, Babe," Agnes laughs. "I'll be eighteen next week. Isn't it high time I'm allowed to walk through my own neighborhood?"

"I don't suppose I can stop you walking anywhere you please. Why don't you walk into Harlem and see what happens?"

"There's an idea. But today I only went to the O'Tooles'."

"What O'Tooles?"

"Don't you remember? From St. Francis?"

So Aggie's seen Babe trailing her, and she's constructed an elaborate lie to cover herself. Very clever. Babe's never actually seen her granddaughter duck into Calabrese's—how could she possibly keep up with Aggie's pace?—so it's not a bad bluff. But does Aggie really think she'll let it go at that? "What sort of O'Toole would be living on Fifth?"

"Do you really not remember? Monica's mother was Italian too."

Aggie gives her time to recover from all the implications of *that,* but Babe stands her ground and keeps her silence. Aggie gives her a sly look:

"Lately we've been visiting again. Didn't you read my note?"

Before Babe has time to recover from these shocking lies, Aggie's back in the girls' room burying herself in a book. Oh, she thinks she's so smart. So smug. Irish and Italian indeed. The whole story's sufficiently diabolical to give Babe a rare attack of memory fever, not entirely sure that there wasn't, after all, an O'Toole family who lived down the Slope. A tawny-haired swarthy Monica.

By the time they've finished their after-dinner coffee, Babe's narrowed it two possibilities: either Aggie's having fun with her—just like her father, hilarious fun at her grandmother's expense—or there really are O'Tooles living on Fifth and she's imagined the whole Calabrese business. When Agnes does the wiping up, she produces a scrap of paper, supposedly swept out from under the counter, with her own handwritten note: "Happy Fourth! I've gone to Monica O'Toole's. Back for dinner."

But Aggie's cleverness is not going to ruin Babe's plans or her obligations to DiMaggio. The Yanks have rescheduled the Gehrig memorial for Sunday, and for all Babe recognized a great man when she saw him, she's not about to endure a doubleheader on a Sunday, not even for Lou Gehrig. The class of fan you get on Sunday is not the class of fan Lou deserves, and not the class of fan she deserves, either. She'll slip into the Saturday game instead, with the true believers. It will buy her time out of the apartment, away from the innocent looks Agnes beams her way.

Babe leaves for the game even earlier than usual—she'll have her first, not her second, breakfast at the Purity, and before that she'll walk a circuitous route up Fifth Avenue, the same way she walks when she follows Agnes, that long looping detour to see if she'll be able to remember any O'Tooles along the way. Aggie's too clever by half, but cleverness runs in the genes and her grandmother means to outsmart her.

On the landing she hears Bruscelli's door creak open. For the first time, it strikes her as comical that while she's keeping an eye on Agnes,

Bruscelli's keeping an eye on her. Not the same intelligence behind the two kinds of spying, nor the same moral imperative, but still. You have to admit it's droll.

And on the ground floor, she even gives Nosey a smile (a little imperious, she would admit if pressed) as they exchange their ritual greeting.

"You must be going up to the Stadium, Mrs. O'Leary."

"Mrs. Bruscelli, I make it a practice to keep my plans flexible and private."

"You're a great kidder, Mrs. O. Say, how about that DiMaggio? You know, he comes from Sicily."

What on earth this signifies Babe could not possibly trouble herself to imagine. Bruscelli has never breathed the slightest interest in baseball, much less the Yankees, and has only latched on because now everybody in New York, even in Brooklyn, is Joe's best friend. Or maybe that's not it. The way Nosey's worked Italy into the conversation . . . The papers are full of spies: the Gestapo is sending them right into America, disguised as Jews so that people will feel sorry for them, and anything Hitler does Mussolini wants to copy. What's become of Bruscelli's nephew, anyway? Is he lingering still in a jail cell with the other busboys from El Morocco? That must have been some spy ring they were running. But she doesn't inquire about Nosey's nephew. She decides to throw the old busybody off balance instead:

"DiMaggio's a prince."

Nosey shakes her head in vigorous denial. "He's a king. An emperor."

A duce perhaps? These people do not know how to quit when they're ahead. Babe lets the front door slam behind her. Ordinarily Bruscelli makes her hip throb, but today it's the knee that gives as soon as the sidewalks run the least angle downhill. The walk to Fifth Avenue is all downhill. She's resisted a cane for years but she won't be able to manage the trip to the Stadium much longer without one. Ah, well. Better a cane than a lifetime spent in a dark apartment, listening for the neighbors the way Bruscelli does. She winces till she reaches Fifth, where the sidewalks more or less level out.

Now that she doesn't have to keep her eye on Agnes, she turns her

attention to the avenue itself, grubbier than it's been in any of the thirteen unlucky years she's suffered Brooklyn. Even on a Saturday morning, miniature gangsters crowd outside the candy stores and block a respectable woman's passage. She's invisible to them—how can they not see her standing there—and she'd like to twist their ears. Instead she puts a firm hand on a shoulder here, a jutting boy backbone there, and pushes past them. They barely notice her touch, the little hoodlums. And the smells from the trash barrels! While Vito was riding the wave of funereal prosperity up at the north end of the avenue, down here the sidewalks were sinking and stinking. These people don't even understand that the Depression's over.

Crossing First Street, she's more than halfway to the subway. She should be seriously winded at this point, but she picks up her pace to spite her aging body. This stretch is, at least, more reputable. She can breathe again—or could, till she sees a man in a gray summer suit approaching: the only man in a suit on a Saturday in July. Even from this distance she could swear it's Vito coming her way: short but muscular, manly, hatless in the summer heat, his hair as thick and as dark as Mickey's. Thicker and darker, if she'd admit the truth. It *is* Vito. Now she sees the fleshy lips, the one eyebrow raised as he strolls along. She comes to a full stop on the sidewalk and admires him the way those candy-store punks will soon be admiring pretty girls. He's a tank rolling toward her, and he glances carelessly from side to side, taking in the sidewalk as if he owns it. He'll be up to her in half a block, and she finds herself craving the encounter. She hasn't had a battle of wits with a man her age in a long time. Truth be told, she hasn't spoken to a man her age in a long time.

She begins to walk again, slowly so she won't betray her limp, and sucks her belly in beneath her girdle. She doesn't know she's reaching up to straighten her hat and the hair beneath it, but she feels her glove brush her ear, so she must be primping. Here he is. Here.

"Vito."

She must not have spoken his name loud enough, because he rolls past. He's not snubbing her. No, his pace is steady, unbothered, his attention focused elsewhere. See there: over her shoulder, she watches him return a wave sent by an aproned butcher sneaking in his cigarette break across  the street. No, he hasn't seen her. She turns up her volume, as loud as a lone woman on the street can afford to do:

"Vito!"

Perhaps he's going deaf, the way she's going lame. He's in the crosswalk already, wading through a large family on their way to Saturday haircuts. He won't be able to hear her now, not unless she runs after him, and even if she could run she wouldn't. Hasn't she always told the girls that a man must do the pursuing, or at the very least be tricked into thinking he's the one chasing after? It's astonishing that she spoke his name as easily as she did, that she felt that flutter of anticipation after all these long years.

Fulvia's dead now—that's what passed through her mind at the sight of him. Not the way he threatened Mickey, not the histrionic way he carried on, not the way she's forbidden the girls to see him. No, she thought of him as *available,* and she hasn't thought of any man that way in twenty years.

Maybe he did see her after all. Maybe he did snub her. Or worse, much worse: maybe he didn't notice her because she's a fat old limping woman, a nobody on the street to a man like Vito, who is by now probably married to some skinny Italian slut half his age. She retracts *slut.* The word's beneath her, the way the man's beneath her. Her momentary delight at the sight of him was as much an aberration as her loss of control with Mickey yesterday.

She's so disgusted by the whole episode that she barely recognizes Calabrese's itself when she turns the corner and marches past the red brick. If she's beneath Vito's notice, Vito's building—once so impressive, if only for its sheer size—is beneath her notice too. She refuses even to glance at the first side door, portal to stiffs, and the second, which admits both the renters who have paid the note on this building and the landlord himself, Vito Calabrese, the strutting cock of the walk. Thank God she rescued the girls from growing up in those premises.

She won't look at his building, but she can't stop herself from seeing Vito sobbing shamelessly, railing at Monsignor the very morning of Gloria's funeral: the last morning, he vowed, he would ever enter a Catholic church for purposes other than business. She trudges up the hill toward the Purity. She's forgotten entirely the purpose of this long detour: to see if she remembers O'Tooles from the parish who will exonerate Agnes. To hell with the O'Tooles. If she doesn't get her breakfast soon she really will disappear on the sidewalk, and nobody but nobody will notice her then.

In the Purity, it takes forever for her pancakes and eggs to arrive, and she must leave the last bites behind if she's to have a prayer of arriving in time for the National Anthem. She never misses the beginning of a game, that time when she can scan the program and line up the opposing team. But on the train, where she always begins her pregame meditations, she finds herself in a rare mood. No one so much as glances her way, and again she feels the curtain of invisibility separating her from the rest of the city. She's never thought of herself as old, but there it is.

She's an old lady, a fat old lady. Her car's full of foreigners, oily-haired refugees, and for all she knows more spies among them, but even the foreigners don't look her way. She's of no interest, even to the Gestapo. For the first time she allows herself to think of an attack on the subways. La Guardia's asked FDR for gas masks to defend the city, a request she has heretofore dismissed as operatic. Now she imagines what it would be like if one of these strangers tried to release a poisonous gas on the New Lots Express. She'd wrestle them to the floor, she would, and then they'd notice Babe O'Leary.

After she's changed to the Lex, she stares out blankly, exhausted and gloomy, till the sight of her own face in the window opposite brings her up short. She's wearing her red-and-white hat, the brim scalloped to frame her handsome square face. She looks pretty damn good for a woman her age. She takes a deep cleansing breath of subway air. She's always told the girls that the blues will not settle in if only you'll chase them away. Vito's loss, that he wouldn't admire a woman in such a hat.

On River Avenue, she must push herself past her pain, she's running so late. What a day this has been, what a silly lot of trouble she's put herself through. At last she manages to settle herself into her seat before her boys come out on the field to a mighty roar. The Stadium's only half-full but these are the solid Saturday fans, the men who can't wait another day, once their workweek is over, to get out to the ballpark. All around her, the bellows are for Joe and his superhuman feat. The rain and the Fourth of July might have interrupted the celebrations, but these fans are ready to start the party all over again.

"DiMag, DiMag, DiMagggggggggio!" The very bleachers sway with their chants. It's all coasting and carousing from here on in. No more anxieties about whether he'll make it or whether he'll fold. Now it's just a matter of counting up the hits over and above the record, the hits that will pile up like coins in a till. Babe's sure he'll drive the record up to some impossible number, sixty-five or seventy. She allows herself, briefly, to dream of seventy-five.

In the bottom of the first, the Yanks loom so large at the plate that she feels a little redundant in the stands, beaming them the win. Of course they'll win, though Babe does strain for a glimpse of Connie Mack down in the visitors' dugout. She has to admit that Mack still looks sprightly. Not fair that men should be able to age however their bodies choose, that they can broaden and enlarge themselves at will. Nobody overlooks *them* as they pass in the street. Nobody treats *them* as if they're invisible.

Here's DiMaggio up to bat. As the streak stretches out, as the hits pile up, so too will the adoring shouts, the laurel wreath sitting higher on DiMag's Roman head. Or, according to Bruscelli, his Sicilian head. Babe shakes her own head at the fickle, faithless fans, who didn't notice the streak at first, who were absent from all the crucial games, but who now—now that it's accomplished—act as if they knew all along.

A skinny young man she's watching for the first time, Marchildon, winds up to throw the Dago his first pitch. To compensate for his youth, Marchildon tries to give Joe the heebie-jeebie stare and the crowd's roar increases. Marchildon serves Joe up a nice, juicy fastball, and Joe takes a bite. The ball slams past the bleachers so fast that Babe must actually rise to see where it's landed: outside the Yankee bullpen. A gorgeous home run, four hundred feet if it's an inch, on the first pitch thrown his way. Her dear boy really is superhuman. The crowd chants "Forty-six! Forty-six!" and Babe's heart swells with love for this Joe, this kid, this young man who trots around the bases with his shy embarrassed smile, the very smile the papers are plastering all over the city. His first swing.

No wonder she's fallen in love with Joe DiMaggio. He'll never threaten to throw himself out the window, or steal her son away from her. He'll never ignore her on the street—remember how he waved on River Avenue when he and Lefty sped past?

Joe DiMaggio sees Babe O'Leary whether the rest of the world does or doesn't. He stands outside the dugout tipping his hat in her direction, and even if he's so shy he doesn't exactly look up, they both know that the broken record, the home run, the tip of the hat were all for her and her alone. She sits in a stadium of so-called fans, but she's the only one who knows all Joe's been through, the only one who knows all he must still endure. She might be invisible to the rest of them, but Joe knows she's there.

The Yanks have all risen to greet their conquering hero, and as Babe watches them stand there patiently, as if they're on a reception line, she has the strangest vision: she sees a line of refugees, a line at a dock where no ship berths, a line of overdressed families and battered suitcases, a line that snakes out past the docks and into the streets, into the railway stations, a line snaking around the world, across the oceans, into Yankee Stadium where Babe O'Leary is trying to watch a ballgame. How Vito's unnerved her, that such an image should come to mind!

One last wave from Joe before he ducks down into the dugout, and in the stretch of his arm Babe sees her dear boy flying above the war, swooping down to pluck refugees out of their endless lines so he can plant them back on firm ground. What silliness. Joe DiMaggio's not Superman. How strange that she should have to remind herself of such a thing.

But how sublime, what he's gone and done.

SCHEMES

The July weather plays muggy hot-and-cold games with New York. Joe D'Ambrosio throws his gray sheet off and on all night, and when he's not flinging the sheet he's offering up the bites on his ankles, his wrists, his neck. Pete and Pauley stretch out into the space he left behind in their bed on Twelfth Street, but down here on Mott the mattress bunches till he's crowded up against the wall with no one to keep him company.

He's hungry. That's the constant, day and night, not hungry the way starving people are, only hungry enough to think of nothing else. He sees now that being peckish before a meal does not constitute hunger. This—this constant distracted light-headed unfocused vague waking in the middle of the night longing—is hunger.

When he finally rises for a trip to the kitchen, the clock on the wall seems to say 5:03 A.M. It doesn't even make sense to go back to bed if he wants to get to the seven-fifteen Mass. How many hours of sleep could he have managed? He fumbles for the light string above the table and when the bulb finally flickers on sees that he's not the only one up before dawn.

Dorothy Day gives him a wry smile. Behind her the clock still says 5:03 A.M. She's been sitting in the dark with her rosary beads in one fist, the other clenched in her lap. She's dressed already, naturally. Whenever she emerges from her apartment in the front of the front building, she's always ready for business, even at five o'clock in the morning. Now that he too clothes himself out of the giveaway boxes, choosing among shirts too short in the sleeve and pants that never quite reach his ankle, he has a new respect for the good lines of her suits. She should lose those dreary scarves, but even his father, who thinks the words *clothing* and *dignity* are synonyms, would approve of the suits.

"Looking for food?"

He's mortified. He's not only interrupted her prayers, he's been caught raiding the pantry, and it's hopeless anyway. Can he eat raw potatoes? Dried navy beans? They don't go out for milk till morning and as for a scrap of bread—there's never a scrap of bread. His body grows leaner by the day, or by the Day. Dorothy herself is a greyhound. No wonder her dresses hang well on her.

"That's what I woke up for too," she says. Lately she seems to have warmed to him. Her clenched fist unfolds and she holds out a dry old wedge of white cheese and breaks it in two to share. She may have been saying her prayers, but even Dorothy Day gets hungry on Catholic Worker rations. Of course he's never heard her bellyache the way the rest of them do. She spoons her soup languorously, as if it will actually provide enough nourishment to get through their days. As if it's loaves and fishes. Maybe when she goes off to the farm she gorges on fresh cream and butter.

He accepts the cheese, resists scarfing it down, sits. God knows his mother fed him enough all his life that he should be able to last a month without sinking this low.

"How old are you, eighteen? You might even still be growing. You ought not have to rummage for food in the middle of the night."

"It's not the food," he lies. "It's the bug bites."

She perks right up. "Lice? Or bedbugs?"

He holds out his wrists for her examination. The welts, beginning to crust where he's scratched, are bigger than he imagined. His wrists look the way they did when he was seven and clawing his way through chickenpox. A vision of his mother, gooping on the calamine lotion.

But it's only Dorothy Day turning his hands over to pronounce, "Fleas!" as if she's some kind of naturalist. "I thought we were all done with fleas. We're not harboring cats and dogs back there, are we?"

He thinks of the rats he hears in the cellar, of the plague. If fleas are joining bedbugs in the nightly attacks . . .

"On the farm," she says, "we get mosquitoes the size of bumblebees. We have to get you out there."

He nods miserably—can't wait to meet the mosquitoes—and chews on his cheese as slowly as is humanly possible. Now he's broken his fast, and if he can't take communion he might as well savor every minuscule bite.

"Of course you'll be there for the August retreat."

This makes him more miserable still. She's been planning this retreat for weeks, a chance for Workers from Boston and Chicago and New York to ponder the war and their part in it. Or their part out of it. But he already knows his part, and anyway, except for his trips to Yankee Stadium, he's never in his life been off the island of Manhattan, and he'd rather not leave it for the Pennsylvania farm. He'd rather not encounter any large farm animals.

Food's been the only argument in favor of her retreat to the countryside but why, after all, should there be more food at the farm if volunteers are coming from all over the country to compete for every ear of corn? "You'll need somebody to keep the place going. I'd be glad to stay—" He sits up, trying to look like the sort of fellow she'd like to keep the place going, like Joe Zarella, her right-hand man, like someone not much older than himself who stays up nights worrying over the unpaid bills instead of bugs and hunger.

But Dorothy says, "Oh, Julie can see to the house." He, with his dirty sheets and his unwashed socks, he whose mother checked the cleanliness of behind his ears until the day he entered military school, would not be capable of running a houseful of derelicts. But an innocent high school girl is up to the task.

He would rather not, in any case, think of Julie. When they're in the kitchen together she casts her large doleful eyes his way. He'd *like* to take up with her again, now that Agnes is forever and always out of the picture, but Father Stepaniack, his new confessor, says that if he's truly serious about pacifism then he's to steer clear of girls till he's got an idea what the future holds. It's not fair, says Father S., to string along a girl if he's going to jail. For Father Stepaniack having a conversation with a girl is tantamount to asking her to marry you. The priest's pitted skin makes Joe conclude it's never been too much of a problem for *him* to keep his distance. He tries to squelch his own sense of pride around the man, but there's a big difference between the kind of advice he got from the Jesuits and the kind he gets from this parish priest.

"They might have lowered the draft age by then," he says, and watches Dorothy perk up again. She knows all about the letter he's sent to his draft board. *Foolhardy,* she called it, sending a letter before they're even calling up eighteen-year-olds, but she said the word with as much relish as she pronounced *fleas.* She hasn't been doing such a great job, shielding Catholic Workers from the Army. They're leaving the houses in droves, all over the country, renouncing their pacifism this time, and this time only, to fight a madman. No wonder Dorothy wants him at the retreat. She needs all the steady war resisters she can get.

"When you come out to Pennsylvania," Dorothy says, "we can introduce you to some Mennonites, some Brethren. The real peace churches. We're Johnny-come-latelies to this game, you know."

"Any chance of meeting somebody working to get more refugees in?"

She gets the same look she wears when the Workers discuss their money-raising schemes, a look that suggests someone's calling her name in the distance. "They've been doing the same letter writing we've been doing. And pamphlets," she adds. This time she adds the wry smile. They all know the impact of pamphlets.

"See, I've had this idea." He takes himself by surprise. He's thought of telling her his Mexico plan—eventually, he'll have to—but it's still so vague he's held off. Now what does he say?

"Before I get a draft notice, I thought I might go down to Mexico City. Try to get some refugees back across the border."

She's pretty good at hiding her surprise, too.

"I'd help them get to the Chicago house, or ours. I mean, I know it's illegal, but I'm already going to jail. I imagine they'll take the risk too. After what they've been through."

"Wait a second, Joe. Just where are you going to find these people?"

"I thought I'd write to the Quakers down there."

Another look of surprise. "All right, let's say they put you in touch with some refugees who want to get into America. And let's say those refugees are willing to risk life and limb. You don't suppose you're going to sweet-talk some border guard? During wartime?"

He laughs. "*Gee sir, if you'll let me explain . . .*" The first time he read Gandhi, he really was that naive. And maybe he's been naive more recently than he lets on. Only a few weeks since he thought you just approached Joe DiMaggio on the street and spoke the word *refugees*. "I guess I'm just going to have to sneak them in."

Any other Catholic, any other American, would blanch at this mention of sneaking, of flat-out lawbreaking, but Dorothy Day turns the bright pink of pleasure and gets right to the heart of it: "How?"

"Guides. I met a man at the War Resisters League who says you can pay people to get you across the desert."

"The desert!" The word itself captivates her. "Of course. You would be thinking of the desert fathers."

He would be? He tries, again, to read her. People look so different in the early morning, when you and they are sleep deprived. Dorothy's face is simultaneously sharper and softer. Her words float toward him and he feels he could catch them in his palm, like moths, like fleas. *Desert fathers, temptation, the devil. Hungry, hungry, hungry.*

"I hope you're not planning on having any visions out there," she goes on. "I must say, after living with some of the men around here I'm not as big on visions as I used to be."

He grimaces. Crazy Louie had two weeks of visions and two trips back to St. Vincent's before he finally succeeded in slicing his wrists deep enough to bleed to death. In an alley three blocks over, all alone. Nothing he could do to help. That's mostly been his story since he came here. He might as well be on his way.

"Do you know the legend," she says, "that Mary Magdalene lived in the desert for thirty years?"

"I wasn't planning to stay that long." There, he's made her smile for once in his life. "Once the guide gets us over the border—"

"Wait. Where will you get the money to pay this guide?"

And where will he get the money to pay for the Greyhound bus, and where will he get the money to eat in Mexico City or to push the long way north? This is the one question he can answer, because it's the same answer that keeps the House going and keeps them hungry, all at the same time. "I'll beg the money."

Nothing she can say to that. She knows already that he'll be begging the money from her, that he's luring her into his scheme the same way she's lured everybody else. The House will be emptying out, once the war starts: not just the volunteers but the homeless men, too, who will hear there's a war on and find themselves rising earlier, drinking less.

She contemplates her rosary beads and it seems to him that she clutches them tighter, as if to defend herself. When she finally looks up, he's surprised to hear her say, "I suppose you'd better go ahead and write to those Quakers in Mexico City."

"You're a visionary." People call her that all the time, that and *saint,* but she likes his irony and they both laugh wryly at the word, to distract themselves from their hunger, from all that begging they'll soon have to do. The cheese is gone.

Once a week he walks past his folks' building on East Twelfth Street. He figures it won't count as open defiance if he just happens to run into his mother, or his brothers, or Uncle Fran. But he hasn't run into anybody yet, and this time when he turns the corner on First Avenue he loops back around the block. It's a physical longing he feels (when he lets himself feel it): his little brothers' feet twining around his in bed, his mother's light touch on his shoulder when he's bent over a book. And when's the last time he bent over a book? He misses that, too: the steadiness, the order, of study. Maybe when he's in jail.

He stops himself from circling the block a third time. It's three fifteen. If this were September, Pete and Pauley would be meandering home from the parish school, but it's only July. He could scout the playgrounds, but it occurs to him that his brothers must be where he was, the last five or six summers, helping Pop. Well, he can't go there.

And so he begins his journey back to Mott Street, where he's supposed to be on letter-writing duty this afternoon. It's the big joke lately: if you need a letter written, D'Ambrosio's your man. A week ago, when Dorothy was gone to the farm to be with her daughter, they all sat around drink-

ing a bottle of plum brandy dropped off by a benefactor who didn't realize you can't keep alcohol around a house occupied mostly by drunks. They used their best judgment and drank the bottle down, to remove temptation. Tipsier than he ever got from high school swizzling, he talked up a storm, allowed that he's not only written to Quakers, he's written three letters to DiMaggio himself.

The other Workers thought that was hysterical. The fellow's the toast of New York now, mobbed wherever he goes. Joe tried to explain that look DiMag gave him on West End Avenue, but that only made the other Workers laugh all the harder. They refer now to the D'Ambrosio Plan to Save the World.

By now even he sees the joke. They're right, he played the fool when he accosted DiMag. He was drunk with adrenaline after his fight with Bernie.

What would Bernie say if he knew Dorothy Day herself gave him the go-ahead on Mexico City? He's already been down to the Greyhound ticket desk to calculate the cost and the route. He'll take a bus due south to South Carolina, they tell him, and then head west: Georgia, Alabama, Mississippi—Mississippi. Then on to Texas, on to Mexico.

He pauses at a trash barrel to pluck out a newspaper. He's in luck today: a *Post,* nearly new. Jimmy Cannon's the best sportswriter in New York. Getting the scores late has been a greater torment than bugs and hunger. The Yanks are on a long road trip and last night—Sunday—he went out into Mott Street to ask passersby if they knew what happened in the Chicago doubleheader. The third man he stopped told him the streak was up to fifty-three. It was almost enough to allow him a good night's sleep.

He digs into the *Post* to check the box scores. DiMag had three hits in the first game. The man's on fire. If Joe DiMaggio can hit safely in fifty-three games, Joe D'Ambrosio can get himself through Mississippi. Maybe they'll even know about the streak down there, and won't be so as hard on Italians as he suspects they are otherwise inclined to be.

Back to the front of the paper, to see the war news he'd rather avoid. Tomorrow's the second draft lottery (numbers pulled from a goldfish bowl by pretty girls: perfect). He scans down the page. This drawing's still for men over twenty-one. Is it possible he'll have three more years? In three years he could be back and forth to Mexico a dozen times. But the Germans are outside Kiev, bearing down on Leningrad. Stalin's making deals with Churchill and they'll be drafting eighteen-year-olds soon enough. He'll go to jail soon enough.

It *was* foolhardy to write a letter before they've even called him, but putting his intention into writing made it real the way that telling Dorothy made the Mexico plan real, the way that telling Agnes about jail cleared the path. Agnes. She crosses his mind as many times as hunger. She's behind every headline (he unzips her dress and it falls from her white shoulders). Today he can't chase the idea of getting on the subway and going to find her (the dress slips to the floor). He decided long ago that he'd never subject himself to risking her job, to being overheard, to begging out in public. If he's going to prostrate himself, it's not going to be in B. Altman, for God's sake. If he goes after her, he's going to Brooklyn. All he has to figure out is how to get to the Brooklyn Twelfth Street (she stands there in her white lacy underthings). It could be a kind of baptism, his preparation for the journey south. He feels himself yielding. Today he actually has a couple of nickels in his pocket: Dorothy has persuaded him that he's supposed to take a little change. He's just not supposed to spend it.

He approaches another stranger on the avenue, a businessman who looks as if he possesses the directions to get anywhere in the universe. At the word *Brooklyn* the man scratches his head under his hat.

"You better get the IRT, then."

Joe trudges all the way crosstown to catch the IRT. He'll stop at the token booth to chart out a route, the way he's charted his route to Mexico City.

He's stunned when he emerges from the train with the early rush hour crowd and finds himself in the middle of Grand Army Plaza. He can't believe that he's in Brooklyn. He must stop yet another stranger to point him in the direction of Twelfth Street, which is, the man tells him, a good hike. Twelfth and what? Twelfth and he doesn't know. His walk could go on for miles.

Mostly, though, he's stunned by the look of Brooklyn. The apartment buildings on Plaza Street are swell, and when he heads down Eighth Avenue the brownstones are sweller still. The neighborhood's rich, when the one thing he's always loved about Agnes is the way she uses *poor* as a badge of honor.

At Twelfth Street he peers up and down, choosing a direction. If he turns left, he'll run into houses and a leafy park. He turns right, heading down the hill, and after a block senses for the first time that he's on track. He passes a factory. Apartment buildings become tenements. Women in cotton housecoats sit on stoops and front entranceways, watching their toddlers scamper, giving him the evil eye. It's not as crowded as his East Twelfth Street, as anywhere in Manhattan, and not as dirty either. This is why people move to Brooklyn or, he supposes, why they never left in the first place.

It's not such a foreign country (he pictures himself boarding a Greyhound bus). He passes Seventh Avenue, Sixth, Fifth, Fourth. The tenements diminish to shabby frame houses, the houses diminish to shabby warehouses. At Third Avenue he senses he's crossing a boundary, leaving the neighborhood, so he turns and retraces his route.

Going uphill, he slows his pace. Fifth Avenue is crowded with delis and shops, with the first wave of workers returning from their day's labor in Manhattan. He peers up and down the avenue. A vision of stealing nickels from the change jar for a daily trip to Brooklyn. Stupid to come all this way without a clue that would lead him to her address. He strains to remember a landmark she might have mentioned, but Brooklyn was only the place she disappeared to at the end of their nights together. The idea that he would find her here is sheer lunacy. He'll have to remember not to wander Mexico City with as little direction as he has today. It's early, anyway, for her to be getting off work. Best thing to do is hike back up to the train and head back to Mott Street. Best thing to do is forget about Agnes. She knows where to find him. If she wanted to see him, she would have.

He chugs across Seventh Avenue, and with his new momentum nearly smacks into an Agnes look-alike: a brunette, only her hair has a distinctly reddish cast in the sunlight. The look-alike turns her alarmed face away from his stare. He goes another few steps before it hits him. He turns in the crosswalk and calls out: "Miss O'Leary!"

She swivels her head to see who called, looks more alarmed still, and fairly runs in the opposite direction. Joe trots after. He could catch her on the corner but she might screech in fear, so he calls again: "Miss O'Leary!"

And again she turns. She really is one of Agnes's sisters, a stunner. Her eyes are enormous, her lips full. Unusually full. Agnes is attractive, but this one . . . He flushes at his own disloyalty. She cringes there beside a fire hydrant, as if it might provide some distance between them. This would be the youngest one. He can't remember what name Agnes gave her.

"Sorry to startle you." He approaches but keeps that distance she wants. "I'm a friend of Agnes's." He watches her fists come down from her side.

But then stupidly he goes on: "Matter of fact, I'm trying to locate Agnes."

Instantly the look of confusion reappears. This is a girl who won't give a stranger her address no matter who he claims to be. "Agnes is at work," she gets out, in a little-girl voice that almost breaks the spell of her looks.

"I guess she won't show up for another hour or so?"

Again the girl bites her lip rather than give away her sister's schedule. My God, she thinks he's trailing Agnes. Well, he supposes he is.

"Will you tell her Joe D'Ambrosio was around?"

Loretta: that was the name. She finally offers him a wary smile. "I think you met my grandmother at Yankee Stadium."

"I did, I sure did. She's . . . something, your grandmother."

Loretta stops fretting and beams. Standing there in her thin sundress with the modest flounce around the neckline, she's the most gorgeous girl he's seen in a lifetime of ogling gorgeous New York girls. Quite a figure that flounce is supposed to hide. But there's something a little off about her. She's like the princess who's been locked in the tower. She doesn't seem to know how to be around people, how to talk to them.

"So. If you could give them both my regards."

More confusion on Loretta's face. She keeps on beaming till there's nothing for him to do, having said his good-bye, but take off. He gives her a little wave (like an idiot) and enters the crosswalk.

This time she's the one who calls him. "Joe. Joe."

And this time he's the one who fairly flies back.

"I just wondered . . . if you'd like to wait for her. At our place."

Would he. Would he ever. He falls in beside her, but the O'Learys, it turns out, are just around this proverbial corner, in a crummy building like the one he was looking for. He notes the number: now even if Agnes doesn't show, he can write to her. Need a letter written? D'Ambrosio's your man.

The building's a dark and gloomy little walk-up with a knob coming loose from the front door and a bare bulb in the entranceway. A year ago he might have agreed with Agnes that it was poor, but now this building is to poverty as his high school appetite was to hunger. An old crone in a wrapper opens her ground floor door to peer out at them as they pass.

"Who's your fella, Loretta?"

Loretta blushes ruby red and mumbles something before she hurries up the stairs. He gives the woman a grin over his shoulder—he knows a dozen like her, on Mott Street—and she winks back, the old flirt.

Loretta scrambles up to the third floor and he follows. Oddly comforting to be back in a place that houses regular families and old ladies, not dreamers and bums. At her doorway, Loretta fumbles with the key till he'd like to lean over and do it for her. He restrains himself, keeps an invisible yardstick between them. Again he imagines her shrieking if he comes too close—though Loretta's the kind of girl you wouldn't mind comforting.

The grandmother hears them on the landing and opens the door before Loretta manages to turn the key. She recognizes him right away.

"Good grief. What are you doing here?"

Loretta slips inside and hangs her head in shame. He gets the feeling her grandmother subjects her to this sort of thing on a regular basis. He tries flashing the grin again, but Mrs. O'Leary's a tougher old bird than the one downstairs. She wants an answer.

"Your granddaughter found me downstairs and invited me up. To wait for Agnes."

Mrs. O'Leary glowers at Loretta, thinks better of it, waves her hand for him to enter. The three of them crowd together in a dark, narrow hallway till she leads them under a little arch into a tiny living room looking out on an airshaft. She gestures to a sagging couch and takes the armchair. Loretta hugs the arm of the couch, as far from him as she can get. Doilies on the furniture, lace that's seen a better day covering the bottom window.

Agnes's grandmother stares him down. "Joe, isn't it?"

He nods. "D'Ambrosio. Nice to see you again, Mrs. O'Leary."

She waves off all niceties. "So, Joe D'Ambrozhio. What were you doing waiting for Agnes downstairs?"

"I . . . had the afternoon off."

"And you broke your index finger? Is that why you didn't ring the doorbell?"

He can't tell her he didn't have the address, but there's a stranger truth he can offer: "My folks don't have a doorbell. I never remember that other people do."

"Was she expecting you?"

"No." Maybe that was too fast. "No, I haven't seen her in a while and I thought . . ."

"You thought you'd loiter outside."

He smiles pleasantly.

"Tell me, Mister D'Am*brozh*io." He's in trouble—Joe was good enough at Yankee Stadium. "Are you related to the Calabrese family?"

He knew a Calabrese in second grade. "No," he says, prolonging the smile though it's beginning to cause him pain. "Not that I know of."

"Are you quite sure of that?"

He's bewildered, and in his bewilderment glances at Loretta, who's more bewildered still. She stares at her lap, wrings her hands. He's never actually seen anyone do that before.

"I *am* quite sure of that, Mrs. O'Leary."

"Don't you get fresh with me."

"I'm not trying to be fresh." He feels as if she's pushed him up against the wall the way the Jevvies do when the freshmen get out of line.

"Then wipe that silly grin off your face."

He does. Boy, does he.

"Now you'll please tell me what you're really doing here."

A wicked witch has taken the place of the crusty, charming old lady of the ballpark. Joe D'Ambrosio doesn't like the new version. "I'm really here to see Agnes." He says it with an edge, and finally she relaxes in her armchair. He knows the type: a bully, who backs off when you stand up to her. Vindictive, though. The next thing she says is "Agnes is keeping company with another young man."

"I know." This time he doesn't come back so strong. "We're all friends."

"That boy, that Bernie. Jewish, isn't he?"

He can't do anything but stare at her. He knows this type of mick, too: if you don't have red hair and freckles you're too dark for her. Maybe she thinks he's there to rob them blind, though it's a mystery what they might have to rob. Poor Agnes. Poor Loretta. He rises.

"Thank you both for inviting me in. I have to get back to work."

The grandmother rises too and he sees the same conniving gleam she got that time at the ballpark. "Don't go," she says. "Loretta, put the kettle on."

With the tea would come a bite of food, a cookie or a cracker, whatever these strange people related to Agnes have in their cupboard. He wavers. He hasn't eaten since the thin barley soup at lunch, and he's tramped crosstown and then, in Brooklyn, up and down that hill. He wavers, but he's already standing over Loretta and she's already shaking his hand, her fingers light as leaves. He's already crossing over to the wicked witch to shake her hand good-bye. Now he really must give up his chance to see Agnes.

Because what would it be like, sitting with her in this room, the old lady standing guard? Worse than going to see her in a department store. Might even be worse than not seeing her at all. Somebody needs to keep this old woman in check. When he gets Agnes back, it's going to be up to him.

"Thank you for your hospitality." This time he *is* trying to be fresh, challenge her, precisely what somebody should do to her every day for the rest of her life.

"You're welcome," she says brightly. "We'll tell Agnes you were here."

He doubts she will, but Loretta might, and it's no matter anyway. He's going to write to Agnes, he's going to pour out heart and soul in a letter. He's going to get her back. Too bad for Bernie. Too bad for Loretta who, he fears, has already succumbed to his power over women. Too bad for Mrs. O'Leary, who's run her granddaughters' lives long enough.

They haven't even missed him when he gets back to the House. Zarella drifts through the kitchen, looking distracted.

"Anybody seen the light bill?" he says.

Better this purposeful chaos than the order Mrs. O'Leary imposes. He feels as if he understands, whole, why Agnes has been running from him and why he must overtake her, fast. He means to save Agnes from that household, from that monstrous woman, and the sooner the better.

PART IV

PAST THE BAD STUFF

First trip to Cleveland since the beginning of June. For the rest of his life, Cleveland will be where Joe DiMaggio kept his streak alive while Lou Gehrig lay dying, and that's not all Cleveland has to offer in the bad memories department. As he recalls, the lights are especially brutal in Lakefront Stadium. He sure as hell doesn't like fielding in that glare, and as for hitting—better not think about what happens to his batting average under the lights, not when he's trying to keep a streak alive. Lakefront's a monster.

But for all the bad associations with Cleveland, he's got a good feeling about tonight. Suiting up, he hears a swing band's jazzy tunes drifting in from left field. The band's out there—why else?—to celebrate his own visit to town, to celebrate the way he's riding his streak like it's a bucking bronco. Word is, Cleveland's gathered up the biggest night crowd ever tallied.

The rest of the Yankees show up in cheerful gangs, jitterbugging to the music. They use their locker doors for partners, even Charlie Keller, swinging his long, powerful King Kong arms. Crazy. You can hear the crowd's giddiness from in here. Cleveland still thinks it has a shot at the pennant.

DiMag has been a little giddy himself, the last week or so. The streak stopped being agony and started being—well, he wouldn't go so far as *fun*. The gradual slide made it hard to pinpoint when he started feeling as

201

powerful as he'd fooled the fans and the writers and even the other Yanks into thinking he'd been all along. He's whistled past the bad stuff. He knocks wood: a pencil behind Gomez's ear. What's Gomez writing down?

"Gems," Lefty says. "Great thoughts. Brilliant words for the lads in the press box to pass off as their own."

Last year Gomez thought he was all washed up, thought he was done for, but this year he and Lefty, his good-luck charm, are magic. Lefty's pitching tonight, and when Lefty pitches, DiMaggio hits.

"You better wipe that grin off your face, Dago," Lefty counsels him. "Or nobody'll recognize you."

DiMag passes the grin on to Rizzuto, one foot in his uniform pants. Kid's not doing so poorly himself: hit in eighteen games in a row, had a baby streak of his own going there. DiMag basks in the warm glow of collective glory. Hey, maybe he's a socialist. Maybe he's one of those Bolshies the Nazis say they're trying to wipe out. He picks up a Cleveland *Plain Dealer* off the bench. The Japs are up to no good over in China. He has to read a smaller headline twice:

GERMANS AND ITALIANS ASKED TO LEAVE U.S.

WHAT? His eye runs down the column. They're asking diplomats to clear out, the guys who work the embassies. For a second there he actually thought . . .

He throws the paper back down on the bench. What's the matter with him? He was born in this country. He's as American as anybody in *Cleveland.* He feels his cheeks singe.

Shame is a complicated emotion. Take the women who've been throwing themselves at him since the streak began: if he feels any shame over the way he goes for blondes (does he?), it's all wrapped up in whatever it is he's felt since grade school, when his tongue tied every time he was called on to answer. Guinea, wop, dago, greaseball. His mama can't speaka da English. His mama don't like it when he plays the field.

He swallows down his coffee, lights a Camel. Fifty-seven: a better word than *shame.* Tonight's word is *fifty-seven.* Did he say that out loud?

Nah, he knows better. The Heinz people want to cut a deal: Joe D's fifty-seven hits to go with their fifty-seven varieties. The Dago will deliver.

Al Smith is on the mound for Cleveland (didn't somebody famous have that name?). The way DiMaggio sees it, he and Al Smith are soul mates, the pair of them expressionless as judges when they face each other down. Old friends in that regard. The way he and Ken Keltner at third base are old pals: Ken just might be the best infielder in the league, but DiMag remembers how, that last time in Cleveland, he managed to slam the ball past third base just fine. Keltner must remember too, cause he's gone deep, trespassing in left field territory. Joltin' Joe will have to smash it all the harder.

His first at bat, Smith gives him what he needs: a low inside curve. DiMag holds back, holds back, whacks it with all he's got and knows from his follow-through that he's bagged the fifty-seventh game. Only his foot slips on the dirt in the batter's box, still damp from last night's rain. He has to hightail it to first. The throw beats him by a split second and he hears the crowd's wonder match his. How the hell did Keltner manage to snatch that ball off a hop and send it by return mail as fast as he did?

Next round, Smith walks him, and the crowd boos the home-team pitcher. DiMag would rather they didn't. Sure it's a dirty trick, but walking a guy on the fifty-seventh game of his hitting streak just goes to show that Smith, for all his stoniness, is rattled.

In the seventh inning, they don't dare walk him again, but it's like a bad dream coming back: Smith gives him what he needs, he connects perfectly, Keltner grabs it off a hop again. The ball precedes him to first, this time by a second split yet more infinitesimally than the last. Again the crowd whistles its wonder.

Screw it. He'll get another shot. Won't be the first game of the streak played with a stadium full of fans holding their breath. He hears his stomach rumble, but he doesn't feel any of the sting, doesn't taste acid on the back of his tongue the way he did midstreak. He's beyond acid, beyond feeling, beyond thinking. The only way you hit the ball is to leave the premises, go elsewhere. He's already there, in elsewhere land.

He floats through another long inning and watches from the bench as the Indians, trailing, yank Smith for a right-hander. DiMag hides a smirk. The new kid, Bagby, looks like a punk, a know-nothing. Thinks he's a tough guy. When the Dago strides up to the plate, he's looking at his last chance—it's the top of the eighth—but one is all he needs. He lets the kid go to a one–one count and then bye-bye Bagby. *Fica.*

Bagby glowers and for the third time that night DiMaggio connects with the ball in precisely the way he's paid to do. But the pitching change has thrown off his swing, and he knows as soon as the ball leaves the bat that he's grounded it. Lou Boudreau at short scoops it up. Easy double play, but DiMag runs his heart out to first base anyway. The fans deserve that much. This time it's not even close.

And that's it.

Barring a miracle, the streak's over. DiMaggio doesn't really see the fans jumping to their feet, doesn't really feel the clap of his teammates' hands on his back, hasn't really returned to earth. Better this way. No more worries. No more making himself sick over whether he'll keep the streak alive.

By the end of the eighth the score's four–one, which pretty much nails down that coffin. There won't be any extra innings. Won't be any miracle. The least he can do is act like Gehrig, who knew how to take his lumps. He sits up straighter on the bench. Don't let them see you mope and whine and feel sorry for yourself. He trots out to center field looking neither to left nor right, his dignity restored.

Then, as if his torment's not complete, another twist. In the bottom of the ninth the Indians remember they'd like to tug the pennant away from the Yankees. That'd be the nuts, if they pulled themselves together and gave him another shot up at the dish.

In center field, DiMaggio waits for Murphy to warm up—Gomez has been yanked, too, for handing out singles. DiMag shifts his weight, wills himself to think of anything but baseball, lets home pop into his head, sees the *Rosalie* sailing off from the wharf, smaller and smaller until it's a speck. When he was small, he thought the boat and his father might sail over the edge of the universe. Greenberg, sailing away on a troopship. No asking if we're going to war now. The only question, the reporters say, is why it's taking so long. A pang: they'll forget his puny streak, the one that didn't even match his minor league record, when Greenberg lands in Paris and starts saving refugees right and left. Knock it off. Greenberg's a decent guy. What is the matter with him?

Finally Murphy's ready. Even in the outfield, a million miles away, DiMaggio can tell from the way Rosenthal's coiled at home plate that he's ready too, ready to hit the ball for Cleveland. And sure enough, Rosenthal connects for a triple deep into left that drives in two runs. Now it's a four–three ballgame. The tying run's on third with nobody out. If Rosenthal touches home plate, Joe DiMaggio gets another chance to keep the streak alive. If anybody else does, Cleveland's won the game and it's all over. All over one more time.

Steady at his sentry post, DiMaggio listens to the collective heartbeat of the stadium. He hears Henrich's heart in right field and Keller's in left. His own heart has stopped beating, and finally his brain takes pity and shuts down too. Cleveland sends up Trosky to pinch hit. Wasn't that somebody famous too? Trosky grounds out. One away.

Soup Campbell (*What the hell's going on with the names in Cleveland?*) comes in to bat for Bagby and hits the ball straight back to Murphy. Rosenthal—the idiot!—tries to score and gets run down between third and home. Two outs, and now no runner in scoring position.

Still, there's one more shot for Cleveland to tie the game, one more chance for DiMaggio to stay alive. Weatherly ambles up to the plate trying to look nonchalant and DiMaggio does what a ballplayer must never do: he wills his opponent to hit the ball safely. He wills it with all his heart and soul, with all his power. He betrays his team, his teammates, his own hard-won dignity.

So he deserves it and worse when Weatherly grounds out. The last thing Joe DiMaggio sees from center field is Soup Campbell running halfheartedly toward second base. Pretty good punishment for his pride. Swell ending for the hero.

He doesn't even have to live through what happens next to know what happens next. Back in the clubhouse, the reporters want him to play it out over and over and over, the first Keltner snatch, the second Keltner snatch, the heartbreaker at the bottom of the ninth. He says what they want to hear: *It's been a good ride, I just wish it could have gone on forever, that was some fine fielding Ken Keltner pulled off at third base. You gotta hand to it the guy.*

So his heart is evidently ticking again, and his voice box is still working, working better than usual as a matter of fact. He's a regular chatterbox in defeat, Joltin' Joe DiMaggio.

It goes on forever, but finally the last reporter leaves. Rizzuto grins at him as if to say *Can you believe those guys?* "Stick around, will you, Phil."

"You betcha."

The two of them stick around long after the scavenging reporters go to type up their sob story. They stick around long after Lefty leaves to lick his own wounds. They stick around long after the Skipper limps off to celebrate the way his boyos beat back the opposition.

Let 'em go. Joe DiMaggio's not going to face some fan's pity, some fan's *Tough luck, Joe.* He can't bear it. He'll wait till next week to go home if he has to. He'll stay in the clubhouse till the last man in Ohio climbs into bed. Rizzuto knows how to keep a fellow company: he thumbs through the paper like he was planning to spend his night sitting around the clubhouse anyway.

Funny. The Scooter's a clever kid— quick with words, they're finding out—but he knows just how to hold his tongue too. He's been handy, this streak, has tagged along a couple of times when DiMag wanted to see a western. At the movies, he and Rizzuto sit in companionable silence in the dark: what a woman would never do. Dorothy would be reaching for his hand, checking to make sure he laughed at the funny lines and choked at the sad ones.

Fully dressed now, the two of them alone in the clubhouse, they pass that *Plain Dealer* back and forth. Maybe Rizzuto's actually reading an article here and there. He sure as hell isn't. Even the funny pages don't make sense.

Finally he rises and the Scooter follows suit. At the door, Phil sticks his head out first to make sure the coast is clear. They've outlasted the fans, and Joe DiMaggio can finally leave Lakefront without the hordes sticking out their programs and their baseball cards. He breathes a sigh of relief, but why then does he feel all the more desolate, facing an empty Cleveland street in the middle of the night?

Halfway down the block he realizes he's left his wallet back in the locker room, which is surely locked up tight by now. He can't bear the thought of facing a night watchman.

"How much you got on you?" he asks Rizzuto.

Phil counts a ten, a five, three singles. One look at the Dago's face, and he hands it over.

"Thanks." DiMaggio's spent enough time in Cleveland. He knows a corner bar down the block, the kind of bar that stays open till the wee hours and harbors fans who know how to leave a baseball player alone. The locals won't believe their eyes when Joe DiMaggio walks in the door but they'll know enough to give him elbow room. When he veers off, Rizzuto follows.

"Nah, nah," he says, not unkindly. Good man to stick by him, but even Rizzuto can't help but pity him on this day. DiMaggio wants to drink alone, into the morning. He wants to arrive back at the hotel so late there won't even be any blondes waiting for him. He pictures the phone ringing in his hotel room: Dorothy, in New York, at the other end of the line. He can't summon any emotion whatsoever at the sight of her huge belly protruding, her lower lip puffing out her humiliation.

———

He's rip-roaring stumbling-down drunk when he steps out of the cab, the kind of drunk that would make any other man bellow. Not Deadpan DiMaggio. He swallows his words even as he stumbles, even as the door-man catches his elbow and steadies him. He gives the man a nod and thinks, maybe, that the fellow melts into a pool at his feet. Sick, when you think about it, that he has the power to make a grown man go all girly wet. Sick, sick, sick: he's not going to throw up, he never throws up, he won't throw up. Look, he's on the elevator already and even if he's got motion sickness he's not going to fucking throw up.

Lefty has to open the door cause he can't possibly make the key work, and Lefty has to put him to bed. Lefty's his mama, his papa-mama, his sweet big brothers, his big hairy-balled guardian angel. He didn't throw up, he won't throw up. But already the headache pushes its finger against his temple the way Dorothy pushes against . . .

He loses the sentence, loses the thought, drifts into sleep, wakes thirty seconds later. Too late to call Dorothy. Too late to find another woman, too drunk to get it up. Poor Dottie. He leaks tears into his pillow. Poor little baby, born into this loveless marriage, this loveless world at war. His poor papa. Poor pop. The poor refugees with their leaking peaches. He feels his teeth move, feels his hair grow. He sleeps.

The next day—dashing to the crapper, right eye throbbing—he doesn't even know what city he's in.

And then he remembers: streak's over.

NAKED

Babe says: "It must have been a month since your Joe D'Ambromeo tramped over to Brooklyn."

"Joe D'Ambro*sio*."

"I suppose the Sisters didn't trouble to teach you about puns. Not one of their habits."

Agnes cracks a grin despite herself.

"Well, well. A smile from Our Lady of Gloom. What about that letter he sent? Did you answer it?"

Agnes swallows back *None of your beeswax* and stretches out a Mona Lisa smile instead. She should have just burned Joe's letter, but instead she sleeps with it under the mattress and takes it with her every time she leaves the apartment, takes it with her even if she's just going to the bathroom.

"I certainly can't help wondering about a handsome, tall fellow like that." Babe commences to whistle "Joltin' Joe DiMaggio," to signify that she has more important concerns. On Agnes's eighteenth birthday she announced, *You're an adult now, Aggie—Agnes—and you don't have to answer to anyone, least of all me.* Clever Babe. She couldn't turn the screws any tighter.

Weird to see her so cheerful this early in the morning. She's even made French toast for Agnes's day off, out of bread that's gone stale for once. At the beginning of the year the bread would have been already stale when they bought it, but now her dad's been gainfully employed for months and months, and so they have luxuries: fresh bread, a *Post* in the evenings, a new pair of silk stockings that Mickey presented to Babe as shyly as if he were her lover. Every now and again Babe forgets herself and lands a kiss on one of the girls' foreheads, a kiss delivered with what looks suspiciously like affection. She couldn't have read the letter, could she?

Agnes twitches at the very idea. It's five pages of Joe's sweet looping handwriting, a kid's handwriting, a man's words coated in syrup: *I love you, which you must have known all this time. And I want to marry you. I know what a sacrifice I'm asking you to make. I can't imagine you want to wait for me till I get out of jail.*

"Jiminy Cricket," she said aloud, the first time she read it. "You're not *in* jail yet." She was perched on a park bench in Prospect Park, a public space her only hope of privacy, a fool's grin on her face her only defense against the groan she'd otherwise emit.

Now she says, "I thought you didn't like Joe D'Ambrosio because he's a Red. Not that he *is* a Red."

"Precisely," Babe says, but that's not precise at all, it's ambiguous and frustrating. Now she's sweeping the kitchen, though Agnes dawdles still over the big breakfast. Up to no good, her grandmother moves her hips as if the arthritis has all been one big misunderstanding. Agnes feels for the letter, safe in her bathrobe pocket. Maybe she really will have to burn it.

Babe says, "Better a Red pacifist—"

"He's just a plain old pacifist—"

"Better a misguided Red pacifist than a boy who's too short," Babe finishes triumphantly. She's been on an anti-Bernie campaign for weeks, her first step to see that he's thoroughly humiliated.

"Oh, for goodness' sake, Babe. What if he's short? What does that have to do with anything?"

"Do you really not know? If you close your eyes to it now, you'll find out on your wedding night."

"Babe!" Agnes wails. No one's coarse as Babe. The very idea of Bernie's being underendowed in the manly department is—

"—the lowest you've ever sunk. You should be ashamed."

"Who's the elder around here, Agnes? Who's deserving of respect, Miss Now-That-You're-Eighteen-You-Think-You-Can-Speak-to-Your-Grandmother-Any-Way-You-Choose?" Babe's actually smirking. She thinks she's scored the winning point.

"I'm going out." Agnes rises and leaves the dirty plate where it lies.

"Going out where?"

"I don't have to answer that."

"No," Babe says carefully. "We've already agreed you don't have to answer that."

"But I will," Agnes says. She knows she should hold her tongue, she knows she should. But this business about Bernie has her crazed, exactly what Babe wants, and if Babe wants her crazed, she'll just have to deal with the consequences. "I think I'll look in on my grandfather."

The look of jealousy on Babe's face feels worth it, for one split second. But after the second's been halved, a large lump of wet bread lodges in her lower gut, and it's all she can do not to cry out again. She feels for the letter, touches Joe's handwriting. Safe.

"Anyway." She's not sure whether she's trying to lighten the mood or further incense her grandmother. "Bernie says this is the Year of Short Shortstops. If you're so down on short men, what about Pee Wee Reese?"

Rage and contempt drop Babe's lower left lip into a snarl. Her jowls quiver. She advances on Agnes with the broom and pokes the bristles into her side.

"Stop it," Agnes says, with some dignity. "That broom's filthy."

"No, you're the one who's filthy," her grandmother answers. "A filthy little slut. A whoor. Don't you know anything? Pee Wee Reese is a *Dodger*!"

Walking up Fifth Avenue, Agnes is still shaken. Babe's always tended toward low-grade violence—she clunks the O'Leary girls' knuckles with spoons and swats at their backsides—but all through the years it has never once occurred to her that her grandmother hates her.

Now the memory of Babe thrusting the broom is as real as the heat lightning flashing through the muggy sky, but not as startling as the next revelation. The curtains part to reveal what Agnes has known for a long, long time and hasn't been able to admit: she hates her grandmother too. She feels the way she did the first time she realized that she might not believe in God.

She stops in her tracks in front of Campanella's Bakery, the morning bread smells still wafting. *Your mother sent you out for a loaf of semolina.* How can she tell Bernie that she's chosen Joe?  How can she do that to him? When he's been so sweet, when he believes what she believes: about the war, anyway. She has a feeling he'd be more sympathetic to her God doubts than Joe would ever be—though what she believes about everything is all turned inside out again this morning. If Babe wants her to choose Joe, it can't be the right choice. *She tied you at the wrists, so you wouldn't drift away. But would she go down into the street with you? Oh, no. She was too distracted. She was too distraught. She was too consumed with her own problems.*

Bernie seems like the tougher one but he's not, really. He'd never say a word if she told him she was marrying Joe—maybe he'd say *Good luck, Agnes,* and turn his face—but he'd do something crazy, maybe even jump onto the subway tracks the way his father did. Whereas Joe will just drift away to another girl, a prettier girl than she. Joe's loose and Bernie's clenched tight, every fiber of him. Bernie says he's enlisting but pores over the City College course lists. Bernie needs her and somehow—she can't sort it out, it's not meant for sorting—somehow she needs Bernie.

Then why does she long for Joe's flesh, cinnamon colored in the summer light? Why did the letter have to be so *romantic?* He closed with:

My lips, two blushing pilgrims, seal this.

He really did. And Babe knows to call him D'Ambromeo. Somewhere between eighth grade and becoming the monster she's become, her grandmother must have read Shakespeare too. Agnes is so furious—at Babe, at herself, at Joe, at Bernie—that she won't even let herself cry. *Your mother sent you out for a loaf of semolina, and then she found another length of clothesline and looped it round the pipe.*

At Calabrese's the front door is open. Curious. She pulls it shut behind her but her grandfather doesn't appear after she rings the countertop bell. Out in the hot streets fire engines clang, deep and sonorous, mocking the little funeral parlor ping. Maybe her grandfather's gone to see the fire.

She opens the front door to look for him and—curiouser and curiouser—there he is, suited as usual, but running toward her on the sidewalk as fast as Jesse Owens, screaming something she can't make out. She goes to meet him. At the corner of Fifth and President, Vito huffs and puffs and leans on her arm.

"Tell Tommy come now. They're jumping out the windows. Run!"

She runs like Owens herself, back down the block, back through the front door of Calabrese's. She hasn't seen the fire herself, has witnessed no flames shooting, no fire trucks tearing round corners. But she's smelled it, acrid smoke snaking down the avenue and leaving behind the disturbing mysterious scent of whatever's being burned, brownstone and frame window and . . . human flesh? *They're jumping out the windows,* her grandfather said.

She won't let herself picture it—it doesn't help to stop your gaze on horrible things. She makes her way through the office and the parlors. In the second viewing room, that back parlor, there's a side door behind which the basement stairs descend. She steps through the door and into a large foyer off the back entrance where the ambulances and hearses stop. The stairs stretch down beneath ornate sconces on the wall, the dark stripes papering the walls austere and formal and manly. Her grandfather couldn't bring himself to skimp on decorating anything, not even the back stairs. She's never climbed down them before, and makes as big a racket as she can to warn Uncle Tom she's on the way. The wooden steps are soft and yielding. They bring the bodies down on stretchers, and they leave in boxes, men groaning under the deadweight. Surely these old stairs are a safety hazard.

Uncle Tommy doesn't hear her clatter, or doesn't anyway make a move to let her in. She has to pound on the metal door and wait forever. *Awright, awright.* She begins to shout, the way her grandfather did: "They're jumping out the windows. Your father says come right away."

That does it. He flings the door after all, wide enough for her to see into his cavernous space. Two metal tables lie side by side, like siblings' beds—so he can work on two bodies at once? But today there's only one body. Even as her uncle stands there in the doorway listening to her tumbling exhortations he's pulling off his gloves and the rubber apron, covered in small, damp spots like grease stains—chemicals? blood? bile? He hands over the gloves and apron for Agnes to deal with.

"How many alarms?"

Having no idea how many alarms are even possible, she says, "Five."

"Oh my God. Hold the fort, Aggie."

And he, forgetting that he's leaving her to the room where the State of New York and the Family of Calabrese agree she's not allowed, takes off like a track star too, clambering up the uneven stairs she has just descended.

He's gone, gone and left her to the mortuary. There's nothing she can do about the fire. Is there? She'd only be in the way. She's supposed to put the apron and gloves down. So if she has to saunter over past the corpse, it's not as if she's defying anyone.

Her first time alone with a naked stiff. She decides that the only safe place for the gloves and apron is on a shelf on the far side of the metal tables. She'll be able to pass the corpse once, take a glance without having to look too hard, turn, come back and focus on it, and fix the angle she'll use to hold her camera on the day they finally let her photograph a bare body. She swallows three deep breaths, begins the count to ten, changes that to five—they could be back any second—and briskly crosses the room.

It's a fresh corpse. The blood must have been drained already, the body pumped full of gases, yet it's still tinged the faintest blue, the vague color of morning sky. She stretches to push the apron and gloves onto the top shelf, forces herself to turn.

The orifices must already be plugged, thank goodness. That was first, wasn't it, plug the orifices? Then what do they do with the penis? She's never heard the word aloud, has only seen it in books and thinks it's pronounced "pen-is," like "penance." Brotherless, she's never seen one, live or dead: the only sightings have been on statues.

This one is so tiny, so vulnerable, the barest tip of its little head poking through the sack that holds it. It's a worm, not a body part. It's a sad little reminder of life, like the decaying birds on the park walks, like shite in the toilet. She prefers the testicles, the comical way they hide behind the thatch of thinning graying hair. Thank goodness Uncle Tommy hasn't shaved that yet. Poor man.

She feels her mouth hanging open, and that's enough to stir her to leave, but not quite yet: it's indecent to stare at his private parts and not his public. She must look at his face, pay him that much respect.

She stops breathing altogether. The man's her father's age, the same looming circles beneath his eyes, the same jowls. A onetime drinker, like her father. Do all corpses look this spent, or only the corpses of men who think they're failures? His eyes are cemented shut—she can see little traces of the glue, like morning sleep.

He has a big, full mouth (in that, too, he resembles Mickey), a needle dangling from the side of his lower lip by a thread very like a thread of spittle. She wants to reach out and touch the tiny gleaming needle: it looks just like the ones Babe uses to make repairs in the worn-out elastic of their waistbands. She interrupted her Uncle Tommy as he sewed up the lips.

She feels more comfortable with this body than with the dressed-and-gussied ones that hold court in the parlors upstairs. She must get a camera down here, she must photograph this body. She looks around to see if a witness lurks, someone hiding behind the jars of Uncle Tom's face paint to read her thoughts.

On cue a young man pushes open the door, a skulking tall black-haired pimply boy her own age: Nick, who comes to help her uncle lift bodies. His job is down here in the dark, and her grandfather and uncle have never so much as introduced him, their hired hand. He glares at her and won't move beyond the stairway.

"Uncle Tommy's gone to help with the fire."

Still he stares. She wonders if he can talk.

"He asked me to put his gloves and apron away."

"Then you better wash up," the boy says, "and go upstairs." He can talk all right.

Of course she has to write Joe back. You don't get a letter like that and not answer it. She tells him she must meet him: she has to tell him in person that she's chosen Bernie—can't do *that* in a letter—and nearly makes herself weep by reciting the lines she might use:

> *If thou wilt leave me, do not leave me last,*
> *When other petty griefs have done their spite,*
> *But in the onset come, so shall I taste*
> *At first the very worst of fortune's might.*

She owes Joe that much: to tell him now, *in the onset*, before she goes any further with Bernie. She proposes that they meet—where else?—in Washington Square, in a week's time.

And in the space of that week, the early sultry days of August, she changes her mind all over again. It's not Joe's fault that Babe thinks he's the one she should marry. Babe only distracted her by pleading his case. When she closes her eyes on the subway and drifts, it's Joe she pictures. The night before she goes to meet him, she dreams that it's Joe, wearing Jesse Owens's tracksuit, who runs away from her in a vast arena. Just when she's about to overtake him, he descends into a tunnel. When she reaches the mouth of the tunnel, a metal door descends and shuts her out: Joe's lost forever. If that's not a warning to go to him she doesn't know what is.

Along with his letters (now there are two), she's taken to carrying her savings, so Babe won't know how much she has. If she and Joe are overtaken by their passion—why is she thinking such an overblown word? Gracious—if they're overtaken by their feelings, at least she'll have cash to pay for a cheap hotel room in the Village. Who's to stop them?

Joe, of course. He would never do such a thing.

It's been so long since they've seen each other that she can't even remember what he looks like. Does the hair fall down over the left side of his forehead or his right? Would you call his eyes black, or just plain

old brown? When she spots him in the park he's stooping to return a kid's Spaldeen, and it's only his back she sees. It's all she needs to see, taut muscles under a khaki-colored shirt: one of his old school shirts, wearing thin. He rises and returns the ball effortlessly—with his *left* hand. How's she forgotten this, that he's a southpaw? His foot rises in the thick summer air. She decides all over again to marry him. Before he goes to Mexico, before the year is out.

He turns and spies her, and here comes that big Clark Gable what-the-heck grin. The bones of his face are precise as cut glass. He's so graceful, when she can barely cross the street without tripping. So positive, so *happy*, when she's morose. He clings to his faith and she's thrown hers away. Why would he want her for his wife?

For this: he wants to touch every square inch of her. Does he think they're hidden from view, standing here in the middle of the walk, beneath the arch? He swoops in as if they're alone in the dark, kisses her full on the mouth, presses harder till . . . it's just not right, she can feel him stiffening against her, and it's still broad daylight, not even close to dusk. Just not right that the children of Washington Square Park should witness this naked need.

They still haven't said a word to each other. He must feel her own stiffening, the other kind, because he takes her by the hand to a bench, where he grazes her cheek with the back of his hand. Where did he learn to do *that*?

"Agnes," he says. "Come home with me."

She thinks he means his parents' house, thinks he's rushing ahead to introducing her to the folks. Too fast, too fast.

"They've all gone on retreat. I convinced Dorothy I'd have a nervous breakdown in the country. Don't look like that, I'm just joking. I'm in charge of the house while they're gone."

She's speechless yet.

"We can have some privacy, for once. Don't worry. I mean: to talk."

Home to the Catholic Worker House. She decides she mustn't smile up at him and smiles up at him. Her cheeks ache and pull with how much she's missed him, with how foolish she's been. It's the set of his muscles, his bones. The certainty of those lines. A flash of pity for Bernie.

She nods. She still hasn't spoken a word, and she doesn't intend to speak one all night, if she can avoid it.

Mott Street is busier still on a Saturday evening than it was on a Saturday morning, though all the stores are closing up now. It stinks of drippy cheese and rotting meat and slimy fish a monger's selling under the hydrant's drip. Sweating children slick as seals squeal and dash through the sidewalks in their sleeveless undershirts. The grannies have finally taken off their shawls, their great bosoms heaving down on their stoop watch. The cloying August air has made the children giddy and stunned their keepers. They should have started dinner by now, but it's too hot, too hot to go in, too hot to light the stove, too hot to stir.

Joe takes her back through the front house and into the rear. She's astounded by the trick: an entire other building's tucked away back here. He leads her by the damp hand, or maybe that's her own hand that's damp. The walls are the grim color of poverty, the breath of air between the two houses only enough to remind her that she's choking in the heat.

On the ground floor of the back house they meet a resident and even though Agnes has seen the men in the soup line she's shocked by the fel-

low: a little rodent. Is that a long tail swishing as he pushes past them? His whiskers are glued with sweat to his face. Like the children outside, he wears a sleeveless undershirt, only his is filthier still.

"That your sweetheart?" he asks Joe, his voice fluty and lecherous.

"Isn't she something?"

Agnes can't believe he has the presence of mind to pass it all off so blithely. (Another pang—Bernie's favorite word: *blithe.*) They ascend a grim, narrow stairway. A strange comfort, to know that some live sadder lives than the life her father has lived. Joe's tiny room is a fright. Even one of Babe's horrid lace curtains would break this gloom. All is bare—windows, lightbulb, the gouged dresser—and the sheets are gray. Naturally it hasn't occurred to him to make the bed.

As if he's heard her, he leans low to pull the sheet up: "Ta-da!" He's not ashamed of his hovel, not at all. She loves him.

"Where do I sit?"

He gestures and she sinks down to the low, narrow mattress, which perches on a makeshift frame of milk crates and creaks raucously as she descends. Joe, grinning, joins her.

"Can you believe I talked Dorothy into leaving me in charge?"

"You'd talk the newsprint off the *Herald Tribune*." Who does she think she is, Dorothy Parker? How false could a girl possibly sound?

"I'm scared the place is going to go up in flames on my watch. I'm scared we've forgotten to pay the light bill."

"You're not scared of anything."

"I'm a little scared of you."

Well, he's very good at sweet talk, always has been. It's not possible that St. Joe has taken her to his room to seduce her, is it? Her back is turned to the wall, but with the eyes in the back of her head she can still see the crucifix above them: the white body naked but for that swoop of cloth. The tortured Christ.

"You're not scared of me. I'm blushing, thinking what you wrote." And suddenly she is: *If I could touch you, if I could speak with my hands . . .*

"You never answered my question."

She won't answer it still. But she smiles.

"Are you still seeing Bernie?"

She shakes her head no, though she saw him last week. It's not a lie. Last week she didn't know that Joe was the one, and when she sees Bernie next she'll tell him . . .

It's enough for Joe. He decides to speak with his hands again and she must be answering him. One moment they're sitting side by side and the next they're lying side by side, their legs stretched out like diving boards over the wavy, watery floor. She's dizzy from lack of oxygen, from this onslaught of kissing and pressing and squeezing in the damp, hot afternoon. Without knowing she's about to do it, she reaches beneath her skirt to open a garter, and removes her stocking somehow with her one free hand. Joe moans, maybe to signify the vision of a hand peeling silk off a white leg. She's in a very odd position, her knee twisted and bent. She must get out of it somehow. She unbuttons the top button on her blouse, or maybe she dreams that she's unbuttoning her blouse. How could it be that she's stripping herself of clothes, when no one's seen her naked since she was a small child and the sight of Babe in her droopy drawers made her vow she would never submit to such indignity?

Joe kneels above her—the milk-crate bed yowls like a cat—and undresses her himself, button by button, hook by eye. When he flings away her brassiere she wants to grab it back, and when she's left in her panties and girdle, one stocking to go, she closes her eyes and pretends her body is Loretta's. The skin on Joe's fingers is rougher than it was a few months ago, but his touch is gentle. They're going to do this. They're really going to do this. And then there will be no going back.

Too fast, too fast.

He rises again from the bed and she opens her eyes. He's changed his mind. But no. Now he undresses, under the gaze of the crucifix, strips to his shorts. She holds her breath, awaiting the poor, meek pen-is she saw on the corpse. When he pulls down his drawers, she doesn't make a peep, but something's all wrong: he's huge, enormous.

Of course she giggles.

He descends and snuggles close. "Are we so funny looking?"

"An elephant's trunk!"

"The better to deflower you, my dear."

And that's when—Joe sounding like Bernie, Joe trying to make himself sound like an old letch—she panics. She's always been a virgin and now she never will be one again and, furthermore, this doesn't feel so good, whatever Joe is doing so vigorously with his hand between her legs. She wants to move it to the right place, but she doesn't want him to know that she touches herself at night, when Loretta's asleep, or pretending to sleep.

He rolls atop her and dwarfs her, his weight bearing down. She's trapped, pinned. She's wanted this for a long, long time but this is never what she wanted. He pushes into her as if he's running one of his races— how does he even know how to do that, or where? He's too big, he's bigger than other men, he's hurting her. And hurting her more: now she's stretched to the breaking. She burns and stings and doesn't even know what part of her is tearing. He kisses her again, but now even the weight of his face, even the weight of his lips oppresses her.

Something happens. It's over already, when it hasn't even started. He shudders and moans and flops above her. When he rolls off, he's laughing, laughing till the tears stream down. He closes his eyes:

"You did *this* for me."

For him? She closes her eyes too, rolls on her side and flings her arm across his chest, because if she just pretends it's all right it will be all right. They breathe in-out, one-two, in-out together till she realizes that he's fallen into quick and carefree sleep.

She stays there forever, the light dimming outside. Finally she rises without deciding to rise. The sheet below is spotted with her blood, but not so much as she would have thought. Not so much as it hurt. Now in the darkening evening, the overhead bulb glaring and the window bare, she's truly naked. She's never dressed so fast in her life. Joe stirs, and she tiptoes to the door.

He starts awake at the door's creak, but as usual nothing clamps the flow of his speech: "Wait, I'll walk you to the train. I'll ride with you to Brooklyn! There's so much . . . we have to decide, Agnes—"

She puts a finger to her lips and backs out of the door before he can jump up too, to dress, to stop her. The bed screeches as he tumbles up, and she skips downstairs, out the back building, through the front, past a gang of men in dungarees—they don't *live* here, do they?—who would just as soon rape her as look at her. One rushes to hold the door for her but she can't even summon a muttered *thanks*. She doesn't even see what he looks like.

Out in the street, she turns the wrong

way on Mott, to throw Joe off the trail, and hurries round corners till she's sure he can't follow. She's lost, but she's on her own, no other body pressing down. She wanders (in the dark, it feels like miles to Houston Street) till she finds the way to the subway. She's sure that the men she passes on these mean streets—men in dirty work clothes, men in caps pulled low, men who skulk and leer—would take a knife to her throat on a dare. She herself hasn't looked a single person in the eye. What's happened to her, that suddenly she's frightened of poor folks? She's lost her virginity and turned into Babe, all in the space of an afternoon.

On the train she rearranges her skirt a thousand times and imagines the vile stains that will show when she rises. When she gets to Brooklyn and walks in the door, she'll slip first to the bathroom—they'll all think she's on the rag—and she'll wash herself clean of this uncanny feeling that slips through her like fog. She'll change her clothes and eat with the family as if nothing's wrong. She'll just have to pretend that nothing momentous has happened, and it will be good for her too. It will clear her head. She'll just have to find a way to tell Joe and Bernie both that it's too soon, that she can't be pressured this way, she's too young, she's just turned eighteen. She's not the ball they can toss between them. She's not the monkey in the middle.

But Babe will know: Babe will know right away what she's done. Babe knew before she did it. *Slut. Whoor.*

She makes herself look at the people on the train, at other people's faces, at other people's headlines: UKRAINE, RUSSIA, STALIN. JAPAN. DEBATE ON DRAFT. She can't bear to look any closer.

If she's pregnant she'll just have to deal with that too. She doesn't feel like crying. It's more like a nothing, a darkness. The aisle of this subway car might just as well be the tunnel Joe disappeared into in her dream last night. She forces herself to look up again.

That man, sitting just past the door. It's the photographer, it's that Walker Evans. It couldn't be—he rides the Lex—but it has to be, with the rumpled raincoat, the fedora pushed back. Sure enough, his hand's in the pocket of his coat, when everyone else in the car is stripped to the least possible clothing. It must be a hundred degrees down here.

He spies her too, as if she's reached him with her brain waves. He bows his head as formally as a man taking surreptitious pictures on the train can bow, and cracks a slow-breaking grin, a grin very like the one Joe cracked when he first spotted her today in Washington Square. She smiles back. She can't help herself. Walker Evans is a famous photographer and he sent her a book a million years ago, and now he's *bowing* to her on the subway. She remembers, dimly, falling in love with him that day they all stood on the platform at Astor Place.

He's not shooting her, is he? She lowers her head and shakes it back and forth: *Please don't take my picture.*

He grins again, pulls his hands from his pockets, holds them up: *Look ma, no shutter release. No picture.* It's astounding. She's having a wordless conversation with a famous man on the train to Brooklyn. What on earth could he want in Brooklyn? If she struck up a conversation with him, she could tell him that she's become a photographer too, that she means to photograph corpses and that they will tell the world something, her corpses.

But what they will tell the world she doesn't know—she must be crazy, dead bodies—and anyway they've pulled into the first station in Brooklyn, York Street, and Walker Evans rises. Of course. He knows someone in Brooklyn Heights, where all the artists and the writers live. He smiles at her again and on his way through the doors he says, over his shoulder, "You're still onto me"—or does she dream it? Already he's gone.

He was *flirting* with her. She could have struck up a conversation with him and who knows, he might have seduced her too, might have known, looking at her face, that she's not a virgin anymore, that the schoolgirl's all grown up. If she doesn't watch herself, she might go off to Brooklyn Heights and sleep with artists and become a bohemian and . . .

O Joe. O Joe on his gray sheets, thinking she will marry him. She can hardly believe that she thought it too, thought it this morning when she rose and this afternoon when she left her stocking counter.

And now she knows she never will. And loves him somehow all the more.

BROOKLYN, BEWITCHED

All Brooklyn is under a spell.

Radios blare from every apartment—the game sounds like it's being broadcast from one distorted loudspeaker—and the moment the last out is called, the wailing begins. Babe O'Leary hears the cacophony from every direction: every driver in Brooklyn must be leaning on his horn.

By the time she gets herself down the stairs and out into the street, the borough's gone mad. Even sleepy Twelfth Street is jammed. A cabbie pulls his hack over and jumps out to kiss the cheeks of housewives who look like they're auditioning for a burlesque routine. Down the street two young mamas who've brought out pots and spoons to join the racket dance around like trained monkeys, their toddlers pirouetting at their feet.

Babe says, "Whoopdeedoo," but she doesn't need to lower her voice to assure her safety in this mob. No one hears her. The Brooklyn Dodgers are the National League champs and no one is paying the least attention to Babe O'Leary. Nosey Bruscelli perches up against a fire hydrant, shaking her fist like a demented demon. When's the last time Babe saw Nosey outside the building? Has she ever, in fact, seen Nosey outside the building? She approaches warily.

"I thought you were a DiMaggio fan." In the crisp fall light, every steel hair on Nosey's quavering chin stands out in stark relief, and Babe feels a wave of panic about her own mustache, which she cannot see to tweeze out properly, not with her failing vision and the apartment's dim light. Babe doesn't ordinarily feel panic. It's all of a piece with this Dodger madness.

"Everybody loves Joe," Nosey warbles. "And everybody loves the Bums."

"Oh, for pete's sake."

"Pete Reiser!" Nosey cries—this is the closest Babe has ever heard her come to wit—and a passing trio of schoolboy hooligans picks up her cry:

"Reiser! Reiser! Reiser!" In the distance they shift their chant to "Reese! Reese! Reese!"

The Yankees clinched their own pennant three weeks ago, the earliest ever, and did you see the Bronx losing itself this way? Did you see schoolboys marching down the streets drumming out "Rizzuto! Rizzuto! Rizzuto!" No, you most certainly did not. This is pathetic, this carrying on, this childish racket. And the jammed traffic means, furthermore, that everything will be backed up—subways, trolleys, sidewalks—and everyone in the family will be late for dinner, today of all days. Babe's starving. Listening to the game (she doesn't often tune in to the Other League) has enlarged her appetite.

"Don't bother going up the avenue," Bruscelli says helpfully. "Not nothing open."

Babe ignores her. Does she think Italians will ever be accepted if they can't at the very least show fidelity to their own? She ignores the bewitched crowd, too, and proceeds up the block.

On Seventh Avenue, a simian young man greets her as if they're old pals: "How 'bout those bums, hunh? How 'bout our boys?"

She refuses to smile.

"Aw, c'mon. Live a little."

She relents and offers a cagey half smile, playing along with this cheery schmeary business so that no Dodger fan can take pleasure in her displeasure. Won't she have the last laugh, when the Yankees ride roughshod over Durocher and his clowns.

Bruscelli was right about the butcher—he hasn't locked up, exactly, but he's abandoned his post—and, to punish him, she drags herself the extra block to buy cod, though everyone will think she's gone mad along with the rest of Brooklyn, buying fish on Thursday when they must eat it Friday as well. Her hip is worse than usual (has to be the aggravation) and a headache pushes oddly, lumpily, up against the top of her head.

Babe doesn't get headaches, and she won't abide this one. A World Series looms, and she hasn't long to campaign for seats. Yankees vs. Dodgers: one team respected by the quick and the intelligent, one team the object of blind, dimwitted infatuation. A subway Series! The first two battles will be in the Bronx, the next three in Brooklyn—if indeed three more are required. Babe wouldn't be a bit surprised if the Yanks swept it in four, which means that she can't afford to wait. She, who has sacrificed everything she holds dear to live in Brooklyn, deserves to be at Yankee Stadium for the opener.

At dinner, when they're finally all crowded in—a rare event, now that Agnes has started college and has abandoned all pretense of keeping regular hours—Babe waits for the proper moment as Mame spills out a report of what's happening on the street: "There are *hundreds* of men down there."

"Down where?"

"Fifth Avenue. They've got a bonfire going. They could burn down the neighborhood!"

In the corner Loretta looks—yet again—as if she might burst into panicked tears.

Agnes says, "They're only burning a Cardinal effigy," and Mickey chimes in, in completely uncharacteristic excitement. "The Dodgers started out down there," he instructs his daughters. "In Washington Park. Did you know that? The Dodgers were *spawned* in this neighborhood."

Nosey Bruscelli's infidelity is one thing, but her son's is quite another. Babe feels the wound as a screw turning in her aching head. "Enough of the *Dodgers*," she says briskly and acidly. "I have to calculate how I'm going to get a bleacher seat for the first game."

Mickey says the obvious: "Hard to come by."

"Opening day, they throw open the gate for the bleachers at 10:00 AM on the dot. If I'm there by three o'clock, I should think, I'll be near the head of the line."

"Three o'clock," Mickey whistles. "We can't put you on the subway in the middle of the night."

Babe sniffs at his ignorance, but not too obnoxiously. She needs him. "No, Mickey, not three o'clock in the morning. They're Series tickets! I'd have to be waiting outside the afternoon before, don't you see."

"Good God, ma."

"Don't be spineless. I'll be part of a crowd, well patrolled I can assure you. It will be perfectly safe."

"But outside the Stadium all night? Where would you sleep? On the sidewalk?"

Mame and RoseMarie titter.

"Very droll, Mickey. I wouldn't sleep at all, don't you know. I'd have to stand all night to secure my place."

"Gee, ma, on those hips? We'd be visiting you in some godforsaken Bronx hospital before the dawn cracked." Never mind that Mickey was born in the godforsaken Bronx. Of course she doesn't mean she'll actually spend the night on the sidewalk—a woman her age, and in her condition, couldn't possibly consider such a thing. She's asking *him* to spend the night on the sidewalk, to buy her the bleacher seats. Do you suppose he'll be the only man in Brooklyn or the Bronx playing hooky from work? It's not the sort of errand you can outright ask your grown son to do, but you'd think he could meet her halfway.

She's not at all ready, though, for the halfway route he proposes. "Tell you what," Mickey says. "I'll see what I can do about seats at Ebbets Field."

Babe counsels herself to remain calm. If Mickey, after all those years, does not understand what it would mean for her to watch a World Series game in Brooklyn, she will just have to explain it to him. "It's out of the question. I cannot sit myself down among the—well, they've named themselves, haven't they? The bums."

"Come on ma, we'll take the trolley."

He means to go with her? She's indulged in solitary baseball for so long that she cannot allow herself even the fantasy of an escort. "Inconceivable," she says. "Who knows what riffraff they let into the bleachers at Ebbets?"

"Aw don't worry, ma, they'll let you in if I buy the tickets."

At this all four girls laugh outright. Babe would like to fling her fury in Aggie's direction, but when she stares her down Agnes gazes back, a half smile still playing on her lips. Aggie's calmed down, the last few weeks.

You'd think she'd be weeping her eyes out, now that both her boyfriends have deserted her, but she's strangely peaceful. When she's at home, that is, which is hardly ever. And not a sign of either of those clowns in Brooklyn, not a doorbell pressed since Aggie rushed in that night, shame tattooed to her cheeks. Coming in the door so late and so secretive, she threw Babe a look, and Babe threw her a look back, and both knew what the other knew. Aggie gave herself to one of them, the handsome, smooth Italian or the short, Jewish pretender—that's all Babe *doesn't* know, the details—and whichever it was must have told the other. Well, now Agnes O'Leary has found out for herself what boys think of you when you give it away for free. (She was not exactly married herself when she and Albert decided to bed, but that was entirely different. She was completely assured of his affections, and he did marry her, did he not? Eventually.)

In these long weeks since that night Babe has wondered, of course, if Agnes could be pregnant, but pregnancy would never account for her sudden calm. Even when Aggie speaks of the war in Europe, that war that used to drive her to distracted tears, she speaks now with resignation. The other night, lecturing them all so self-righteously about what was going on in the ghettos of Poland—starvation, according to Agnes, starvation and worse (Babe stopped her before she could tell the tale any more vividly at the dinner table)—she didn't exactly hector them. She cut her speech short: *It's all in the paper for anybody to see,* knowing full well that not a single member of her family would open the newspaper to verify her account. She's stopped expecting anything of them. Maybe she's stopped expecting anything of herself. Maybe Vito has promised her money, or an apartment, or a fur coat.

Now Babe decides to take a leaf from Aggie's Book of Control. She has a day or two more to persuade Mickey of the right thing to do, and maybe she can even coax Loretta into giving him the hint he requires. She does not intend to miss this World Series. She does not intend to miss her Joe.

But by the very next morning her ticket campaign is stopped dead before it has started. Mickey calls her from the office (the reinstalled telephone receiver she holds yet another luxury returned to their lives) and says he has great good news to give her: Matt McClary has offered them two tickets, to game five. He pauses for dramatic effect. Box seats.

Babe is rendered very nearly speechless. There may not even be a game five. She may miss the World Series entirely, and if by chance the Dodgers manage to eke out a win that buys them a game five, she will have to endure it in *Brooklyn*. Her son's completely thwarted her. He must have known all along what she was asking, and now he knows that she can't possibly beg him to make the trek to Yankee Stadium and then escort her to Ebbets besides. She's trapped. She doesn't even make the effort to think how grand it will be, sitting in box seats—she's been sitting in the bleachers for thirty years and has long since stopped wanting better.

"Where did Matt McClary secure these tickets?" she demands, because a light company man like McClary, a slick smiling mick, could only have come by something so valuable through nefarious means.

"Dunno," Mickey says, tuning out as usual the accusation. "Ours is not to question why."

"I'm questioning why. I'm questioning why, if he has two tickets, he's giving them to you."

"He has four tickets," Mickey says in triumph. "And he wants to go with his old pal to the ballpark."

"I doubt he wants to go with his old pal's mother."

"He wants to go with any dame of my choosing."

"I beg your pardon?"

"Oh, don't take yourself so seriously, ma. The Dodgers are in the World Series."

And with that he hangs up the phone. Extraordinary. He is truly under a spell: the *Dodgers* are in the Series, with no mention of *their* team, their men, the substitute fathers she so painstakingly introduced to him when he was a boy.

That headache pushes again, on the dome of her head, where her fontanel was when she herself was a baby: a babe. The aging Babe pushes back. Sometimes she actually thinks Mickey resents her for coming to take his wife's place, though *he* is the one who asked *her* to give up an apartment so convenient to Yankee Stadium.

They don't take the streetcar after all. Matt McClary drives them to Ebbets Field in his big, black Packard. His date is another boyo from the neighborhood, name of Slippery Quinn. The name fits. He resembles an eel, long and skinny with slicked-back black hair. Babe resists the temptation to tell him so.

As they inch round Grand Army Plaza, Mickey sits on the edge of the backseat, the better to talk to his middle-aged buddies up front. The traffic is stop-and-go—all Brooklyn's headed to Ebbets Field—and it's hot, hot, hot. The thermometer's supposed to hit ninety today, a freak October occurrence befitting this hellish outing. Heat like this is nothing less than a sign from God (Who also had the good sense to rain out game three when the Series moved to Brooklyn). It's pretty clear whom the Almighty favors. The choking air rushes in the back window, threatening her hat, every time they pick up speed.

"Can you believe it?" Mickey says to the front seat. "The bottom of the ninth?"

"Strike three? Three outs in the bag?" McClary twitters.

Babe is, despite herself, fascinated by the way the three men speak to one another. They sound like small boys, stating the obvious to make sure they've got it right, replaying yesterday's game that's been replayed over the sound waves and in the papers ad infinitum, since the Yankees pulled it out of a hat. Brooklyn was leading yesterday, leading all the way into the ninth inning. With two men out, Tommy Henrich swung for strike three, and the Dodgers won the game—only then they decided to throw it away.

Behind home plate, Owen the butterfingered catcher dropped the ball and the clever Henrich ran for first, like the dickens according to eyewitnesses. DiMag, naturally, followed up with heroics: a good, strong hit and then a demon run of the bases on Keller's double. A stylish, impossible slide into home. When they finished their half of the ninth the Yankees were leading seven–four, and the Dodgers didn't have the heart or the guts to take it back. They lost a ball game they'd already won, a ball game that would have tied the Series at two all.

"They say the fans just sat there when it was all over. Glued to their seats. I'da sat there too," Slippery Quinn says.

The other two men make sympathetic clucking noises: they'da sat there with him. Babe should be getting accustomed to Mickey's infidelity, but it shocks her anew, shocks her almost as much as this boyish flirting the three men do with one another.

As if to defend his manliness, Quinn twists himself around to address her. "The boys tell me you're quite the fan, Mrs. O'Leary."

"I am," she replies crisply.

"But maybe not on our side."

"I know which team will win today."

"Care to place a friendly bet?"

This Quinn, this middle-aged chum of her son's, is toying with her as if she's some adorable old lady. Friendly bet indeed.

"Is your own mother living?" she inquires sweetly.

"She is, actually. But she don't care for baseball."

"I'll bet her life on it, then."

"Ma!"

Quinn laughs uproariously. "'S'all right, Mickey. Your ma's a card."

A card indeed. They have no idea what powers she possesses. Quinn finally stops his false hooting. Babe doesn't trust him any more than she trusts Matt McClary, who's brought Quinn to the ballpark because he has no wife to take. She's willing to wager there's no Mrs. Quinn, either. Not likely any of this trio will attract a bride at this stage of the game, not in their lifetimes. Certainly not in hers.

A car ride is a rare treat for her, or should be, but her knees throb and a shooting pain travels down her side, hip to toes. She curls her feet upward to stop the spasm. The ride across Flatbush is as slow as a funeral procession, but it's her companions who will be doing the weeping tonight.

The plan is to drop her off right at Ebbets, to spare her the walk from a parking place. Mickey will get out with her at the Rotunda. The Rotunda. She's managed to keep her lah-dee-dahs to herself. She's aghast to think that her son's even been in Ebbets Field, but from the way the three men talk it's evident he's been there more than once. What a secret to keep from your mother.

They don't even get close to the designated intersection, McKeever and Sullivan, because cops wave them away from every turn they want to take. The line of cars slows, stops dead, inches forward. McClary finally pulls in at the first fireplug with an inch to spare for the Packard.

"Tell you what, Matt," Mickey says. "I'll park the car and you go with my mother. I don't want you missing the first three innings on account of us."

McClary demurs from the front seat, but Mickey—treacherous Mickey—presses the point. "They're your tickets."

"We'd a done better walking over through Prospect Park," Quinn says.

"Perhaps it's not apparent to you that one of us would have had a difficult time, walking through the park." Babe's sour tone evidently seals the deal for McClary, because he hops out of the driver's seat and opens her car door with a flourish and a most unseemly grin. He crooks an elbow for her to grab—as if she would hang onto his flesh.

The Packard pulls away from the curb, speeding more quickly than it's moved through traffic all morning, and she stands there a moment, mouth open and arms akimbo. Then there's nothing to do but trudge along beside Matt McClary, surrounded by dark hordes. Dodger fans are notoriously Jewish, but she wouldn't say she could pick them out. They look normal enough. Suppose they think she's McClary's mother.

McClary, for his part, keeps his distance too. When she stumbles on

 a crack, he smiles back cruelly. "Worried about your Yanks?"

"Not for two seconds."

He smiles again. They never got on, and McClary doesn't darken their door anymore. In the beginning, after Gloria died, he was there every night, dragging Mickey out to some speakeasy to drown his misplaced sorrow. But Babe laid down the law soon enough, and Mickey got sober enough to realize it wasn't entirely safe to have his friend and his mother in the same room. McClary's smiles turned into sneers.

As, it seems to Babe, they're doing right now. McClary gets ahead again, looks back to locate her, smiles that unctuous grin that soon enough turns threatening, ominous even. Well, this is the very same McClary, after all, who gave Agnes the rides home, the same McClary who taught Agnes, in his own darkroom, to develop her pictures. Entirely inappropriate, a middle-aged bachelor and a schoolgirl. She's sorry she ever let Agnes get in a car with the man, much less a basement room, in the first place. She has a terrible thought but puts it in its place. Agnes has too much spit and fire in her. And McClary wouldn't dare walk beside her now if he had so much as laid a finger on Agnes. Of course, he's not exactly walking beside her. He points ahead to Ebbets, and Babe spies the famous striped awning. She's already short of breath and sweating under the navy boater she's worn to honor the Yanks.

McClary leads her through the Rotunda without a word, but it's obvious his goal is to make her gape and gawk. He takes his time, sweeps them round the crowds and the gilded ticket windows. The center chandelier is enormous and gaudy, fashioned to look like a dozen bats balancing a dozen balls of light, but even its glare cannot match the bright day they've just departed. Going from outside to in has sent a spike crashing down through the top of her head. For one second she can't see, but quickly enough she regains her vision. The spike does a U-turn and reascends until only the tip of it pokes through her damp scalp.

She keeps her head down and her mouth shut. McClary, of course, has his head stuck up his royal Brooklyn arse. When she stops in her tracks he throws his palms up to the domed ceiling, as if to say *I don't suppose the Yankees have anything like this.* His attitude is enough to get her past the momentary thrust of pain. No, the Yankees don't have anything like this. They have River Avenue and the smell of hot dogs and good beer and honest strapping men with hair on their chest. She and McClary smile falsely, transparently, at each other, and soon enough they're climbing the ramp to find their seats.

The ramp is so dark that she must slow herself. She's almost surprised when McClary slows too, and again offers his elbow. In the crowd of bums surging forward, Babe almost allows herself to take the proffered arm, but waves him off instead and presses herself against the rail. She feels the walls closing in, a sensation she most certainly never experienced at Yankee Stadium.

"Mrs. O'Leary? You OK?"

The grating sound of his concern infuriates her and she's able to proceed. They've only climbed the lowest of hills. When they reach their gate and she can finally look out onto the field, she stands for a moment to slow her breathing. The view of the infield is astounding. She could reach out and touch her boys. When Joe DiMaggio takes his place in center field she will for once be able to look him in the eye.

"A toy stadium!" she says to McClary, but he pretends not to hear and moves ahead to nab an usher. It *is* a toy stadium, a miniature ball field for miniature men. No wonder they call their shortstop Pee Wee.

McClary holds out a hand to her till she's reached him. At the box, he makes a grand gesture of tipping the usher—what's he give him, all of two bits?—and they take their seats, inside the jaunty, red rail. Very grand. They're surrounded by substantial men in suits, men who must work for the likes of Consolidated Edison, too, only as executives. They give McClary and her the once-over nod and then not a second glance.

She can't help but admit, even with this sensation of dizziness, that it's a splendid view from behind third plate. The seat's far roomier than the bleacher allotment she's accustomed to. Droll, that she's pitying the fans out there all squeezed together when a month ago she was sitting in the bleachers herself. But she doesn't know how she's going to make it through this ball game sitting next to McClary. They don't exchange a word, and not a sign of Mickey, either. She wouldn't be a bit surprised if he missed the entire World Series game. The story of Mickey's life.

Finally, in the third—the Yanks have pulled ahead two–zip—Mickey and the odious Slippery Quinn show up, sweating through their shirt-sleeves, their cheap jackets dragging behind them. They climb in behind McClary and the sun beats down on them all. She would sorely love a sip of beer, but when the men inquire after her health she assures them that she doesn't require a thing. The strange thing about these seats is that the view has diminished over the course of the game, or perhaps that's a haze rising from the diamond. Whatever it is, the infield blurs at the edges. Her Joe is a tall exclamation point out in center field, where he's seen precious little action. McClary passes a flask—oh, for God's sake, how ill-bred—and Quinn, behind them, grabs it up. A spoonful of whisky splashes onto her lap, but before she can properly admonish anyone Tommy Henrich goes back, back, back to strain for the ball Pete Reiser's hit so high. The Dodgers score a run and of course the place goes wild, everyone standing it appears but herself.

The Bums are still alive, which is more than Babe can say for her own abused body. Again she feels the walls closing in, though this time the walls are made of her own son and his two friends, drinking like the working-class men they are while the men in suits pretend they don't smell the diesel aroma of the whisky. One of them is sure to fetch an usher, sure to betray them. They'll be ejected, and she'll lose this chance to see the Yankees crush the Dodgers.

No usher arrives. Quinn and McClary and her Mickey keep up a steady chatter, like monkeys—where else has she heard monkeys recently?

"That Packard handles like a dreamboat," Mickey tells McClary. She could twist his ears for talking through a Series game.

"She's a beaut," Quinn adds. They speak from a script.

"Great day at the ballpark, huh, ma?" Her own son, whom she taught to cherish language!

"Swell." It was supposed to get up to ninety, not a hundred and twenty, which is what it feels like now, and the sun was not supposed to beat down this mercilessly. She tries to calculate how much longer they will have to endure it before they fall under shadow. The men carry on their schoolboy conversation over, around, through her. Nausea joins her dizziness to keep it company, and the fourth inning passes in a blur as shapeless as the field is becoming.

In the fifth, after Rolfe grounds out, some inspiration, some drifting spirit, appears out of the hazy field and summons her to remember her role. She gives herself a good talking to. No matter that it's Ebbets Field, no matter that she could be dying of heatstroke, she's still the one with the powers to rally her fellows and if she doesn't attend to her business here and now this two–one game could slip away from them.

No sooner does she focus on the win than Tommy Henrich slams the first pitch delivered to him over the right field wall. Not much of a distance in this playhouse, but good for a homer. Good for her recollection of what she can accomplish—what she must accomplish—when she puts her mind to it. Mickey and his pals give her gentle congratulatory pats, as if she's the one who homered. Could they possibly have an inkling?

Now Joe's up. Her heart pounds recklessly, a young girl's heart, as if it doesn't remember how much it's pounded already in this season of his streak. She's back in the ball game, swollen with love. Her companions chatter and natter.

"How's Agnes doing with her pictures then?" she hears McClary ask Mickey, but she wills herself to focus only on DiMaggio at the plate.

"You should see the setup her granddad's given her. You'd drool, Mc-Clary."

Babe's throat muscles briefly cease to function. *Her granddad!* From Mickey's lips. The very man who tried to kill him. She coughs to make sure she's still breathing.

"Well, why don't you invite me over to see it sometime?"

"Say the word," Mickey says blithely. "He put it down in the cellar at Calabrese's."

"Creeping Jesus. A darkroom in a funeral parlor?"

"Don't laugh. It's first class all the way."

So Aggie and Vito and Mickey all have secret lives she knows nothing about. So they've been all carrying on together, one big, happy family, and she's not invited, and no one's even had the decency to tell her they left her off the list. Wyatt winds up and she has the strangest sensation: staring at the Dodger pitcher, for just an instant she feels as if she's staring at Gloria's wide long-suffering smile. Silly. Wyatt isn't even smiling. Pitchers never smile.

But worse is yet to come. Wyatt seems to know how intently she's watching him. He winks at her and pulls his mouth in so that now it's Gloria's sweeter, smaller smile he wears: so passive, so pleasant. The smile she saved for after the babies came. She doesn't feel the least bit of guilt for instructing Mickey that he must put her in an institution. He didn't take her advice, in any case—and look what happened.

Wyatt delivers the pitch and Babe watches Gloria's face spin on the fastball hurtling over the foggy infield toward DiMaggio. She turns half-way round to see if Mickey knows she's in trouble—if he has any idea that his wife is haunting her—but his eyes are on the ball game. A flush of terror such as she hasn't known since Albert died. The only cure for it is to follow her son's example, to keep her eyes on the ball field, that field that wavers now below her. She tells herself to snap out of it. She's always had a vivid imagination.

It works. She's back in reality: DiMaggio slams the ball to center field. She sees it fly too high and she sees Reiser make the easy catch. She sees Joe round first at full speed and get almost to second before he registers the out and pulls up short. She even sees her beloved DiMaggio cross the infield to make a remark to Wyatt. But that's not right: that's not her shy Joe. He's no wiseacre, he doesn't taunt the pitcher. Hell's bells, everything is upside down and inside out. Joe DiMaggio never instigates a fight, he's never even *in* a fight. He's a prince, but these bums, these clowns, these Dodgers have set him off, have incensed him the way Gloria Calabrese—Gloria O'Leary, God help us—once incensed Babe.

Down on the field, Wyatt and DiMaggio advance on each other, fists raised, trading insults. All of Ebbets Field joins them, roaring its own insults down on Joe DiMaggio. The language is appalling. You simply do not hear that word at Yankee Stadium. Babe does her best to shout out, but she can't see properly and she can't hear, either.

Below her, the four sides of the diamond push in on each other. The diamond frame becomes an oval, and the crowd's roar stops. DiMaggio and Wyatt battle on in a shrinking cameo outside of which little creatures swarm. Little girls? Monkeys? No, no, the little creatures must be  ballplayers, must be Yankees and Dodgers come to defend their warriors. Babe leans forward as if she could touch them, as if she could use her magical powers to stop them. But the figures jumble together, and then the strangest thing of all happens. Babe O'Leary ceases to care.

The spike presses itself back down into her brain and the field below is nothing but blackness, nothing but heat and night. Maybe the devil's finally claimed her because she allowed herself to be escorted to a World Series game in Brooklyn. It's almost enough to give her a good laugh, but she hasn't the time to laugh about this, not while she's flailing, reaching out for McClary's arm so she can hang onto him instead of pitching forward. Funny she hasn't reached for Mickey. With no game to distract her, she feels time slow in her entire body. She tries to cry out that you can't blame Joe for losing his temper, not after this long season of his streak, of the fans' brutal expectations. You can't blame McClary for bringing a flask to the ballpark. He's only lonely, the old bachelor, and Mickey's only lonely too. But that's not right, they have each other, they have that slippery Quinn fellow, while she herself . . .

She herself has gone deaf in the roaring stadium, deaf and blind, and evidently she's lost all other sensation as well, because she doesn't know if she's standing or sitting or falling head over heels onto the miniature toy diamond at Ebbets Field, Brooklyn, New York, borough of Jews and coloreds, borough of the aged, the infirm, and the lonely, borough of weeping young mothers. Borough of the slippery, the nefarious, the smug, the wicked. Borough of the bewitched and the smitten, borough of Pete Reiser and Pee Wee Reese, borough of the living, the dead, the haunted. Borough of those who wait for war to begin, for the Dodgers to win. Borough of those who float, as Babe O'Leary does now, in some mist that cannot decide whether to settle in one world or the next.

CORPUS

MEUM

They sit crowded together in the back of DeRobertis. Their table, like all the others, is too small to allow for breathing, and their shared plate is piled high with cannoli. It's even Saturday night.

Only one difference between this Saturday night and all the Saturday nights the three of them have sat in this exact spot: Joe's brought Julie, who looks breathtakingly beautiful with her snood of blond curls and her skin lightening to pink in the October air. Her eyes are as dark as Agnes's are light. If he had a sister, she'd look like Julie.

Agnes, following his game plan, sneaks a peak at Julie every now and again. Of course, there's the complication of her grandmother's stroke: Agnes has sneaked away from her hospital vigil to say good-bye, and if she could leave a possibly dying relative for one last word with him, he still holds out hope against hope.

He prods her: "When will they know? I mean, how bad?"

She shrugs, which alarms him. This isn't the Agnes O'Leary he knows, or even the Agnes O'Leary he doesn't know, the one who slept with him—hell, gave herself to him, no questions asked—and then shut him out. The one who returned his letters with a frigging POEM instead of straight talk. Instead of having the decency to just say right out that she doesn't love him. Bernie says she won't go out with him either. A lie? Or an equivocation? Pretty suspicious the way Keller got back in touch, patched it up between them just in time to arrange for this good-bye party: he showed up at the Worker House, carrying his City College books. Rubbing it in. Now Bernie's pressing his thigh into Agnes's, rubbing it in all the harder.

"Gee, I'm not leaving till four o'clock on Monday. I ought to get over to that hospital to say good-bye. She was kind to me."

"No Joe, it's O.K." Agnes knows precisely how kind her grandmother was. He hates himself.

"It's not even clear she knows anybody's in the room." So Bernie's been to the hospital room in Brooklyn and wants him to know it.

When Julie clears her throat, he squeezes her hand beneath the table. He knows what he's doing—he's trying to provoke Agnes into saying something, anything. What he wrote to her was this: *We've shared the most sacred*—aw, he can't bear to think what he wrote. Is that it? He's corny? Isn't that what a girl wants after she gives you her virginity? A little lovemaking, a little serious romance? Is she punishing him with a poem because she figured out he had some experience? He told her they didn't have to do it again. God almighty, he told her he wanted to marry her. And she told him nothing. Nothing but *If thou wilt leave me* written out in crisp handwriting that didn't even waver. Talk about corny. Talk about cheeseball. Talk about cold. He squeezes Julie's hand all the harder while he gazes on Agnes's face and pictures her naked body stretched out on his bed that afternoon: she's sturdy, small breasted. Her shoulders and her hips are broader than he imagined, her thighs stockier. She'll grow fat like Babe, probably.

"My goodness," is what Julie's saying to Agnes. "How will your family pay for all that time in the hospital?"

Wonder of wonders, she's made Agnes giggle. "My grandfather said she could stay on a hospital bed in his funeral parlor."

Bernie, in the new and obnoxious Brooklyn accent he's been playing with all night, says, "Den where would dose corpses go?"

Agnes descends into sputters that begin to sound unhinged. "He'd have to move her"—pause for more hysteria—"he'd have to move her into his office. Whenever a stiff needed the parlor."

Julie says, "This must be so hard for you."

Agnes regards her with a puzzled look. "Well, it might do her some good. Being speechless for a while, I mean."

That last has no doubt horrified Julie, but then she's never met Babe. "She can't speak at all?"

"She's trying her damnedest." That's new—Agnes must have picked up *damnedest* in college. Or from a new boyfriend? "She moves her left eye back and forth. The right one won't open. The last few days, she's making some kind of sound. A chatter, like a bird or a monkey, almost."

"Then maybe she *will* recover?"

"They still don't know, the doctors. But I do. She can't wait to get out of that bed and whack one of us, probably me. With a nice hard spoon."

Julie says, "You must have quite a grandmother," and Joe's wildly, extravagantly ashamed that he brought her. She sounds so . . . sweet. So . . . innocent. So dumb. She still has one more year of Cathedral High to go, so his kisses haven't gone past her mouth. Julie would be horrified if he went further and he might be horrified too. Dorothy would banish them both from the House if she knew even kisses were involved.

What happened with Agnes wasn't even in the same ballpark. What happened with Agnes was body merging with body, spirit with spirit, the so-called mortal sin which he can only regard as what was bound to be. He still hasn't confessed it, doesn't intend to confess it. No, he's been to communion every morning since. What he did with Agnes was sacred, a sacrament in and of itself. He's not ashamed of it.

Even now Agnes reads his mind, and sounds almost sweet herself when she teases him: "What will you eat on your bus trip, Joe?"

She's signaling him, sure as Babe's been signaling with one darting eye. "You'll box me cannolis, Agnes, cannolis for the journey."

Julie says, "Cannolis! You'll be sick as a dog if you eat pastries on the bus, Joe. The fumes!"

"Nah, it's just an old joke between us. From when Agnes worked the counter."

"Well," Julie says, "you don't have to worry about the food. You know what Dorothy always says: *Ask and ye shall receive. Lilies of the field.*"

"*Toil not!*" Bernie adds. A joke, and a poor one.

"Hey, I'll be toiling."

"Sure you will. Toiling away with all those señoritas."

Julie's indignant on his behalf. "Joe has his work cut out for him. He's got to make contact with those Quakers in Mexico City and then . . ."

And then he's got to escort the couple they've located for him, with their three little girls—it would have to be *three,* one still a toddler. They're Austrians who got out via Portugal: they waited three years for passage. The man talked their way into Mexico but now Mexico doesn't want them and they'd rather be illegal in America than illegal south of the border: they don't speak Spanish. And neither does Joe, and he doesn't speak German either, so it should be some fun locating a smuggler to get these people he can't communicate with into Texas. Maybe they'll have a little high school French, the way he does? They sure won't know Latin. The Quaker fellow he's corresponding with writes, in perfect English, of the grave responsibility: he's leading these people into a journey they never would have contemplat-

ed on their own, they never would have undertaken if Joe D'Ambrosio hadn't suggested it, via handwritten letters from Mott Street, New York, from a community of dreamers. The Friend writes as if Joe's their persecutor, not the Nazis, as if Joe doesn't spend every night waking on the half hour to imagine what it will be like in a Mexican jail, the cries of the little girls uncannily like the cries of his little brothers when they get a good hard smack from Pop.

He's completely lost the thread of the conversation. Bernie, for some reason, is talking about Moscow.

"Has it fallen?" He hasn't read the news in days.

"It doesn't look, uhm, hopeful."

Agnes says, "Moscow won't fall. They're on fire, the Russians."

"Since when did you get to be an optimist?" Bernie says.

"I've been reading Babe the papers. Funny. She never wanted to hear the news unless it was baseball."

Julie says, "Oh dear."

Agnes sneaks a peak at him, Joe, and he catches her. Something so strange about her coloring, flushed and pale at the same time. And the way she drifts away from the conversation, then flashes back. Here she goes: "All Moscow needs is a miracle. A little hocus-pocus."

"Hocus-pocus," Bernie says. "You know where that comes from? It's corrupted, from the Latin: *Hoc est corpus meum*."

But Joe says, more sharply than he's ever said anything to Agnes, "I thought you didn't believe in miracles."

She gives him that strange look, that look that's supposed to tell him something. Her face is stripped of a smile but suffused with something new, a softening of her pale mouth, a somber tenderness that isn't like Agnes at all. "I don't believe in the magic kind of miracle."

"I thought it was the religious kind you didn't believe in."

"Same thing," she says, but not unkindly. "I believe in whatever Babe's got. And maybe those people in Moscow too."

"Oh, you Brooklynites," Bernie says. He's in rare form tonight. "Sentimentalists, each and every one of you."

They all fall silent. It's not just Brooklyn that's sentimental and Bernie knows it. It's the three of them saying their good-byes. Might not ever see each other again, he thinks tragically, and envisions again that jail cell, presided over by a hairy, mustachioed Mexican jailer. He sees Bernie in Army green, splayed on the battlefield. Oh hell. That's just Bernie on the sidewalk on West End Avenue, after he decked him. Which he wouldn't mind doing again tonight. *Oh you Brooklynites.*

"How you like Marymount, Agnes?" he says finally, maybe to point out that Bernie's not the only one who's figured out how to get to college.

She almost whispers it: "I'm not going."

Bernie grabs her wrist, resting on the table. "What do you mean you're not going?"

Her volume comes up a notch. "I mean I'm not going. I'm taking pictures." She shakes her wrist loose. "And reading. I'm reading."

"Agnes!" Bernie's an old man, lecturing her. "Why didn't you tell one of us?"

She smiles unexpectedly, mysteriously. "We haven't exactly been palling around, the three of us. Not lately."

Bernie groans, loudly, and Joe feels like groaning too. If Agnes decided not to go to college, everything he thinks he knows about her is wrong. Taking pictures? With a Brownie? He can hear his own old man's response to *that* as a plan for the rest of her life. Hell, she could come with him to Mexico and take all the snapshots she pleased.

"What about next semester?" Now Bernie sounds almost panicked. "Did they hold your scholarship for you?"

Agnes doesn't even turn to face him and Joe knows she's given the scholarship away, turned it down, her once-in-a-lifetime shot at having her education paid for. So she can take pictures? It makes no sense.

"What about you, Bernie?" she says, and now she doesn't sound gentle at all. "Will you be taking classes next semester?"

They all shut down at that bit of cruelty. It's coming closer and closer, the war. That's why they're here tonight, that's why the friends who don't even speak to him anymore have come to wish him bon voyage. How would you say that in Spanish?

They finish their coffee in silence—even Julie knows not to chatter—and make their way outside for the false and confused good-bye hugs on the avenue. It would have been better if Bernie'd just left well enough alone instead of setting up this torture. And why did he have to pick DeRobertis? Rubbing that in too, meeting him around the corner from the family he's not allowed to see? He has to keep an eye out for them when all he wants to do is keep Agnes in his sights. *What will you eat on the bus?* Maybe she was saying that one day she'd join him.

The way she goes to hug him good-bye, though, tells him just the opposite. This time she holds her body back even more stiffly, so that her breasts won't even graze him, and she's out of his arms before he's had the time to so much as squeeze her shoulders. She gazes down at the sidewalk, her misery granting him one last burst of hope.

"I really admire what you're doing, Joe."

He should float away at that, he should ascend to heaven at the news that Agnes approves of his crazy mission, but instead he hears the line for what it is: it's what her head told her to say, not her heart, not her gut. She admires what he's doing. What is she, a goddamn war resisters' critic? He puts his arm around Julie's shoulder, squeezes tight, watches Agnes flinch. Not another word. They've said their good-byes and this time the good-bye's forever. Good-bye, Agnes O'Leary. Good-bye, bitch.

When they're far enough away to be out of hearing range, his own ears pounding with blood, he tells Julie he's afraid that Agnes is turning as hard as her grandmother.

Julie says, "Poor old lady. Imagine, lying in that hospital bed, trying to communicate."

He feels as if he could retch cannolis. The car fumes come at him in a wave. Agnes didn't even ask if she could take a picture of him, to remember him by when he's in prison.

And there's still one more tortuous good-bye to go. His mother's finally willing to defy his father, finally willing to meet him on the sly. She's terrified about Mexico. And not terrified, at the same time. She was a small child when her own family made the journey over. She knows that sometimes you can't stay put, you have to move on. And she's always been on Joe's side, or at least mostly on his side. When he needed his birth certificate for the passport—he had visions of slipping back and forth across borders and borders and borders, Guatemala and Honduras and who knows, on past the Panama Canal, down to South America where the most refugees are—she sent it to him at the Worker House, with a note: "I pray for you." There was more, more about peace with his father, more about a father being the head of the family, but only that one line, *I pray for you,* stuck, the futility of it suggesting the futility of his own prayers for the refugees.

They meet in the one place Joe can think of where there's not a chance his father will have spies: on the steps of the library at Forty-Second Street, between the lions. He's sitting on the top step as she approaches, and from the confused way she looks around he can tell that she's never climbed these steps before. How about that, practically your whole life in this city, thirty-nine years, and you've never been north of Fourteenth Street before this secret assignation with your own son. A stab of hurt, or anger, or dismay. It's almost funny. It would make Agnes giggle.

His mother still looks good, though, still looks young. Old-fashioned, but with a face like that—big eyes, good sharp cheekbones, ash-blond hair against golden skin—she can get away with it. She's slender, and she's got a figure, and if her dress is longer than the other dresses, if her jacket's a little frayed at the wrists, if her hat's a dark straw hat that would be better worn in the springtime (for some reason he pictures Agnes's grandmother wearing this hat), she's still a beautiful woman and he's proud of her even as he's ashamed of her. No wonder she never wanted to walk along Fifth Avenue. She was always needed at home, always waiting, always waiting for the boys to get out of school, for Uncle Fran to come home from his prowling, anxious in his guilt to boss her around. She made a big joke of it: servant to a household full of men. She *liked* it. He's pretty sure she liked it.

They hug each other so long and so hard that you'd think they were lovers. She's weeping, too, something he hasn't prepared himself for: his mother's not a weeper. She can't afford to be, not around his pop.

"Oh Joey, how can it be. All this time missing you and now you go away?"

Well, why didn't you come see me, Ma? He doesn't say it, doesn't point out that the only reason he's been banned from his own childhood home, the only reason he's not allowed to say good-bye to the brothers who are probably already forgetting what he looks like, already forgetting what he used to do in bed at night, under the crucifix, is because of his mother's blind obedience to a good man who is nonetheless a tyrant. Aw, maybe he's not a good man at all. What does it matter. The point is, the point is, the point is. The point is he has to do this, he has to go. Has to do *something* for the refugees. Señor Quaker in Mexico City is absolutely right, it can't be half-baked and it can't be half-assed, but whatever it is it has to start somewhere and it starts here, with him. Starts now, weeping mother and all.

This is like having a conversation with Agnes. There they sit, joined in misery, mother and son, holding hands on the top step of the New York Public Library, not even seeing below them the hordes of Monday morning people streaming past, hurrying on in their oblivion while a war rages across Europe, Africa, Asia. The papers are full of Japan now. He doesn't read the papers anymore. He only sees the headlines as they float past him on city streets, only hears a radio when a shopkeeper broadcasts it onto the street. What good could more information do him now? Who needs the details when it comes to slaughter?

"Joey, maybe you could get in big trouble doing this?"

She wants him to deny it. He can't think how to put it in a way that will ease her mind.

"Tell me again, what it is you're supposed to be doing."

He hasn't said anything about sneaking back across the border or escorting a family or his nightmares about a Mexican jail. And he won't tell her now, won't tell her that he can't back out now, not with his wallet stuffed with cash and the address of American Express in Mexico City. He won't even tell her that Dorothy's come through for him, Dorothy and all the other Workers who've been handing over every nickel and dime and praying up a storm for the success of this pilgrimage. He can't have his mother envisioning that journey across the desert that Dorothy's so excited about. He sees whitened bones, parched lips. He hears the evil chortle of movie Mexicans and so would his mother. He won't have her waking in the middle of the night to the same nightmares he's been having.

He repeats what he's already told her: "The Catholic Workers are sending me down to Mexico City, to meet with some Quakers."

"But Joey, if the war comes like everybody says, can't you get in trouble being down there when they need you up here?"

"Ma, that's what I've been trying to get you to understand. I'm not going to war, I'm not going to . . ."

What's the point. She can't even begin to understand what he's talking about, she'll only bring up his pop again, his pop's horror that a son of his would not put on the uniform of the country that has saved them, rescued them, from poverty. His cousin Dom's already let the NYPD know that he will have to go if war's declared, that he'll join the rest of the D'Ambrosio clan who have a pact that they'll all show up at the recruiting station together, fifteen males below the age of thirty, five of them married. They'll volunteer together to go fight the very country where some of them were born. He can't begin to explain to his mother what he believes in the face of the D'Ambrosio wall of unwavering belief.

She doesn't press it. Maybe she can imagine it. Maybe he doesn't do her justice. Maybe she'd rather have him in jail than blown up on a battlefield. Wouldn't that be a maternal response? For one brief shining moment he wishes he could rest his head on her lap, that they could form a pietà right there on the library steps.

"Father Salvati says—"

"Aw, Ma."

"Joey. I have to. I have to tell you at least what he says."

"What does he say."

"He says this woman, this Dorothy, she's not right in the head. He says she doesn't obey the Church, doesn't respect it. He says it's not right for you to live there. He told me, Joey, he said I should go down there and help you pack your clothes to come back home. If you hadn't called . . ."

"Ma, you never listened to Father Salvati in your life. He's been picking on Petey and Pauly since they started school. Why you listening to him now?"

She begins to weep again.

"Listen, Ma, he's got it all wrong. Dorothy's obedient, Jesus God Ma, if there's one thing she is it's obedient. Father Salvati's full of crap."

She moans. "He got you into that Jesuit school," and he sees how this could go on, the two of them talking past each other all morning long. He pulls her to him, squeezes her tight as he knows how. She's too thin, too frail, her frame so much smaller than Agnes's that he feels he's holding a child. And he feels her calming, knows he's soothed her, knows that now she's the one who wishes she could rest her head in his lap, that if they are to be a pietà, it's a pietà in reverse, a perversion. Her tears let up. She doesn't try to say anything. This, he supposes, is what he thought Agnes might do last night: yield to him, signal with the least give of her body that she loves him. So this is comical too, that it's his mother he's snuggling on the way out of town. He loosens his hold, settles her upright, rises. "I guess I better go get my kit together. Bus leaves at four."

"I'll pray for you, Joey. Oh."

"Maybe you'd like to window-shop a little, Ma, as long as you're up here? I could take you by some nice stores, Lord & Taylor, B. Altman, they're all right here."

She shakes her head in her stubborn way and brushes off her jacket, though there's not so much as a stray bit of lint. She's not going any place where she'd have to be ashamed of herself.

"I'll walk you to the train then," he says, and she nods at that. He'll walk her to the subway, and then there will be his own bus to catch.

Dorothy's not always home in the middle of the day, but she's told him she'll make a point of being there today. He passes through the front house, down the long, narrow corridor, borrowed duffel bag in hand, and knocks on the front office door to ask her for her benediction. She's barricaded in there behind stacks of her beloved papers, but the desktop where she's writing out her column with a chewed-down pencil is bare but for the paper. No tears from Dorothy at the sight of him: sometimes he thinks she's past ordinary emotion. It's hard to imagine she ever cried, even as a baby.

"In a pinch, if someone hints at a bribe, we could wire you—"

"I know, I know. Go to American Express. But I won't."

"If you have to—"

"I know," he says. "I know."

He thrusts his hand out across the desk for the good-bye shake and she takes him by surprise. She rises, tugs her sweater down, comes around to the front of the desk just as slowly as if this were a ballet. When she reaches him he thrusts the hand out again, but she wraps her arms around him instead. What beautiful irony, that two middle-aged women touch him this way when Agnes . . . He hugs Dorothy back, with more power than he thought he had to give her, and is shocked at the spongy feel of her breasts against his chest. He pulls away.

From her pocket she extracts a slip of paper with names. "Every priest and Sister I could locate in Mexico City," she says. "It's not much. They've had their own troubles, God knows."

The no-nonsense dark-eyed gaze Dorothy bestows on him doesn't betray any of the terror that Agnes or Julie or his mother have betrayed these last few days. Dorothy looks at him as if she knows that he'll pull it off. She smiles a firm and businesslike smile. You put one foot in front of the other, her unblinking eyes say. You get on the bus. She tugs at a strand of gray escaping her bun: not like her, to have a loose bit of hair. She pulls her apron string tighter.

"All right," she says. "Off with you. *Vaya con Díos.*"

Of course: *bon voyage* in Spanish. He nods, because for the first time saying good-bye he finds he cannot speak. Well, it's a foreign language. You don't have to say a word, saying good-bye. You just put one foot in front of the other. You just get on the bus.

Outside the fall light is gray, depressed. A good day to leave New York. A good day to head to Charleston, South Carolina, first stop, where Dorothy's arranged for a nun to meet him at the station and feed him tonight. Dorothy swears there are Catholics in Carolina, Italians even, but he doesn't believe it. He sees that book of pictures Agnes carted around for weeks, as if it were a prayer book, those grim visions of the South.

One foot in front of the other. He walks up Mott Street, the duffel lighter than the gym bags he used to carry, and must resist the urge to run—first time in weeks he's thought of trotting. But he has a way to go, north to Thirty-Fourth Street, to the Greyhound Station. It won't do to arrive for his bus journey sweating. Won't do to have a seatmate repelled by his smell, and then there's that poor nun who has to see to him when he arrives.

Charleston, South Carolina, and then Georgia, Alabama, Mississippi, Louisiana, Texas. He won't let himself imagine anything past that first stop. Hell, he won't allow himself anything but this moment in this city, maybe the last time he'll see New York for years. He swallows city air and tastes (not for the first time) bread, cheese, wine, blood. In front of him the butcher's boy descends to the bowels of the shop. Children liberated from school push each other in little gangs and tumble at his feet. He turns left on Kenmare, passes the old Cathedral, crosses himself, feels his body lightening. His body's whipping up more adrenaline than he ever brought to any track meet. He should have stopped by Xavier to say good-bye to Father Phelan. And he should have stopped by the stand, too, should have said good-bye to his father, whether his father offered his hand or made a fist or turned his back to him. He's not a good son, he's a lousy son, and there's no time now to make amends.

Is there? Checking the pocket watch Joe Zarella dug up for him, he nearly runs into a baby carriage. Zarella probably lifted it from a corpse. No, there's no time left to say good-bye to his father. He fights the terrible sensation that he's about to leak boyish tears, but then he sees Agnes naked, stretched out on his sheets: those little breasts, those nipples pale as putty. The sturdy efficiency of her body. Funny that Agnes is always reciting poetry when really, when you think about it, she's all prose, body and soul. First time he saw her in the Xavier gym she was standing apart from the other Dominican girls, looking lost. She wasn't wearing her glasses and he thought she was a little dizzy and a little ditsy too, the way she peered and then stared off. He was the one who asked her if she was looking for somebody—Bernie had nothing to do with it, only horned in as soon as Agnes giggled and blushed and ran her hand back through black hair curled off a high pink forehead. Later, when it was time to see what punch she was drinking, when she put the glasses on, she was all business: sharper, prettier even. Oh come on, it wasn't Agnes's looks that ever sucked him in. It was the idea that she knew something about him, knew what he was trying to say. When Agnes listened, you knew she had turned off every other sound in the city—the honking taxis and the rattling trolleys and the subway rumble—and she was only listening to you, listening so hard she went past the words and down into the confusion that made you say the words in the first place, so you could make some sense of yourself. What the hell is she thinking of, quitting school to take pictures?

Agnes pulls him up Sixth Avenue, where he removes his jacket and flings it over his shoulder. At least this time she's memory, not fantasy.

Was he too rough with her? Too tender? He retraces her body, runs his hand down her round, still belly, knows he's driving himself nuts, not to mention making himself hard. He stares in the passing coffee shop windows, as if another Agnes will appear there to save him. She wanted it too. But she was paralyzed that afternoon, still as death, submitting to him as if it was all his choice and not the two of them who decided, falling back onto the sheets.

For some reason he remembers standing next to that colored man in Times Square, back when DiMag was still chasing the record. Lost in their sad handshake, the man's dry, rugged palm pressing into his own, he passes Fourteenth Street without even realizing it. Now the street sign says 17TH STREET, and seventeen blocks to go till the Greyhound station comes into sight, till the big buses blowing their noxious fumes swallow him up. His throat's tight, his eyes—aw say it isn't so—his eyes are watering after all. He makes himself smell Sixth Avenue now: taxi exhaust, knishes, the rank smell of too many people too close together. He makes himself gaze on the buildings rising up like prayers to heaven, finds his pace. You put one foot in front of the other. You put one foot in front of the other, and then you get on the bus.

PART V
FALL, 1941

DEADPAN

SMILES

"Joe. Joe. Joe. Joe."

It's been like this half the night, her breathless chant, but the doctor said don't call back till the contractions are—he's forgotten how many minutes, but Dorothy knows. Dottie stares down the clock by the bed as if she can will it into cooperation.

He rises from the living room couch where he's spent half the night trying to catch a catnap. Forget it. Every time he drifts into sleep, into the edges of some strange dream, she calls again. He begged her to let him bring his mother out to New York, his mother who's been through this nine times herself and who knows how many times with the daughters and the sons' wives and the cousins and the nieces. He's begged her tonight to let him call June Gomez to come sit by the bed. This isn't right, a family shrunk down to two, one of them utterly lost. He doesn't have a clue what he's supposed to be doing for her, but still she calls: like clockwork, like contractions.

He pads down the endless hall and, one more time, pokes his head into the bedroom without pulling his body behind. "Getting to be time?"

"Almost."

"Hurt?"

"Like hell." She gets a bare-lipped smile going, but even from the doorway he can see that her eyes are swimming. She looks queer, pale enough to scare him, but then he's hardly ever seen her without her lipstick, even going to bed at night when she takes off the top layer but always leaves gaudy color behind. Her showgirl makeup stains the pillowcases so that she buys them by the dozen, the easier to throw them away. Maybe it's  good his mother's not here, to see how many silk pillowcases are stacked in the linen closet, to see his enormous pregnant wife's skimpy negligees.

"Maybe you could get up? Walk around a little?" That's what he'd do if he was in a fix like this: walk the city streets, walk through Central Park, look in the silly windows on Madison Avenue. He'd walk for hours, the way he used to walk during the streak, till the baby was ready to drop.

"The doctor said just lie quiet."

Her teary gaze is a plea but what can he do for her? A washcloth to hold against her forehead? That's no good, that's for a fever. "How's about I call June?" Has to be the tenth time he's suggested it.

"June's never had a baby!" she cries out. "She won't know any better than I do."

"She might know better than *I* do."

"Couldn't you just sit here Joe, for a minute? Hold my hand?"

She says it so simply that he obeys for once, goes to sit on his empty side of the bed to keep her company.

"No honey, this side."

Again he obeys, over to her side where there's hardly enough room for a woman, much less a man, to squeeze in. He makes himself smile down at her and squeezes her hand and feels her forehead for a fever after all.

Dorothy closes her eyes and her tears run silently down onto the expensive stained pillowcase. Not a man living on Planet Earth who knows what to do at a time like this. How long will she want him to sit here? He's got his back twisted up funny. She looks like she's drifting off to sleep—if she does, maybe he could just slip his hand away and rise ever so slowly to sneak off and call June.

A shadow crosses her face and he shivers: *Dear God, don't let this child be choked by the cord.* The words come back unbidden—must have heard them in North Beach from his mother's lips. God would have listened to childbirth prayers from Rosalie DiMaggio, but maybe not Joe D, ballplayer and philanderer. *Blessed Mary, ever Virgin. If you could please put in a word for me.* He hasn't been to Mass since his own wedding.

Dottie lies silent. Last night when she first woke him, he started up from the pillow, but it was only a dream: he was down by Fisherman's Wharf, and a screeching bird turned into a big looming plane flying lower and lower to buzz him. He knows what that was all about. Lefty's been trotting out an old story lately, how in the '37 Series he stopped the game to watch a big plane float over the Polo Grounds. That's all it was.

Maybe he's sandy eyed and helpless at the crack of dawn, but at least he's not crazy the way he was before the streak. That was more pressure than any man should bear, but this will end the way it's supposed to, with a baby on the other end: a boy, if he's not mistaken. A clean, normal, regular, everyday thing, the opposite of the Streak, and that will make him, for a change, the opposite of a Freak or a Hero. Just a regular guy, with a kid to call him Pop.

He wants to ring up Lefty but Dottie says no, she's not about to ride to the hospital with that maniac, so he gets her down on the elevator and the doorman fetches them a cab in no time.

Dorothy says, "Thanks, Sol," clear as day. She *would* know the doorman's name. He won't forget it now, the fellow who got them a cab the morning his son was born. His heart flutters like the flags above the Stadium and he lets out a little laugh, settling into the backseat.

"What's so funny?" At least she can still talk, between gasps. She looks swell, now that the doc's given them the green light. Between pains she painted her face and crimped her hair and now, from the neck up, she looks like the showgirl she was born to be.

"I farted." That's another thing he'll remember, the great Joe DiMaggio, scrambling for a tip, farting, while the poor doorman—Sol—hovered.

"Jumping Jehoshaphat." Dorothy gasps with the pain and giggles at the same time, moans so hard that the best thing that could possibly happen happens. This beautiful woman who dolled herself up for him in the middle of labor farts too. And claps her hand over her mouth and bites a finger, it's so funny. From her huge belly an echo sounds: the baby inside, maybe even farting along. Before she even dabs at the scarlet-stained finger she snuggles up into him like this was meant to be, husband and wife and baby makes three, the Farting DiMaggios. She moans all the harder.

He sees that the driver's watching them in the rearview and ducks his head down farther. Leave us in peace, huh, bub? She's having a baby, and anyway it was a classy little toot. A woman's entitled, in the throes of childbirth, to her privacy.

When the nurse finally comes out to tell him the scoop, she flirts with him, flutters her hand back through carrot curls all the way to her cap, thrusts her chest out. Plain as paste, but cute all the same. "She's doing just fine, but it's a breech birth, Mr. DiMaggio, so it might take a while."

"Breech!"

"Feet first," she tells him in a confidential whisper, "but don't you worry. We handle plenty of those around here." He pictures Rizzuto sliding into home, feet higher than his head for the tag out, hears his mother's whisper: *Poor picciriddu stuck in there hour after hour. Time the doctor got there, nothing he could do to save either one.* If Lefty were here, he'd say forget it, Rosalie was telling a story from the old country, and this is New York, this is 1941—but Lefty's not here and he's light-headed from hunger and worry and a sleepless night.

He tries to sit still, but he's a cartoon papa who jumps up to pace. The waiting room's almost empty this hour of the morning: only two other fathers to be, lawyers or bankers from the looks of them, ties flapping and shirtsleeves rolled up identically, like they're wearing a uniform. They gape like visitors to the zoo: the great Joe D, in the very same father's waiting room. He bolts for the elevator to take that walk he wanted Dottie to take. You have to do *something.*

He never walks out alone anymore, he always has the company of Lefty or Toots or the Scooter, and in the elevator he needs them more than ever. A pair of knuckleheads, a father and son with an empty wheelchair between them, stare at his back till the younger one blurts out, "Say, will you give us an autograph, Joe?"

Joe. Like they grew up on the same street. Kid can't be more than eighteen, but DiMaggio handles it the way he always handles it away from the ballpark, when it's a man and not a boy groveling. He doesn't even see them, doesn't hear what they're asking. Before the elevator's touched down on the ground floor he feels their fury zapping into his back.

The doors open and they follow close behind. "Prince Charming," the kid says, and the father's worse: "What would it cost him?"

When he was a younger man, a single man, he might have wheeled on them. He's never been a fighter—doesn't need to be, muscled as he is—but he's never backed down and he deserves as much respect as the next fellow waiting for his wife to give birth. He doesn't want to give these wiseacres a pass anymore than he wanted to give Wyatt a pass in that last game of the Series, when the asshole thought Joe D, now that the streak was over, was fair game for insults and insinuations.

But this is the morning of his son's birth, and he's trying to set things right with the Blessed Virgin so his prayers will go through on the right track, and he doesn't have time to tootle around with a couple of clowns. He pictures that other kid, the crazy one who stood on West End Avenue with a bloody nose yelling about refugees.

But that was different. At least that kid was willing to take a chance and not for some crappy autograph. Before Sol came and chased him away, DiMaggio was inclined to march right up to him, stare him down eye to eye, say:

"What the fuck do you want me to do?"

Because what he wanted to do was tell somebody, in person, man-to-man, head-to-head, that he was sick and tired of being everybody's goddamned hero. The president of the U.S. of A. can't do anything for the refugees but Joe DiMaggio's supposed to?

He even stepped into the street, as if he was going to jaywalk right up to the kid, who was yelling like he was saying a goddamn prayer—*You could save them, Joe DiMaggio. You could*—the boy's nose swelling and oozing like he'd been hurling himself against a brick wall over and over and over. Something about him so single-minded, so *what the fuck if the whole world is watching,* that made DiMaggio want to take him by the scruff of his neck, look at him extra close, see how this boy could possibly know about Joe DiMaggio's nightmares. But then Sol rushed out and ran into traffic, after the kid, and a crowd gathered. DiMaggio does not stick around for crowds.

He circles through the revolving door, back out into the bright day, and the terror washes over him anew. What if the baby gets stuck, foot or head or culu, what if they have to cut Dottie open to get him out of there? What if he chokes in the meantime? *Blessed Mary, ever Virgin.* He can't finish the prayer.

He strides along, chin up, face staring straight ahead, looking neither to left or right as office workers crane their necks back to see if that's who they thought it was. After half a block he knows that the baby will be all right, that he'll make it out with no trouble. Joe Jr. He knows it whole, the way he knew things all through the streak. They'll have to use the forceps and Dorothy, at the sight of him, will think he's maimed for life, but he'll be fine, just marked up with two bright welts for his first couple of days. He knows the rest whole too, knows that most of this kid's life won't be so easy either, not for father, not for son.

He walks harder, close to a trot now, pushes east toward the river and light that's brighter still, feels the acid drip. Stress, Doc Painter would say. *Don't let the stress get to you,* the way upstairs some doctor is telling his wife not to let the pains of childbirth get to her.

Which is why he's taking a walk in the first place, why he's pounding out all his hopes and fears for that poor kid, still waiting to be hatched upstairs while his father runs away from the whole birthing show. Where does he think he's going, anyhow?

He turns back for the hospital, back to wait for the plain, cute, red-headed nurse and the gorgeous, blond, suffering wife, back for news of Joe Jr., born into a country that's gearing up for war.

Running away must have made the baby come fast down the chute. One of the lawyer or banker fathers tells him the nurse was out to fetch him, and before too long they've got the little monkey cleaned up and they let him take a peek, behind glass. Face like a red onion, scrunched and bewildered, an outer space creature. The nurse tells him the big welts are from the forceps—they'll fade away—but he recognizes his premonition and feels his back, that old demon, clench again. Can he see Dottie now? No, she's sleeping off the gas.

He stares in again at this wrinkled little being they tell him is the flesh of his flesh. The way the little fella's curled into himself makes his father float above the universe, but there's nobody in this hospital who could possibly fathom how utterly alone he is now, in the hour of his son's birth. His wife needs a little time, the nurse drones on. She wouldn't want him to see her as confused as she'll be when she wakes up.

So he walks west, then south to Fifty-First, down to Toots Shor's place. Or maybe it would be more accurate to say he flies, cruising above the city streets, buzzing through construction sites, smiling on every man, woman, and child he passes. He signs a thousand autographs but it doesn't slow him down. Fifty-first turns from a street into a broad avenue cleared for his welcome-home parade. Women are so surprised to see him they wave their delicate hands, gloved now in autumnal fawn, as they pass.

He doesn't remember flying through the door of Shor's, but he must have, the way the crowd stares, expectant. He scans the joint as usual for sight of Toots, makes his way twice around the circular bar, a couple of reporters scribbling no doubt the remarkable observation that today Joe DiMaggio, news flash, smiles. Finally he spies Toots schmoozing and their eyes meet. They both wend their ways through the late-lunch crowd to his table up front, awaiting him as usual. It's worth the look of shock on Tootsie's face when he bursts out with it before he sits himself down:

"Joseph Paul DiMaggio Junior."

Toots claps him on the back and then squeezes tight—the fat man's always touching him, but not like this, not down past muscle into some soft spot with his thick, knowing, fatherly fingers. Finally they break apart and he sees the whole restaurant looking up at him with the same shock and delight: could this possibly be their Joe D, who always sits so defensively, surrounded by a floating and ever-shifting array of bodyguards waiting to beat off dumb out-of-towners who don't know any better than to approach? He sits, but when they all burst into giddy applause he jumps up again and reaches for the wooden box he picked up on Sixth Avenue, the biggest, brownest Cuban cigars anybody in Shor's ever got a load of. He remembers the proprietor's hands shaking in the presence of star dazzle, but he doesn't remember buying the cigars.

Toots leans over the table: "I'll call the front office, let 'em know to put out a press release."

He starts to say *Yeah, sure, I didn't think of that,* but his mouth clams up at the sight of his old friend, his old protector—the Pretty Jew, Toots calls himself, but one thing's for sure: Toots ain't pretty. And Toots is plenty worried about the refugees but never once has he asked Joe DiMaggio to save them. Never once has Toots acted like he's anything but an ordinary mortal. He finds himself throwing his arms around Tootsie's fat neck to choke out:

"We farted, all three of us."

And the room behind Toots fades gradually to black. No one in this crowd, not the strangers, not the writers, not the show people, not the tourists, not even Toots, could possibly understand. Even his own family, babies crawling every which way for generations to come, couldn't understand how this one child changes everything utterly. He says a prayer—bypasses Mary entirely, because he's finally found the courage to go straight to the Skipper—and doesn't lose it or forget it, because it's only a single word:

"Thanks."

And then, maybe because it sounded inadequate, he says it again. "Thanks," says Joe DiMaggio, on the afternoon his son is born, and doesn't understand why, in the midst of this crazy, terrifying joy, he still for some reason feels guilty too.

THE

FORTUNE-TELLER

Babe's sounds resemble words: the question is what words. "Airs ur oyen?" she says from her wheelchair and Agnes, passing through the living room, holds her hands up to signify she can't make out the question. Babe turns a shocking shade of salmon, as she does every time she can't be understood. One side of her mouth droops down so comically that Agnes pictures a cigarette dangling, Babe a gun moll.

Agnes turns down the Philco to translate: "Airs ur oyen? Where's your oyen. Oy en. Boyfriend. Where's your boyfriend?"

Babe clenches the working fist in triumph, her half smile grotesque. Agnes has considered photographing her grandmother, of course—she's considered a whole gallery show of Babe O'Leary, one side of her formerly imposing body withered—but it wouldn't be right to take advantage of Babe in the first helpless minutes of her life. All Brooklyn, even Mame and RoseMarie, talk of nothing but Pearl Harbor, and Babe for once can't direct the dialogue.

"Bernie's probably signed up by now. And no, I don't know why he wouldn't call me with news like that. Except—as you might recall—you ran him off with that nasty Jewish stuff of yours."

Babe raises her good eyebrow, which Agnes considers cheating. It's not true that Babe ran him off—Bernie wasn't the least bit scared of her.

He's been sulking the last month because Agnes won't go back to snuggling with him, but she can't, can't possibly, can't smooch innocently with Bernie when she's been to bed with Joe. And now Bernie will be going off to war. Which means Babe will take the credit for his departure and wheel around looking positively half-pleased with herself.

"I'm going to grab two seconds of privacy."

Her grandmother's good eye registers the irony of *privacy* being invoked in this household. Before, at least, they hid their bodies from each other, even when there were no doors to hide behind. Now they must help Babe to the bathroom, which has been the worst, the absolute worst, of this entire affliction. It's not the moving her which is, God knows, backbreaking. It's not even the wiping her arse. It's the sight of her bald, naked privates exposed for all the world to see. All four sisters have entered into a conspiracy to keep Mickey from being alone with her when she might have to use the toilet, and not just because she blames him for the stroke and punishes him with every half gesture. The O'Leary girls don't want their father to connect Babe's terrifying swollen nakedness with their own. If that's womanhood, they'll stay girls forever, even the one O'Leary acutely aware that she's not a virgin anymore.

Babe sits half of herself up taller in the wheelchair and sends the good eye in the direction of the kitchen. Meaning that Agnes, who was hoping to run out, should instead fetch her grandmother's lunch and feed it to her, one trembling spoonful at a time. And if Aggie really pretends to have any mercy, Babe's eye continues, she'll follow lunch with a trimming of her grandmother's whiskers, those thick white hairs that spring from her chin more vigorous and defiant than ever.

Loretta's stopped going to school to care for Babe while the rest of them head off to work—she says she was quitting anyway—but on Saturdays the duty always seems to fall to Agnes. It's hours before she can palm Babe off on Mame, hours before she can slip out to have a private conversation in a public call box. In the bustling drugstore she makes her way to the big wooden phone booth and she's finally alone, finally brave enough to make the call she's been dying to make. A week's passed, almost, but it took Babe's nudging to push her over the line no self-respecting girl crosses. For the first time in her life, she's calling a boy.

"AGnes," Bernie says when he hears her voice. His own is breathless. She pictures his mother hovering in the background.

Yes, he signed up, he says: yes, in Times Square, Monday morning. And then stayed around Forty-Second Street all day to wait for the head-line from Congress:

U.S. Declares War.

He sounds like he's swallowed a dozen cups of coffee. He's already passed the physical. She just caught him in time. He reports for duty as soon as the Army figures out where they're going to bunk all those extra soldiers. He's never seen his mother cry before, not even when his father died, but she's crying now. "I guess Joe was down in Mexico applauding Miss Jeanette Rankin."

"Who's Miss Jeanette Rankin?"

"Republican of Montana. The only no vote."

Agnes falls silent. He's going off to war and still he has to get his digs in. "So will you let me see you now?"

"Of course I'll see you." She doesn't correct him, doesn't say that she's never refused to see him, she's only refused to be his girl.

"Tonight?"

She laughs. "It's Saturday night."

"I don't want to go to DeRobertis." He spits it out, as if he's been saving it up, fantasizing this conversation, waiting by the phone.

"No," she says. "No, you pick the place."

And he says "Toots Shor's" so instantaneously that she believes he *has* rehearsed it all, has waited by the phone. All right. She may not have heard of Representative Jeanette Rankin of Montana, but she's certainly heard of Toots Shor's. "Gee, Bernie, it doesn't have to be such a fancy place."

"I'll dip into next year's book money. I don't need it now."

"Don't come out to Brooklyn, Bernie. I'll meet you there."

"Agnes are you—"

"I can't wait to see you, Bernie," she says, and she means it. Only what in God's name will she wear to a restaurant like that, where all the swells go? And how's he going to get a reservation, on a Saturday night? He'll have to tell them he's a soldier, getting ready to ship out. It's not real yet. She tries to picture him in uniform, but can only summon his Xavier dress grays. If he can just hang on to his glasses. All along that's what she's dreaded: Bernie on a battlefield without his glasses.

She's twenty minutes early—the trains *would* be running ahead of schedule tonight—so she circles as many midtown blocks as she can to kill time, then waits under the awning in her plaid tweed coat. All the women coming and going are dressed in fur. At least Loretta's done a good job with her hair—or had done a good job, before the evening mist got to it. Underneath the tweed coat, Loretta's dressed her in a tight blue number she produced, like a magician's assistant, from the back of the shared closet: turns out she's been hoarding their mother's clothes. Tonight Agnes wears a suicide's clinging satin.

Finally Bernie sidles up, looking taller than usual, pecking her on the cheek like a middle-aged man and taking her by the hand through Shor's front door and the crush of bustling bodies inside. She ogles the circular bar, bigger than the entire Brooklyn apartment. Bernie seems to know what he's doing: he maneuvers her halfway round the bar till he finds two empty stools and awaits her coat. He'll check it, he says, as if he checks a date's coat every night of the week, and moves off, nonchalant, to find out about their table. On her own, she orders the first drink she's ever ordered for herself: a Manhattan, straight up. Her voice comes out squeaking.

But here's Bernie back already, resting a proprietary hand on her shoulder and leaning in close: "Fifteen minutes for the table. You all right there?" Astounding. She, who's always made her way in the world, who got herself through rich girls' school, is squeaking in Toots Shor's, but Bernie sounds like a man who stands at this bar night after night shooting the breeze with actors and nightclub singers.

"I'm fine." Thank God her own voice is pitched more or less right this time. "Nice place."

The fifteen minutes stretch to twenty-five, then thirty-five, and Bernie orders her another Manhattan. That's a lot of book money down the tubes, a lot of Manhattan down the hatch. The wonder is, the two cock-tails steady her walk and when they go to claim the table that's finally ready she feels middle-aged men gaze after her. She's never slid so grace-fully into a chair in her life.

"Did you see, walking by? You're looking right at him now."

She smiles enigmatically. Does he really not know she can't see a thing?

"*DiMaggio.* And his wife. And another couple, I think it's Gomez."

She can't see the table Bernie means, much less its occupants. "Want to switch places?"

Bernie's grin is big enough for even her to see. They rise and trade chairs, Agnes reaching out a hand to graze Bernie's as they pass. She shouldn't do that, not after all those weeks Bernie pleaded with her, but it comes naturally, like the way she feels now in the blue satin, as if it's molded itself to fit her skin.

Bernie pretends he's not spying but he's tight on martinis and can't restrain himself: he laughs out loud. "Joe D is probably the best present you could possibly give a soldier going off to war." He speaks the lines as if the two of them are the Barrymores, dining onstage. "Well, maybe not the *best* present."

He wouldn't say such a thing if he weren't tipsy. He couldn't possibly know what she gave Joe. Bernie scans the room elaborately, pretends he's not zooming in on the DiMaggio table, lowers his voice. "Joe's just kind of quiet, kind of staring off. Poor guy."

"Rich guy!"

"He's been under a lot of pressure." Bernie sounds, again, like a man of the world, a man who's seen a lot of other men under pressure.

"Going to get his autograph?"

"Nah," Bernie says, ever so casual. "He hates that, in a place like this."

This new Bernie—she can't even recognize his *accent*—makes her swell with a longing for something she can't name, something that has to do with her mother and father back when they were courting, when Gloria was that girl in the photograph her father hides away, the girl who smiled such a carefree trusting smile. Such a blithe smile.

"Oh Bernie," she says—it's not so much the Manhattan speaking as it is some voice that hasn't spoken in a long, long time—"I wish you didn't have to go fight."

He throws one arm over the back of the chair, thrusts out his chest. So that's how he's going to handle it. So that's how he *has* to handle it. "I'll be all right," he says. "You wait and see. Not a scratch on this soldier."

It's enough to make her want to see his expression and she digs in her pocketbook till she realizes that the glasses are in her coat, checked away.

"I'll go—" he says, half-rising, but she stops him with a raised palm. That plaid and those glasses are not making another appearance till the clock strikes midnight. Doesn't Bernie know what Dorothy Parker says: *Men seldom make passes . . .*

"No," she says. "You order for me, Bernie."

It's not like her, but it feels good to let someone else do the ordering. Feels good, just for this one night, to have someone take over for a change.

And it feels good when they finally board the Brooklyn-bound train at one o'clock in the morning, to sit in utter silence, sleepy, drunk, leaning against each other in a dream time. After Shor's, they went down to Times Square and slipped in and out of bars they'd never even noticed before, bars crowded with boys shipping out and girls contemplating what good-bye present to give them. They've been misty-eyed with complete strangers. Now they drift off on the rocking train and miss Agnes's stop. Now they must trudge home from the south side of the park.

Funny that Bernie hasn't made a pass after all this time. Funny he hasn't asked what she thought he would, back in Manhattan. They should be cold, but they're not: they're pickled. They take their sweet time, strolling along the park.

"You're quiet tonight."

"Must be Joe D's influence."

"Think this is our last time together? Before you go?" Their footsteps thump along in the damp dark night.

Finally: "Yes. Unless."

Maybe she jumps in too soon. "Unless?"

Again she has the sense that he's stored the answer up, memorized it. It springs out whole: "Unless we get married."

She peals out the most delighted laugh she'll ever give him. After his crack about the best present she could give him, she was waiting for him to take the rest of his book money for a hotel room, and after they left Manhattan without checking into a hotel she's been waiting for him to pull her out of the lamplight, maybe into the park. But no, not dear, corny Bernie: he wants to marry her. "Oh Bernie, you're the sweetest guy who ever walked the face of the earth. But I wouldn't do that to you, I wouldn't tie you down."

"*Tie me down.* I could be dead in—"

Dead goes through her like a cold current. Her footsteps slow, and she trips on her too-high heel. Dead doesn't even mean anything. She wakes every morning to a vision of Joe, stumbling across some Mexican desert. Now she'll wake to a vision of Bernie, stumbling in front of some Nazi tank.

She stops and feels the cracked sidewalk beneath her rise. She doesn't know which way is up. "I have to stop a minute."

He presses forward anyway. He presses forward and wraps her in his short, sturdy arms and gives her a decent, drunken, worthy-of-Joe-D, man-of-the-world tongue-thrusting deep-breathing Clark Gable kiss.

The next morning, when Babe wheels her chair one-handed to the side of the bed to shake her awake for Mass, Agnes senses—not for the first

time—that Babe knows everything that transpired last night. She flinches.

"Sick. Let me sleep please. I'm sick."

Babe spews vowels that signify *hell* and *mortal sin* but wheels away. By the time Agnes finally rises her sisters have all gone off to church and Mickey, it appears, has gone with them for a change. Anything, evidently, to get away from Babe. She lurches through the hallway, not even attempting to translate the foreign sounds Babe projects from the living room. In the bathroom, she tries to retch but can't. Did she leave Bernie with the impression that *she might marry him*? Their good-bye floats back: *I have to think. I have to think.*

And that second kiss, at her door frame, when she could barely stand, when he pressed his body hard against her. There has to be a word for that, for when you're good as making love with all your clothes on. Is that what enlisting does to a boy? What war does? After he kissed her, after he pressed himself so hard against her that he sucked all the breath from her body, she could barely climb the stairs. Now she finds herself praying he didn't fall asleep on the train and get himself robbed or knifed or clobbered. But she doesn't pray anymore. It's as hard for her to summon language this morning as it is for Babe. She stares into the toilet's brown water.

Out in the hallway Babe recommences her incantations. Agnes has never had a hangover before, so it's never before occurred to her that she could maintain complete and utter silence in the face of Babe's roaring. Wordless, she brings her grandmother a cup of coffee. Babe, furious, pushes it away, grunting heathen sounds. Her grandmother doesn't want coffee, she wants to talk war, or baseball, or how Aggie should run her life. But Agnes's right eye must be swollen to twice its size, and she can't bear to gaze on Babe's twisted fallen face.

She pours Babe's coffee, then her own, down the kitchen sink. Mass is out by now. Her grandmother will be all right, till the others get home. Babe doesn't even utter a peep when she slams the front door and retreats to the street. She's ready to retch again, and now it's the whole side of her head that's swollen.

The funeral parlor's locked up tight—no stiffs today—so she rings the back bell and waits for Vito's heavy step on the stair. He throws his arms wide at the sight of her and doesn't even chastise her for how long it's been. He knows what's wrong: at least, he knows half of what's wrong. "Late night, huh, kid?"

He leads her up the back stairs. "Only one cure. I'm gonna make you a sorta egg cream, with a slug." She can't imagine sipping a drop without gagging, but she does feel better trailing his broad back, running her hand along the nubby cream-colored wallpaper. The mahogany stair rail's as elegant as anything on the *Queen Mary*. A chandelier with glass jewels dangling, its circumference wide as the wheels on Babe's wheelchair, beckons from the landing. As always, she waits for the childhood memories of these stairs. As always, they elude her.

One flight up he leads her, as he has before, straight through his open front door into the long, narrow kitchen at the back, where she can sit at the long, narrow table he made himself, from the coffin maker's leftover planks. He doesn't like her to wander the rest of the apartment, doesn't like her to see what she's already seen, sneaking her peeks: the walls covered with monumental prints of Rome and watery prints of Venice, when he never passed through either city on his journey from Cosenza to Brooklyn. The elegant little side tables that surely once held pictures now bear ornate and empty silver bud vases. Not a photograph on display in all the six rooms of this apartment. He promised to give her a picture of her mother, but he looked so panicked that she doesn't dare ask again.

As soon as she's sitting, he fusses, sets down an enormous crystal goblet, spritzes seltzer from the blue bottle on the counter. "Some terrible thing, huh, this Pearl Harbor? Your Uncle Frank'll be over there before we know it."

Her uncle the marine: she's forgotten him entirely. He could be dead before she even meets him.

"And some of the fellas you know. They'll be getting called up."

"That's where I was last night," she says. "Saying good-bye."

"Aw. Sweetie." He closes the icebox door and comes to knead her shoulders. "That Italian kid?"

She begins to sob: she, Agnes, who hasn't shed a tear in years, sobs like one of her grandfather's mourners, not because she sees that Italian kid but because she can't see him, can't imagine anymore what he looks like or what it was like that afternoon he made such god-awful love to her. "Not the Italian one." It comes out like a hiccup. "*Ger*man."

Above her, behind her, her grandfather stretches his arms around her, chair and all, his embrace as awkward as any hug Joe ever gave her. He bends to kiss the top of her head. He's whispering *all right, all right, all right.*

"He wants me to marry him before he goes and oh God I don't know what to do. I don't know."

"What do you *want* to do?"

"I mustn't." Not *I don't want to.*

"Well, we got that answer pretty fast." Her grandfather squeezes her tighter. She knows somehow—maybe there's still a little psychologist in her—that it's not really her, it's her mother he's squeezing now. She can feel his fingers trembling even as he tries to comfort her: he's on the verge of weeping himself.

Her first sight when she finally, miserably, heads for home and pushes open the front door is Mickey, standing over Babe, trying to interpret.

"Come here, see can you understand what she's saying." For once he can't hide his frustration. It's a wonder his patience has lasted this long, the way Babe's been haranguing him in her mystery language day and night. At the sight of Agnes approaching she bellows, "Nooooo." She gets that *N* out all right.

Mickey shrugs. "Looks like you're on the shit list too."

"Dad." She doesn't mean to berate him, it just pops out: she's not used to this sort of language from her father.

"Now you're correcting me?" She watches her father's jaw pulse with anger. "Maybe you two deserve each other." He wheels on his mother, brushes past Agnes, storms out the front door she's only just entered. But that's not possible. Her father doesn't storm anywhere, doesn't turn on her with the same venom his mother's been spraying his way. This is not sweet suffering-in-silence Mickey O'Leary.

He was right about the shit list, anyway. Now she'll be stuck again, all Sunday afternoon. Where are her sisters? They've certainly made themselves scarce since the stroke. She dashes down the hall, looking for Loretta at least, but the apartment's empty. They've all deserted her, and now she'll have lunch and dinner duty besides. Her good cry and her grandfather's drink eased her headache for a while, but now it's back with a vengeance.

She returns to the living room but won't come in past the arch.

"Look what you've done to every single person in this family." Babe shakes her good fist. You have to give it to her. She can't form her words any better than a two-year-old, but by God she can get her point across. She's FDR's equal when it comes to getting her way. Agnes, transfixed at the sight of the speechless, unstoppable Babe, stands in the doorway, the listener Babe intends her to be. She knows from the great effort Babe takes with her mouth that she's about to give her some terrible injunction.

"Ont. Oo. Arry."

"I thought you'd given up telling me what to do."

Babe only says it harder, faster. "Ont oo arry."

"I don't know how you figured it out."

Babe's lower lip curls down like a dying flower and she says it a third time: "Ont oo arry."

"Don't you marry." Agnes translates in a cold fury, knowing what word will come next, knowing somehow—how could she possibly?—that Babe will even get out the difficult starting consonant. She recites along:

"Don't you marry . . . that Jew? I'll marry whom I please, you tyrannical old bitch."

Sweet suffering Jesus, she and her father both, and she worse, a thousand times worse. She thinks to run from the apartment herself, to follow after Mickey, but she has no idea when the others are coming home. She sees Babe yowling for the family she's driven away, sees her grandmother working herself into such a rage that she has another stroke and falls from the wheelchair, cracking her head open—finally, fatally. A split melon, on the gray threadbare rug.

Now she's the one who can't speak. She stomps to the girls' room, flings herself headfirst on the bed, kicks her legs up and down, a childish tantrum that eases the swelling in her eye and consoles her. Who else is there to console her? Who's there ever been, in this household?

"The funny part is, he's not even Jewish," she bellows. "I wish he were."

Silence from the living room. Maybe Babe's slipped in her urine-soaked seat. Maybe she's dangling down from her chair, about to hang herself with her own twisted dress.

"Joke's on you, Babe." She's the one who's yowling now, the one who's regressed past childhood and gone all the way to primitive animal life. Wouldn't it just serve Babe right if she did marry Bernie, if she went to live with Bernie's German mother, if Babe spent the rest of her days sputtering over the imaginary Jewish in-laws.

She burrows her head into the flat, moldy pillow but she can't make herself cry again. She's reduced to these spilling sounds coming from deep in her belly: Babe's vengeance, her granddaughter sentenced to the same wordless fate.

She rolls over on her back and Bernie leans down to kiss her the way he did last night. He presses his newly exercised chest hard against her breasts, his thigh against her thighs. Bernie takes over for her, orders for her, gives her a rest for once from this constant working, worrying, caregiving, slips his tongue into her mouth, his hand onto her breast, his soldierly tidy body into her own.

She closes her eyes.

She's always loved him, she has. She'll go stay with Bernie's mother, a sane woman who takes care of herself. She'll get better and better with the camera her grandfather buys her, and she'll get an assignment from *Life* and she'll go find Bernie on an Italian battlefield. She'll cradle him— no. He'll cradle her, he'll take over for her, he'll comfort her.

A deep breath. Another. A third.

She rises as she always does, turns once more into the dutiful daughter, the dutiful granddaughter who spoons the soup and wipes the arse and listens to the incomprehensible bitterness of a miserable old woman. But this time as she rises she has a secret to keep: and won't it be a supreme pleasure, to keep it from Babe.

There's no time. Bernie goes straightaway to see Father Phelan and reports that he's agreed to push everything forward—if they get the license on time (she has to go, pronto, for a SYPHILIS test), Father Phelan will forgo the usual instruction in favor of an hour's conversation with the pair of them. And he'll announce the banns in three weekday Masses instead of posting them three weeks running, a bending of rules he seems to think don't count anyway in wartime. Father Phelan, the same seducer who persuaded Joe to be a pacifist, now agrees to marry Bernie on his way to war. He's their Friar Lawrence.

> *I have a faint cold fear thrills through my veins*
> *That almost freezes up the heat of life.*

Those can't be the lines she should be thinking.

Bernie gets the word that he has ten days till he leaves for Fort Jackson. Nine days. Eight days. On five-days-and-counting Agnes picks up the blood test results. Why this strange sensation, so close to disappointment? On day four, they go to pick up the license. They'll have three days together as husband and wife. If Bernie works out that she's not a virgin, he'll go off to war with murder on his mind.

They meet at Chambers Street and stroll together, hand awkwardly in hand. Bernie's still flying, still full of some juice stronger than the caffeine they pour at Horn & Hardart. He already looks like he's been in the Army forever, more like a soldier home on leave, in his white dress shirt, than a kid about to go off to boot camp.

"Still can't believe you said yes, m'dear." Even his Noel Coward sounds older and wiser.

She aims for blithe, to please him, but somehow her voice comes out squeaking again: "You're so much handsomer than Babe."

He doesn't take offense: he takes a bow instead, right on the sidewalk, his glasses slipping precariously.

Loretta's to be her maid of honor, only she doesn't know it yet. Agnes doesn't dare tell her what's up till the wedding day, though she'd sorely love a consultation about which dress of Gloria's to pick. Instead she resorts to base deceit: she sneaks downstairs to Bruscelli's, asks the old lady to sit with Babe for the afternoon while she and her sister go off shopping for a surprise present. *Surprise present* is sudden inspiration and terrible irony: she's getting married on Babe's birthday, her sixty-ninth. Babe looks like eighty now, and she could live to be eighty too. Or ninety. Babe, being Babe, could live to be a hundred.

On the appointed morning, veins thrilling, Agnes wraps her black high heels in tissue, rests them in the bottom of a B. Altman shopping bag, and folds her mother's dove-gray dress suit on top. She'll change in the subway station. Already she can smell the urine round the base of the toilet. Already she clutches the hem of her dress, to keep it from touching the filthy floor.

"Happy Birthday, Babe." She stands looking in on the living room where Babe has been posted in her wheelchair since dawn. Loretta has her up and dressed for Mickey's good-bye kiss every morning, but Agnes herself hasn't kissed her grandmother in ages and she's not about to rile her suspicions by starting now, not even for a sixty-ninth birthday.

"I aren u a erk?"

"I took the day off, to do a little . . . shopping." The left side of Babe's mouth creeps up at the thought of tonight's birthday dinner. Agnes summons every ounce of shamelessness to take Loretta showily by the elbow into the hallway, to whisper just loudly enough for Babe to catch the edges: "Will you help me shop for Babe's present?"

And here's the snag: Loretta looks at her knowing that something's up, that Agnes is lying, that they won't be going shopping at all. She stares at Agnes for the longest time. They never should have let Loretta leave school, should never have left her holed up here, day after day. She's always been strange. Who will she be after a few years waiting hand and foot on Babe?

Agnes pulls her sister into the bedroom, where Babe truly can't hear them. She wants to tell her now, now, wants to ask if gray's all wrong for a wedding, a bad omen, but she only says: "Bruscelli's coming upstairs to sit with her."

"*Bruscelli?*" Her sister looks as if Agnes proposes to bring a Nazi spy into the house.

"I couldn't think of anybody else. Anyway, she's tickled to death."

But as Bruscelli knocks gaily, musically, on the O'Leary door, Agnes knows she's made a terrible mistake. Babe, from her sentry post in the living room, spies her jaunty old nemesis passing through the door she's never entered before.

"Us ee oo-in ere?"

Agnes leads Bruscelli to the wheelchair, where half of Babe shrinks back.

"She's come to sit with you, while Loretta and I go shopping."

A look of terror crosses Babe's face, a look that passes from the still-living side to the dead. Her grandmother's usual fear of anyone darker? Bruscelli leans forward to pat Babe's hand, to reassure her, and a curious thing happens. Babe's terror passes onto another level, one that doesn't have anything to do with Bruscelli or Italians or even her own helpless position in the chair. Her good eye flashes back and forth as if she's watching a newsreel or a matinee, as if she's reliving some scene from her own life: the stroke? Or from before that? Is she watching her past life, or her future?

"What is it, Babe?" Agnes's tongue is sharp and she knows it, but Babe looks up at her with that one eye and an expression Agnes has never seen before, a quivering beseeching look you might see on a starving dog or one of those hopeless defeated men in Dorothy Day's soup line. The big querulous eye begins to twitch wildly, as if it's conducting an electric current. The other sinks into her cheek.

"What is it? What do you want?"

Babe lowers her head. "Umaee."

"Umaee. Uma ee. Company? Oh, sweet Jesus, Babe, that's why Bruscelli's here. She's here to keep you company."

Babe won't lift her head: "Urs."

Yours. Your company. Your company, Agnes, you on your way out the door to your wedding. Your scheming conniving grandmother, the one who hates you, the one you've decided you hate right back, wants you to keep her company.

Agnes goes on high alert. Her heart, inflamed with rage, rips through her chest. This is the lowest trick the slithery Babe has ever played. She gazes down on her cowering grandmother and spits flames: this fat distorted antisemite, this malingering manipulator who broke her father's heart. Somehow Babe has tricked her into pity. Somehow Babe has tricked her into a loyalty she didn't know she still possessed. This sick Babe, who can't for once fend for herself, who's wanted her company so jealously all these years she'd rather drive her away than share it. Agnes would like to throttle her.

She clicks her tongue against the roof of her mouth: once, twice, a third time. She tastes ashes. "Mrs. Bruscelli, I'm sorry. It looks like she's not ready." Babe has the decency to keep her head lowered, her triumph to herself.

"Sorry, Loretta. I'll be back in no time. I'll keep Babe *com*pany. I just have to . . ."

She just has to go to Manhattan, prowl through the halls of Xavier where she used to go dancing, find Father Phelan's office—where Bernie waits, mother in tow. She has to tell Bernie she can't marry him. She knows as if she's always known it that it would have come to this, that it was coming to this, she just didn't see it yet. Babe has spared her an operatic scene—a *Shakespearean* scene—in the dove-gray suit, with Loretta and a couple of hundred high school cadets as witnesses. Now at least she can offer up her grandmother as meager excuse, to save Bernie's pride in front of his mother, in front of the accommodating priest. At least Loretta won't have to know the worst about her.

She grabs up her glasses and two tokens, clatters down the stairs before Bruscelli can even collect herself to leave. She doesn't so much as wave good-bye to that spiteful old woman, her grandmother, doesn't give Loretta so much as a rueful smile on her way out the door.

She can't bear to look at any of them, because she's started to see how it will be, now that she's witnessed her grandmother's terror. The future rolls out before her, and the first thing she sees is that she won't be able to desert her grandmother any more than Joe can desert that family he's dragging through the wilds of Texas.

She'll play the martyr. No silent suffering from her, the closest to Babe, the most like Babe of all the granddaughters. She sees as if in a vision how she'll tramp the streets of Spuyten Duyvil, where Babe's been threatening to return ever since she came to claim Gloria's place. Spite the devil indeed. She sees how she'll knock on superintendents' doors until she finds a cheap enough rent, how she'll finally move Babe out of Brooklyn after all these years. Babe can have the bedroom and she'll sleep in the living room, the way her father does now. Someone has to save him. Someone has to save Loretta. Oh, she'll play the martyr all right.

 She'll have another job by then. She'll answer a classified in the *Times* and charm Mr. Leon Gottlieb, portrait photographer and German refugee, into hiring her as his darkroom assistant. His accent will be harder to understand than Babe's, and he'll be a stern taskmaster, and he'll show her more tricks than poor old Mr. McClary ever dreamed of.

Mr. Gottlieb will help her grandfather buy her the camera she needs, will come stand beside her for the Brooklyn funeral when her grandfather, heartbroken over his fallen marine son, dies too soon.

But Babe will live on and on. In a few years, Babe will be the cantankerous queen of Spuyten Duyvil, the other side of her body back in business, back at Yankee Stadium once a week during baseball season, now that they live so close. She'll sing Joe DiMaggio's praises—*the great war hero*—when everybody knows DiMaggio dodged the Army as long as he could, then stood on his head to stay out of combat. Agnes will bring Babe to lunch with Mr. Gottlieb and will take great pleasure in the way Mr. Gottlieb wrestles Babe to the ground, conversationally speaking.

She's already charging down the subway steps, off to tell Bernie she can't, mustn't, won't be his wife. It's too soon, she'll say. She doesn't know quite how she knows it—she can't say, pushing her token into the slot, whether it's a vision or a daydream or just the way the facts fit together so logically—but she knows that the Army will soon find out about Bernie's fluent German and when they do they won't send him off to Europe at all, they'll send him to the Pentagon to translate. He'll call her when he comes to town, but they'll never talk about the war or the body count or Joe or Babe. Certainly they'll never talk about how close they once came to marrying. Bernie will have another girl by the second year of the war, another wife, a sensible, boring, adoring girl.

And when the war winds down in Europe, when Bernie begs them to send him into action after all, he'll ship out the other way, to Okinawa. He'll get his horrific battles. When he finally comes home, when Agnes makes her way out to his wife's trim little house on Long Island, she'll be stunned by the awful silence from dear old Bernie, the terrible silence that leaves him unable, for a time, to say anything in any accent to her or anyone else. He'll stare at her through the glasses he's managed to hang onto as if he remembers her perfectly well and hasn't the slightest interest in why she came to call.

Joe, though. Joe will be the opposite, chattering on when she visits every month in Danbury. Joe will laugh raucously at himself, showing up for his own arrest at his Manhattan draft board when he never even had the chance to break the law properly, at the Mexican border. That refugee family took one look at the weaselly guide, Joe will say, one look at the noonday sun and the desert stretching out, and fled back to Mexico City, where they're living still. Without papers and without Joe D'Ambrosio's help.

Joe will tell her anything, everything, even the terrible things that hardened federal prisoners—mobsters and kidnappers and drug runners—do to pacifists. He'll tell Loretta too, though Agnes will put a stop to Loretta's visits as brutally as Babe might have done. She won't have Joe breaking Loretta's heart from a prison cell. She won't have Loretta tying herself to a man who will drift without a dime his whole life from one hopeless cause to another, his handsome head cracked open again and again, marching for condemned prisoners and civil rights and the farmworkers' union.

Joe will even egg her on, from his prison cell, as she cajoles editor after editor into giving her a break. She'll blush as she begs for journeyman work, she'll blush as she pays her dues on the city beat, she'll blush as she photographs more corpses on the streets of Manhattan than Weegee ever did. Still Joe will push her, to get over to Europe even as the war is winding down, to do what she feels called to do, to call on the editors whose names Mr. Gottlieb's photographer friends give her, to wheedle credentials and a berth on the last troopship sailing east. *To witness,* he'll say, over and over: just what you'd expect from a pacifist sitting in federal prison. She'll feel him behind her, him and his witnessing, Joe and Babe thrusting her farther out into the world than she might ever have ventured on her own.

She'll never tell either of them what she sees when her blushing finally ceases, when she angles her way onto that first convoy of Jeeps rolling into the liberated camp. It's not an extermination camp, not like the ones the Russians are finding: the people who died here died of disease, of starvation. She'll get corpses, the captain will tell her, corpses piled high, but she'll get the living too. Take your pick.

As she makes her way from gray-green barracks to barracks, drab, ordinary buildings, her camera will dangle useless from her hand. It's as if she's there but not there, as if she has transported herself to some other familiar place—a narrow bathroom, a basement, a darkroom, a coffin—where it is difficult for the eye to register what it is seeing. The prisoners, the ones who can walk, press the bones of their fingers against her shirt. A young skeleton leads her through the buildings, where the men who do not have the strength to rise huddle four and five together in bunks stacked on bunks.

No words for this sight, or for the thick, acid-sweet smell of death and dying that has entered every corner. Not even her beloved Shakespeare will have a couplet to suit this occasion, to prettify it, to make it bearable. This is beyond language: not even Joe would know how to *witness* this. She will stand in the dark corner of the barracks ashamed to look on these men, but one of them will catch her eye: an old, bald man with swollen eyes rimmed with sores, an old man anchoring the men who lie behind him. He will roll his eye to Agnes's camera and manage a slight dignified nod of assent, though later Agnes will decide it wasn't so much assent as it was command. Wordless, she will agree to make a record of what the world can't bring itself to imagine.

And after all those early years of preparing herself, of steeling herself with her mother's picture and her grandfather's mortuary and the mean streets of Manhattan, she won't, after all, photograph a single corpse in that camp. The dead bodies won't be able to give her their permission, and she will decide in any case to pick the living.

None of it will seem possible, or real, and after she has published the pictures it will seem less real still. She will never pull out the yellowing tear sheets to look at the photographs again, but she will see those pictures—in flashes, in slices, in the corners of her dreams—for the rest of her life.

She'll sleep with Joe every now and again, down through the years, when she's between lovers and he's between wives (once, even, when he's not quite between wives). He'll coax her out of bed and down into the street to demonstrate with him or, better yet, to photograph the demonstrators whose zeal is so hard to capture in black and white. She'll never tell him that she almost married Bernie. She loves them both still, loves them both more as the years go by, as she freeze-frames them into who they were, so charged up, so pure of heart. (Pure of heart: wouldn't they both find that unbearably corny.)

Bernie will speak again, in accents, will study German literature, as if he means somehow to understand that darkness they lived through by reading stories. Joe will surprise them when he's the one to finally and utterly lose his faith. And Babe will love that nonchalant slugger DiMaggio with unwavering fidelity until her dying day.

The train lumbers into the station and Agnes steps aboard. She straightens her hat—the raspberry-colored beret, meant to look gay on her wedding day—and grabs a strap. The car is full of empty seats at midmorning, but it's not a day to sit, not on her way to give Bernie this news. She tries to read the advertising placards, but behind her glasses her eyes won't rest, won't read a single line through to the end. She rides the train standing, hanging on, rocking to and fro, rehearsing the lines she must speak, as soon as she finds her voice and the words to tell Bernie the truth. Or as close to the truth as human decency will allow.

Photography Credits

Dwight D. Eisenhower Presidential Library: portholes on SS *St. Louis,* 29, 78, and 33, 108, 243

Courtesy of E. R. Fuetsch family: soldier, 261, 273, 283, soldiers, 289

Courtesy of Sealy Gilles: wedding toast, 276, 279

Copyright © Estate of Helen Levitt, courtesy Laurence Miller Gallery, New York: boy with chalk drawing, 44

Copyright © Hulton-Deutsch Collection/CORBIS: two girls, 29

International Center of Photography/Getty Images: Weegee (Arthur Felig) self-portrait, 18, 21, 146, 216

The following images are all courtesy of the Farm Security Administration–Office of War Information Collection, Prints and Photographs Division, Library of Congress: Jack Allison: peanut wagon, 238; Esther Bubley: window shopping, 264; John Collier: priest, 154; church, sky, 254; Marjory Collins: iceman, 166; storefront, 191, 237, crossing street, 212, typist, 229, 241, newsroom, 232, flag, 286, Army doctor, 290; Jack Delano: locomotive, 143; studying, 250; lunch counter, 258; Jack Delano/Arthur Rothstein/Christian Jara: desk collage, 137; Sheldon Dick: kids on steps, 175; Walker Evans: two girls, 62, 65, 71; Walker Evans/Christian Jara: woman in building, 39, woman with witch hat, 54; Christian Jara/Marjory Collins/unknown photographers: face collage, 242; Dorothea Lange: street meeting, 67, 219, street scene, 259; Gordon Parks: longshoreman, 177, stevedores, 227, 228, 234, 269; Edwin Rosskam: Washington Square arch, 217; Arthur Rothstein: beat cop, cop with old lady, 55, 62, 113, 114, 158, 161, shoeshine, 58, boys with gun, 70, 71, 112, street band, 95, 203, carrots, 121, seamen, 128, kids, 218; Lee Russell: three young men, 9, 173, men outside shack, 93, two men, 176, teenagers, 222, department store, 256; Arthur S. Siegel: smiling girls, 102, 164, 280, *Social Justice,* 105, 119, fireplace, 141, 145, back of head, 152, 207, walking along, 169, fashion show, 189, at the bar, 206, overboard, 209, bottom of stairs, 213, toast, 270, New Year's Eve, 271; John Vachon: billboard, Times Square, 79, 132, sleeping, 130; John

Vachon/Arthur S. Siegel/Christian Jara: night watch collage, 208; unknown photographers: priest, 72, 87, 98, 186, night out, 90, hair, 117, dreamy, 139, 183, 189, flag, 151, 156, 160, storefront, 152, 287, pretty face, 192, blond man, 197, 236, anxious boy, 199, 245, 254, hats against wall, 231, standing man, 239, roller skates, 266, recruiting, 274, fashion model, 191

Department of Special Collections and University Archives, Raynor Memorial Libraries, Marquette University: Catholic Workers, 51
Metropolitan Museum of Art, Walker Evans Archive, 1994 (1994.253.502.3), copyright © Walker Evans Archive, Metropolitan Museum of Art: man on subway, 22, 27, 225

National Archives and Records Administration: SS *St. Louis,* 81, 149; at dock, 181

New York Times Co./Archive Photos/Getty Images: Dorothy Arnold, 41, 201

pdimages.com: Babe Ruth, 37

Sporting News Archives: Joe DiMaggio, iii, 5, 7, 10

The following images are all reprinted with permission of the United States Holocaust Memorial Museum. The views or opinions expressed in this book, and the context in which the images are used, do not necessarily reflect the views or policy of, nor imply approval or endorsement by, the United States Holocaust Memorial Museum: four passengers, 23, 36, 281, young men, 165, 181, and two images of skaters, 295, all on SS *St. Louis,* courtesy of Fred Buff; young boy, 75, 85, 145, 268, United States Holocaust Memorial Museum and American Joint Distribution Committee, courtesy of Aviva Kempner; two young passengers on SS *St. Louis,* 111, courtesy of Peter Chraplewski; the Arndt family on SS *St. Louis,* 123, 189, courtesy of Lottie Brown; passengers on SS *St. Louis,* 181, courtesy of Dr. Liane Reif-Lehrer; passengers on SS *St. Louis,* 248, courtesy of Ruth Heilbrun Windmuller; baby, 263, 265, courtesy Dr. Rudolph Jacobson; passengers on SS *St. Louis,* 292, courtesy Don Altman